MOONSHINE

PATH
OF
THE
RAVEN

MAX SHIPPEE

Edited by Alice Kuo Shippee
Cover Art & Maps by Tim Byrne

Reader's Guide
www.readmoonshine.com/readersguide

Teacher's Guide with Curriculum
www.teachmoonshine.com

A Magenta Creators Collaboration
www.magentacreators.com

WGA Registration: 2270841
Hardcover ISBN: 979-8-9922062-1-0
Paperback ISBN: 979-8-9922062-0-3
eBook ISBN: 979-8-9922062-2-7

Jim,
Thanks for looking
over my shoulder.

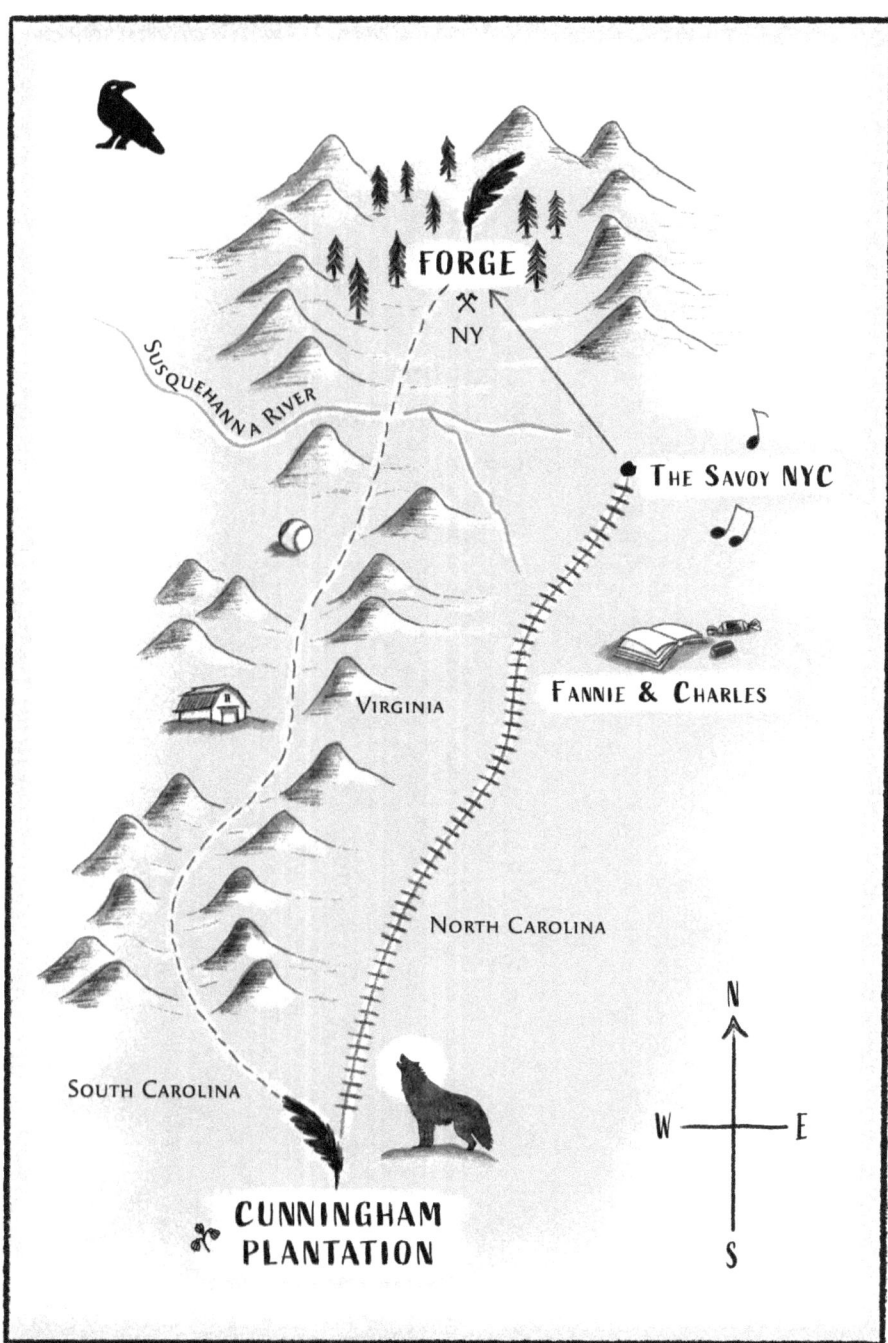

For those who wish to return to the woods
With a blade by their side and a cloak and hood

1

Full Moon

The Woods Outside Cunningham's Plantation
South Carolina, Winter 1909

He was on a dead run.

Branches scraped at his arms.

Barking swelled in the distance.

In a moment, the dogs—and the men behind them—would be upon young Sam.

Fear shot through his body.

His bleached and bloodied shirt caught the moonlight and made him stand out against the trees. With his good arm, Sam pulled his shirt over his head and flung it to the ground. His dark African skin would prove an advantage in the night.

He splashed across a shallow stream and scrambled up an embankment into a small clearing, suddenly trapped by thick underbrush and briars.

There was nowhere to go.

He turned back, only to hear the barking grow louder. The water churned with the sound of what must have been a dozen dogs. At the age of twelve, this was how his life would end.

Or not.

High in the sky, the full moon threw her jagged beams through the tops of the trees. Pain pulsed a rhythm through Sam's mangled arm as a song of strength stirred deep. Blood dripped from his elbow as he raised both fists, ready to face what was coming.

Two Weeks Before

2

New Moon

The Outskirts of Forge, New York

Letha's cabin window was a flickering yellow square in the darkness of the forest. Snow gently fell, muffling the cold winter night.

Inside, Arthur lay in the bed beneath an old black wolfskin, his breaths shallow. Letha pulled up the wooden rocking chair, leaving trails in the dirt floor. Next to him in these final hours, she carefully watched Arthur's tired face in the steady glow of an oil lamp. Her own paper-thin skin showed signs of many trips around the sun.

Noticing a bit of sweat on Arthur's forehead, Letha pulled the wolfskin off his body, leaving him covered by a single light muslin sheet. She draped the wolf skin carefully at the foot of the simple bed, then gently took his hand, placing it in hers.

Arthur's eyes slowly opened, and he looked expectantly towards the door.

"They're all gone," Letha comforted. She had been waiting for him to wake. "For a few days now." Arthur shifted his eyes to Letha.

"A few days?"

Letha nodded and dabbed Arthur's forehead with a cloth. They both knew Arthur's grasp of time, like his grasp on life, was slipping more and more. She was pleased to see a slight smile crease the corners of his mouth as he relaxed his head back onto his pillow.

He took another labored breath in, then out, gathering his thoughts. "I suppose now is as good a time as any." He was finally ready. "One final spell?"

Letha took a deep breath and gently stroked his hair. Arthur reached up and took her hand.

"Till next time, then?"

Letha admired his humor to the end, "Ha...yes, next time."

Arthur took another breath before his request, "My axe."

Arthur's axe held his strength and soul. Like him it was tarnished and etched with time. It held stories of his past, of enemies and forests felled.

Letha reverently placed the axe in Arthur's hand. His curled fingers gripped the worn handle.

Outside, the snow ceased, and the clouds swiftly parted over the cabin, opening the sky to the Milky Way above.

With his last bit of remaining strength, Arthur strained and raised the axe high. The silvery scarred surface glinted, and the edge sang sharp in the firelight. Arthur lowered the axe into Letha's open hand.

Letha's unwavering voice filled the cabin.

"Since Gilgamesh your song was sung
By silver moon and silver tongue,
Here a blade to cut the skin,
From these words a spell begins."

Letha held Arthur's wrist in one hand and gripped the axe close to its head in the other. In a swift motion, she slit Arthur's wrist with skilled precision. He winced as Letha placed the axe on his chest, and the blood flowed down his open palm. Letha carefully held a wooden bowl beneath his hand, catching each drop from his fingertips. As the color drained from Arthur's face, Letha recited,

"Blood of death is blood of birth,
My body a bridge made by earth,
Forever remembered and tethered we,
This blood buys immortality."

Letha held the bowl over Arthur. He closed his eyes, his body relaxed.

"Rise, rise through blood thine own,
Destinies together sewn,
From this death, life passes on,
From ages old, to newborn fawn."

Letha carefully poured drops over the axe on Arthur's chest. The drops slid into the crevices and imperfections before seeping into the metal itself. She then raised the bowl to her own lips.

"I drink now from the River of Lethe,
Forfeit all the memories we've shared
From the floods of Noah to the fires of Salem,
You shall carry our story and prayer."

Letha drank, then moved to the foot of the bed and poured blood from the bowl onto the wolfskin pelt.

"This coat now, thy spirit holds
Soul released and body unfolds.
The boatman waits to take thy fare,
To cross the Styx and find an heir."

Letha grabbed the pelt and called out.

"Release your shield and shed your skin,
A curing force held within,
I give you leave to take your flight,
Journey strong throughout the night."

Pulling hard on the wolfskin, she flung it high into the air toward the shadowed corner of the cabin. It fell to the bare ground in a heap. Arthur's breaths were barely perceptible, yet each time his chest rose and fell, the wolfskin ever-so-slightly did the same. Letha stood, took her staff, and gestured towards the pelt on the ground.

"As this death does give you heart,
New path at hand and destiny chart,
Take form now and beast contain,
With this loss, new life is gained."

The fur stirred with a primordial crackling. It rose from the ground, squirming and stretching until finally taking the full form of a large, dark wolf. It was tall enough to look Letha directly in her eyes. Her gaze locked at the Wolf, she reached for the bowl and carefully offered it.

The Wolf bowed its head and drank what was left of Arthur's blood, then licked its snout clean with its long tongue. It silently padded over to the bed and sat, gazing straight at Arthur.

With great effort, Arthur turned his head to the Wolf, his breaths barely perceptible. The Wolf found Arthur's rhythm and matched it. A shadowy mist of breath moved between them.

In...

    out...

        in...

            ...out.

As Arthur let go of his final breath, the Wolf took it in.

All was still. Too still.

The Wolf slowly stood, shaking and twisting its coat from head to tail, flinging tiny droplets of blood that sizzled onto the walls. It walked circles on the dirt floor of the cabin, sneezing as its movements devolved into an erratic pacing. As bloody foam dripped from its mouth, it stopped and looked directly at Letha. The cabin was too small for the both of them.

She chanted again,

"Move now, beast, from conjured spell,
Moon and sun together meld,
Like a swift, take fast the lead,
Then just as swift, return to me."

Letha swung her staff, pointing to the door of the cabin. It flung open and the Wolf burst through into the darkness beyond, turning directly south, as fast as it could move. It knew exactly where it needed to go, and there was nothing that would stop it.

From a pocket in her cloak, Letha pulled an old black sock with two buttons sewn at the toe and laid it in her hand. She pulled two leaves from her staff and placed them with the sock. She clicked her tongue then blew hard into her palm. The sock and leaves flew up and out of her hand, transforming into shiny black feathers, wings, and claws. A Raven. It softly landed on her shoulder. She whispered to it.

"Bird of wing and thorn and claw,
Take flight and tell of all you saw,
Bring him here, that I may confer,
To follow the beast this night has stirred."

The Raven blinked twice and cocked its head sideways to look at Letha with one eye. It paused, then cocked its head to the other side.

Letha waited.

The bird waited.

Letha rolled her eyes.

"Just...get John," she finally added.

The Raven nodded, opened its wings, and flapped twice before taking off. It squawked as it flew out the door into the moonless night and turned North, away from the Wolf. Another wave of Letha's staff, and the door closed.

Letha took her staff in both hands and drove it into the dirt of the cabin floor. Small glowing roots grew from its end into the

10

ground, dimming into the dirt as they spread. The staff remained standing upright without her hand. Letha walked to the fire and stirred it a bit, causing a few sparks to leap into the air. With a wave of her hand, the sparks gathered and swirled above her palm. She moved back to the staff and lowered her hand until the glowing swirl balanced at the top. She put her palm over the swirl and pressed it down into the top of the standing staff. The glow travelled down and into the roots that had spread, favoring the ones to the west. Once in the roots, the glow traveled underground rapidly out of the cabin.

On the western outskirts of the village, an amber light filled another cabin. Constance turned over in her bed. She looked to her own staff, standing in the middle of the room. From its roots, an amber glow rose up the length until it swirled into a glowing swirl in the air.

Constance pulled her covers off and put her feet on the floor. She took a breath.

"Good bye, Arthur," she said aloud.

The still air held her voice in a cocoon of quiet. Constance could feel the space that Arthur had left behind.

In the silence, the plants spoke to her. She knew it was time to prepare her Wolf for the journey ahead. John would need her potent magic for the next full moon.

She pulled a mason jar from the cupboard and began at the kitchen table. From the low ceiling, she pulled dried herbs and remedies to place in the jar. She knew John's brew by heart. He would arrive at Letha's soon. There was no time for a fire; the tea would have to steep on his journey.

Constance covered the jar and grabbed her winter's cape. She reached for her glowing staff and gestured to open the door then stepped into the night.

3

The Raven's feathers pulled at the still, dark air as it soon found the river heading north out of town towards John. Only the glint of stars heard the rush of the rapids. The bird pushed on until underneath her the river gave way to trees, then the black glass of the snowless, frozen lake. Set back on one shore sat a long, one room, rectangular cabin. Small dying wisps of smoke came from a single large stove pipe at one end. The fire needed tending soon. Arthur's death had been no more than an hour ago.

Inside, rows of bunks lined the walls from the door, while at the far end a large wooden cook stove stood marking the front of the kitchen. Between the bunks and kitchen, a long table and benches waited for breakfast, still several hours away. John was in a deep sleep despite the snores and sounds of a dozen other dozing men. He was such a big fellow that his feet stuck out past the end of his bunk. One foot was bare, while the other had a sock bunched up at his toes.

The Raven flew down the row of bunks and landed on John's bare foot. It picked at John's bunched up sock until it finally got a good pull and tugged it off entirely. John twitched awake and looked down at his feet. The Raven looked back and dropped the sock.

"How did you—?" John's question was cut short by the Raven jumping from John's foot up to his leg, over his stomach, and onto his chest. It cocked its head sideways, one of its eyes looking straight at him.

"Ah, so it's my turn, is it?" John said softly.

The Raven opened its wings and flapped twice, then gently pecked at John's chest. John sat up in his bunk. *We best get a move-on, then*, he thought.

John slipped his shirt over his head, then bent to lace his boots. When he stood, the Raven took a perch on his shoulder and playfully picked at the white streak that blazed through his otherwise dark hair. John slid his two hand-axes into his belt. He grabbed his pelt-skin satchel, then tried to keep his boots from clomping as he tip-toed, the best he could, through the rows of wooden bunks, and gently nudged the heavy timber door open.

John stepped into the cold, then turned to pull the door closed behind him when he heard a voice from inside, lightly chiding him.

"Hey now, don't go hungry."

The cook of the lumber camp, "Soup," emerged holding a small paper-wrapped package. The lantern he held threw just enough light to illuminate the men in their bunks, now sitting up behind him on the moonless night. John's dark skin made the glow from the lantern seem warm, even in the winter. Soup's pale complexion matched the flour always on his hands. John smelled cinnamon as he took the package.

"Are these cookies?" John asked with surprise. *When the hell did he manage to make these?* he thought. *And keep them away from Rowan?*

"Easy, John, they're to help you on your trip. And a good gesture for the new guy, too. Don't eat 'em all the first night."

"Don't eat 'em all the first night?" John playfully mocked, then added, "Thanks."

"Godspeed." Soup gave John a solid slap on the back. John looked back through the door and saw the rest of the lumberjacks offering a mix of smiles, nods, and gestures of goodbye and good luck. John gave them a slight bow in return then stepped into the night. The Raven spread its wings and took flight from his shoulder, leading the way South. John soon found himself at an easy run, pacing the best he could behind the bird.

From behind him, the cabin echoed with the sound of men sending him strength for the miles ahead, their voices deep and rhythmic, it sounded almost like a rumbling bark from the wild.

His journey to catch the Wolf had begun.

—-

An hour later, John arrived at Letha's cabin. The Raven landed on Letha's shoulder as she stepped outside. She mocked surprise as John came into view.

"So you're the lucky one?"

"The chosen one, eh?" John joked back. Constance stepped out from the cabin behind Letha and gave John a knowing nod.

15

"You're making good time," Constance said.

The Raven squawked on Letha's shoulder, as if to take credit for the fast pace of the evening. Letha rolled her eyes at the Raven, then passed John a small pouch clinking of coins.

"In case you need to buy someone's good graces," Letha added.

Constance handed John the mason jar full of steeping herbs. "Think you can keep this intact for two weeks?" she jested.

"No promises," he grimaced, looking at the muddy concoction. "Looks delicious."

"It doesn't have to taste good to work. The further apart we are, the stronger it has to be."

Constance pressed a bindle of seeds into John's palm.

"Plant these seeds at his home, give it words to keep him connected," Constance said.

John carefully tucked the items into his satchel next to Soup's cookies.

Letha looked south and took a breath. "Arthur's Wolf is probably coming up on Utica soon."

"I can keep up as long as the Raven does," John reassured. The Raven flapped its wings.

"'Course...be careful and all that," Constance offered.

"'Course," John teased, though neither Constance nor Letha believed him. Letha addressed the bird on her shoulder directly.

"Now, one more thing. Are you going to give me one, or make me take it?"

The bird looked her up and down. Letha made a pinching motion with her fingers towards the Raven. It squawked.

"Come on, now," she coaxed. The Raven ruffled and preened at its feathers. It repeated the movement again, only this time it's preening produced a single black feather in its beak. It held it

16

for a moment, then cocked its head toward Letha and offered it to her. Letha took the long feather graciously.

"There, that wasn't so bad was it?"

The Raven squawked again, and cocked its head sideways.

"Go on now!" Letha encouraged. "That Pelt's got quite a head start on you!" The Raven opened its wings, looked south, and took off.

John's eyes followed the Raven as he adjusted his satchel one last time. He gave both ladies a wink and bow.

"I'll be back before you know it."

John turned and his boots made fresh tracks in the snow. He followed the Raven's squawks, with the whispers of Letha's voice in his head.

"Godspeed as you go find the one,
Pass this down from old to young.
Bring this one before it's done,
From not the father, but still a son.

Letha shut the door behind her and inspected the Raven's feather in the firelight. Constance took a small empty glass jar from the mantel and pulled the cork. She put her nose to it and smelled.

"Hm, lavender," she said out loud as she offered the opening to Letha. "Should be fine."

Letha dropped the feather inside the jar. Constance replaced the cork and set the jar back on the mantel. The single black feather stood upright on the point of its quill. Letha looked at Arthur's body, addressing him even though his spirit had already left. "All we can do now is wait, old friend."

Constance looked Letha up and down. She looked tired.

17

"Would you like me to stay?" she asked.

"I'm sure the boys'll come by tomorrow," Letha answered.

"Well, then," Constance pulled the rocking chair closer to the fire, making new tracks in the ground, and offered it to Letha. "Here you are. Try for a bit of rest, dear. You'll be needing it before too long, if you don't already." Letha pulled her shawl around herself and sat. Constance found another blanket to tuck around her in the chair then threw a few more logs on the fire. When she turned back, Letha had already drifted off to sleep.

—-

Through the night, the Raven would call every so often. John could never tell if it was chiding him for being slow, or simply calling a Raven's version of *This way!*

Miles ahead, the Wolf was still on a dead run, a supernatural determination pushing it ever forward.

4

"How's that oldest one comin' along?" Uncle asked. His Pa stood behind Sam and put hand on his shoulder, and spoke the words with truth.

"He's a helpful one for sure, a good worker."

Over the first decade or so of Sam's life, a day's work had become obvious, as it was often the same or an extension of what had happened the day before. Collecting eggs, weeding, checking the wood pile; they were all things that Sam had to give little thought to as he went through his day. In fact, so relaxed were his days, he almost always sang a tune to himself as he worked, a wonderful side effect of having a musical mother.

Changes in the seasons happened with equal predictability, and Sam knew that early spring meant planting the big sharecrop of tobacco, as well as the smaller personal staples for themselves. Each would be harvested at slightly different times, meaning the end of summer and into autumn was busy with much to do.

After enough years, it was almost like he could tell the future. During the longest days of summer he noted how the sun would rise on the left of the dirt road to the east, and set over the trees at the edge of the fields to the west. When the days were shorter in the winter, the sun rose more southernly on the other side of the road. He'd watch the moon trace similar paths through the sky, still east to west, though it rarely followed the sun's line exactly. His father had a special affinity for the night sky, and had taught Sam how to connect the tiny glinting specks into animals, a hunter, and something his dad called "The Big Dipper."

His father also taught Sam how many nights between new and full moons. Sam loved to stay up late and watch the primrose flowers open as the blue of the full moon touched their petals.

"Gonna have thirteen moons this year," his father mentioned as they stepped outside after dinner one night to check the chicken coop.

"Thirteen?" Sam asked. "It's twelve, isn't it?"

"Most years," he replied, "This years' got one extra. That's what the almanac says. Happens every few years or so."

"So there's gonna be a month with two full moons?"

"Yes, there is," his father replied. "That second one is the blue moon. Extra special."

"It really look more blue?" Sam asked.

"I guess we'll have to see," smiled his father.

Sam learned how to make steady progress on one task before moving on to another, without any reminding from his Ma or Pa. He learned that being a "good worker" didn't just mean doing what you were told. It meant you were paying attention. It meant that you proudly took responsibility without being asked. It meant you were helpful. After all, there was always somethin' to be done.

If he saw the water in his mother's sink bucket was low, he'd bring more from the well; same with the wood pile for cooking. His little sister would collect eggs, but Sam made any repairs on the chicken coop, and he'd even do the butchering from time to time.

Sam soon realized, there was always somethin' that needed doing *before* the doing. Every so often, when he was getting water from the well, the rope would break on the first pull. He'd have to find a new rope, figure out a way to fish the bucket out, then reattach it before he even started the job of pulling water. If he had to fix the chicken coop, he would run out of nails, and he'd have to go out to the scrap wood pile and pull nails from older boards.

Even when things were going well, there would be bumps in the road. They'd be harvesting the corn and sure enough, the weight would tear a hole in the garden basket. Indeed, there was "always somethin'."

Of all the jobs he had, he liked the planting the best. Whenever he plunged his hands deep into the dirt, he felt a sense of calm. Naturally, he was happy to take any seed or partially cut tuber his mother would offer and try to grow it. He loved the root vegetables the most; they grew deep. His mother would often brag to others about how she never had to have her hands in the garden as Sam would take care of everything.

He had a good rotation of onions, sweet potatoes, carrots, and even ginger. Above ground he had vines, including peas and tomatoes. There was okra, and even tall stalks of sweet corn, as long as they could keep the raccoons out. Growing things never felt like work to Sam; it always felt like a playing in the dirt with a little added patience that gave a reward after a time.

It wasn't long after Sam learned about the blue moon that his father mentioned a bit more help was needed out at the Cunningham's plantation, and in addition to the jobs Sam already did around their small homestead, he'd soon be making money by working at alongside his father and others.

His father came to him and said, "Time to make yourself useful." Of course, Sam was already proud that he was quite useful to his own family. Now he'd be useful for someone else and get to put a little something in his pocket.

The very next day, Sam started at the Cunningham's plantation, where his father had worked since Sam was a baby. Abbot Cunningham, the owner, was giving Sam's father an extra twenty cents a day to have Sam join him anywhere they needed help on the property.

His father reminded him this would be a starter job. A reputation for good work could take you many places in the world. There was more to life than feeding horses and cooking for people in big houses.

"I've done better than the ones before me, and you'll do better still for you and yours," his father had told him. "Work makes the man, and the man makes the family."

If Sam's mother was around, his father would add, "A good woman helps too." That last part would usually get a smile from his mother, and sometimes a playful swat that made his father laugh.

Sam's mother had made a name for herself with music, playing piano at three different churches. She even managed to get an old upright on loan, and she put it to good use. She made sure to sing with her children every evening. She'd play while Sam did the dishes, or swept up. On Saturdays, Sam would sing along as he helped bathe the twins, his little brother Ben and sister Ruthie. Sam sang so much and so well that his mother would bring him along to sing at the services.

"That child's got the voice of an angel," the ladies in church would say.

While Sam enjoyed the praise and attention he got at church, it did made for busy Sundays.

Sam's mother had promised him she would find even more places for him to sing when spring came this year. Sam wondered where those places were.

"Church ain't the only place people sing. You got the gift of song. You gotta use it," his mother pronounced one day with a confidence only mothers have.

"He does, he does," his father nodded in agreement. "After all, you sure were singin' when we made him."

His mother slapped his father across the back over and over as he giggled in mock protest. Sam couldn't tell if his father's tears were from his mother's slapping or his father's own laughter. His father turned to Sam, a huge smile on his face and a twinkle in his eye as he wiped his cheek and kissed the air towards his mother. He spoke to Sam with a warmth that all proud fathers have.

"Ain't a better gift a soul can give than bringing a smile with a song. That voice you got? That music you got in ya? That'll take ya places, yes it will. Don't you never stop, you hear?"

His father wasn't a singer himself, which made him even more proud that Sam was. On hot summer nights, his mother would play that piano hotter than a skillet, while Sam let his voice wail and fly. His father would scoop up Ben and Ruthie in the kitchen and spin them high in the air. Maybe his father couldn't sing, but nothing could stop that man from dancing, and there was nothing that filled Sam up more than a kitchen full of song and dance.

—-

The day Sam started working, Mr. Cunningham told Sam's father it would be in the garden. Sam quickly discovered "in the garden" meant anywhere there was dirt; weeding flower beds, clearing drainage ditches, felling old trees, and even digging fishing worms for Mr. Cunningham's son, Seamus. It all fit within the definition of "gardening," and that was fine with Sam. After all, he liked the dirt even more than most boys did. In the middle of working, he'd often drive his hands deep into the earth, burying them completely into the thickening coolness and try to feel what seed would plant best underneath.

Singing with his mother had taught him to listen for the harmonies and Sam always felt there was a faint voice, or a song, or maybe a rhythm, coming from beneath the ground that he couldn't quite hear. He swore he could almost feel them in the earth. Sometimes, a melody would occur to him, and he wondered if it was a song from his own head, or if he was finally hearing the music from deep within the ground itself.

Today, he found himself humming one such tune as he weeded and tended the rose bushes lining the sides of the main house. It was a pale yellow plantation style home with a wide porch that welcomed guests to the front door. Sam stared past the second story of the house and up into the clouds.

I wonder if there are even bigger houses are out there, he thought.

He had heard that in the cities up north, the houses were close together, so close their chimneys almost touched.

I wonder where they grow their food? he mused.

He wondered if there were churches in those cities where he could sing with his mother. He heard stories of places up north where the winter brought snow so deep you needed shovels to clear it away. He'd only seen snow a couple times in his life, and it never stuck around longer than a day.

This day, in addition to pulling weeds, he had been tasked with making sure there weren't any dead leaves or old brown petals hanging from the blossoming stems. It was an easy enough job. If he was back home, he would have been cleaning out the pig pen, so getting to work around the flowers was considerably cleaner.

Sam was on hands and knees pulling a deep rooted weed when he heard the hesitant staccato sounds of a piano through the open window just above his head.

Inside the music room, ten-year-old Arabella swung her feet under the piano bench as she sat practicing. The rest of the room held carefully arranged cases of a banjo, a guitar, a mandolin, and a fiddle. Featured in the center of the room was a shiny, black, grand piano. There was nothing grand about Arabella's playing, however. She was currently making a sour face while working on a simplified version of "Fur Elise." Each time she played through, there were a few notes where something didn't sound quite right. She made another attempt, but once again something made her scrunch up her nose. She sat discouraged, looking at the music, then at the keys in front of her when her ears perked up from a sound coming from outside.

"Ooooo," a voice sang.

Arabella looked over at the window, then down at the piano keys.

"Ooooo," the voice sang again.

Arabella reached forward and played a note on the piano. It was close, but not quite the same as the voice outside. Again, the voice sang the note.

"Ooooo!"

Arabella eagerly played another note, then another, and another until she finally found the one that matched the voice.

Excitedly, Arabella started the phrase of "Fur Elise" again, slowing at the part with trouble, but playing through it correctly! She stopped, clapped her hands, and ran to the window. She couldn't wait to meet the person that belonged to the helpful voice.

"Thank you so much!" she exclaimed. "I couldn't find that note for the life of me!"

Her head poked out the window and she looked back and forth, but the only person outside was a young boy, one of the help, pulling weeds.

"Who was that, singing that note out here?" she asked.

"That was me." Sam sang the right note again. "Ooooo. Weren't nothin'."

"Well, I'll be," Arabella said under her breath. "Do you play piano?"

"Mostly sing in church is all."

Arabella looked Sam up and down, and noticed the colorful weeds in his hand, "Are those for me?"

Sam followed Arabella's gaze down to the uprooted short stalks he was holding. They were weeds, but they were also small purple flowers called *vetch,* or so he had been told.

"You want *these*?" Sam asked as he held them up.

"Well, if you're giving them to me, of course I'll take them!" She leaned as far as she could out the window and over the rose bushes, but the vetch, and Sam, were well out of reach.

Sam took a minute and looked at the girl who was hanging out the window, staring at him.

Guess she really likes weeds, he thought.

Sam took a couple steps and reached over the rose bush to hold out the cluster of vetch, the dirt still on the roots, while Arabella graciously received them.

Once in hand, Arabella pulled them to her nose and dramatically inhaled. She smiled, and looked at the flowers as she asked Sam another question.

"Thank you...wait, what's your name?" She asked.

"Sam, Miss," he answered automatically. Having no hat to tip, he nodded his head slightly before adding, "Nice to meet you."

"I'm Arabella, nice to meet you as well," Arabella responded with a curtsy. "Since you're at the window now, do you want to watch me play?"

"I should be weedin'."

"Should or shouldn't, that's always the question isn't it?" She finally took her eyes off the flowers and turned her gaze to Sam, sizing him up with a quick up and down. "Suit yourself."

Sam stepped back to where he left off, and got his hands back in the dirt.

Arabella returned to her piano and sat with a poof of her dress. She set the flowers down, dirty roots and all, on the bench next to her, and started to play.

5

Once they saw John leave with the Raven in the night, Amasa, Rowan, and Kofi knew they should head to Letha's cabin down in Forge to help with Arthur's body. They rose a little earlier than usual to find King already hitching up the horses. All four took the logging sled down to town while the orange-tinged clouds still held onto the morning, before the sky returned to the usual overcast grey.

Amasa, with his blue eyes and silver hair, looked a healthy and dignified fifty, though his stories came from much older times. Rowan was as Irish as they come, with the bright red, full beard and easy wit of youth. Kofi spoke English with his native Nigerian accent, his inner strength carved out of the same black granite as his physique. He and Rowan loved each other like brothers, and they fought like brothers too. King's gift for horses was given to him by his Mongolian ancestors, though they were a world and many lifetimes away.

Letha appeared in the doorway of the cabin just as they arrived, and soon all the men joined her for a moment of respectful silence at Arthur's bedside. Arthur had left his body only a few hours before, and in death looked smaller and more frail than any of them remembered. King broke the solemn moment with a small bow, then stepped out to go ready the sled. They'd be moving Arthur to the vault until it was time for the fire. Amasa turned to Letha.

"Everything went as it should?"

"So far," she replied. "'Course we'll have to see who John comes back with."

"Let's hope there's no surprises," Amasa added.

Rowan gave Letha a quick look up and down.

"Looks like you made it through alright, eh, ma'am?" He asked. He knew she was in the middle of one of her most important spells.

"A bit more aches in my bones, but Arthur was always a headache, so it's hard to tell if this is any worse."

Rowan put his hand on her shoulder and they shared a smile. "Let's hope the next one's a little less headache then," he said.

Kofi and Rowan carefully wrapped Arthur's body in blankets from the bed, and were surprised to find him already as stiff as one of the timbers he'd cut in years past.

"I got 'im," announced Rowan.

"Do you?" replied Kofi, "Careful, now."

"'Course, I'm careful, it's Arthur for Chrissake. Step back."

Kofi put his hands up and stepped back. Rowan picked up Arthur's stiff, unbending body and tried to balance him on his shoulder like a log. As he turned to exit, Kofi and Amasa both ducked just in time to avoid being hit by Arthur's feet. Instead of their heads, Arthur's feet smashed into the mantel above the fireplace, knocking over the jar with the Raven's feather. Somehow it stayed intact, but the cork top popped off and the feather ended up half in and half out of the bottle on the ground.

"Oh, dear," remarked Letha.

"Watch it! What the hell are ya doin', man?" fired off Kofi.

"I'm trying to get the bastard out of here!" shot back Rowan.

"Well, get him out of here then! Stop dancing with him for god's sake!"

Rowan clumsily made it to the door of the cabin and kicked it open. In his embarrassed rush to exit, the door bounced back on Arthur's head with a *whack!*

"Dammit," Rowan said under his breath. The door hit Arthur's legs and finally shut behind him as Letha tried—and failed—to stifle a laugh at the irreverence of it all.

Kofi grabbed new blankets from the foot of the bed and offered an apology on behalf of Rowan, "I swear. I'm sorry, Letha."

"Ah...no worries, none at all. He's already gone, that's just the shell." Kofi gave a laugh of understanding as he and Amasa finished making up the bed, tucking the sheets just right.

"That should do it, dear," Kofi turned to Letha and gave her a gentle but meaningful hug. Letha looked up at Kofi from her old, hunched posture. She placed a hand on his chest and paused for just a moment as she looked at him with a pride that only the aged have earned.

"Ah, Kofi," she said, "You always were my favorite." Kofi's smile could brighten even the darkest rooms.

"And you mine, dear," he whispered back at her as he took her hand and gave it a light kiss. He made a gratuitous bow as he stepped backwards towards the door.

"Ah, stop it!" Letha rolled her eyes.

"Never!" Kofi stood with wink, and stepped outside.

Only Amasa was left. He was picking up the jar and carefully placing the feather back inside. He slid the cork in just so before setting it back in its place on the mantle. He turned to Letha.

"You planning to go with Arthur, or will you stay?" he asked her frankly.

"I'll stay, for now. Alma seems to be brewing a girl, I should stay until at least then. Perhaps the new moon will bring the magic of a new baby."

"And if it doesn't? Or if John doesn't return in time?" A bit of concern tinged Amasa's voice.

"One thing at a time, Amasa." Letha took a breath. "I'm not the only one that can feel it then, am I?"

"I feel it, too," Amasa replied. "Arthur's passing...things are shifting. It feels like there is more change on the way, though what it is, or where it's coming from I cannot tell."

"We'll all know soon enough. We'll just have to trust the timing." Letha went quiet. She looked wistfully into the air, like she was lost in thought or in a time long passed.

"Amasa?" She finally said.

"Ma'am?" Amasa replied.

"Bring a long saw out to the vault with you. It'll be time to fell the tree."

Amasa looked to the ground. He knew what Letha was saying, and he knew that she was right, but he still didn't like what he and the other Jacks had to do. At last, he nodded, then held out his arms to her. Letha took the invitation and embraced him.

"See you soon," Amasa said. He opened the door to take his leave, letting in the sounds from outside. Letha heard the boys on the wagon, Rowan's vocal protests were loud and clear.

"*You're* her favorite?!"

31

Letha's smile was genuine, even with the solemn atmosphere, it was still fun to tease the boys.

"Trouble to the end," Amasa said with a smirk, shaking his head. Letha's eye twinkled.

"To the end."

Amasa stepped out into the cold of the morning, Letha made a gesture with her staff, and the door to the cabin closed.

6

John and the Raven found a swift pace trailing the Wolf together that first night. The Raven would fly ahead to get a bearing on the Wolf, then circle back to steer John accordingly with a *Caw!* In the darkness, they left Forge behind and quickly found themselves moving around the outskirts of Utica, across the Erie Canal, then bearing slightly west to keep the valley on their right.

Valleys are better than over mountains, John thought.

At the continued coaxing of the Raven, John made his way through Norwich, then across Nineveh Bridge, just outside of Harpursville, New York. They followed the edges of the Susquehanna River, running south all the way until its namesake town in Pennsylvania. Another hour or so south, and John finally watched the river turn away west.

Here come the mountains, he thought as he climbed southeast instead. John figured he'd covered a good hundred and fifty miles or so that first night. As the sky hinted at the start of day, the Raven took a perch in a tree and stopped. No caws, no urging on.

Must be time to rest.

The sun pushed its way into the brightening sky while John wasted no time finding a spot of shade to settle into, unfolding his wolfskin-satchel to pull it up and around his shoulders. He closed his eyes, knowing once the sun made its trip across the sky, the smallest hint of a crescent moon would show itself, and the Wolf would be on the move again.

—-

Sure enough, John woke with a loud and clear *CAW!* at sunset. He opened his eyes and saw the Raven perched above him on a branch. Following the sun towards the horizon, a sharp, thin curve of a moon hung in the sky. He sat up, rubbed his eyes, and was pleased to feel his strength had returned during his sleep. He took a sip from his canteen and tried not to think of the cookies Soup had given him the night before. Keeping up with a bird's flight while his feet were on the ground took some doing. After quickly collecting his things, he was on the move again. He found his pace as the final stretches of sunset orange set over the mountains to the west of Wilsonville along the Lackawaxan River.

An hour later, the slivered moon started to touch the horizon. As it disappeared and the night darkened, John and the Raven soon left the Poconos Mountains behind them.

For the whole night, John's mind wandered as his feet made the miles pass. Much had been set into motion in Forge. He did not know when he would return, but Constance would no doubt be making preparations with Letha to welcome them home.

Eventually, he realized the Wolf was following the arc of the Appalachians to the West.

John's gait was unbroken for the entire night, and after crossing the river in Duncannon, another dawn was on the horizon. The Raven stopped calling and perched. Its silence told John it was again time to rest. Sleep found John quickly.

—-

John was surprised when the call of the Raven woke him during daylight. The sun was inching into later afternoon and still had a good hour or two before it would leave the sky. It would be unusual for the Wolf to start moving already, but the Raven was persistent, and John stirred himself, gathered his things, and followed the squawking.

This could mean good fortune, he thought.

John knew this whole process could easily take a month or more. He had only been following the Wolf for a few days, and it would be quite the stroke of luck to find someone so soon.

After barely a hundred yards, he found the Raven perched; the Wolf was close.

John stopped and took a deep breath. Sure enough he picked up an earthy, feral odor. John crouched and pushed through a bit of underbrush and found himself at the edge of a large clearing, the ground and grass brown.

Where are you? he thought, scanning left and right over the field.

Across the clearing a large group of boys was playing a game of scratch baseball. With a wide stance at home, one boy held a stick high over his shoulder. Another stood in the middle of the makeshift diamond, winding up to pitch a barely stitched, well-worn ball. A few of the boys had gloves; most didn't. Shirts and planks of wood marked the bases. With all eyes on the pitcher and batter, they didn't notice John watching from the edge of what was deep left field.

"Aye, batter! Aye, aye batter!" the boys in the field called to the boy at bat. Raising the bat up and back, one of the batter's elbows was skinned. His trousers stopped midway down his shins, hand-me-downs he'd already outgrown from an older brother. He squinted a keen look of determination as he gripped the bat.

"Swing battah! Swing battah! Hey! Battah, battah!" the razzing continued. The pitcher wound up and threw the ball hard, putting speed on it he thought would be impossible to hit. He was wrong. The batter stepped his left foot forward and turned his hips, the end of the stick following the twist in his shoulders. *CRACK!*

The ball launched up and over the infield and deep toward the right side of the outfield, bouncing twice before almost rolling into the woods. As John's eyes followed the ball, he finally spied the Wolf in the bushes. It was lying low, a bit of foamy drool at the edge of its mouth. The ball had landed within ten yards of it, right at the edge of the field.

Its eyes were twitching from one boy to another. As the batter rounded first base at full speed, the Wolf snapped its attention to the one who was fast approaching the ball.

Both teams erupted in cheers.

"GO! GO! GO!!!"

"Throw it!!"

"He's headed home!"

The outfielder was almost to the ball. The Wolf crouched on its haunches, ready to pounce. In one motion, the boy grabbed the ball, whipped around, and hurled it back toward second base, just as the batter made the turn. The outfielder watched the ball's high arc, behind him, the Wolf licked its lips.

The shortstop snagged the ball from the air as the batter touched third. The only play left was at home, and the shortstop fired it hard.

"THROW IT!!! THROW IT!!" shouted the boys in the outfield.

"HOME!! HOME!!" shouted the boys from the sidelines.

The batter's speed brought him quickly within a few strides of scoring the winning run. The shortstop's throw was magnificent—the ball was coming in fast, just in front of home plate, a foot off the ground.

"SLIDE!! SLIDE!!"

Out of the corner of his eye, the batter could see the ball coming. He took two more strides and leaned back, slipping his foot under the empty catcher's mitt just as he heard the sound of the ball *slap* into it. As his body followed through, he kicked up a huge cloud of dust, and everything came to a stop.

Silence.

Somewhere above, the baseball gods blew just enough of a breeze to clear the dust. The batter was leaning back, his leading foot on home. The catcher's mitt was on his leg, ball caught.

In a voice-cracking thunderous eruption, the boys at the side sprinted over the baseline and the outfield rushed in.

"SAFE!! HE'S SAFE!!!

"OUT! HE'S OUT!! OUUUUUT!"

It took mere seconds for fists and dirt to start flying every which way, a mass of pubescent energy unleashed at opposing teams. John thought of breaking up the fight, but instead chuckled to himself.

To be so passionate, he thought. It tickled him because he completely understood.

John scanned the woods behind the boys, then back to the underbrush of the outfield, but there was no sign of the Wolf. The Raven cawed again and John looked up to see it take flight, heading south.

He considered staying hidden and picking his way through the woods around the game, but upon looking towards the pile of boys he thought, *They'll never even notice.*

So passionate was the fight at home plate that John, a six-foot-four, two-hundred-thirty-five-pound black man, went completely unnoticed as he jogged out in the open across the outfield, then into the woods.

The chase for the Wolf was on again.

7

Almost four decades ago, Arthur and Letha had arrived in Forge after the iron mining had already gone bust. Even though the town was deserted, they saw no reason to change the name. A family named Twitchell owned a great deal of land in and around Forge, and offered Arthur a sizable sum to take down the timber on the property. Arthur had accepted the deal, provided he could rebuild the small town as he saw fit, and he made a simple, strong request to be left alone. And of course, no questions.

"I already owe you my life," Twitchell had responded. Then, forever the businessman, added, "As long as you deliver."

And deliver Arthur did.

Even with Twitchell's basic knowledge of Arthur's gifts, he was still surprised at how fast Arthur and his crew could work. It wasn't hard for Twitchell to be generous, since Arthur's crew would cut three to four times as much as any other, and often over rougher terrain and through worse weather. Funny enough, it made Arthur's crew both the best paid, and the most profitable there ever was. The hard work and good profits made it easy to keep the deal going, and as such, Twitchell kept up his side and never asked any questions.

Those same profits let Arthur's crew live and even establish small personal farms on the very land they were cutting. Arthur found it refreshing to finally be able to settle into the land, and stop his nomadic life for the first time. As it turned out, Arthur wasn't the only one looking for a more permanent place to hang his hat; when good men find honorable work, it's hard to hold them back. Before long, John, Kofi, Rowan, Amasa, King, their Witches, and even more of their kind had come to live and work alongside Letha and him.

As with any working crew, each new addition caused a few bumps that needed smoothing over, but once all found a rhythm together, they grew stronger. Together, they couldn't be stopped.

Arthur's crew of lumberjacks, or "Jacks" at it were, developed a reputation, one that they earned repeatedly each and every year. They proved tight-knit and supremely skilled, floating more wood down Adirondack streams in the spring than two or three other normal crews could manage. Others that had passed muster with Arthur, Letha, and the rest began to populate Forge and as such, earned the title, "townsfolk." These townsfolk each had deep, personal ties to one of Arthur's crew. All of them credited one of Arthur's men, or women, for stepping in during a time of need and giving them a second chance at life. They'd each decided the best way to honor that second chance was to come to Forge themselves.

The townsfolk also knew to not ask too many questions. Truth be told, not knowing some things was easier than knowing and saying you didn't.

Every so often, some logger from away would come into town thinking he could bully or cajole his way onto Arthur's crew. Even with the townsfolk telling the newcomer to leave it alone, it never worked, and soon enough, such a man would find himself waking up far downriver, cold and wet, with anyone within a hundred miles echoing, "I told you so."

Some outsiders saw Arthur's crew as elite or egotistical, others saw it as simply particular. It did take a certain type of man to spend days and nights on end in the wilds and cold of the northern forests.

All the towns around, even as far away as Utica, generally agreed Arthur's crew was generous and kind, as lumberjacks go. On the occasions they did come into the bigger towns, they seemed nice enough. As most other lumbermen, Arthur's crew would have a mighty fine time dancing in the dance halls, even if they did tear up the floors with their spiked boots. Surprising to most, Arthur's crew never partook in any of the extra services the dance halls provided, no matter how graciously and low-priced they were, puzzling the women that worked there as much as the regulars that frequented them.

When they made it far enough out of Forge to their traditional stop into Paddy Ryan's pub, they would eat as much as Paddy himself could cook, but they would never touch rum, beer, or any alcohol. The kegs lining the walls never seemed to hold their interest at all. All this did, of course, was add to the crew's strange reputation and mystique, making them even more renowned.

Local legend said crossing Arthur and his men was a mistake. At best, such mistakes would end in a mild humiliation, either in a river or a snowbank. At worst, a man could find himself a limb short. This reputation had allowed Arthur and his crew to make sure their legend stayed as local as possible. Any extra attention was unwanted by Arthur, and he felt he had done well to keep his own little part of the land honorable and peaceful.

It had always been Arthur's hope this relative peace and prosperity would continue, even without him. While it wasn't entirely up to Arthur to choose a successor, crews need a boss, and someone had to eventually take the reins. Arthur was confident there were many who could do the job. They'd all been together for so long that only time would tell who could, and should, rise to the occasion. Arthur had learned from the history of others that while blood passed down many things, rarely did it decide a leader. A leader was inspired and decided by those who were willing to follow. With any luck, such a person would still have a bit of Arthur's influence to guide them.

—-

The first sign of Arthur's decline had been his limp.

Maybe a dozen years ago, on an otherwise normal winter day of cutting and loading timbers, Arthur caught his foot as he tried to stop a pile of logs from rolling into the horses. While he kept the horses safe, his ankle never quite fully healed, even with Letha's help. Over time, it progressed to a persistent limp, becoming more and more noticeable to others, and more bothersome to Arthur.

Without the balance of a good stance, he soon found his axe didn't make the chips of timber fly as far as they used to, nor did his swings make the pleasant and familiar *pop* when metal sunk into wood. Rowan would occasionally offer him a slender gnarled length of oak for a walking stick (not a cane, mind you), but Arthur repeated refused. In addition to the limp, he noticed himself starting to squint to see into the distance, and having to lean in to hear people talk. He had always led his crew by example, and didn't like to think his own link in the chain was weakening.

When he finally did reluctantly accept the walking stick, he took a bit of friendly ribbing from the boys. They thought they were clever to call it a Witch's staff, but Arthur got the last laugh by using it as an instrument of correction; a Witch's staff had great power after all.

Even with the growing hints of his last chapter of life, he did his best to keep the mood light. He preferred to focus on the days he had left, instead of the days he would soon be missing. No one lived forever, not even Arthur, and his soul had made many, many trips around the sun. Knowing there weren't many more, he felt blessed to witness each new dusk and dawn. He was happy he would be able to leave on his own terms. Many others hadn't been so lucky.

It was Letha who planted the idea of a gathering in Arthur's head during one of her more playful jabs:

"Too bad you'll miss your funeral," she said. "It'll be a helluva time!"

After a good laugh, Arthur actually gave it some thought. *It is,* he considered, *a shame to miss a party given in your honor, with all those that've been a part of your life.*

"More of a reunion, isn't it?" he corrected with eyebrows raised. "That's all a funeral is after all...a reunion minus one."

"A reunion? Now?" Letha couldn't help but laugh, Arthur's strange, humorous perspective was the gift she would miss the most. Even now, she wasn't sure if Arthur was playfully waxing philosophical, or actually wanting to plan a gathering.

"Call it a funeral plus one," Arthur suggested with a smirk, and the gathering was on.

The news went out far and wide that Arthur was having a last call of sorts, and any that wished to share a story or two, while he was still around to deny it, were invited to attend.

That spring, people began to trickle into Forge in the days leading up to the reunion, eventually referring to it as "Arthur's Last Call and Festival," spinning a bit of humor and rhyme into the grief of a goodbye on the horizon. Soon the town swelled from its normal few dozen to hundreds.

On the official day that spring, the feeling was indeed fiercely festive. Food was aplenty and games from log rolling to axe throwing to Viking chess spontaneously took place. Music filled the air while dance pounded at the earth and filled their souls. Of course, Letha and the other women had made sure the weather was appropriate, with just a quick shower in the afternoon, so the little ones could run in the rain. The clouds had long ago moved away when the sun set, revealing a clear sky with no moon to outshine the stars. The children and adults challenged each other to name the most constellations in the sky.

As intended, the affair had been more sweet than bitter. At the end of the night, when Arthur's legs would dance no more, he felt he had done good by his crew and then some, freely giving some of his last time on the earth to those that he held most dear.

People would trickle away over the next few days, and Arthur made sure to say each goodbye with a smile. He was grateful for his long life, and it was important he share that warmth before his body went cold.

Arthur held on for four more winters before Letha performed the final spells on a cold and moonless night, and sent the Raven to trail his own spirit south.

———

Years later, when Arthur passed, Rowan, Kofi, Amasa, and King moved his body to a small hill at the outskirts of town in which there was an earthen, underground vault, with a door on one end. Arthur would rest here until it was time for the final ceremony.

Next to the vault, a once majestic pine reached into the sky, its trunk at least six feet through. Like Arthur, the tree was worn from its many years. Its top was scraggly and bare of needles and only a few low branches still showed lingering signs of life.

Outside the vault, each of the Jacks took a turn on watch. Not that Arthur was going anywhere, but it was important that someone was present to make conversation and receive the small gifts many were bringing to honor his long life.

Naturally, in addition to word of his passing spreading around town, there were also whispers.

"Who's next then?"

"What now?"

"Have they picked someone yet?"

"What about Letha?"

Some questions would be answered sooner than others.

Amasa had also brought up a long saw from the logging camp as Letha had suggested. Though the Jacks all preferred their axes, there was no doubt the long saw made a straight,

45

clean cut. Amasa stepped up to the thick, majestic pine and placed a hand on its trunk.

"Looks like it's time, old friend," he said.

He laid the saw sideways at the base of the tree and gave the first few pulls, setting the teeth into a horizontal groove. He stopped and left the saw in the tree, leaving the job for others to continue.

In the coming days and nights, as each Jack stood watch, they would reverently give a few pulls and cut a little further into the tree. There was no rush to take it down, but they all knew, just as Letha did, that it had to be done.

Forge had been home to Arthur for quite some time and he had suspected it would be the place where he finally let go of this world. He just hoped that whoever would be reborn in his spirit would be able to carry on the peace he had fought so hard to find.

8

Arabella had found a vase for the purple vetch all by herself and put the flowers on display right on top of the piano. The flowers were a pleasant reminder of that boy, Sam, that helped her find the right note. Even if the dirty roots made the water muddy, she thought they looked lovely in the music room.

It had been a few days, but she hoped to see him again; after all, he had been quite helpful for her playing. The same as previous days, she pushed herself off the bench and stepped to the window. She looked back and forth, up and down the sides of the house, but there was no Sam to be seen.

She sat on the piano bench and played "Für Elise" once through with wonderful mediocrity. She glanced toward the window and waited. When Sam failed to appear, she replayed the phrase with a purposeful wrong note or two, or three. She waited again, but still, no Sam. She turned on the piano bench and walked to the window again.

He must be out here somewhere, she thought.

She looked right and left again, then, disappointed, she let her eyes drift out onto the lawn that stretched to the woods.

There was the long driveway, and across it the horse pastures. One of the foals raised its head from the field, shook its mane, and playfully jumped away from its mother. Arabella brought her gaze back across the lawn towards the garden at the back of the house. It was growing well this year, Betsie from the kitchen said the carrots and peas would be ready any day—

Wait, there he is! There's Sam! In the garden!

Sam was on all fours, humming a tune to himself as he made his way through the carrots. His job today was to weed and pick. Weeds trailed his progress on the ground, while the carrots were in a basket he filled at his side. This was his final job of the day, and once he got to the end of the row, he could be on his way home. With how well the garden was doing this year, Sam figured he'd be working till almost dusk. Even so, he was once again happy to be in the garden and not the pig-pen.

Arabella came up so fast that Sam didn't even hear her until the questions started.

"Whatcha doin'?" she chimed.

"Wha-?" Sam startled a bit, "Oh. Carrots."

"Why don't you come back by the window and listen to me play?" she asked with a smile.

"'Cuz the carrots are over here."

"Well...," Arabella looked down the rows in the garden. There were a *lot* of carrots.

"Miss Betsie says I gotta finish this whole row before I can go home," Sam continued.

"Is that all?" Arabella replied. "It'll go much faster if I help, won't it?"

Sam blinked a couple times.

She must be lonely, he thought.

Before Sam could make his thoughts into words, Arabella was in the dirt next to him. She grabbed a carrot and yanked, snapping off the greens but leaving the carrot itself in the ground. She held the greens in her hand and looked at Sam.

"Um... I didn't get the carrot part."

She's not going to be much help, Sam thought.

"Ya gotta wiggle it a little 'fore you pull," Sam explained. He grabbed the next carrot where the greens met the orange of the root, and made small circles, loosening the dirt around it. "And ya gotta be gentle when you pull." Small snapping sounds escaped the dirt as Sam gently but firmly drew the carrot out of the ground. He tapped it a few times on his other hand to get most of the dirt off.

"You make it look so easy," Arabella remarked, wide eyed.

"'Spose it is...once you get the hang of it."

Arabella, however, could not get the hang of it.

The next carrot she pulled broke and she left half in the ground before going in and digging for it. She pulled the tops off the next two, and had to dig those out as well. Sam could see her frustration, so before she made even more of a mess, he offered a solution.

"How 'bout I do the carrots, and you do the weeds?" suggested Sam. "It don't take as much of a wiggle...you can pull them out any way you want."

"If you think it would be helpful. I wouldn't want to mess anything up."

"Y'already done a bit of that, I'd say," Sam nodded to the unsuccessfully-pulled, broken carrots still in the ground.

"Well, momma says mistakes are just a chance for a lesson. So I guess I'm getting my lessons in today," she said with too much emphasis.

"Guess so," Sam replied.

Even though there were more of them, Arabella was much better with the weeds. Dirt, roots, and weed stalks sprung into the air with every pull she made.

She's quite determined, Sam thought as he watched her pulling with bewildering enthusiasm.

With half his task taken care of, things progressed more quickly, and soon they found themselves at the end of the row. There was a pile of carrots in the basket as well as a trail of weeds heaped behind them.

"Now, come on!" Arabella squealed. She reached for Sam's hand but found he was already holding the basket of carrots.

"I gotta get these to Miss Betsie," he said.

"Well, hurry up!"

She sure always seems in a hurry, Sam thought.

"I'll be waiting!" she called as Sam walked to the back door by the kitchen, "You come to the window!"

Sam dropped off the carrots in the kitchen to Miss Betsie, who complimented him on how fast he got the job done.

"My, that was quick!" she said. "I suppose you can go along home now. I'll tell your Pa when he comes around. Git now, before I think of something else for you to do!"

Sam came out of the back kitchen, gave a last look over his shoulder to the garden before stepping away from the main house to head towards his own home. Arabella's head poked out of the music room window.

"Where you going? Come on!" she urged, beckoning with her hand. Sam took a deep breath before reluctantly walking towards the window.

Hope it's better than last time, he thought.

50

"Let me know if this sounds right," she said as Sam approached and casually leaned his elbows up on the window sill. His work was done for the day, after all.

Arabella came around the piano bench and sat down, her dress making a bit off a *poof* as she sat. She gave one more look over her shoulder to make sure Sam was still watching and started to play. Her tongue stuck out of her mouth as her fingers sounded the same simple version of "Für Elise" she had played before. She slowed the tempo slightly to make sure she got the right notes, glancing back to see Sam smiling a little. It made her smile too.

Arabella's mother, Caroline, stepped through the door and into the music room. Her voice had a subtle southern drawl that made her sound proper, even when she was scolding.

"There you are, my dear, I swear I've barely heard you play a full song the whole time you've been in here, what have you been —" Caroline stopped when she saw Sam leaning on the window sill. She looked over at her daughter and saw that Arabella's cotton sun dress was dirtied with two large brown patches where her knees were. Dirt from her unwashed hands was smeared on every note in the key of G.

"What have you been doing, young lady?!" her mother cried. "Just look at your dress! The piano—"

"It's from the garden, Momma!" Arabella said. "I helped Sam finish the carrots and now he's listening to me play!"

"Sam? Who?" Caroline wracked her brain for anyone her daughter knew named Sam before she followed Arabella's gesture towards the window. "Well...Is that right? How nice of you to help," she said to Arabella before turning to scold Sam. "And how rude of you to let her!"

Arabella's father appeared in the doorway. He was a slender but stern, traditional southern man.

"Now what's all the shoutin—," he saw Sam standing at the window sill and looked him dead in the eye. "Shouldn't you be workin'?"

"Miss Betsie said once I finished the carrots I could go along home," replied Sam.

"You finish 'em?"

"Yes, sir," Sam replied.

"Then you best be gettin' home." It was an order.

"Yes, sir." Sam left, happy to be done with his work, but somehow sorry about Arabella's dress.

9

The miles were adding up. For the past several days, over hills, through valleys, across pastures and streams, John had been chasing the Raven, and by extension, the Wolf. He figured they must now be somewhere well south of Maryland, maybe even through all of Virginia.

Morning was still far in the distance when the Raven perched in the moonlight on the naked branch of a dying elm. Stopping in the middle of the night was unusual for the Wolf, even with the full moon a few nights away...unless the Wolf had found what he was looking for.

"A stop in the night, eh?" John asked the bird out loud. He was never sure if the bird actually understood him. Sometimes it seemed to, other times it didn't. This time the Raven stayed at its perch and stared down, unblinking at John in the still night. No squawks.

With the Raven motionless at its perch, John didn't bother to set up any kind of camp. Instead he let his axes fall to the ground and sat with his back against a tree, quickly tucking his satchel behind his neck. He gave the Raven one more glance to make sure it hadn't moved, then took a deep breath and closed his eyes. Now further south, the nights were warmer, and he was looking forward to his rest.

Before he even started to dream, John was startled awake by the Raven pecking at his hand.

"Already?" he said out loud.

He stood and stretched, then paused when he heard a strange clamor some distance off. In an otherwise still night, there was the voice of a man shouting and swearing. John shook off his brief sleep and gathered his satchel and axes. The Raven perched on his shoulder, gave a squawk, and took off in the direction of the commotion. John followed.

Within a dozen strides, he came upon a fence at the edge of a large, flat pasture. The swelling three quarter moon gave light for John's keen eyes to behold the side of a barn at the other end of the field, and a little further along, a farmhouse. In the open doors of the barn, the shifting light from a lantern spilled out. A voice yelled:

"Get the gun! Get the gun! Quick!"

A woman ran out of the barn and towards the house, her night dress making her steps short. John easily vaulted the fence and his powerful strides took him across the pasture in the same time the woman took to disappear into the house. Turning the corner to the open doors of the barn, John saw that a farmer had the Wolf, mouth foaming, cornered inside.

"Sir," said John.

"Jesus!" the surprised Farmer jumped. He turned his lantern to look John up and down, then quickly put his eyes back on the Wolf. "Who the hell are you?"

"That don't matter," John said to the Farmer. "Let him go."

"What? Go? He's gonna tear up the calves and half the sheep! Where's that fool woman?!"

"Let him go... sir," John said. "It's important."

"Important! What about my damn homestead? There she is..."

The Farmer's Wife rushed into the barn, then startled at the sight of John's massive frame. Mesmerized, her eyes stayed glued to John as she turned the single shot shotgun over to her husband.

"Jesus, woman, watch where you're pointing that thing!" the Farmer scolded. "Now give me that—here, take the lantern."

The Farmer's Wife couldn't take her eyes off John, while the Farmer couldn't stop staring at the Wolf. As a result, somewhere in the lantern-gun-shuffle, the lantern dropped, crashed, and broke on the floor of the barn. The splattering kerosene made the flames rise in an instant.

"Dammit, woman!" cried the Farmer, "Jesus H. Christ!"

The Wolf, spooked by the burning fire before it, drew back in confusion.

The Farmer brought the gun up to aim, but the growing flames blocked his shot. He fired anyway— *BLAM!* The shot missed and instead blew a hole in the side of the barn.

"Gol' dang it!" He popped open the shotgun and the empty shell sprung out. He held out his hand. "Another!" The Farmer's Wife looked down at the Farmer's empty hand, dumbfounded.

"You didn't grab no more shells!?!?" He yelled, "Now what the hell am I supposed to—"

John leapt over the flames, pulling his axes from his belt. Locking eyes with the Wolf, he made his way to the wall of the barn. With three of John's powerful swings, the shotgun hole became big enough for the Wolf to escape through. John stepped back and gestured with his axes towards the hole. The Wolf looked at his only way out, then with a snarl and a growl pushed through to the outside.

John added more swings and the hole was soon big enough for John himself to step through. Outside, John holstered his axes and watched the Wolf as it ducked under the fence at the edge of the pasture. The Raven swooped close to John's head and gave a *CAW!* as it flew off to follow. John hesitated as he heard the Farmer's voice from inside.

"Dammit woman...WATER!!"

Looking back through the hole he made, John saw the flames rising inside, higher into the rest of the barn, lapping at the hay loft above. It wouldn't be long before the whole thing was ablaze.

The Farmer's voice hollered in a panic, "We need to get to the calves!"

John looked across the pasture at the fence where the Wolf disappeared. Behind him the orange flames climbed higher. He looked into the sky at the three quarter moon, knowing the Wolf was getting further ahead by the second. He took his axes out of the holsters again and squeezed the handles, letting his shoulders rise and flex, gathering power from the night.

Inside, the flames crackled, and the Farmer was trying in vain to get to his calf pen when he heard the splintering of wood. Whipping his head toward the sound, he saw John's axe come through the barn from outside. Two more strikes and a hole was made in the stable wall wide enough for the calves to stream out.

Chickens clucked wildly and flew every which way, trying to keep away from the flames. The sheep were bleating desperately, and the horses neighed louder and louder. Over the cacophony, the powerful splintering of wood exploded again, this time coming from the sheep pen. Within seconds another hole was torn in the side of the barn, and the Farmer heard short whistles from outside beckoning the sheep as they pushed through the hole into the night.

The Farmer himself finally made it to the heifers and managed to get all three of them outside the front of the barn before he was almost run over by one of his own mares. As it galloped away, he ran down the side of the barn to find flames filling huge holes cut through the side of each horse pen.

The Farmer looked left and right, scanning for the strange man that had saved his livestock, and in some ways, the most valuable part of his entire homestead. He continued to circle the barn, but found no one. Looking out toward the edges of the pasture, the farmer only caught the glint of an axe in the moonlight as John vaulted the fence and slipped into the woods.

The Farmer turned back to the barn behind him. It was now fully engulfed in flames with his livestock running amuck all over the barnyard. The Farmer's Wife ran up to his side with a single bucket of water, eagerly handing it to him. He took the bucket from her, looked up at the flames of the barn, then down to the single bucket of water again. He dropped it on the ground.

"Gol' dangit."

10

Full Moon

A few days after finishing the carrots, Sam found himself with pruners in his hand, climbing over limbs higher and higher into the air. He had heard the Cunninghams were hosting guests this evening and Mrs. Caroline, the lady of the house, had insisted on getting the trees trimmed before they arrived. He had spent the better part of a cloudless, humid day thinning out the branches of a pair of willows; two of the main features of the plantation. He would clip and prune a few branches and drop them to the ground, where his father would periodically come by and carry them to a burn pile past the main house aways off. As usual, Sam hummed a melody as he worked.

Near the end of the day, his father whistled up from the base of the tree to get Sam's attention. "Mr. Abbot told me to tend the horse's. You finish up here," his father called up. "See you at home."

"See you at home," Sam called back down.

Sam spent another good half hour trimming before dropping his pruners into his trouser pocket and looking west. The limbs he stood upon shifted and swayed as the wind stirred. The evening would bring a cool winter's breeze. The sun stretched its last rays into the few long clouds above the horizon, its warmth touching Sam's face. As he climbed down, he left the final orange of the day tickling the top of the willow tree. When he was halfway down, he paused and watched yet another carriage pull up to the front door of the main house. The well dressed visitors stepped out of the carriage and inside without even a glance to the trees he had spent the day trimming.

Sam dropped down out of the willow and found himself in the cooling shade of early evening. The easy breeze rustled and stirred the recently trimmed branches above.

He was gathering the last of the clippings under his arm when he heard a voice from behind him.

"You missed one!" Arabella smiled and held up a branch, then poked and tucked it into the bunch under Sam's arm. She was dressed even fancier than usual.

"Well...thank you," Sam replied as he poked a few branches in himself.

"I want you to come listen. I learned a new one!"

"A new one?"

"Yes, a new song. You wanna hear it? I wanna play it for you before the rest of the stuffy guests arrive. Once they're here I'll have to be on lady behavior."

"I'm s'posed to finish up here, bring these back to the burn pile behind the shed, then—"

"Well, it's on the way, isn't it? You could just stop by the window for a quick listen."

Sam looked at the growing bundle under his arm, then at Arabella. He remembered the look Arabella's father had given him at the window.

"I should be on my way home, Miss," Sam replied.

"Look, my dress is perfectly clean, there won't be any trouble this time," Arabella assured him. "You're gonna walk by the window anyway, just stop for a moment. Please?"

Sam shrugged.

Just don't lean on the window, he thought.

Arabella ran ahead and into the music room, poked her head out of the window, and waited for Sam. With the last willow branches and clippings gathered, he reluctantly walked toward the house.

"Ooo! Look!" Arabella squealed as a few blue fireflies rose from the lawn and started an early dance into the air around the approaching Sam. Sam was careful to stand just outside the window, happy to have his arms filled with willow trimmings so he wouldn't lean on the window sill.

A minute later, Arabella finished a simple, square version of "Amazing Grace." She looked out the window to Sam.

"No wrong notes!" Arabella announced proudly. "I've been practicing!"

"Yeah...sure," Sam trailed off, then considered out loud, "I sure heard it different in church though."

"Well...that's what the notes say." Arabella pointed to the loose sheet music placed on the piano.

"The music?" Sam pondered, glancing at the papers filled with lines and dots. "I thought the music was the sounds."

Arabella laughed, "Well, of course the music is the sounds, silly, but the paper is...it's like a book for the music, so it's like I was reading it."

"A book for the music? Huh," Sam thought for a moment. "In church they just play from how it sounds."

"I played it just right, see?" Arabella took the pages of loose sheet music off the piano and was soon leaning out the window to show Sam. "See? These are all notes that—"

A long howl echoed from the surrounding woods. Sam's hair stood on end.

"What was that?" Arabella said, eyes wide and searching the edge of the woods. A gust of wind pulled the pages up and out of her hand, sending them down the huge lawn and toward the willow tree.

"Oh no!" Arabella cried.

On instinct, Sam dropped the branches he was holding and chased the pages. Arabella tumbled out of the window and followed as fast as she could. The sheets scattered and tumbled across the lawn. Finally, Sam caught the first page under the willow tree and handed it to Arabella. He took off again and caught a second and third just as they reached the edge of the forest. Arabella looked down and counted.

"One, two...four...oh no! I'm missing page three!"

As if on cue, page three flew past them and into the darkening underbrush of the forest. Arabella leapt for the final sheet but missed as it flitted further into the tangle of oaks, sycamore, and pine. Arabella led the chase all over again while Sam followed behind, never to leave a job undone.

With the sun down and night upon them, it only took an instant for Sam to lose sight of her.

"Wait! Miss?!" he called. "Miss 'Bella?"

"I got it! I'm right over—" Her voice stopped short.

Sam moved toward her voice, swatting and pushing through a thicket. He broke through to find her standing frozen.

"Miss?"

Arabella wasn't moving. The last page of music dropped from her hand. Sam finally realized she was staring at something, and her eyes were filled with fear. He followed Arabella's stare, and felt his own fear rise up within.

It was the Wolf.

Its lip rose to reveal a row of sharp teeth, and a low growl came from its belly. A foamy drool dripped from its mouth. Even darker than the shadows cast by the rising moon, its head was tall enough to look a man in the chest. Its piercing eyes shone in the moonlight.

Sam kept his voice low. "Miss, you best be gettin' out of here," he instructed. Sam stepped slowly, his eyes only on the Wolf as he put himself between the beast and Arabella.

"Sam—?"

"You go on, now."

Arabella glanced at Sam for a split second, then back to the Wolf.

"Go on, slow…," Sam added.

Gingerly, she stepped back. One foot, another, inching away…her foot landed on the fallen page of music…*crunch*.

The Wolf lunged with its mouth wide. Sam jumped and jammed his forearm between the beast's teeth. The Wolf's fangs sank deep as it thrashed back and forth, shredding Sam's arm. Sam could feel the heat of the Wolf's foamy drool as it seeped into his arm. With a powerful flick of its head, the Wolf launched Sam into the air, slamming him into a tree, and knocking the wind out of him before he crashed to the ground.

"No!" Arabella cried.

The Wolf turned back to Arabella, licking Sam's blood from its snout.

Sam gasped for air. He looked down at his arm and saw the white of bone through the gnawed flesh.

Arabella screamed. The Wolf was closing in.

Finally catching his breath, Sam reached into his pocket and grabbed his pruners before scrambling back toward Arabella. With the Wolf trained on her, Sam had only an instant to charge the beast with his last bit of strength.

He lunged. The Wolf snapped its head and closed its powerful jaws on Sam's thigh. He was thrashed back and forth, the Wolf's teeth cutting and sinking deeper and deeper into his leg. Screams filled the forest. Sam and the Wolf crashed to the ground, but the Wolf wouldn't let go.

Sam raised the pruners and brought them down as hard as he could, jabbing the beast straight in the eye. He twisted and pushed as hard as he could. A yelp escaped the Wolf's throat and its legs gave way as it slumped to the ground.

Arabella was on her knees and at Sam's side in a flash. She reached down and pried the jaws from Sam's leg. His blood flowed out and onto her hands. She bunched the edge of her dress and pressed the fabric to Sam's wound the best she could.

Sam grimaced against the pain.

"You're bleeding—there's so much—"

Sam's eyes fluttered. The bushes shifted behind her, and Arabella snapped her head toward the sound.

Her father broke through the underbrush, with her brother Seamus close behind.

"Girl, what are you screamin'—" Abbot's eyes widened as he took in the scene. "What in the—" The blood stained dress of his daughter filled him with fear as he rushed to her side.

"What's he done to you? What has he DONE?!" her father yelled as he pulled her up and away from Sam and the Wolf.

63

"It's not my blood, Pa! It's his! It chewed him up! It—"

Her father looked at Sam and the Wolf, then inspected his daughter. "What are you doing out here with him? You shouldn't be out here at all!"

Arabella stood up. "Pa, we have to—"

Abbot roughly pulled Arabella by the arm. He glanced over his shoulder at the wounded and dying Sam. "Serves him right for being out here with you. Who knows what could've happened?"

Arabella struggled against her father, but there was no way she could overpower him.

"Pa! PA! We can't—!"

"Leave him be!"

"NO! NO!!" Arabella cried, but it was no use. Her father yanked her away. Her brother turned back and bent low to look Sam in the eye.

"Serves you right for trying to git with my sister," he hissed. "You're gonna die...alone."

Sam's vision went blurry, and everything went black.

Tears streamed down Arabella's face as Abbot dragged her across the lawn and up the stairs of the front porch.

"We can't just—" she cried as she finally broke free.

"I've heard enough!" Abbot grabbed her again. "That's enough out of you. What's done is done. If there was *one* of those beasts out there, there's bound to be more, and we're not risking our lives for a—"

"Maybe he's still alive!"

"That's the end of it!" Abbott yelled. Caroline eased the front door open and stepped onto the porch.

"Abbott, my dear, what's all the fuss about? We have guests."

"Get her cleaned up!" Abbott barked. "And send her to bed for giving so much lip!"

Caroline swept up Arabella as the guests filtered out of the house, gasping and whispering at her bloodied appearance.

In the forest, Sam regained consciousness for a brief moment. He blinked his eyes open, and touched his leg. It felt sticky. He could smell pine. Through blurry vision, he saw a huge black figure pulling the Wolf away from him. The figure flopped the Wolf on its back, then looked up just as Sam's eyes fluttered into the back of his head. Sam heard soft chanting as darkness surrounded him and he passed out again.

Arabella hugged her knees in the bathtub while her mother poured water down her back, offering words that should've been soothing, but weren't. "It'll be okay, don't you worry. Your Pa's just lookin' out for you."

Arabella stepped out of the tub in silence as her mother dried her off. Caroline slipped a nightgown over her daughter's head, laid her down in bed, gave her a kiss, and gently closed the door behind her.

The moon shone through the window as the breeze pushed the bedroom curtains into her room. Arabella looked down to her hand, where a red stain streaked across her palm. A silver beam set her face aglow in the lonely darkness. Her eyes were wide open and full of tears.

In the days leading up to the full moon, the Wolf had been circling the plantation, unseen by anyone except John and the Raven. For the first time in almost two weeks, John sensed the Wolf had found its mark.

This must be the place, John thought. *Best get ready.*

He spent the next couple days getting the lay of the land. He watched the large yellow house from the woods, seeing workers and the owners of the plantation go about their daily lives. One of those lives was about to change.

John's own change was coming too, as it had every month for centuries. He would need a place unseen by human eyes and unheard by human ears. The woods were always the perfect hiding place. Trees muffled sound and kept sight lines short. In the night, the darkness beneath the canopy was so complete and shadows so deep an entire beast could hide within them.

John set up camp in the forest nearby among some tall, friendly pines. He dug two small holes next to each other to make a hidden, smokeless Dakota fire. A stream close by made for easy water.

On the night of the full moon, as Sam was climbing down from the willow tree, and the last of the Cunningham's guests were arriving, John was at his camp.

He reached into his pelt-satchel and pulled out the jar of tea Constance had given him. It had been steeping since he left

Forge; no doubt it would be potent. He held it up against the golden glow of the sky, watching the swirling herbs and other mysterious ingredients. Constance would never actually tell him what was in it. He just hoped she added some maple syrup. He pulled the lid off, and immediately smelled valerian and skullcap. He did not smell maple syrup.

Dammit, he thought.

He took a deep breath and downed the whole thing in one gulp. Making a face, he remembered Soup's cookies and shoved one in his mouth as quickly as he could. After a few breaths, he began feeling the calming effects of Constance's powerful concoction.

Thinking ahead, John shed his clothes and put them in a neat pile, revealing a muted scar running from his upper arm to his neck. It started to tingle.

John braced himself. Constance's magic would help with the suffering, but not the pain.

At the first glimpse of the moon, his scar itched and burned.

Hair rose fast from the rugged skin.

The muscle under the scar pulled and stretched, and John felt his bones softening and hardening as they elongated and rebuilt themselves. The ligaments and tendons groaned inside from the tension. His heart pounded in his chest as it enlarged chamber by chamber. Agony pierced his mind as the structure of his skull extended into a snout.

His eyes rolled back and memories flashed through his mind: regret after painful regret, experiences he wished he could go back and change.

His ears rose high on his head.

His teeth bled as they shifted forward, his canines lengthening.

It only took the moon seven minutes to rise, but in that time, John's body completely changed. With it, his mind had experienced lifetimes of pain, anguish, and grief. It was the price he paid for the power he held.

He stood tall and wrapped his pelt around his waist. He was as much beast as man. Instinctively, he filled his lungs with air and howled.

He was ready.

Several hundred yards away the Wolf growled, and John's keen ears made him turn his head.

John's huge strides closed the distance quickly. He watched through the trees as Arabella chased her fluttering sheet music unknowingly to the waiting Wolf. An unseen witness, John patiently remained in the shadows as Sam bravely saved Arabella and impressively managed to subdue the Wolf with the small blade of his pruners.

It was imperative that John hold himself back. He knew once the Wolf had found its mark, there was nothing that could change it. The Wolf, and Arthur, had made the choice, and that choice was Sam.

John also didn't intervene when Arabella was dragged away by her father. Now he didn't need to navigate around the girl, and even better, they assumed they had left Sam for dead.

If John didn't act quickly, they would be right.

He finally stepped out of the shadows and pulled the Wolf away. Then in one motion, he threw Sam over his shoulder, grabbed one leg of the Wolf, and started to walk. His night was just beginning. Letha's spell had worked.

When he came upon his small camp, he carefully laid Sam and the Wolf in the shadows. He pulled out his journal and opened to a dog-eared page to refresh his memory. Trading the journal for an axe, he began to chant as he made the first cut through the belly of the Wolf.

"This coat now, thy spirit holds
Soul released and body unfolds.
Release your shield and shed your skin,
A curing force held within."

The process of the transference was already underway, and John made quick work of skinning the Wolf. Every so often, he would hear a groan and look over to see Sam struggling to make it through his dreams.

Sam looked like he was both trying to wake up and stay asleep at the same time, a common occurrence for this first night. John knew the dreams were vivid and strange. After the bite comes a state of shock, naturally followed by a black out that leads into a strange space between awake and asleep. The whole body is immobilized while it recovers through a series of fever induced dreams lasting at least several hours and often days.

This was the initial integration. Inside Sam, the blood from the Wolf's bite—the very same blood Letha had pulled from Arthur on the new moon two weeks ago—was beginning to pulse. It was finding a way to integrate. Like all transformations, it was painful.

With John's skill and extra strength from his own transformation, his axe blade cut quickly under the skin of the Wolf as he sliced and pulled it away. Each pass of his axe gently shaved the fascia from the muscle, and left the Wolf's body naked and pink in the moonlight. Steam rose from the exposed flesh. Once he passed the spine, John flipped the Wolf onto its other side. It was a bloody job, but it needed to be finished, and soon.

Getting the Wolf-skin off the Wolf and onto Sam would not only ensure a good bond, but also help tremendously in the healing of Sam's wounds. In fact, the hide might be the only thing that could keep Sam alive. Healing was the most potent of the Pelt's magic, and truth be told, the secret to Arthur's long life, and John's too.

John's satchel-pelt unfolded so its fur side was out, and it crawled along the ground and up onto John's back to witness the last few cuts. The Pelts didn't have eyes, but they seemed to see everything, and know all that was going on around them. Like a lot of magic John had experienced over the years, he wasn't sure how it all worked, he just knew that it did.

John made the final slice, drew the Pelt off the Wolf, and flopped it onto Sam. He then pulled, tucked, and wrapped the Wolf's Pelt all around Sam's wounded body. It settled and clung to Sam, the fascia under the fur melding with Sam's own skin, embracing its new partner.

John dragged the Wolf's body into a circle of moonlight. As the cold blue beams struck the skinned carcass, smokey wisps rose and swirled from the glazed pink flesh and dove down into the Pelt. The bonding and healing had begun. John's own Pelt slithered on the ground back and forth as if it was pacing, a strange witness to the whole process.

Butchering the fresh kill had covered John in blood. He was quite a mess. He purposefully perked his ears and smelled the

70

air. Not sensing any danger, he made his way to the stream nearby to wash the blood away.

Even though John had tucked it in, Sam's Wolf Pelt continued to move on its own. It shifted and slithered up and down Sam's body, searching out what needed to be healed the most. It squeezed around his mangled arm and shredded leg, sliding over and winding around them tightly. With the rest of his body released from the Pelt's gentle squeeze, Sam twitched himself awake. He opened his eyes to a moon so full and bright that it cast shadows onto the forest floor. On the ground next to him lay the pale and thin body of the Wolf. A grey mist rose and whirled toward him, as if the beams from the moon were evaporating the body before his eyes.

He struggled to his feet and after another look, realized the Wolf had been completely skinned. The muscle and sinew glistened pink and shiny in the moonlight, yet the body was evaporating with a subtle *hiss* before his eyes. As the last of the mist enveloped them, the naked carcass dissolved into the ground, becoming indistinguishable from the dirt. Sam blinked.

Dizzy from the effort of simply standing, he braced himself against the trunk of a tree. A squishing sound caught Sam's attention and he looked down to see it was coming from where the thick, dark Pelt was clinging to his arm and leg. Sam shuddered, then scratched and pulled to get it off. While the Pelt held firm to his leg, he managed to free his arm. In the moonlight, he could see that somehow the skin had closed and there was no longer bone showing. Even more strange, it didn't hurt to move. With the Pelt still squishy and clinging onto his leg, he pushed off the tree and realized he could actually walk with some limping and a great effort.

71

He caught movement out of the corner of his eye, and his ears tracked a scurrying that trailed away through the bushes. He managed to whisper.

"Help!"

No one answered.

He gathered as much strength as he could and tried again, breathlessly.

"HELP!"

From her bed, Arabella sat up into the moonlight. Did she hear something? She turned her head sideways to listen, then slid out of bed and tiptoed to the open window.

John stopped washing his hands in the stream nearby and stood, cocking his head to listen over the gurgle of the water. His own Pelt, a strange eyeless pet, broke through the under brush and beckoned him.

Sam hobbled forward with less pain than he expected. He pushed himself through the woods towards the main house as the Pelt squeezed his leg.

"Arabella?" he whispered.

"It's too bad...I was looking forward to hearing her play," gossiped a lady with a tall hat as she fanned herself.

"Abbott had no choice. She was very disrespectful," replied another in a canary yellow dress.

Above the music room, Arabella stood at her window and squinted into the night over the great lawn. Something stirred the shrubs. Was it the wind? Or was there something moving along the border of the tree line? Something in the shadows?

From the darkness, just where the lawn met the woods, Sam appeared. He limped forward.

"Sam!" gasped Arabella under her breath. She bolted out of her room, down the stairs, and straight out the front door, running barefoot across the lawn as fast as she could. Her nightgown trailed behind her like a ghost.

In the music room, the lady with a tall hat caught a glimpse of the moon now high over the trees. She gestured and remarked to her friend, "My, my, look at that moon tonight." She squinted out the window, a gossamer figure catching her attention. She turned to her hosts.

"I say, Abbott, is that Arabella?"

Water still dripping from his hands, John arrived at his campsite to find Sam was gone. Before John had a chance to panic, the Raven swooped low and gave a loud *CAW!* as it flew towards the Cunningham's plantation.

Sam was limping fast across the lawn as Arabella rushed to him under the willow tree. Sam could barely hold himself up as she hugged him tight.

"SAM! Oh! We need to—"

BLAM!

A gunshot rang through the night air, freezinging both of them.

John snapped his head towards the sound.

"Get back here, girl!" Abbott called as he reloaded the gun. "So I can get a clear shot!" Other men from the evening's guest list began to gather behind him.

"Pa! It's Sam!" Arabella looked down at Sam's arm, then at the strange fur-skin that was wrapped around his leg. "He needs a doctor!"

"GET AWAY!" Abbot yelled.

"Pa! Don't—" she cried, but before she could finish, her father fired another gunshot in the air. *BLAM!*

Sam didn't have any choice. He pushed Arabella away and ran as fast as he could back toward the woods. His injured leg sent shocks through his body with every stride.

"Seamus, get the dogs!" ordered Abbot. "Torches, too!" He turned to his guests with a smile. "Gentlemen, if you're in a hunting mood, there's a few more guns inside."

Sam sprinted from the lawn into the forest as Abbot's men stepped onto the porch armed with an assortment of pistols and rifles. Abbot kept the only shotgun for himself. Seamus released the dogs from their chains and their barking announced the chase was on.

Arabella fell to her knees, her heart broken. The dogs dashed past her toward the woods. Her father, brother, and the other men followed close behind, rushing past her as she looked at the sky and pleaded, her tears glistening in the moonlight like dew.

"Pa! NO!" she cried.

Sam's breath echoed in his ears as he ran. Adrenaline took over, deadening Sam's pain as he picked up speed. He ran into the woods so fast, he didn't notice the shadow of John's beast standing by the same tree Sam had been slammed into hours before.

As the dogs entered the underbrush, Sam had no choice but to push deeper into the forest and the night.

11

He was on a dead run.

Sam's injured arm dangled at his side as he wove the spaces between trees. Barking swelled in the distance. In a moment the dogs—and the men behind them—would be upon young Sam. The moonlight caught his bleached and bloodied plantation shirt, making him stand out against the trees. He used his good arm to pull it up and over his head, flinging it to the ground. His African skin would now be an advantage in the night.

Branches scraped at his body as he splashed across a shallow stream and scrambled up the embankment on the other side. He stepped into a small clearing, surrounded by thick underbrush and briars in every direction. There was nowhere to go.

The barking sounded closer.

He turned to rush back across the stream, but the water churned from what must have been a dozen dogs. The calls of the men were quickly approaching. He was out of breath, and out of room. There was no escape. His heart pounding, Sam fell to his hands and knees in exhaustion. The full moon threw her jagged beams through the tops of the trees and onto Sam's back. The same moonlight struck the faces of the dogs as they leapt into the clearing and surrounded him. This was how his life would end, at the age of twelve.

Or not.

Sam gripped the earth and clenched his eyes shut. In his mind's eye, his mother's fingers danced across piano keys and struck a deep chord. His father's feet pounded a dancing rhythm.

A thousand miles north, Letha gripped her staff and thumped a rhythm into the ground. She softly called out, "Rise."

Fists full of soil, pain surged up from the earth and pulsed a rhythm through Sam's mangled arm; a song of strength stirred deep. Sam stood. Blood dripped from his elbow as he raised his fists.

A deep, resonating growl filled the air behind him, pressing waves of sound through Sam and penetrating the surrounding woods. Every hair on his body came alive. Sam didn't dare move. The dogs ceased their barking and froze in their tracks.

The Pelt squeezed tight around Sam's injured leg. The pulse in his mangled arm gave way to a heat traveling up and into his chest. The heat brought courage that pushed back at the fear. From deep within his own body, Sam somehow knew whatever made the penetrating rumble was *with* him.

The Raven landed on Sam's shoulder.

Another growl caused sudden dread as it reached all the men, slowing them to a stop on the other side of the stream. They searched each other for an explanation for the sound; it had driven fear down into their bones. Seamus finally asked the obvious question.

"What was that?"

Torches illuminated each of the men's confused faces. Some even raised their guns, searching the darkness. Finally, one man offered a clue, gesturing ahead.

"It's from up the other side of the stream there. The dogs got 'im rounded up." He pointed his torch towards the small clearing, where he glimpsed the dogs and Sam through the trees.

"Up there, he's cornered now!" Abbot called as the men sprung back into action.

In the clearing, Sam heard a low snort from behind him. All the dogs sat, focused up and over Sam's head at the shadow that blocked out the moonlight.

The men's boots splashed through the stream, their torches flickered through the trees as they ran up the embankment and emerged just behind the dogs. Their voices were threatening.

"You're gonna get a learnin' tonight for sure!"

"Can't get away now, can yuh boy?"

Their jeers suddenly ceased. The light of the torches revealed Sam surrounded by the docile dogs, and *something* behind him.

"What the devil?" Abbott finally managed under his breath. A gun broke the silence.

BLAM!

The shadow disappeared from behind Sam just as he felt the slug whizz past his ear. A shift in the air pushed all the flames of the torches sideways. There was a sound, like a muffled slice, and the shadow was back behind Sam, once more blocking out the moon. Barely a second had passed.

The gun dropped to the ground. Sam looked down in the flickering torchlight to find a hand was still partially wrapped around the grip behind the trigger, and an arm, or part of one.

There was screaming.

Sam scanned the men, finding one who held up a bleeding stub of an arm. His screams turned to whimpers.

From behind Sam came a voice deep and resonant.

"We'll be going now."

There was a moment of complete silence, even the gurgling of the stream seemed to stop. The voice continued.

"I advise you keep your bullets, and you can keep your limbs. There'll be no killin' tonight."

CAW! The Raven added.

"Kill 'em both!" Seamus raised his gun. *BLAM!*

Sam caught a glint of silver and a spark of metal on metal as the slug ricocheted away and into the trunk of a tree with a muffled *thunk*. In front of him, Sam beheld a massive, hairy claw gripping an axe. It had deflected the bullet. Then the axe and the shadow were gone again, and Sam heard shrieking and the sound of flesh being torn; this time it came from Seamus.

Another gun went off with a *BLAM!* Sam felt a sharpness in his good leg. Warmth ran down into the back of his knee.

Silhouetted against the full moon, another gun was flung into the air, a hand still gripping the trigger. An arm cut at the elbow followed, still holding a torch. Blood fell back in arcs toward the earth. More men hollered in pain. The deadly darkness was everywhere and nowhere. More gunfire echoed, as did the sound of limbs being severed from bodies, like branches being ripped from trees in a storm.

The presence finally returned behind Sam, once again casting its protective shadow over him.

Each and every man collapsed in one form or another. Some leaned on trees, others knelt and clenched what remained of a bloodied appendage. Every single one was missing at least one hand; not one had escaped the mutilation.

"We're done here," the creature behind Sam said. Sam turned and found the creature kneeling.

"Get on," it said.

Sam reached for its shoulders, clutching two handfuls of fur as he pulled himself onto its back. As he climbed, Sam felt throbbing in his leg. A heat rose from the wound up Sam's body and into his head. He felt his face flush, and his grip went weak. The world started spinning, and everything went dark.

Sam's eyes blinked open for a moment. He was upside down and bouncing slightly. He felt the roughness of fur on his face, below him the ground sped by. He realized he was being carried over the shoulder of the creature that had saved him. The dogs were giving chase at full speed, but they weren't barking. Instead, their tongues were out and their tails were wagging.

Sam's head felt heavy, and his eyes flickered closed.

Even with Sam slung over his shoulder, John's beastly form allowed him to cover the half mile to his camp in no time. Sam was still unconscious when John gently laid him by the fire for the second time that evening.

"Now...you stay put," John said aloud.

The dogs trailing them circled and sniffed Sam up and down as he lay motionless. John could still hear the voices of suffering in the distance as the men made their way back to Cunningham's plantation. Against his more primal urges, John had left them all alive. He had relieved them of their guns, and in the process, a hand or an arm. He purposefully left them all with legs to carry themselves home and was confident that they would all heal from their wounds; his cuts were clean. He was also confident that they would remember him, the beast in the woods.

In addition to the wounds from the jaws of the Wolf, Sam's good leg was now bleeding from a gun shot. John pulled at the Pelt to cover the additional wound. He knew that healing three wounds would take the better part of the night. But more importantly, making sure Arthur's blood properly integrated into Sam would take more time. In fact, this night was only the initial step in the process. Once he brought Sam and his family back north to Forge, there would be Proving Night.

John hadn't anticipated Sam's will to be so strong. He certainly hadn't expected Sam to go searching for Arabella.

It was a shame that Abbott's own stubbornness meant the loss of an arm for himself, his son, and their guests. As is often the case, it was easier to make the dogs behave than the men.

John did keep his word, though; there had been no killing on this night.

Now that the unplanned drama was over, and John had Sam back at his camp, he was hopeful they could take their time. He could meet Sam's family, give Sam a day or two to heal up, and start their trek north.

Tomorrow, when Sam awoke, they would go to Sam's home and speak to his parents. It was up to John to convince them that it was in Sam's best interest to come north with him. Sam's family could come too, or not, but Sam must come. There would be no spells of persuasion to help. John had to use his brain, not his brawn. Truth, no lies.

Letha had shown insight in choosing John. His history in the South as a black man would provide a bridge to talk with Sam's parents. Sending Rowan, with his bright red hair, or Amasa with his blue eyes, would've made swaying Sam's parents more difficult. This was a job for John from the beginning. Of course, he had his own deep history with the South of this country. Some of those memories were fond. Some, but not all.

This journey's memories would not be about him, they would be about Sam. And for now Sam was sleeping, wrapped in the fresh Pelt from Arthur's conjured Wolf. John would find no sleep with the full moon high in the sky, instead he alternated between periodic checks on Sam and making notes in his journal. There was new history being made, and before the memories faded, they needed to be accounted for as they happened. On the way back North, he'd give these first few pages to Charles, one of the Holders, to copy and chronicle.

As the sun came up hours later, John went through his transformation again in reverse, from the Wolf-like beast back to man. He checked on Sam one last time, finding him sweaty but still sleeping soundly. For the first time since his travels started on the new moon two weeks ago, he felt calm.

John's body wanted to relax while his mind continued to race through his mental checklist for all the tasks he accomplished the night before; witnessing the event, skinning the wolf, applying the pelt, protecting Sam... He convinced himself all was in order and knew after such a dramatic night his own sleep would come fast. He leaned himself up against a tree in front of Sam and gestured to his own Pelt to curl up under his head for a pillow. He gave one last look to the fire and Sam before letting his eyes close and allowing sleep to find him.

As John drifted off, the ever-watchful Raven gave a light squawk and took a perch above him in the very tree he was leaning on.

12

With the gunshots sounding from deep in the woods, Arabella feared the worst. Her mother pulled her from the lawn, through the crowd of bewildered guests, and back upstairs to her bedroom. Left alone, all Arabella could think of was Sam. Exhausted, her eyes were almost closed when she heard muffled groans of men and gasps from the women downstairs. When she came out to investigate, her mother loudly scolded her to get back to her room and shut the door. She obeyed.

With her ear pressed to the door, she could make out voices talking about rags, bandages, and calls for a doctor. Eventually, the initial commotion calmed, Arabella moved to her bed, and with her eyes drained of tears, she finally succumbed to sleep.

———

The early sun cast an orange glow into Arabella's room. She opened her eyes to a familiar space, but an unfamiliar voice filtered into her room. She sat up in bed and listened, barely making out the faint words from downstairs. She cracked her door and listened carefully.

"If you know where they are, then me and my boys can take care of it quite quickly, ma'am." The man's voice was high and obsequious.

Slipping out of her room, Arabella crept down the hall to the top of the stairs. She saw the front door open and her mother, Caroline, speaking to a man at the threshold. He looked plain enough, holding his hat by his side.

"Of course," her mother replied. "I can write that down for you. We know exactly where they are."

Unnoticed, Arabella hunched between the railings of the stairs, straining to listen.

"As regards to the...rate," the Man with a Hat paused for a moment and continued in his distinct southern drawl. "I realize you are in the middle of a troubling time, ma'am. I must admit I feel rude discussing money at a time like this."

"It has been more than a troubling night for all of us," Caroline responded, "but, please go ahead."

"In that case, most of our...clients...do pay half up front."

Her mother looked at the Man with a Hat, waiting. After a moment, he leaned forward and said something more into her ear. Her mother nodded.

"Please wait here," her mother gestured inside the door. The Man with a Hat stepped into the foyer as Caroline turned and walked down the hall and into Abbot's study. A woman emerged from the front parlor with bloodied bandages in her hand, her canary yellow dress marred with red stains. She gave the Man with a Hat a minimal nod before she hurried back towards the kitchen, shaking her head in disbelief along the way. In her haste, she left the door to the front parlor slightly ajar. The Man

84

with a Hat caught Abbot's eye through the open door. He gave a slight bow before stepping back to the foot of the stairs. Arabella's mother came from the study.

"Please, let me confer with my husband," she said.

"Of course, ma'am."

Caroline went into the front parlor and closed the door behind her.

Seemingly alone, the Man with a Hat placed his hand on the banister of the staircase, moving it back and forth, feeling its smoothness. He turned and took a couple steps into the open front door, put his hand in his pocket, and pulled out a small lollipop wrapped in a shiny bit of wax paper. He twisted the wax paper off unconsciously and put the lollipop in his mouth, then folded the wrapper twice and put it back in his pocket. He looked out over the front lawn of the house, almost as if it was all his.

I should have asked for more, he thought.

Arabella's mother stepped out of the parlor with an envelope, thick with what could only be money, and approached the porch. The Man with a Hat pulled the lollipop from his mouth and held it behind his back as he bowed slightly and extended the other hand to receive the envelope.

"When should I expect this to be taken care of?" Caroline asked. The Man with a Hat looked at the envelope in his hand, an address was written on the front.

"Ma'am, since you've provided me with an address, we should have the job finished by tomorrow. Perhaps even today."

"Today? Why, that's very...efficient."

He gestured towards the front parlor, where the men were being tended, "It does seem urgent."

"Yes. Yes it is," Caroline agreed. "I don't know if I'll have the rest of the...the balance, so quickly," she considered out loud.

"Don't you worry about that, ma'am. I can come back just as easy the day after tomorrow, or even the next."

"Tuesday then," her mother responded.

"Ma'am," he nodded. He stuffed the envelope into his front pocket, tipped his hat as he put it on, and quickly walked down the front steps.

Her mother stepped back inside and closed the door. She paused for a second, deep in thought, then turned to see Arabella standing at the top of the stairs in her nightgown.

"Who was that?" Arabella asked. "And where's Pa?"

Her mother's glance into the parlor betrayed her desire for secrecy, and Arabella rushed down the stairs.

There, in the parlor room, were the men from the party last night. Each one was bandaged and being tended to by the wives. A white-coated doctor made his way around the room, checking the wrapping on each of their wounds. Every man bore a bloodied stump, some above the elbow, some at the wrist. Before her mother could stop her, Arabella ran to her father.

"Gentle now," Caroline called from behind.

A wrap of bandages was stained red at Abbot's shoulder, where his arm should've been. Arabella gently sat on his lap, then gingerly wrapped her arms around his neck and squeezed. As she pulled away, Abbott looked her up and down, and noticed the red on her hand.

"Are you hurt?" He asked.

"No," Arabella rubbed her palm, but the stain remained. Abbot seemed relieved.

"Don't you worry," Abbot said. "We'll get that boy."

He looked to his wife, who turned to the window as the Man with a Hat reached the end of the driveway.

The Man with a Hat paused for just a moment, pulled the package from his pocket to inspect the address, and turned right.

13

There are many ways to do it, but mostly its personal preference.

The hard part wasn't the fire. After all, a fire really isn't that hard to get going, especially with a can of kerosene. The hard part was making sure the people you wanted in the house were actually in the house. It's a complete waste of a good fire if there's nobody inside. He didn't particularly like that part of it. The part where he had to drag, cajole, and tie up the people. It would be so much easier if they just stayed put on their own. But here he was, rope in hand, yet again stuffing a torn piece of old shirt into a woman's mouth and tying it around the back of her head.

Of course the kids were easier, because they would just cling to their mother. He didn't have to worry about them going for help, necessarily, but he was a detail-oriented person, so he cut a few more lengths of rope and made sure they were anchored securely with their mother to the one wooden pillar in the middle of the house.

He had learned over the years that their little arms would sometimes slip out of the knots he would tie. At first he was frustrated by this, because every so often one would get away. But then he realized it allowed him to practice tying the knots better and tighter. He was actually quite proud of how nice his knots looked. He had never seen the ocean, but he was confident that any sailor would marvel at his proficiency with a rope.

With the little ones and their mother tied up to his satisfaction, he grabbed the can of kerosene. Starting at the center of the shack, he was careful to pour without splashing. For the fire to spread efficiently, it was best if the kerosene was continuous. Splashing some here and some there was fine, but it didn't make for a satisfying *whump!* when he threw the match.

He made sure the mother and the children's clothing had soaked up enough, continued around the kitchen, and made sure to douse the upright piano. He walked backwards, carefully wetting a trail to the bedroom. He nonchalantly flung a few extra splashes onto the husband's body. The lone bullet hole through his head kept him dead still.

He brought the kerosene trail all the way to the window. This was a more creative choice on his part. Most people would assume you would make the fire start at the front door, but that was a trite choice. Not to mention the slight risk of being seen.

With the can in hand, he jumped out the bedroom window effortlessly. He splashed the last of the kerosene on the window sill and against the side of the house, then pulled a box of matches from his pocket.

With a flourish, he lit a single match on the box. His eyes were wide with anticipation as he brought it down to the window sill. Before the match even touched wood, the flame jumped and chased the soaked trail with frightening speed. He pulled the match away as the sound of the fire filled his ears.

The job was done.

He knew not to linger long. The neighbors were a ways off across the cotton field, but once the flames got high enough and the smoke thickened, they would notice. Still, he couldn't help but step back for a moment and watch as the flames lapped out the windows at the clapboards, getting hotter and higher by the second.

The muffled cries of the mother and children faded as the crackling of the fire grew. The Man with a Hat gently patted the thick envelope in his front pocket then picked up his empty metal can and stepped away from the scene.

Down the road a piece, he spied one of the neighbors come running out of their shack of a home in the distance. He could make out a faint yelling and arms waving as they pointed towards the flames. He angled away from the dirt path, across the back field, and into the woods, away from the neighbors.

The black smoke rose high in the sky behind him.

14

It wasn't always the case the Wolf would find its mark by the first full moon. Sometimes it took several cycles before it found someone worthy to pass its blood. John's own Wolf had taken six weeks to find him. All the journeys were different, though they were also all the same.

John thought his nights and days of chasing the Raven were over, but instead, he was staring at the unflappable bird. He had only found an hour or two of sleep this morning before the Raven's incessant *cawing* pulled him from his slumber. As he forced his eyes open, he realized he had neglected an important addendum to the ceremony: telling Letha the blood had moved from the Wolf to the Chosen, Sam. Once she knew, she would start preparing for John's return, and eventually the rest of the ceremony.

I should've remembered last night, John thought. Catching the Raven would have been much easier in his more beastly form. Of course, it also would be easier if the damn bird just cooperated. Instead, John had spent a good portion of the morning pursuing the Raven in circles around the camp. All John needed was a single feather to send Letha the news.

John knew it. The bird knew it. John knew the bird knew it, and the bird knew that John knew. With the moon now under the horizon, John was still faster and stronger than any normal man, but a bird has flight, and a witch's bird is particularly savvy.

He couldn't help feeling a little resentful. He had travelled over a thousand miles in the past two weeks, following the Raven through valleys, fields, and over small mountains. He even overcame last night's trouble with Abbott and his men and managed to complete every task required of him.

Well, all except the feather.

He tried to reason with the bird, perched just out of reach in a tree.

"It's just one feather. You knew this was part of the deal."

The Raven squawked and nimbly flew to a higher branch.

"I'd rather you just gave it to me," he tried, but the Raven didn't move.

Looks like I'm climbing, John thought. He grabbed a branch, pulled himself up, and began his ascent.

"Come on, bird. That's a nice birdie."

The Raven curiously watched John as he made his way up the tree. John was a good thirty feet off the ground when he finally was high enough to reach for the bird.

"Come on, now...I just need one feather... You can even choose which one...," he called gently.

But the Raven wasn't done toying with John quite yet. It gently flapped its wings and landed a few trees away, higher still.

Dammit.

John looked down at the ground far below. Sam was still soundly sleeping with the Wolf's Pelt wrapped tightly around him. John had checked the bullet wound earlier. Only a small pock mark was left where it had gone through.

John mentally measured the distance between him and the bird, and him and the ground.

No sense in climbing down, just to climb all the way back up, John thought. *I can jump it....it's not that far.*

John set his feet on the branch the best he could, bent his knees, and jumped up and away from the tree. He reached out and sure enough nabbed a branch at the peak of his leap. His legs swung a bit, and his feet soon found the crook of a limb just below. A laugh of relief escaped him.

"Haha!" *Not bad after a thousand miles of running.*

The Raven was two trees away, preening and pulling at its feathers. John was sure it was mocking him.

So much for this being a friendly, easy event.

John calculated it was only one more jump between him and the Raven, but it was a big one.

Come on, John. You can get that bird... make the jump... and grab it at the same time.

He turned away from the bird, and called out loudly.

"No worries, I can just head north without the feather!" he tracked the Raven at the edge of his vision.

"I'll just tell Letha what happened," he continued. "I'm sure she'll love to hear about how 'helpful' you were about sending word." He moved his feet, it looked like he was going to start climbing down.

Sure enough, the Raven gave a gentle caw and coo, like a sort of Raven's compromise. It shuffled on its branch a little, then jumped and opened its wings, quickly gliding to the tree right next to John. John saw the move out of the corner of his eye.

Perfect.

He turned, jumped, and reached for the Raven.

Mid-glide, the Raven flapped its wings a single time and rose *just* far enough in the air that John's hand missed by an inch. Flailing, he grabbed at any branch he could, finding only a small offshoot to precariously hang from high above the ground. He clung to it, but could feel it giving way.

CRACK!

There was no limb on the trunk to plant his feet, and he was too far away from any other branch to swing. He was running out of tree.

SNAP!

John fell backwards. The tops of the trees reached into the sky faster and further as he fell. He had just enough time to see the bird *squawk* with Raven laughter as he braced himself for the impact of the ground fast approaching below.

"Son of a—"

Suddenly, he was suspended mid-air.

Phew.

All two hundred-plus pounds of him hung in the leather of his own Pelt for a split second before giving way and plopping the last few feet to the ground with a *thud!* John crawled off his Pelt and came to his knees, rubbing and stretching his back. He reached over and gave the Pelt an appreciative rub as well.

"Good boy," he said. The Pelt leaned into his hand.

From above, the Raven's *caw*s sounded like laughter. It took off from the tree and swooped down at John's head, taunting him. John instinctively reached up and grabbed at the bird, but missed. The Raven turned and swooped again, lower this time.

SQUAWK!

There was surprise in the Raven's call as it sunk to the ground. The edge of John's Pelt had caught the bird's legs and pulled it from the air. In an instant, it had the Raven wrapped up completely. John smiled and gave the Pelt another scratch of appreciation.

"Well done."

John brushed himself off and approached the bundled bird. He smiled as he looked down at the Raven. He methodically chose a feather, taking his time for a little "gotcha" emphasis. Finally, he reached out and pulled.

Pluck.

"Thank you so much," John said with over-sincerity, and his Pelt let the Raven go. The bird squawked resentfully as it flew to a new perch above.

Back at the campfire, John grabbed a stick and stirred the smoldering embers, finding a few that still had a red-orange glow. He pinched the quill and bent forward to gently touch the tip to the coals. With a small *puff,* it caught fire. John brought it up to watch it burn. The bright yellow flame gave off hints of purple and green as it crept down the edges.

Over a thousand miles northeast, Letha looked up from her rocker to see her own Raven's feather catch fire in the jar on the mantel. She watched it burn with the same subtle hues of green and purple John was seeing at his campfire. Soon, it was ash.

"Well done, John," Letha said aloud.

The feather business done, John sat, settled in, and reached for his journal to chronicle the drama of the morning. Instead, he soon found his pencil trailing a squiggled line across the page. Sleep was fast descending upon him in the shade of the very tree he had fallen out of.

He and Sam both slept while the sun arced into the sky and traced patterns on the forest floor. As it reached its apex, beams streamed down through the old growth canopy onto a sleeping Sam. His eyes fluttered under his eyelids, and beads of sweat formed on his forehead. In his dreams, images flashed of torches and dogs. There were sounds of screams—of Arabella and the group of men. An old woman's voice murmured something over him while he was being tucked into bed. The glint of a blade in candlelight blended into the canopies of giant trees reaching into the sky, blocking the sun. One of the tallest, oldest trees started to fall, and just as it crashed into the ground, Sam twitched himself awake.

Sam lay still, taking in his surroundings. The Raven flew overhead, blocking the sun from Sam's face for a brief second before it disappeared again amongst the trees.

Sam's brain was spinning from the strange images his mind had conjured. Were they dreams, or was it the night before? The Wolf, Arabella, the dogs and men, the large ferocious creature— it was the stuff of terrible dreams, but it felt so real.

Where am I? This isn't my house, Sam thought. *Is this a dream too?*

Sam slowly looked around. A few feet away, a hole in the ground held a smoldering campfire, only a periodic wisp of smoke escaped the coals left from the night before. A tingling, then a deep ache came from his injured arm and leg. His instinct was to get up and move, but Sam didn't want to disturb...*him.*

Across the coals of the fire, a huge man was sleeping with his back against a large pine tree, an open journal on his chest. There was something he recognized in the man, but Sam was also sure he'd never met him. Perhaps it was the distinct white streak that blazed through his otherwise dark hair. Even with his hands folded on his lap, there seemed something ferocious and dangerous about him. He was the type of character a boy wouldn't forget.

The Raven landed just above the sleeping man, on a thin, scraggly branch. It twitched its head, looked at the man, then over at Sam. It gave a *squawk*, stirring the man from his sleep.

"What now?" The man groaned as he stretched his arms high and his legs long. He inhaled and exhaled as he moved, as if he could breathe out the stiffness. Sam tried to stay quiet, but his leg and arm were burning.

He looked down and found he was covered a wolf skin.

Wait, this isn't the wolf skin? Sam thought.

He sat up with a jerk and tried to pull it away, but there was a strange, pink, jelly-like substance making it cling into his skin. A chuckle came from the man.

"Afternoon," he said. His voice was deep. The man glanced at Sam's arm and leg.

Sam remembered flashes of the night before—teeth sinking into his flesh—but when he looked down to his arm and leg they only showed scarring, as if the attack had happened weeks, or even months ago. He could feel the scar on his arm pulsing and throbbing. Sam reached down and tried to wipe off the pink goo.

"Rubbing it in 'll be better," the man offered.

Sam raised his eyebrows.

"It'll help you heal up." The man nodded, *go ahead*, then rubbed his own arm as an example. Sam reluctantly stroked his hand up and down his scarred arm. The goo was tingly and cooling as it seeped into his wound. To Sam's surprise, the throbbing diminished. He rubbed it into his leg too. Sam looked

97

back up at the man, who offered a smile with a hint of *I told you so*. Sam traced the slick skin around the small circle of the gun shot wound on his leg and wondered how long it would take to heal.

He returned his attention to the man across from him. Sam's mother had always taught him to introduce himself, so he did.

"I'm Sam."

"John," came the reply.

"You a friend of my Pa's or somethin'?" Sam asked.

"Not yet, but I hope to be once I meet him. If he's your Pa, I'm sure he's a nice fellow."

Sam's ears recognized something in the voice of the man. Sam suspected this was, indeed, the large dark figure from his strange dreams last night. Was it all a strange a dream? Or was it one of the few fleeting moments of consciousness in the night? He remembered Arabella on the lawn, then pushing her away to run from the gunshots and dogs. There was also a huge creature, something with teeth, covered in fur. There was screaming. Sam shook his head to clear his thought before managing a question.

"Were you in my dream, last night?"

"I was around last night, yes," John paused. "Usually getting your First Bite is an event all on its own. But last night...well... last night was...a little messy." The Raven squawked as added punctuation. "It was the beginning of a journey we're on together now."

"First Bite?" Sam asked as he looked down at his scar, then scanned the woods for another wolf. "How many are there?"

John laughed, "Ha! Only one, funny enough." John trailed off as he thought out loud, "Huh. Why *do* we call it First Bite? It's not like there's a second and third."

"I got a second one," Sam held up his arm and pointed to his leg. "One. Two."

"I 'spose you did, didn't you?" John let out another chuckle at the humor of Sam's observation.

"That your bird?" Sam continued, pointing at the Raven above John's head.

"For now," John replied. "I'll return him when we get back home."

Home, Sam thought.

He quickly got to his feet, tugging at the Pelt clinging firm to his leg. Sam was surprised he felt no pain in either scar as he moved. Half a night ago, both his arm and his leg were almost bitten clean off, but now he stood tall as if nothing had ever happened.

He had to get to back to his family. They'd be worried. He stood still for a moment, searching his instincts for a direction to go. He felt himself drawn South. He finally managed to rip the Pelt from his body and ran.

"Where are you—?" John started, but Sam was already out of sight between the trees.

The Raven squawked.

"Dang it," John said under his breath. "He sure likes to run off."

Sam knew his mother would be worried and his father would be mad when he came through the door, but he ran as fast as he could anyway. Despite his injuries, he felt faster than usual. At the pace he was going, he'd be home in no time.

John packed up camp as fast as he could. Funny enough, following Sam would allow him to finish with the very last thing on his list before heading north; convincing Sam to come to Forge with him.

If Sam was older, perhaps offering honest, well-paid work would do the trick. But with Sam's younger age, it was prudent to confer with his parents. Convincing a boy's parents he should head north with a stranger would be a challenge, even though John saved the boy's life. He'd have to tell them that Sam was also chosen, then he would have to explain the Wolf and the significance of the bites without sounding like a crazy person. He wasn't exactly looking forward to it.

As a last resort, he had the small pouch of gold. It was still surprising to John how clearly money could talk when people couldn't.

Sam came out of the woods and into a field of cotton. He picked up the smell of smoke, and the images of torches arching into the moonlight flashed through his mind. Around him, tiny pieces of grey ash fell like dark snowflakes from the sky. Sam had a feeling, a very bad feeling, that he knew where the blackened flakes were coming from.

Sam reached the edge of the cotton field and leapt onto the dirt road running alongside. Finding it familiar, he turned left and realized the smell of smoke grew stronger as he ran in the direction of his home. There was a swelling certainty that something was terribly wrong. He looked ahead, but there was an absence on the horizon. The fear inside him grew, congealing into a single thought.

Where's my house?

As he ran, every so often a loud snap sounded and resounded with a strange twang, it seemed to come from where his house should be.

Finally, Sam slowed in front of a pile of black and gray ash. The cast iron stove still stood where the kitchen should be, but only a few blackened studs were still standing. A small section of the metal roof leaned up on the thick wood of the upright piano, still throwing small flames. Another snap and twang resounded. Sam realized the sounds he had been hearing were the piano strings snapping as the thick hardwood of the back weakened from the burning.

The shack that Sam had called home his entire life was burnt to the ground.

Sam scanned for his mother, father, and the twins, but they were nowhere to be found. In the backyard, the pigs and chickens were squealing in their pens. The swing that hung from the tree, his sister's favorite place, was empty. From the well behind the tree came Auntie, his old neighbor with a filled bucket in hand. She dropped the bucket and ran.

"SAM! My SAM!" she cried as she looked him up and down. "My boy! We thought for sure you were..." her eyes looked toward the pile of ashes.

Sam couldn't move. All the feelings inside him settled into his stomach and everything just, stopped. He dropped to the ground. He reached into the soil, a place he could usually find comfort, but there was none to be had. It felt empty, dry.

Silence.

He felt the heat from the pile of ashes on his face and bare shoulders. The lingering smoke seeped into his nose, and a swirl of wind sent gray dust into the air. Inside Sam there was no fear, no sadness. He felt nothing. His song ceased.

Auntie's husband, Uncle, approached holding a shovel coated in wet ash. His voice was compassionately matter-of-fact.

"Son," he said. "They're gone, it's all gone."

Uncle and Auntie hadn't been able to stop the flames, only the spread of the fire. They had raked and shoveled a circle around the shack, stomping and throwing dirt onto any of the flames that spread along the ground. In their old age, it was all they could do. Now, only the piano and a few other spots still smoldered in the blackened pile that was once Sam's home.

Auntie and Uncle felt a presence over them and turned to see John.

"Dammit," John said.

Sam put his hands on the ground and rose from his knees— onto all fours, like an animal. He paced back and forth at the edge of the ashes of the house, snorting through his nose, like he was trying to get the smoke to leave his mind. His movements quickened as he grew more and more agitated. Confusion and rage were erupting inside him, an aggressive frustration that he'd never felt before. He wanted to tear something apart.

"You best stand back," John said to Auntie and Uncle.

Sam clawed at the ground, bared his teeth, and ran right at Uncle, but John stepped in his path. Sam pounded his fists against John's chest. John didn't budge.

Sam turned and lunged at Auntie, but John again blocked his way.

"Oh my lord!" cried Auntie.

Sam tried to shove John's immovable mass. Then with a grunt of Herculean effort, Sam lifted John off the ground. Even John was surprised at Sam's display of strength.

John took a deep breath and made himself heavier. Sam strained with all his might, but it wasn't enough. Sam's knees buckled and he released his grip, crumbling to the ground.

"Pelt!" John yelled.

Sam's Pelt leapt onto Sam's back and enveloped him in a tight cocoon. As Sam struggled, John wrapped his arms around him in a fiercely gentle embrace.

Swaddled in his Pelt, Sam's body stopped fighting and he went limp. The hurricane of emotions subsided. His mind went still.

John felt Sam, tearless, break in two.

The confusion on Sam's face made John's heart ache. No matter how dire a person's life, if they have their own people, their own family, they can get through most anything. Sam's family had been stripped away from him, and there was an emptiness John recognized. He, too, had lost many along the way.

"Breathe," John offered quietly.

The Pelt relaxed its grip. John knelt next to Sam and put a hand on him. He let a moment pass, counting Sam's breaths. The Raven squawked from a tree behind them. John wished they had more time.

"I need to take you north," John said quietly. He turned to Auntie and Uncle. "Are you family?"

"We've known Sam his whole life," Uncle offered. "We're Aunt and Uncle by heart, but not by blood. Are *you* family?"

John took a moment to consider the question.

"In a way, yes," he said. "I came to speak with his father, or his mother, today," John looked to the pile of smoldering ash, "but it seems as if that's not in the cards."

"Some sad cards today," remarked Auntie.

"I came to offer the boy a place...a job. I found Sam last night and was coming today for his family's blessing to bring him north. Is there no next of kin?" John turned to Uncle. "Should I be asking you, sir?"

Uncle's age had made him wise. He would not make choices for another man's life. He had lived and fought through a war many years ago that freed him to choose his own path, and he was not about to take that choice from someone else.

"He's twelve. He can decide on his own," Uncle replied. "I was ten when I left home." He looked at Sam, and tried to give him a little hope. "You have work here, if you want it. I'm sure Mr. Cunningham will have you."

Mr. Cunningham's name brought flashbacks of the night before through Sam's mind. There was Arabella and the Wolf, then Abbott Cunningham firing his gun, the beast, John. There was blood and screaming. A dark figure in the moonlight. Sam tried pushing the thoughts from his mind, but they wouldn't stay buried.

"No. No, Mr. Cunningham," replied Sam softly. John gave no betrayal about the night before.

Sam looked over the smoldering pile. He had no reason to stay. His family was gone, as was his shared room and the few possessions they had. All of it was burned to ash.

Nothing in this world was permanent, everything had an ending. John knew this truth would someday lead to understanding, but the pain would remain.

Sam knew things had changed forever. For the rest of his life, there would be before the fire and after the fire. He heard his own father's voice in his mind.

"Make yourself useful, now."

Without thinking, Sam's feet brought him to his garden at the side of the ash pile that used to be his home. All of the green growth above ground had been burned away by the heat of the fire. With his bare hands, he dug into the soil and his fingers found something intact. He pulled out a sweet potato and brought it reverently to Auntie.

"I planted these," he said.

"Don't you worry about them now," Auntie replied.

Sam looked back at the ashes of his house again, then let his gaze drift to the animal pens.

"We ain't gonna need the chickens and such?" Sam asked John.

"We've got a long ways," John replied. "Best if we travel light."

Sam turned to Auntie and Uncle, "They make nice eggs. And the pig, Pa said we'd smoke 'im come Easter."

Sam had made up his mind.

A moment of silence settled in, as Sam remembered the words of pride his father had spoken about him. He looked up at John.

"I'm a good worker."

John blinked. The statement caught him off guard.

"How's that?" John asked carefully.

"I'm a good worker, sir," Sam replied.

John didn't know how to respond.

"I'll earn my keep," Sam continued. There was a pause before he added, "North?"

John nodded yes.

Sam put the potato in his pocket. He started walking. It felt better than just standing there.

As Sam's feet took him away from his family home, Auntie's tears flowed. She ran after him and embraced him one last time. When she pulled away, Auntie's chin was quivering, but she still managed a smile. With her thumb, she wiped a tear from her cheek onto Sam's. Her eyes shimmered with hope.

"Many years, many tears." She let Sam go.

Auntie stepped back to Uncle and found comfort on his shoulder.

"He'll be alright," comforted Uncle. He turned to John, "He's a good one." John took a breath, he felt honored to witness Sam's simple act of courage.

"He's got strong blood," John replied. He put his hand on Uncle's shoulder, and gave Auntie a nod.

He stepped into the ashes and found the center of what was once the simple shack that Sam called home. He knelt and pulled out a small pouch. He spoke aloud to the lingering spirits.

"Your son will be taken care of." John took a few seeds from one of the pouches Letha had given him and pressed them into the ashes. He swirled his hand on the ground, both covering the seeds and collecting a small handful of ash, easing it back into the same pouch. He placed his hand over the spot on the ground and spoke truth.

"In the ashes of the past are the seeds of the future."

He stood, gave one more look over the burnt remains, and followed Sam.

Auntie and Uncle watched John and Sam until they were specks in the distance, blending into the trees. Behind them, neither noticed the small bud already sprouting from the seed John had planted in the ash.

15

As the afternoon stretched on, John let Sam lead the way and embraced his slower rhythm of smaller steps. John was pleasantly surprised to find that Sam possessed a pretty good sense of direction.

Following John's initial instruction to "head north" Sam did just that. If a road presented itself, they would walk it for a length, then detour in and out of wooded areas and along the edges of fields to stay on course. For miles, there was nothing between them but the sounds of the wind and June bugs. Every so often, the Raven would call impatiently; it had grown accustomed to John's faster pace.

The clear skies eventually gave way to tall, puffy clouds. Crossing a fallow field, the Raven drew Sam's gaze upward. He stopped walking and took a long look at the rising clouds above. Finally, after the miles of silence, he spoke.

"How long?"

John considered the question.

"I'm hoping to catch a train car if we can," John shared. "It'll be much faster than walking." John wasn't sure how long until Sam would need a rest. His wounds were mostly healed, but the journey was long. "If our luck holds, should be less than two weeks to make it all the way back."

"Oh."

"We've got quite a ways to go."

Silence settled in for a moment before Sam spoke again, still looking at the sky.

"I was askin' 'bout them."

John looked up into the sky, then back to Sam, a little perplexed.

"Them?"

"My Ma & Pa, sister and brother...How long does it take 'em to get up there?" Sam gestured to the clouds.

John realized what occupied Sam's thoughts during the miles of silence. The question was unexpected and even heartbreaking, but not surprising. John felt a touch of pressure; after all, he wanted to offer hope and relief to the boy. He took a deep breath as he carefully chose his words.

"I suspect it's right quick, seein' how...angels got wings and all."

John watched patiently as Sam's eyes traced the edges of the clouds, the wheels in his mind turning.

"Ain't nothin' that flies slow," Sam stated.

John smiled as he repeated the truth out loud to himself, "Ain't nothin' that flies slow."

Sam smiled back. The Raven let out a *caw!* of agreement. In the distance, a train whistle blew.

John turned toward Sam, "You ever been on a train before?"

"No, sir," came Sam's reply.

"Well, pick up your feet then," John said. "This one might be ours."

John led the way towards the whistle at a good trot. He looked back, expecting to see Sam lingering, but instead found him right at his heels. There was a look of anticipation in his eyes, and John was glad that Sam had something to look forward to.

Most boys do like trains, he thought.

16

Long before John and Sam could see the train through the trees, they could hear its rumbling and its occasional whistle. The closer they got, the more John picked up the pace. Each time, to John's pleasant surprise, Sam was always close behind.

John didn't realize that Sam had his own reasons for getting to the train.

———

Every so often, on an early Sunday before church, Sam would feel a gentle shaking at his bed and wake to see his father over him. His father was a tall, slender man with a stern look but an easy laugh. On these early mornings, Sam knew they were headed to the tracks.

Sam didn't know how, but his father always had perfect timing. They would step out of the trees at the side of the tracks just before the engine would churn by. They would wave at the engineer, and the engineer would blow the horn, making Sam hold his ears. His father would laugh.

Sam learned all about trains from his father. Sam knew they shoveled coal into the burner to make enough heat for the steam. He knew the huge train cars were heavy enough to just lay on the wheel assemblies, without any additional bolts. His father had told him how the wheels were forged at angles so they wouldn't derail when going around corners. On one hand, it was all quite simple, a powerful engine pulling the cars, like a horse pulling a carriage. On the other hand, there were hundreds of pieces that had to be tuned to work together. Sam found it exciting.

The workings of the train were one thing, but even more, Sam looked forward to the stories his father would tell. In these stories, his father hopped from train to train all up and down the rails, as far north as Boston, and all the way down to the Bayou. Even more exciting, his father had promised to do the same thing with Sam one day.

In fact, his father would still be doing it if it wasn't for Sam's mother. His father told him Sam's mother was someone "worth staying in one place for." Even so, his father couldn't help but sit and steal a look at the trains chug by from time to time, just to feel the rumble of his past.

———-

Sam and John popped out of the trees just as the train made its way past them. Perfect timing. Sam excitedly made a break towards the tracks, all he could think about was his father's stories, and how he wanted to make some of his own. He was gathering speed to jump on when he felt John grab his arm and slow him to a stop.

"Easy there," said John. "Not this one. It's headed the wrong way."

Sam looked up and down the tracks. It was, indeed, headed south.

"We want north, huh?" asked Sam.

"That's right, north," answered John.

Sam took a breath, he had been excited to finally catch a train. He hoped the next one would be headed in the right direction. For now, all Sam could do was to be patient and wait.

As the train chugged past, John started north. "Once it passes, we can walk the tracks until the next one."

The caboose of the train finally clanged past them and John stepped sideways into the middle of the tracks. Sam balanced on one of the rails, feeling the subtle rumblings that matched the sound of the train fading into the distance. He counted his steps as he walked, trying to stay atop the rail as long as he could. He surprised himself by getting well past a hundred. He finally lost his balance at a hundred and seventy-three, further than he ever got before. He jumped back on the rail and started counting again.

John jumped up onto the other rail.

Sam broke the silence.

"Train's are comin' through all the time," Sam offered.

"Is that right?" John was happy that this silence was shorter than the last.

"If they go one way, they gotta come back and go the other, right?" Sam asked.

John couldn't argue with Sam's logic, "Guess we just have to wait for th' other,'" he said.

"Guess so," Sam replied as he whispered his step-count on the rail again. "Twenny three, four, five..."

"That's good news for us, isn't it? Waiting's easy." John pondered for a moment, "You been on a train before?"

"Not yet," Sam replied. "Pa always said he'd take me." Sam's footing slipped off the track. He stood for a moment, looking down. He swallowed, took a deep breath, and stepped back up onto the tracks and started counting again. John stayed silent, and Sam got all the way to forty two before talking again.

"S'pose I'm gonna miss church."

"S'pose," replied John. "Unless they got a preacher on the train."

John knew the more Sam talked, the easier this change to his new life would be. Yesterday, Sam's life was as normal as any other. Today, Sam had woken up without his family. John knew one of the best ways to quiet and comfort the mind was to condense feelings and thoughts into words, even if those words didn't make much sense at the time.

Sam could talk them, write them, sing them. It wasn't important how he got them out; it was just important that he did. All Sam needed was someone to listen, to simply be a witness, and John had plenty of time for that.

Most great men kept a journal as a practice. Often what can't be said can be more comfortably written. As such, all the men at the lumber-camp wrote things down on a regular basis. At least whatever they felt was worth writing about.

For Sam, that meant he had a duty to keep his family's history alive. Sam's memories would fade, as memories do, but words on a page remind us of times long past and lessons long learned.

John had brought a stack of blank pages to chronicle the journey. He'd already added an estimate to the miles he and the Raven had travelled, as well as mentioning the fire in the

113

farmer's barn with the simple line, "Helped farmer release stock from barn fire."

John didn't know if Sam could read or write. If needed, John would do the listening and the writing as long as Sam was willing to do the talking. Both would be easier if they could sit for a bit, while still making progress north. The train would be good for that, once they actually got on one.

For now, John let the silence breathe while they walked.

A good hour or two later, Sam started to think that waiting on a train only made them come by slower. When he was working at the plantation, or helping around the house, it seemed he would hear them in the distance all the time. But he had made it past a hundred steps several times and even past two hundred steps twice and still there was no train.

This is like watching a chicken lay an egg, he thought.

He had tried to watch a chicken lay an egg once when he was younger; had spent all day, in fact, staring at the chicken coop as one of the hens made circles and pecked all day. He even rushed through dinner only to find that the egg had been laid while he was away.

As they walked the tracks, every so often they would cross a road, and Sam would wonder if they would leave the tracks and take the road instead, but John always kept to the tracks. Dusk was offering her orange hue to the sky when John turned to Sam.

"We best find a spot before the moon shows itself." John stepped from the middle of the tracks off to the side and quickly scouted a place to set up camp a few yards into the bushes.

As Sam collected a few branches for a fire, John pulled Soup's cookies from his satchel.

"You're lucky I kept myself from eating these," John said with a smile. "It's not often Soup makes cookies."

Sam was sure he'd never tasted anything so delicious in his life. They were somehow both salty and sweet, with cinnamon and small pieces of bacon. The were also dense and filling. Even after walking all day, one was enough for fill his belly for the evening.

"We gonna camp all night?" Sam asked as he chewed.

"Hopefully not, we're still tryin' to get the next train north," replied John. He couldn't travel as fast with Sam in tow, and a train was still the best way to make better time than being on foot.

The sun dipped under the horizon. John realized he didn't have much time before the moon would rise.

John turned to Sam and said. "I'm going to be changing soon. It'll come on when the moon rises."

"What do you mean changin'?"

John knew this moment had been coming, and he wanted to do right by Arthur. He stood up, rubbed his hands together, and suddenly wished he had more time to prepare.

"So...Lots of things change as they grow," he started. "You know how a tadpole turns into a frog?"

"Yessir," Sam nodded. "They lose their tails."

"They do, they do. Good, good...and, uh, caterpillars turn into—"

"Butterflies!"

"Exactly!" John took a deep breath. This was going well. "Those changes, are like...magic. Changin' from one thing into another, right?"

"I guess."

115

"And…people go through changes too. Some of us go through really big changes…as we grow up. Mighty big."

Sam was pretty sure his Pa already gave him this talk, but he didn't want to interrupt.

"Matter of fact, *I'm* gonna be changing."

Sam thought maybe this wasn't the same talk.

"You know how an animal changes into another animal?" John continued.

Sam nodded.

"I'm going to be changing into another animal, too."

Sam stared at John. He tried to imagine a six-foot butterfly, but that seemed just silly. So he asked the only logical thing he could.

"Are you gonna…turn into a frog?"

John stared. *Dammit.* He realized that he needed to take a straighter line to get to the truth.

"Do you remember me from last night?" John asked.

"Sorta," Sam replied. "I saw you skinnin' the Wolf?"

"You did, you did. I was also there when the men surrounded you."

Sam looked John up and down.

"You did that to those men."

John nodded.

The top of the moon peaked over the horizon.

John pulled off his shirt revealing a large mangled scar on his shoulder that led up to the base of his neck. It looked markedly similar to Sam's arm and leg. He kicked off his boots.

Sam felt a stir within him, like something was producing a great tugging from his insides, and was trying to get out. The Pelt of the Wolf slithered up and around Sam, gently applying pressure all around his body.

The moon rose into the night sky.

John dropped to all fours and grit his teeth hard while his back arched and a low growl escaped his throat. Thick fur grew rapidly from the scar on his shoulder and spread to the rest of his body. John got both taller and thicker, his hands extending into claws, and the bones in his ankles and feet shifted longer and wider. Sam thought he had imagined the beast last night, but there in front of him, he watched John transform.

Sam was mesmerized. He didn't know why, but he wasn't fearful at all. Instead, he was astonished, and even a little... jealous?

Way better than a frog, he whispered aloud.

Sam's Pelt loosened its squeeze and eased to the ground.

John stood even taller than before. Dark brown fur covered his entire body. His long snout ended sharp, ivory canines. His feet had become long powerful claws.

He turned to the moon and let out a howl that echoed over the trees and through Sam's body.

The Raven landed on his shoulder.

John tilted his neck from side to side, smiling after the pleasant *crack!* His Pelt slithered up and wrapped around him; a lively, mobile kilt.

"There we are," John exhaled.

"Good thing you took off your shoes," Sam said wide-eyed.

John chuckled.

Sam reached out and touched John's arm. The hair was coarse.

"What does it feel like?" asked Sam.

"Itchy," quipped John. Sam walked a circle around him.

"The inside is worse than the outside," John's voice was deep and more gruff. "Probably because of last night." He saw the

117

wheels turning in Sam's head, putting together both parts of John. The part that had journeyed with him all day, and the part that had saved him last night.

"Do you know what part of us is the most human?"

"The talkin'?" Sam offered.

John put his hand on Sam's shoulder. "It's the mistakes that we make. The regrets. Every time the moon comes, you feel all of them. Remorse helps you keep control. It connects to your human part when you're not so human anymore."

A blister of regret swelled inside Sam. If he had woken up earlier...or gotten there sooner...maybe, just maybe, he could have saved his family.

John continued, "I could've killed those men last night. Easily. I tried not to." John sighed. "When you turn into the Wolf, it's easy to kill people...and you shouldn't."

John sighed. "Last night, I changed their lives, but not their minds. I did what I had to do to save you. But violence has consequences." Sam didn't know that John was thinking about the death of Sam's family too.

In fact, John had wanted to stay and avenge the deaths of Sam's family. Had it not been for Sam himself walking away from the ashes of his own home, John would have been more than happy to finish what he had started.

Last night, he had one mission above all: protect Sam. Even with John's incredible restraint, there had been bloodshed. He knew repercussions could be likely and swift. He just didn't realize how swift, and how devastating for Sam.

A silence hung between them, against the sounds of the fire crackling.

Squawk!

The moonlight caught the Raven as it landed in the top of the large oak behind John.

Sam heard the whistle of another train far in the distance. John turned his massive head and pointed his ears to the south.

"That's us," he said. "We'll have to be careful. Generally it's bad to be seen with me looking like...this."

John picked up his boots and shirt, and kicked dirt on the fire. Sam was anxious to catch the train and broke through the tree-line towards the tracks.

"Easy there." John gently pulled Sam back into the underbrush. "We don't want the train conductor to see either of us. Wait for the engine to pass."

Sam could hear the rumbling getting closer and closer, and with it, his excitement grew. He remembered his father telling him that jumping onto a train took skill, speed, and patience. If you made the smallest mistake, it could literally be the death of you. He felt confident he wouldn't let his father down.

Soon the light of the locomotive zoomed by, and John and Sam carefully stepped forward. The wind from the cars came in bursts, matching the clickity-clack and the shrill cry of metal on metal as the wheels slid over the tracks. There was no other light from any of the train cars.

"Freight," John remarked. "Perfect." His eyes scanned down the side of the train. "He's moving quick. We're gonna have to pick up some speed before we make the jump."

"We're jumpin' on a train?" Sam asked.

"*I'm* jumping on a train. You? I'll probably have to throw you."

Throw? Sam thought.

"Here we go," John started to run with the train. Sam surprised himself by keeping pace alongside John.

Fast as they were, they still weren't fast enough to match the speed of the train. Sam felt John's clawed hand on his back, gently pushing him to go even faster. Sam's feet were moving so fast he was on the verge of toppling over.

"Get ready," John yelled as an open box car approached.

Sam felt the back of his trousers slide up his butt crack and his feet left the ground. He was airborne, heading face first toward the moving train, arms reflexively outstretched to brace for the impact. Just before slamming into the side the train car, a large open cargo door appeared before him. He somersaulted through it and tumbled to a stop.

A second later, the beast that was John landed upright on his feet in the open door of the boxcar. John's Pelt got caught on the latch and several loose pages from his journal flew out of the train.

"Dammit," John said under his breath.

Amidst the commotion, John spied a shape in the corner of the box car. A hobo sat up from underneath a pile of hay and burlap sacks and looked at both John and Sam. The moon light made a majestic silhouette of John's beastly form through the open door. The hobo blinked and pulled a bottle of booze from under his blanket. He looked at the bottle, then back at the beast that was John, then back again at the bottle. He raised his eyebrows and shrugged, took a swig, and pulled the burlap back over his head as he laid back down.

John chuckled.

He took a quick inventory of the almost empty boxcar: a dozen bales of hay. A couple carts of chickens. The hobo.

"This should do for a while." John pulled a bit of the hay down and spread it for him and Sam to sleep on. As he lay down, Sam found his legs tired from a full day of travel. Even with the

120

hay poking him a bit here and there, the rumble of the train quickly soothed him off to sleep.

John stepped back to the open door. Judging from the moon in the sky, it was somewhere a little past midnight. He turned and saw Sam wrapped in his Pelt, sound asleep.

This should help us make good time, John thought.

Sam's Pelt would continue to help heal his wounds, and it surely would provide comfort, as any thing that a man constantly carries does. Still, John knew what was ahead for Sam, and he was unsure how to tell him. He was a man of selective words, and he felt a continued nervousness.

John had been ready to teach Sam the tricks of the lumber trade, and even more importantly, how to manage the change when it came time. While being a mentor was one thing, John hadn't expected to be a substitute father for Sam, a father Sam had only lost this morning. John was feeling a growing, persistent pressure, the same pressure one feels when something is deeply important, but there is little time.

Let's just get him home, first, he thought.

John took a breath and stepped away from the door of the box car. He bunched the hay next to Sam a bit, then circled it a few times before settling down.

John tried to sleep, but even with the rhythmic rocking of the train, the Sandman was elusive. Eventually he sat up and looked out the box car door, watching the woods and world pass by in the moonlight. After a while, his gaze fell back to Sam, his chest slowly rising and falling as he slept.

He's been through a lot, John thought. He reached over and placed a gentle hand on Sam's shoulder, a subtle comfort children often feel in their sleep, but never see.

Pulling his hand away, John gave Sam's Pelt a slight rub. His own Pelt wrapped itself up and over John's shoulders. The rest of the night, John's thoughts were like the world passing by outside, familiar but unable to calm.

In the twilight of the morning, Sam woke to the controlled sounds of John's transformation back to human form. John was trying his best to keep his grunting quiet. Sam was relieved the hobo didn't stir. Perhaps the drink still was in him.

Later that morning, the hobo pushed the burlap aside and sat up. After a few blinks, he could make out John and Sam sitting with their feet out the open door of the car, the amber morning light making them seem almost statuesque. John turned and caught his eye.

"Mornin'. How far this one going?" John asked.

"Last stop is the Capitol, far as I can tell. I seem to have lost my ticket, ya know?"

John gave a chuckle, "Hard to hold onto a ticket these days."

The hobo raised himself and came to sit next John and Sam. As he hung his feet off the side, he brought out his bottle and offered it.

"No. Thanks," John replied. The hobo looked John up and down, then offered the bottle to Sam.

"Him neither," John responded. The hobo looked John up and down again, quickly deducing John meant what he said.

"More for me, then," the hobo replied with a smile. He took a swig. "Tastes same as dinner last night."

Sam had heard about fast trains headed all the way to the west coast without hardly a stop, but the trains headed north must've been slower, since it seemed to stop constantly. John wanted to take the train as far as they could, so each time they pulled into a station they would join the hobo in hiding behind the bales of hay until they felt the train clang to life again and they heard the Raven squawk from somewhere outside. They must've picked a good box car, since all the workers ever did was glance in or pull the door closed from the outside.

On a couple occasions, instead of hiding, John jumped out of the box car and soon returned with bread, fruit, or some other simple food. To Sam's surprised, he even brought back a new bottle for the hobo. The hobo expressed great gratitude to John for the food and the bottle seemed to keep him in good spirits. Sam quickly realized it also kept him unconscious when John transformed each evening.

Even if he managed to sleep as the sun went down, Sam's scar would awaken him each night with itching and burning. He would open his eyes just in time to witness the last of John's transformation. Just like the waning moon rise, John's change would happen a little later every night. With each change, he would look a little less beastly and a little more like John. Each morning, when the sun rose, he would change back to himself.

"That scar itching, burning, and such?" John asked one night after he transformed.

"Yeah," Sam replied, "Seems a li'l less each night. Kinda how you seem less, too."

"That *is* how it works," John said.

Sam wondered if John meant that his own scar would always be itchy, or if Sam's itchy scar would lead to something more beastly and transformative in the future.

Sam made good on his claim of being a good worker. Each morning, he would re-stack the hay they had slept on and he'd move the chicken cages around throughout the day, just for a change. He'd even use a handful of hay on his hands and knees to sweep out the box car from time to time.

Sam thought he had a grasp of how much time had passed, but he still wasn't sure if it was the seventh or eighth day when the sun set and they finally saw the distant lights of Washington D.C.

"We should be off before it stops," John said. "Be a lot of people in the train yard."

Sam took the hint and helped quickly gather their things. Sam was no longer in any kind of pain. His Pelt had literally worked its magic, and Sam's arm and leg only had a shade of a scar left. Now, his Pelt folded itself into the shape of a satchel, just like John's, and Sam slung it over his shoulder and stepped to the open door. John gave Sam a nudge as the train slowed.

"Ready?"

John moved to grab Sam by the back of the trousers again.

"I got it!" Sam held his hand up. He figured he'd take his own chances rather than be hauled up by the backside again. He leaned out and tried to find a rhythm as the railroad ties passed by, scanning ahead for a place to land. He stopped and started a few times, gaining more courage each time before he got fed up with his own indecision.

No sense in just waitin', he thought.

Sam jumped.

His feet hit the ground hard, but he kept them moving and managed to run for a few steps before falling forward and rolling his momentum out on the ground. When he settled and managed to get back to his feet, John was already standing next to him.

"You good?" John asked with a chuckle. From close by in the darkening night, the Raven squawked laughter at Sam's landing.

"We've got places to be," John added.

Where they had to be Sam couldn't imagine. They had just spent several nights on a freight train, making it further north than Sam ever thought he would go.

"Toward the lights?" Sam asked.

"Toward some friends," responded John. "We should be able to get there well before I'll be changing. Stay close." Sam's Pelt shifted and slung itself like a backpack, ready for the journey. John drew his Pelt-satchel tight and lead the way as they left the train tracks behind them and picked up the pace towards the electric lights of Washington D.C.

17

Sam noticed the first stray dog within minutes of leaving the train yard. To his delight, there was soon another, and another until John and Sam were accompanied by a small pack. Each mutt was a bit mangled and rough around the edges, and they were all as scrappy and ready to fight as any Sam had seen, but as they followed John and Sam, all had their ears perked and tails wagging. John was still looking very human, or at least he was for now.

John looked up and called to the Raven, "Let Fannie and Charles know we're on our way!"

The Raven flapped its wings a few extra times and continued ahead. John turned to Sam, "It's best not to show up unannounced."

Sam wondered if Fannie and Charles were nice people, and if Charles had transformations too.

As they tried to stay in the shadows of the city, they would slow from time to time, and the dogs would crowd around Sam and his Pelt. The Pelt would shift from side to side on Sam, gingerly touching the snouts of each dog as they approached. Sam would reach out and give a scratch behind the ear or under a neck.

"Making friends, eh?" John commented. He was too busy scanning the streets to give the dogs much mind.

Sam wished he had something more to offer the dogs than scratches, perhaps a scrap of food, or a bone. Then again, for some dogs a bit of scratching behind the ear was the best treat of all.

The night was still moonless and dark when they finally stepped from the shadows of the city down a lamp-lit street. They stopped at a small gate in front of what city folk would consider a modest house, but Sam's country roots told him it was fancy. There was grass in the front, instead of dirt or a garden, with stones placed just so to make a path to the front steps. A bright burning lamp stood tall halfway to the house, lighting the way to the ornate door. The Raven called from its perch at the peak of the roof as if to say, *It's about time!*

At the gate, John held up his hand and all the dogs sat. At the front door, John gave a firm knock. He turned to Sam as they waited for an answer.

"You're gonna like Fannie," John said. "She always knows just what you need."

A well-dressed black man opened the door.

"Charles," John said with a smile.

"We thought the bird showing up might be you." Charles revealed a smile of his own as he leaned on the door frame and looked John up and down. "How are you, John? You look well." Charles gave a glance to Sam. "And who's this?"

"My name is Sam, sir," answered Sam, unsure whether to bow or to shake his hand. Thankfully, Charles extended his hand, and Sam gripped it firmly, just as his father had taught him. Charles returned the grip, as men do, then gave the slightest wink as he addressed Sam directly.

"Well, Sam, I hope that John here hasn't been getting you into too much trouble."

"He threw me on a train," Sam answered without hesitation.

"Did he now?" Charles turned to John with a bit of a laugh. "Did he throw you off it too?"

"No sir, I jumped off myself. Lost my footin', but the trippin' was still better than the tossin'."

"I imagine it was," Charles replied with a chuckle. "We are still trying to civilize that John," he added conspiratorially. "Come on in." He ushered them through the door as he held it open and asked, "Will you be visiting long?"

"Just tonight," John replied. "You know how these things go. It's hard enough traveling in this skin, let alone the fur. We've got to keep moving while the moving is good."

"You're always welcome, John, regardless of how much you're shedding."

Once inside, Sam was stunned by a large library to the left of the entryway. His eyes grew wide with astonishment. There were so many books that there was a ladder, *inside*, just to reach the top shelves. At his own home, there was only ever one book: the Bible.

"It's the only book a boy needs," his mother had told him. His mother taught him to read with that Bible. He would read it to himself and sometimes out loud at dinner when he had found a Psalm or Proverb that he particularly liked. Over the past few years, he had paged through it multiple times. While he enjoyed reading about the gardens and whales and the wise men following a star and such, he found a lot of the middle parts rather boring.

He had dreamed of having another book to read, but had never had the means to get one. He had glimpsed books here and there through the windows of the plantation, but they were not for him to borrow. Charles noticed the boy's wide-eyed gaze.

"You like books?" Charles asked. It took a moment for Sam to finally blink and offer an answer.

"I ain't never seen so many in one place before," confessed Sam.

"Well, come on then, come have a look, maybe I'll let you pick one to take with you," Charles said with a smile. "The next best thing to reading a book is sharing one."

Sam stepped cautiously into the library. All four walls had shelves filled with tomes. Some with large printed bindings, others looking simply like carefully folded pages that had been hand sewn together. Two armchairs, a writing desk holding a few open books, and two lamps took up the middle of the room, all arranged to take advantage of the heat coming from the fireplace.

Surrounded by so many wonderful volumes, Sam couldn't believe that only a few hours ago, he was sleeping next to a burlap covered hobo. Now here he was, standing in the refined library of a proper gentleman, dwarfed by more books than anyone could possibly read in a lifetime.

Sam reached out and gently traced his finger across the bindings of one shelf, then another. His hand suddenly stopped moving and he felt the hair on his body rise. His scar felt warm. Sam's finger was fixed to the spine of a book with letters he knew, but words that he didn't: *Le Morte d'Arthur*. He tilted it,

129

pulled it off the shelf, and held it in his hand. Sam found himself smiling. On the cover, pink flowers grew in a vine around an illustration of two men in armor, their heads bowed. Standing in front of them was a haloed figure that looked like Jesus himself. He felt Charles looking over his shoulder.

"Have you read this one?" Sam asked.

Charles graciously took the book from Sam's hand and gave a knowing glance to John. Sam felt the hair on his body relax.

"Of course," he said, gesturing to the room. "I've read everything here except what's on my desk there. Those are next. But your friend John has read all these and then some."

"And then some?" Sam asked in astonishment.

"Yes, more than this for sure," Charles replied.

"For sure," added John.

"You must read fast," said Sam to John. "It took me almost a year to read the whole Bible."

"Hmm, not bad," John raised his eyebrows. "But you'll need to read a little faster to catch up to me," he added playfully.

"The Bible's not a bad one to start with," offered Charles. "Though, I can see why it would take a lad a while to get through. Truth be told, it *is* quite boring around the middle part...lots of *begats*."

Sam liked Charles already.

Charles tucked *Le Morte d'Arthur* under his arm as he stepped forward to the huge main bookshelf, moving the ladder aside.

"You'll read this one soon enough, I'm sure. For now, let's see if there's something a little more befitting a young man your age." Charles looked up and down the stacks of books, scratching his chin from time to time, and finally sighted the one he was looking for.

"Ah, this one might be a little more your flavor." Charles slid the book off the shelf. "It's even signed by the author. He and my father were friends."

Sam took the book from Charles. The cover was the same dark green of the forests of the south. He turned it in his hands and ran his finger over the gold embossed "H" and "F" on the front. He read the cover softly aloud.

"*Adventures of Huckleberry Finn.*"

Sam opened the book. There on the title page, scrawled in a masculine calligraphy, were the words:

To Mr. Douglas,
Yours in word and spirit,
Mark Twain.

"It's an adventure of sorts. I think you'll like it," said Charles. "Funny enough, the author has your same name, *Sam.*" Sam tilted his head.

"It says here it was written by Mark Twain," Sam replied.

"Yes, of course, that's his *nom de plume*, his pen name. It's a name that he gave himself as a writer. Kind of like a person with a secret. You may even know someone else with a secret or two, isn't that right, John?"

"You're funny, Charles, but Sam knows quite a bit about me already. No secrets."

"How much is quite a bit?"

"Let's just say we've been traveling both days, and nights."

Charles arched one of his brows, "It's nice to know you're not holding anything back." Sam was half listening, still looking at beautiful lettering on the cover of the book in his hands. He handed it back to Charles.

"Oh, no, no," Charles gently pushed the book back to Sam. "Bring it back when you've finished, and you can pick another. Or you can send it down. We've got a few people in Forge we lend to quite often. Matter of fact, I have a feeling John here will be taking a book or two back with him on this trip."

Sam stared at the book. He had only just met Charles and couldn't believe he was giving him something so amazing. Sam had hoped for years to read another book, to imagine another adventure the likes of Moses, Sampson, and Esther. And here it was, literally a new adventure in his hands.

A book.

"Thank you kindly, sir," Sam finally managed. "I'll be sure to get it back to you when I finish."

"Take your time. Enjoy it. Maybe even read it twice," said Charles.

In awe of the gift, Sam couldn't help himself, he thumbed to the first page and took a good long look at the first illustration. It was a boy, about the same age as Sam, with a wide brimmed straw hat, a rabbit in one hand and a gun in the other.

He must be a good shot, thought Sam.

Sam felt a gentle hand on his back and heard a woman's voice, sweet as honey, "You hungry?"

Sam turned to see the kind eyes and warm smile of Fannie, the proud woman of the house. An apron covered her full floor-length skirt, and a high collared blouse with long puffed sleeves. Her touch made him feel welcome and protected at the same time.

"We wouldn't turn down any of your cooking, Fannie," said John as he took his satchel-pelt off and placed it on one of the armchairs. He nodded for Sam to do the same.

"You're lucky I made a little extra," Fannie quipped back with a smile. She then turned to Sam, "Hope you like potatoes, young man. We may even have a little ham left over."

"We'll start some coffee too," added Charles. "We've got more than a little catching up to do."

Sam followed the adults through the narrow hallway, passing a formal dining room with a table piled high with fabrics and a foot powered sewing machine next to the window. At the back of the house they entered the kitchen.

The first thing Sam saw was the ornate cast iron cook stove with silver edging, easily twice the size of the stove Sam's family had. On one side of the kitchen, a basin with a hand pump sat at the end of a dark wood countertop. Above that, open shelving held a mix of plates, metal cups, cooking bowls and the like. A well stocked pantry and icebox took up the other side. In the middle of the kitchen sat a sturdy wood table, stained-with-love, probably meant for four people, but no doubt often seating more.

"There's the sink there, wash up. Go ahead and splash some water on your faces too while you're at it. From the looks I should probably fill the tub for you."

"Yes, 'm," said Sam as he stepped to the sink. "Ma'am?"

"Yes?" said Fannie.

"You've got a pump in the kitchen?"

"Yes, child," she responded, "It's a very modern kitchen."

Sam had pulled buckets from a well, and pumped water from a pump at the plantation, but it was always outside. He had never seen, or even thought of having a pump *inside* before. Its spout poured straight into the sink; you could fill a whole pot for soup and never have to leave the kitchen or even touch a bucket at all.

He raised the arm of the pump a few times and watched as the water flowed straight into the basin. It was amazing.

Charles came over with a kettle, "Can you fill me up?" he asked. Sam gladly pumped until the kettle was full, and Charles took it to the cook stove to start the coffee. Sam finished washing his hands and noticed a small bowl of wrapped candy in the middle of the kitchen table.

"What are those?" Sam asked.

"Those're sweets," replied Fanny. "If it's alright with John here, you can have one now, or two after dinner, as a treat." Sam looked at John, who shrugged his shoulders as if to say, *Fine with me.*

Sam reached into the bowl and took one out. It was a brown wrapper with red stripes and white ends.

"They're midgees," said Fanny.

Sam pondered for a moment. He brought the candy up to his nose and smelled. *Delicious.* His mouth started to water. Having one now sounded pretty good to him. *But..two is better than one, isn't it?*

"How long's dinner last?" Sam asked.

"'Till it's done," Fannie smiled.

The midgee smelled *so* good. Sam took a deep breath and carefully put the candy back into the bowl.

"Two after," he said. Out of the corner of his eye, he saw Fannie give John a nod of approval.

Sam didn't do much talking at dinner; he was too busy using his fork as a shovel. He was sure Fannie had added some kind of magic to the potatoes. Every so often, his eyes would land on the candy bowl.

Two after dinner, he kept thinking.

He listened as Charles, Fannie, and John talked about people that Sam didn't know. First was Arthur. Charles and Fannie gave their condolences as they looked Sam up and down. Then John mentioned a bunch of others: Letha, Amasa, Kofi, Rowan, Alma, Constance, a baby on the way... Sam eventually lost track. Instead, he sat back from his empty plate, his stomach wonderfully stretched from the fine meal that was Fannie's "leftovers."

"You think he liked it?" John asked Fannie with a smile.

"If he grows like he eats, you'll be buying him new trousers soon," Fannie replied.

John leaned back in his chair and patted his stomach, "You always know just what we need, don't you Fannie?"

"Men do tend to be happy with a full belly," Fannie smiled.

"Say your 'thank-you's," John reminded Sam politely.

"Thank you for dinner, ma'am, sir." Sam stood up and took his plate to the sink.

"Well, now. How helpful," Fannie remarked. Sam returned to the table, and took all the plates in turn, then all the silverware. He left the tin cups when he noticed they weren't finished with the coffee.

"I think he wants to use the pump again," joked John.

"Can I?" asked Sam.

Fannie considered the etiquette of letting a guest do the dishes.

"He says he's a good worker," John offered. "Let him earn his keep."

"I suppose you're already up from the table," Fannie relented.

Sam smiled and set to work on the dishes. He had always done them at home, and now with all that had happened, he found a familiar comfort with his hands in the dishpan, listening to the adults talking behind him. He found himself humming as he worked. He did the dishes first, then silverware, and lastly the pan Fannie used to make dinner itself. Just as he finished, Fannie rose from her chair.

"Would you like a bath, young man?" Fannie asked.

"Is it Saturday already?" Sam asked. "That's bath night, 'fore Sunday, of course."

"Matter fact it is," Fannie replied with a smile. "Gimme the lifter there," Fannie gestured. She pried up the cover of a holding tank in the back of the cook stove. It was filled with water, and judging from the steam rising off of it, it was quite hot.

"If you wanna lug the water, you'll be havin' a warm one," explained Fannie.

"A warm bath?" Sam asked. "My momma said I used to have warm baths when I was a baby, but it's too much trouble now."

"It's no trouble tonight, dear. Grab the pail there and let's get to it."

Sam did his best not to spill any of the hot or cold water as he lugged bucket after bucket to the tub in a small room just behind the kitchen. It took five buckets of cold water from the kitchen pump and two hot from the wood stove before Fannie reached down and tested the temperature.

"Well, there we are," she said with satisfaction. "Now go ahead and refill the stove tank before we put you in." Sam obliged and when he returned, Fannie was draping a towel, knickers, and a night shirt on a small chair next to the tub.

She tossed in a new bar of soap and told Sam he could stay in the tub as long as he liked, and that's exactly what Sam planned to do.

136

As he eased into the tub, he watched the water rise on the sides and almost spill over. He felt the heat sink in and his whole body relax.

This is just what I needed, he thought.

He looked at the scars on both his arm and leg. Thanks to the Pelt, there was no pain at all. Funny enough it was just then that the Pelt sneakily slithered under the door of the small room, then inched itself up and pushed a corner of itself over the side of the tub. Sam watched as it tested the water, then slipped all the way in. Before he could stop it, it was under the bubbles, then rising back up to scrub itself against the side of the tub. Sam grabbed the soap and reached out to the Pelt, rubbing the soap in. The Pelt loved it, and wrapped Sam up, scrubbing against him. Sam and the Pelt were a splashed-up, soapy sight, and in the process actually seemed to get cleaner.

Fannie knocked at the door, startling Sam and the Pelt.

"What's going on in there? You best not be makin' a mess!" she playfully scolded from the other side. Sam stared at the Pelt and wondered if Fannie knew it was the one doing most of the splashing.

"Dry off and put those knickers and shirt on!" She continued. "I'll give your other clothes a wash. If I put 'em in front of the stove, they should be dry by mornin'."

Sam stepped out of the tub while the Pelt lingered under the bubbles. He wondered if Charles and Fannie knew about John's nightly changes, and what it meant if they did. Sam figured John wouldn't exactly go around bragging about being a wolfman-beast. Charles and Fannie seemed to be old friends of John, but should Sam tell them?

Sam pulled the shirt over his head, then stepped into the knickers as the Pelt finally climbed out of the tub and shook itself like a dog, getting Sam and his new clothes wet.

Rrrggg! Sam thought as he grabbed the towel once more. Wait, did Charles and Fannie know about the Pelt?

Finally dressed, his clothes were far too big. Sam rolled up the Pelt and tucked it under his arm before holding his pants up and stepping back into the kitchen.

"There you are, Sir Sam," said Charles with a smile, "Smelling much better than John here."

Sam looked John up and down, thought a moment, then said, "You're going to need a bigger soap."

Charles let out a guffaw that immediately spread to Fannie. Even John laughed too.

"Lord, when he's right, he's right!" Fannie managed between slapping her knee and the table. When John could finally compose himself, he playfully scolded Sam.

"Sounds to me like it's bedtime."

Sam realized it had been almost two weeks since he'd slept in anything resembling a bed. His travel north with John had brought him through woods, fields, streams, and quite a bit of time on the train, but not yet a bed. The thought of it made him excitedly tired.

"Of course, of course," Fannie said, finally calming herself. She wiped away the tears of laughter with her apron. "Let me show you where you'll be sleepin', dear." Sam held up his too big knickers with one hand while Fannie drove him by the shoulders and walked him out of the kitchen. She bent down to speak in his ear.

"If ever there was someone needed a bigger soap, it's that man in there," Fannie joked softly as they walked down the narrow hall. Sam smiled. Having Fannie's hand on his shoulders was comforting.

Sam was surprised when Fannie led him up the flight of stairs to a small bedroom. While he saw the tall house from the outside when he arrived, he had forgotten that it had a second floor. He realized that this was the first time that he had been in a house where the man and women of the house were black, and there were also two floors.

It's funny how you don't notice something until you do, he thought.

"This is Haley's old room," she said. Fannie moved to the window and drew the curtains. "Should help with the draft." There was a small dresser with a few books on it, the window, and a kerosene lantern already lit on the table next to the bed. He plopped the Pelt onto the bed, and noticed *Adventures of Huckleberry Finn* sitting on the pillow. The flame from the lamp made the golden "H" and "F" on the cover dance. A bed and a book. Sam felt excited for two things now.

"Can I read the book tonight, ma'am?" Sam asked.

"I don't suppose I can stop you," Fannie replied with a wink. She opened the covers, and patted the bed for Sam to sit next to her. Sam obliged and Fannie tussled his hair, "You *do* smell much better," she remarked with a smile. "I'll see you in the morning for breakfast." Fannie started to stand, but stopped and sat back down. "Well now, I almost forgot." She reached both hands into her apron then held out two fists. "Pick one," she smiled.

Sam wasn't sure what he was going to get, but tapped Fannie's left hand. She turned it over and opened it. There in her palm was one of the midgee sweets that Sam had been staring at all night. She opened her right hand to show there was one there too. She handed the left one to Sam.

"Two after dinner," she winked.

Sam brought the candy carefully up to his nose. It smelled sweet, but deep. He had only ever had a bit of honey here and there, and the Abbot family would give all the hired help, including his father, rock candy on Christmas, but this was different. He finally got a good look at the wrapper. Sounding it out as he read aloud.

"*Tootsie Roll.*"

"That's right. Go on now," said Fannie. "Here, pull both th' ends." Fannie took the small wrapped candy and firmly pulled both ends. The roll twisted like magic several times before coming to rest. Fannie slid a finger under the edge of the wrapper and flattened it, then presented it to Sam. He picked the dark brown roll up and bit a small piece off. It was hard on the outside, but somehow softer on the inside. As he chewed, deep cocoa flavors wafted up to his nose, followed by a subtle hint of fruit.

"Pretty good, isn't it?" Fannie smiled. "It's like a chewy chocolate."

Sam smiled, chewed a little more to savor the flavor, then swallowed. He couldn't help himself and plopped the rest of it in his mouth. It was more than delicious—it was delightful.

"Thank you, Miss Fannie."

"Of course, dear," she replied. Fannie placed the other Tootsie Roll on the bedside table next to the lamp. As she stood to leave, she shook her head and let out another giggle, muttering, "Need bigger soap."

"Sleep well," she finally said, leaving with a smile. Sam swallowed his last bite and eyed the other Tootsie Roll on the bedside table. He reached for it, then stopped.

Probably better to save it, he thought. As delicious as it was, Sam liked having something to look forward to on an otherwise unpredictable journey. He reached past the candy and picked up *Adventures of Huckleberry Finn*. He opened the cover and turned past the illustration of the boy with the rabbit, landing on the first page of the story. As he started reading his tongue dug at a bit of Tootsie Roll stuck in his back tooth.

> *"You don't know about me without you have read a book by the name of The Adventures of Tom Sawyer, but that ain't no matter...*

Before long, Sam was so engrossed in the story he barely noticed the Pelt sneak onto his lap.

Sam didn't remember falling asleep. He remembered the voices from the kitchen while he read the pages in his book. It reminded him of his own room with his brother and sister. Many nights, when they should've been sleeping, they'd quietly listen as his parents and Auntie and Uncle carried on in the next room.

At some point, his eyelids got heavy enough that he decided to close them for *juuust* a minute. His dreams blended his own life with Huckleberry Finn's. There was an island on the Mississippi River, where he and John joined Huck and Jim, stashing a raft and waiting out a storm.

Somewhere between the dream and sleep, Sam heard footsteps and felt his legs being lifted up and onto the bed. He was far from being a little boy any more, but he had no protest when he felt himself being tucked in, and glimpsed the glow of the lamp fade into darkness.

—-

Sam's nose woke him the next morning to the smell of bacon. Or was it biscuits? Opening his eyes, it took him a moment or two to shake off the sleep and to piece together where he was. He sat up and saw *Huck Finn* on the small table beside the bed. He picked it up, tucked it under his arm, held his pants up, and poked his head into the hallway. A railing and stairs showed the way down, and before he knew it, his nose had gotten him swiftly to the kitchen. He stood in the doorway for a moment watching Fannie poke at the bacon.

"Wash up for breakfast, now," Fannie said without turning from the stove.

Sam dropped the book on the table and went to the pump. Juggling his pants and the pump, he somehow managed to wash his hands and even rub some of the cold onto his face and neck, shocking him awake. When he finished, not only had the bacon moved from the stove to the table, but John was standing in the doorway, mid-yawn.

"You're up early," said John to Fannie.

"Some of us do take to rest when the men are up too late," she replied. She opened the oven, pulled out a tray of biscuits, and slid it onto the table next to the bacon.

"Well look here," said John, "You didn't make biscuits on account of me now did you?" He turned to Sam, "Fannie's got the best biscuits you ever tasted. Sweet like candy, I tell you. Don't even need gravy."

"Go on, you can have one," offered Fannie to Sam. "Careful, they're hot," she warned. "Don't go flattering yourself, John. It's Sunday is all, and we'll be heading to church before too long. You got time for a sermon?"

Sam remembered it was Sunday and felt a pang thinking about church without his family.

"I'm afraid we don't have the attire," replied John. Looking down at his clothes, it was obvious John had come straight from the woods. Sam was still holding up his too-big knickers from the night before.

"It's probably best we be moving on," said John. "I don't want to show up in Forge all civilized or anything. I'll never hear the end of it."

"Speakin' of civilized, you didn't leave a pile of fur in that bed now, did you?" Fannie grilled John.

I guess they do know all about John, thought Sam.

"Last night was easy, we're almost to the new moon. I was only ornery for about an hour before the sun came up. Lucky for you, the shedding's minimal."

"Well, that's some good news for both of us," Fannie responded with a smile.

Sam interrupted with his mouth full of biscuit. "Thsss 's gggddd."

John and Fannie shared a laugh, "I told you, son. Don't choke yourself." Fannie pumped a tin cup of water and put it in front of Sam. Charles appeared in the kitchen door, buttoning his cuffs.

"You made biscuits!?" he called with surprise. "Well now, look who gets the special treatment!"

"I knew it!" John smiled. He took a biscuit, threw it in the air and chomped it with one gulp, his cheeks bulging.

143

"At least chew the darn thing!" cried Fannie, "I worked on them all morning! Lord help me."

Sam laughed at the whole scene. It was hard to believe how different things were after a train ride, a few miles of walking with some stray dogs, and a bath. Sam missed his own family dearly, but was glad to find there were still seeds of joy inside.

It didn't take long for all four to stuff their bellies with bacon and biscuits. Fannie even produced another entire tray of baked goodness for John and Sam to pack for their travels. She pulled out some wax paper and told Sam to start wrapping while she stepped away to find some "proper attire" for both he and John.

"Proper attire?" Sam asked.

"Didn't John tell you? You're going to be on a proper passenger train," she explained. "You'll need proper attire. We can't have you looking like you just stepped off the plantation." She looked at John, "Or out of the woods."

John shrugged his shoulders at Sam as if to say, "*I'm* not going to argue with Fannie...are you?" Fannie left the kitchen to search for the "proper attire." John turned to Sam.

"We're headed further north," he said. "We'll have to arrive at the station a little early to get tickets."

A new excitement filled Sam. He had loved the time in the boxcar with John, but riding on a passenger train?

Fannie came back in the kitchen with a pile of clothes and split them between John and Sam. Sam said a prompt, "Thank you," while John's "Thanks" seemed to be flavored with a tone of "If you say so."

With their clothes changed, Sam and John actually did look like proper gentlemen. Each wore long pants, a white shirt, a seven-button vest, and a single-breasted jacket. Charles helped Sam with his tie.

John still wore his boots, but Sam got a pair of black leather shoes that were only a size or two too big. Fannie clapped her hands in front of herself, a bright smile from ear to ear.

"That's much better!" she exclaimed. She pulled at John's collar. "I knew I'd get some Sunday-best on you one day!" Sam was so infected with Fannie's delight that he didn't see it fit to mention how chokingly tight this "proper" shirt collar was. He wasn't sure how anyone could move in such a thing.

"Fannie may like the look, but I think the collars are a little tight myself," announced Charles, reading Sam's mind.

As they all stepped outside to say their goodbyes, the same stray dogs from yesterday sat at attention when John stepped out of the house. As they made their way to the front gate, Fannie took notice.

"What's with all these mongrels?" she said with concern. The Raven landed on the lamp in the yard and squawked.

"They're following us," offered Sam.

"Are they now?" Fannie replied.

"They'll follow us out of here, don't you worry," said John.

"Even after your baths?" Fannie chided John.

"I might be clean, but there's still wild in me, dear," John smiled back. "Thanks for the train schedule, we'll be on the nine-o-five."

"At least you'll be traveling with tickets this time," said Charles.

"Someday soon it'll be in the cars up front," remarked John. Charles nodded agreement.

John turned to Charles and Fannie to say a final thank you, "Thanks much for the bed and the food, especially on such short notice."

"Anytime, John," said Charles as they shook hands. Then the tall, squared-shouldered John pulled in Charles for a hug. It was the first time that Sam had seen one man hug another. It wasn't romantic at all, but deeper in a way Sam could sense, even if he didn't completely understand. It was over in a moment, but the connection it made seemed to linger even after they parted.

The embrace that Fannie gave John was much more familiar to Sam. She went up onto her tiptoes (as women often do), squeezed him, then lowered herself and brushed something off one of John's shoulders. Fannie held him at arms length and looked him up and down (as women often do). She seemed to be painting a fast picture of him in her mind. She finally gave him a golden smile that made everything ok. Sam liked her.

"You take care of each other," she said (as women often do).

John took one of the sacks of biscuits from Charles and handed it to Sam, stuffing the other into his own satchel.

Sam addressed Charles.

"Thank you for the bed and the book." Sam reached out and shook hands with Charles. Charles held his hand firm, placing his other hand gently on Sam's shoulder.

"You let me know how you like it," he said. "And when you're finished with that one, I gave John the one you seemed to like so much from last night. Of course, I've been holding many just for you, for quite some time, as a matter of fact."

Sam wondered how Charles could be saving books for him before they even met. And many of them?

He put his hand on the rectangle of Huck Finn in his satchel, happy to have this first one, while looking forward to what else Charles was saving for him. He hoped they weren't traveling too much further as he wanted to be close enough to easily come back soon for whichever book, or two… or three was next on the list.

"I'd like that very much. Thank you, sir."

Charles let go of Sam's hand with a final shake.

Sam smiled at Fannie.

"Thank you for the biscuits, the potatoes, and the bath," he said with a small bow.

"Of course, child," Fannie said. She pulled Sam in close for one of the warmest embraces he'd ever received. If it wasn't for his stiff new shirt, Sam was sure he would've melted. "You give my love to the ladies and fellas up in Forge now, will ya? Ol' John here is sure to forget."

She pushed Sam back and seemed to take a picture in her mind of Sam too. She turned to John with a stern look, playfully wagging her finger at him.

"Don't you let him choke on them biscuits!"

John held his hands up in surrender, "If you didn't make them so good, I wouldn't have to watch him!"

Fannie let out a heartfelt laugh, and Charles gave John one more pat on the back. John and Sam turned down the short path and toward the dogs waiting on the street. Once outside the short gate, they turned right. Sam couldn't resist glancing back over his shoulder, seeing Charles with his arm around Fannie, both smiling. Fannie waved one more time. Sam felt full.

A few blocks later, Sam asked John without turning, "How far is it?"

"Only a bit till we get to the station, but still some miles to go before we sleep," said John. "And a good few days until we're back in Forge."

"Forge?"

"Forge, yes. Same as Fannie mentioned. That's where we're headed."

Sam had only known that they were going north. To have an actual destination, instead of just a direction, was a little something he could hold onto, even if it did bring up a few more questions.

"It's nice. You'll see when we get there," explained John, before Sam even had a chance to ask anything. John turned to the dogs that had been following them.

"That'll do," he said. The dogs all stopped and sat. "Off you go," John added, and as fast as they had found John and Sam the night before, they were gone.

After a half hour of walking, Sam and John arrived at Union Station. It's huge arched ceilings made Sam feel dizzy as he looked up, trying to take it all in. Everything seemed light and shiny, worlds away from the dark freight train they had arrived in.

Once John got their tickets, they shouldered their way through the crowds, found their train, and looked for their passenger car. They walked the entire length of the train before they found it, just in front of the caboose. John gently shook his head as they boarded the car labeled, "For Blacks Only."

John encouraged Sam to take the window seat as he stowed their rolled up Pelts in the rack above. John pulled *Huck Finn* from Sam's Pelt and the book Charles had given him from his own. Sam looked out the window to see the last minute passengers rushing to make their trains. He could almost picture himself as one of the men, with someplace important to be, and some family at home that he worked hard to support.

John leaned to see out the window himself.

"Lot's of people, eh?"

Sam saw a woman dabbing away tears as a young man grabbed a suitcase and stepped towards the train. A young couple, full of excitement and love, held hands as they jogged to their train car. An old man and an old woman stood on the platform waving, the old man blowing kisses.

The train's whistle blew and they lurched forward. Just as the train moved, Sam felt deflated as he realized he had left his second Tootsie Roll on the bedside table.

How could I forget something so delicious?

His mouth watered, but he swallowed his regret and focused out the window, hoping to find a distraction in the city as it passed by. Soon, the passenger platform gave way to the criss-cross of train tracks leading out of the station.

Resting his book on his lap, he felt something pressing against his leg. He pulled the book away, reached into his front pocket, and was stunned as he pulled out two Tootsie Rolls.

Just what I needed, he thought with surprise.

Sam put one back in his pocket, *One for now, one for later.*

He took it by the edges then watched with delight as he pulled both ends and it twisted open. He put his finger under the wrapper and pulled the candy out just like he'd seen Fannie do the night before. Sam smiled.

He bit into it as the scenery clicked by faster and faster. Sam chewed slowly, savoring every bit. He traced the crinkled edges of the wrapper with his thumb and finger while he settled into a thoughtful silence.

Eventually, he took his eyes from the window and spoke to John.

"I'm gonna find me a girl just like Fannie," he said.

A smile slowly worked its way across John's face, "That's a fine idea, Sam...a fine idea."

18

For an hour Sam watched the world tick by as John read the book that Charles had given him. The backsides of warehouses soon gave way to small clapboard homes, all with chimney smoke rising at the same angle. Sam wondered about all the lives people had in each house as the spaces between them grew. Soon there were no more houses, only trees. Sam didn't know when, but the rhythm of the train lulled him to sleep.

John looked up from his book to see Sam dozing in the late-morning light, the Tootsie Roll wrapper still in his hand. He was glad Sam was resting in this moment between places. He knew what was coming. For now, Sam was still a boy.

For now.

John quietly closed his book, reached over, and delicately took the wrapper from Sam's hand. He gave Sam's Pelt a gentle scratch, and it tucked itself around Sam's shoulders.

Three hours after they left D.C., the train slowed into Pennsylvania Station. Sam stirred and opened his eyes with a stretch and yawn. John was packing his book away as he spoke.

"There's gonna be a lot of people. Stay close," he said.

Even a farm boy from the south had heard of New York City, but Sam was still surprised at the throngs of people swarming through the train station, and all dressed so nice. His collar still felt tight, but he was glad that Fannie made them change, so neither he nor John stood out from the crowd. The smell of tobacco filled the air.

John was easy to follow, his size alone made people step out of his way. Sam scurried along in his wake, doing his best to keep up. Sam soon figured out John was following the signs for the Interborough Rapid Transit, which lead them left and right, up and down, through mazes of people and dim, crowded hallways.

So focused was Sam at keeping up that it was only when the floor moved that he realized they were standing in the middle of another train car. It rumbled and clacked a rhythm as it rose up from beneath the city to an elevated rail. The late afternoon sun made Sam squint as the window revealed his first views of the city, buildings speeding by as the train wove through.

Underneath them, people criss-crossed the streets, horses pulled carriages, and motor-cars blew dark smoke as they wove through the mess. Every time the train stopped, people filed off or pushed their way on. Sam noticed everyone seemed to be in a hurry, and instead of talking, people communicated with nods and glances.

Sam counted eleven stops before John nudged him, and they stepped off the subway at 135th Street in Harlem. Sam felt squeezed as it seemed there were even more people here than at Penn Station. As the train pulled away, he realized a crowd had gathered on the narrow platform of the elevated train stop. Some stood on tiptoe while other's craned their heads trying to get a look at what was happening against the wall at the edge of the stairs.

An angry man wearing a derby was yelling at a woman in a long, simple faded-green dress, her hair wrapped in a red scarf that settled around her shoulders to keep the cold out. She had a few playing cards and a small pile of coins on a soapbox table in front of her. Sam couldn't understand everything he was yelling, but it was obvious the Derby Man wasn't happy. The woman held her hands up.

"I don't control the cards, sir!" she pleaded.

"*Riprenditelo*!! Take it back, I say!" he put his finger in her face. "It's lies! Lies!"

A few men in the crowd laughed uproariously, but Derby Man wasn't smiling. Infuriated, he suddenly overturned the table, sending cards and coins into the air. As the woman tried to contain the mess, Derby Man yelled again, "Take it back!" and reached for her.

Instead of the woman's dress, Derby Man got a handful of John's shirt and tie. John had moved between them in a flash and his mass alone instantly halted both Derby Man's yelling and the laughing of the crowd.

Looking down at the man, John said softly but sternly, "You best be goin'."

Derby Man threw his hands up, making a show of his retreat, "What does a raggedy woman know anyway! Keep your damn cards!" With a "*Hrmf*" he turned on his heel.

The crowd realized the fun was over and dispersed, leaving only John, Sam, and the woman on the platform. She was frantically collecting the coins and all of her cards from the ground, speaking to herself as she flipped through the ones in her hand.

"Drat!" she said out loud. "Where are you? Come back to me, King!" The woman's voice had a smooth quality to it, almost like she was singing.

Sam spied the final card, swept it up off the floor, and handing it to the woman. When she looked at Sam to say *thank you,* she stopped short, holding her eyes on him. There was something catlike about her stare.

"Thank you," she said slowly, "Thank you, young man."

It was the first time Sam had been called a "young man" by anyone. He felt rather grown up.

It must be the clothes, he thought.

"The King of Diamonds," the woman said as she slid the card into the deck. "A good card." She turned to John and finally realized just how big he was, "And thank you...Big...Sir."

"No thanks necessary," said John.

"Some are very passionate about the cards," she sighed. "But it's the cards! It's not me!" She raised an eyebrow. "You want I should read some for you? 'Tis for thank you?"

John considered for a moment as he and Sam finished picking up the makeshift soapbox table and putting it right again.

"No trickery, mind you," John said, "It won't work."

"No trickery for these cards," she playfully defended. She looked at the Pelts strapped around John and Sam. As if on cue, the Raven landed on an electric pole at the train stop and gave a *squawk!* The woman's head snapped to the bird, then back to John and Sam. Her eyes widened.

"Maybe is magic around you two, eh?" She placed her hand over her heart, then extended it to John, "Vadoma."

John mimicked her motion, placing his hand over his own heart before extending it.

"John."

Vadoma took his hand and gave a slight bow.

"And this is Sam," John continued. Vadoma brought her hand back to her heart and offered it to Sam. Sam did the same. Her hand felt warm even on this cold day. With her feline eyes, she looked Sam up and down with a smirk, then did the same to John.

"The pleasure is mine," Vadoma said. Sam liked the melodic quality of her voice.

Sam had heard of fortune tellers that used cards to tell the future, or some that used a candle to cast a spell for love. Auntie used dominoes to find out if it was going to rain, or if a baby was going to be a boy or a girl.

"Are you a fortune teller?" Sam asked. Vadoma smiled in mock protest as she shuffled the cards.

"Ah! Fortune teller is a bunch of tricks," she scoffed. "The cards...they tell a story," she held the deck up for emphasis, "I'm a *Vatiz*." In front of her on the table, she balanced the entire deck on edge.

"Let us see what is your story. Give me your hand."

Sam offered his hand eagerly. Vadoma turned his palm down and brought it over the standing deck. A card jumped up, and Sam surprised himself by catching it. A wave of excitement passed through him.

"Put on table, like so," Vadoma instructed. Sam laid the card face up.

"Ah...should've known, same as before, King of Diamonds. Is good." Vadoma thought for a moment, then turned to John.

"What about you, Johnny?" Sam smiled as he wondered if anyone else could get away with calling John's massiveness "Johnny."

"Like this?" John asked as he held his hand over the upright deck. Another card jumped up, and John caught it. Vadoma took it and lay it across Sam's King of Diamonds.

"And the Eight." She looked at John, then at Sam. "Old man crossed with young man." She gestured to each of them, "Good, right?" Sam glanced at John, who didn't seem impressed.

Vadoma rolled her eyes at John, then took the top card from the deck. She looked at it with surprise, then glanced back and forth in the subway station. She raised an eyebrow as she brought it down. Just as the card was about to touch the table, a loud police whistle pierced through the subway station. Sam's hair stood up when he saw Derby Man standing with a police officer and pointing.

"There they are!" he yelled. Vadoma tossed the last card on the table with a flourish.

"Two of Clubs says, 'Time to go!'"

She scooped up the cards, grabbed the soap-box table, and ran. On instinct, John and Sam followed, sprinting down the stairs behind her and down onto the street below.

The sidewalks were lined with people selling everything from newspapers to ducks. Engines from motor-cars made put-put sounds and spewed smoke smelling of motor oil while horses pulled carriages this way and that leaving a lingering of scent of manure. One loud motorcar swerved and barely missed them as it sped by, the driver cursing.

"Damn engines," said John under his breath. He stared daggers into the back of the driver's head as it rushed away. The policeman's whistle screeched again from the top of the stairs.

"This way!" called Vadoma.

Vadoma led the dash through the streets with Sam and John. To Sam, it was almost the same as running through a forest, only here, the trees moved. It became a game of deftly dodging pedestrians and street sellers as they ran.

Sam was so focused on keeping up, he lost track as they turned right, or left, or crossed a busy street. The policeman's whistle faded into the sounds of the city when Sam thought he heard music. A few steps later, he looked up to see Vadoma stopped in front of a young busker playing a jig on a squeeze-box.

"Evening, Jorge!" she called, flipping a coin into his hat. She pulled the deck of cards from her dress pocket and drew one. "Two of diamonds!" she called. She reached into her pocket again and produced another penny.

Tossing it into Jorge's hat she called, "Another one, for later, just in case!"

"I'll be here!" Jorge replied without skipping a beat.

One more block and a right turn around a corner brought them all in front of a three-story, brick building. A striped awning stretched out over the sidewalk, covering the wares of a small grocery shop. The Raven came to rest atop a nearby street lamp as Vadoma handed the soap box she had been carrying to a barrel-chested and mustached man standing amidst the fruit.

"Good day, Ivan. Thank you for the box."

"Vadoma, you back. You clean horse...he make...mush," he held his nose for emphasis, "or no more stay."

"Yes, yes...of course," Vadoma replied. "Good business today?"

"Da. When is cold, apples stay fresh. See?" Ivan held up an apple from one of the open wood boxes in front of his shop. Though quite late in the season, it looked as if it had only been picked a few days ago. They looked delicious. Ivan seemed to read Sam's mind, and his stomach.

"One penny each or six for nickel." His accented voice was gruff, but Ivan seemed friendly enough. Vadoma tossed Ivan a nickel from her dress pocket.

"Six it is then." She grabbed four for herself, and headed down the alleyway next to the store. "You two can pick your own," she called over her shoulder.

Ivan turned his attention to John and Sam as they looked over the apples. He lowered his voice. "You be careful, eh? Sometime, she nice. Sometime, she trouble."

John smiled at Ivan, "Well now, aren't we all?"

Ivan let out a laugh that shook his entire barrel chest and clapped John on the back, "Da! Is true!"

John held up his apple, "Thanks."

Sam did the same, "Thank you, sir!"

The Raven took flight and squawked as they turned down the alley next to the shop. About twenty yards ahead, Vadoma stood in front of a huge Palomino horse, feeding it the apples she had bought. Attached to the horse was something far more sophisticated than a wagon. It was an exquisite and enchanting carriage painted in reds and greens. Carvings of birds flanked either side of the coachman's box, behind it was an intricately etched door in the center of a rounded roof. It was the very definition of ornate.

The horse gave Vadoma a nuzzle as he happily chomped.

"There's a good boy," she said affectionately.

"That's a big horse," Sam said.

"Yes, he is," Vadoma replied as she fed him from her hand. "Seventeen hands. This is Alde. He likes apples."

The Raven landed on top of the ornate carriage with open wings. It fluffed and ruffled before tucking all his feathers back into place. Vadoma looked at John, then Sam.

"That your Raven?" she asked.

"You could say that," answered John. The Raven gave a squawk of protest.

"The Raven says differently," Vadoma laughed while John rolled his eyes. Sam had assumed the Raven was John's; he wondered who else the traveling bird could possibly belong to. Alde shook his bridle and Sam's eyes were drawn to the carriage again.

"Is that your carriage?" Sam asked.

"Carriage? No," Vadoma corrected Sam politely. "Caravan."

"Oh. Caravan," Sam repeated. Looking it up and down, he was sure he wouldn't forget. Sam would later understand that it was a Romani caravan, a *vardo* in many circles, and a source of pride for many Romani people.

Vadoma turned to John. "You were quite useful today. I suppose I should thank you for stepping in at the station. If there's ever anything I can help you with, feel free to ask." She pulled a calling card from her pocket, and turned it over as she handed it to John.

Vadoma - Vatiz

The card was decorated with the same ornate birds that were carved into her caravan. They seemed to move, slowly flying around the edges of the card. John put it into his jacket pocket.

"Now that you're safe, Ma'am, we'll be heading off," he said.

"I imagine you must have some place important to be," she said teasingly.

"Just The Savoy" replied John. "I've got an old friend there to catch up with before we continue north."

"The Savoy, eh? Aren't we very modern? I have a friend or two there as well. It's not far," said Vadoma. "You've got a sly way of asking a lady to dance, Mr. John. Give me a moment."

Vadoma stepped up into the coachman's box, opened the etched door, and disappeared inside. Sam looked at John.

"We're goin' dancin'?"

Before John could answer, the caravan door swung open and Vadoma stepped out. She had changed clothes completely. A velvet green dress hugged her figure and a glittering headpiece wrapped around her forehead. Sam gulped. She reached back inside with one arm and pulled out a long brown wool coat before closing the door. She casually tossed the coat down to John.

She seemed to glide to the ground as she slid her deck of cards into a dress pocket.

Sam's mouth dropped while John shook his head.

"You weren't going to show up at the Savoy without a date now, were you?" she asked. She extended an arm to John who slid her coat on, one arm at a time. It was so smooth, it seemed like they were already dancing. She glanced at Sam and gave an artful turn of her shoulder.

"Shall we, gentlemen?"

She extended her hand and John gently pulled it through the triangle of his elbow, like a lady with a gentleman. Sam had the feeling that he should be learning something in this moment, but couldn't quite put his finger on what.

"I thought there may be something more to your cards," said John.

"We're all a little more than we let on, aren't we?" Vadoma gave Alde a stroke on the nose, "You stay right here 'till I get back, love."

Alde snorted softly, a sort of horse's agreement.

"Now, who's this other gentleman without a lady?" Vadoma smiled.

She extending her other hand, drawing Sam to her other side. She placed her hand just at Sam's elbow, and it felt as natural as could be.

"That's better...The only thing better than one gentleman, is two," she said with a laugh.

Time seemed to stand still and rush forward at the same time. Sam's nose was filled with the lightness of sandalwood, rich and smoky. For the rest of this life, even a hint of the scent would bring him back to this very moment in the city with Vadoma.

They started their walk by passing Ivan, his arms folded on his chest and a suspicious eye brow raised. Soon they also passed the same busker they saw before. After a look at Vadoma's new dress, he switched to an elegant waltz.

"Have fun on the dance floor!" the busker teased as Vadoma strolled passed between John and Sam.

"Always!" She teased back.

Twilight fast approached, and the shadows from the buildings elongating more and more until they reached all the way to the purple of the evening sky. Sam was amazed at how the street lights lit up the city. Even with the moonless night, it almost as bright as day.

John said the lights used something called "lektrisity." He claimed the lamps were burning inside the glass, like a fire, but not burning up, that way they could stay lit. Sam thought that John must be confused, because you couldn't make fire inside a tube; it would snuff out. It may as well have been magic.

John and Vadoma laughed with each other as Sam tried to take in the city around them. There were so many sites and sounds along the way that Sam found it hard to focus on any one thing. Boys younger than himself offered to shine his shoes, or sell him a newspaper. Old women sold bread, while younger ones offered sewing to repair holes in trousers. Even simple things, like men sitting on the steps of high buildings with their pipes, were new to Sam.

Eventually, they stopped in front of a double door with a sign above that read, "The Savoy," in fancy lettering.

The Savoy

"Well, here we are," said Vadoma. "Shall we?"

They stepped to the end of a line of people waiting to enter. Each time the door opened to let people in, the music would try to get out. The line moved quickly and when they reached the front, John asked the doorman, "Bojangles in town tonight?"

"Sure is," the doorman responded. "Duke is too. Got a few opening acts...but Bojangles'll be up before too long." He pulled the door open and gave a small bow as Vadoma and her gentlemen stepped inside.

The rhythm of drums pounded Sam's body. Brass melodies rose and fell while harmonies engulfed his ears and brain. Tobacco smoke curled in the air, cutting grey arcs into a spotlight that threw a beam from the back of the house all the way across the dance floor to the bandstand. A circle of light followed the dapper band-leader as he waved his baton majestically back and forth in front of a dozen gleaming instruments. Each member of the band wore a powder-blue suit as sharp as a tack. The band-leader glanced over his shoulder

162

from time to time, waving and smiling at the dancers filling the floor...and what dancers they were! Sam couldn't believe how they all moved with the music. Each step filled with rhythm and joy.

Sam felt like he was floating as the music swelled around him, like he was being carried aloft through the dance hall. He felt a hand on his shoulder, snapping him out of his trance. A lady in a long scarlet dress politely asked, "Your coat, Young Sir?" She pulled Sam's Pelt off his shoulders and draped it over her arm, adding it to John's Pelt and Vadoma's long coat.

John leaned into Sam's ear and spoke over the music.

"That's Duke," John gestured to the band leader. "Sure can cast a spell can't he?"

Sam couldn't take his eyes from the band. The music washed over him so thick he felt like he was inside it. Singing for his mother's church was moving, of course, but he never imagined music could surround you and lift you out of your body.

Sam didn't know what to do with all the sights, the smells, and the sounds that seemed to all come at him at once. There was nothing like this in South Carolina.

"Lady, gentlemen. This way if you please." A man in tails guided them to a table laid out with a white tablecloth, polished silver, tall glasses, and crisp napkins folded to look like roses. The man in tails pulled out the chair for Vadoma.

"Lovely to see you again, Ma'am," said the man in tails.

"You as well," Vadoma responded. "It seems my associate knows both Duke and Mr. Bojangles," Vadoma gestured to John.

"If you could let him know John from up north is here," John offered.

"Of course, sir," the man in tails said. He nodded to Vadoma and Sam in turn, "Ma'am. Sir." He disappeared into the swelling mass of waitstaff, busboys, and patrons that was the club on this Sunday evening.

"Seems you know everyone," quipped John.

"A girl does best when she has a lot of friends," Vadoma smirked.

Something told Sam that Vadoma and John weren't just talking about what they were talking about. Sometimes his Ma and Pa would talk about one thing, but he knew they were really talking about something else.

"VADOMA!" came a loud voice.

Standing, arms crossed over his grand chest, was a well-dressed man, flanked by two others in matching suits.

"Barba!" said Vadoma with an overly gracious smile. "It's been a while! How are things?"

"Things? *Things* are missing," came his reply. "Do you know where I might find them?"

"Huh, what kinds of things would those be?" Vadoma was unruffled.

Barba looked at John and Sam, "I see you've made some new friends. Do these new friends know they're mixed up with a thief?"

Vadoma's glance to John betrayed a flash of caution as she addressed Barba with a smile.

"I'm surprised to see you here!" Vadoma gestured around the room for added emphasis.

"We came for the food, but it looks like we're blessed with company as well." He beckoned one of the two matching suits next to him. "You know Sal, don't you?" Sal was tall and slender with a cigarette hanging from the edge of his mouth.

Sal nodded, "Vadoma." It was obvious the greeting wasn't entirely friendly.

Barba continued, "It's funny...Sal here told me that he got our shipment ahead of time, which he was very pleased with." Barba turned to Sal, who nodded his head with exaggeration. "But...he was also very surprised at the 'Fast Service Fee'." Sal's nodding changed to shaking of his head, and an exaggerated frown worked its way across his face.

"I was not aware of an additional fee," Barba continued, "Only you were."

Vadoma held her composure, "Well, I did make the delivery ahead of time, did I not?"

Barba nodded.

"Faster than anyone else?"

Barba and Sal both nodded. Vadoma made her point, but the men still didn't look happy.

"We have questions about how, exactly, you were faster than anyone else. Much faster. There is no way a man could get here that fast."

"That's why it's a woman's job," Vadoma said with a smile.

Barba narrowed his eyes, "Perhaps this woman should go for a walk...to discuss the job."

"I'm sorry, Barba, but my date and I were about to have a dance. He's a personal friend of Mr. Bojangles."

Sal interjected, "No one keeps Barba the Greek waiting."

"You're welcome to the next dance, Barba." Vadoma rose from her seat and reached for John, "But this one is taken."

"I don't think you understand," Barba grabbed Vadoma's arm. "It wasn't a question, it was an order."

Suddenly, several other men in suits appeared, Barba's men. "Now let's go for a walk...nice and easy."

"Pardon me, but this doesn't seem a fitting way to treat a lady." John stood. He towered over both Barba and all of his suits. Barba let go of Vadoma's arm.

"And who are you?" Barba asked.

"I'm next on her dance card." John offered Vadoma his elbow.

"Are you now?" Barba smirked. Even though Barba was confident he and his men could take John, The Savoy wasn't the type of place to cause a scene. As much as he wanted "a word" with Vadoma, he didn't want to be blacklisted.

"Now what kind of a gentlemen would I be if didn't honor her dance card?" Barba looked to Sal and the suits, who all had smiles. "One dance."

"Sounds fair enough," said John.

Vadoma turned to Sam and said loudly, "Sam, will you get a lady a drink?" She then pulled him in close and whispered directly into his ear. "Get Alde and the caravan! Bring them here, pronto!"

Sam looked at her wide-eyed as she pushed him away and smiled, continuing loudly, "Be sure to get that drink order right! I have a feeling I'm going to need it!" She took John's arm and they gracefully stepped away.

Barba, Sal, and the other suits kept their eyes on John and Vadoma as they took to the dance floor. Vadoma turned back and stared daggers at Sam.

"What are you waiting for? Go!" she said through gritted teeth.

Blinking, he looked right and left, but for the life of him couldn't figure out which way was out. Suddenly, the Man in Tails was on his shoulder.

"Looking for the door, sir?" he said into Sam's ear. Sam nodded vigorously. "Right this way!" Sam followed the Man in Tails as he wove through the club and to the door, holding it open with a slight bow as he loudly whispered, "Hurry!"

Sam turned right and ran, but only made it to the end of the block before he realized he once again had no idea which way to go. A quick look up and down the streets didn't help; nothing looked familiar. For all the walking at Vadoma's elbow, he hadn't been focused on the road.

I should've been paying attention, he thought.

There was a *squawk!* from atop one of the street signs. The Raven looked down at Sam, then took flight. Sam sprinted after it.

Inside the club, John proved an exceptional dance partner. As the music crooned, John eased Vadoma this way and that, lifting her effortlessly for a turn here or a twirl there. He led confidently, so Vadoma always knew what was coming next. When the final notes of the orchestra came to rest, she knew the fun was over. Barba and his suits were watching from the sides.

Barba was determined to get his money back. In fact, for the entire song, Barba and his suits never took their eyes off the dancing couple. Barba had even used the time to summon more suits. Before a new song began, the additional suits made it quite obvious that any other couples should sit this one out.

As the other patrons stepped out and the suits stepped in, John held Vadoma in place in the center of the dance floor. He was like a statue, his left arm high, and right arm wrapped around her, a firm hand on her upper back.

Sam chased the Raven street after street; zig zagging through pedestrians, around electric lights, and dodging motor cars. After passing the busker with the accordion, the Raven *squawked!* and made a final turn, perching atop the striped awning of Ivan's grocery shop. Ivan watched with arms folded as Sam bolted around the corner and into the alley.

"I told you she sometimes trouble!" Ivan called as Sam sped past.

Sam finally stopped in front of the massive Alde, harnessed to the caravan. He climbed aboard, took the reins with a snap, and called "Hiya!!"

Alde didn't move.

"HeeyYAA!!" Sam called again. Alde looked back at Sam, then forward again, but didn't budge.

Barba stood just off the dance floor, arms folded across his chest with a wicked smile from ear to ear. The band leader stopped and turned to see his dance floor empty, except for John and Vadoma.

John pulled Vadoma in close enough that they were cheek to cheek.

"How quick is your boy?" Vadoma whispered.

"Not quick enough," replied John. "I count eight."

"Skinny guy smoking at the edge of the stage makes nine." Vadoma answered.

"Nine it is. How well can you follow?" John asked. Vadoma raised an eyebrow.

"Try me."

John called out to the band, "Duke?!"

The band leader squinted through the lights. "John? Is that-"

"Gimme some Poppin', Duke!"

Duke spun to the orchestra and hollered, "You heard the man! Hellzapoppin'!" He punched his baton down and the bongos kicked in a rapid rhythm while the piano and bass doubled down with a wicked walking baseline. The trumpets let out a diabolical scream.

John snapped his wrist and pushed Vadoma hard with his shoulder. She spun across him and away, unfurling at the end of her turn with a back-hand across the jaw of Suit One.

WHACK!

John tugged her hand and Vadoma came back with tight spin. Suit One fell to the ground.

"Eight," Vadoma said.

They shared a smile; this wasn't going to be an ordinary dance.

Sam planted his feet in front of Alde and heaved on the bridle, but the horse wouldn't budge.

"Come on, Alde! Vadoma said to hurry!"

Sam looked to the sky for some kind of help, only to see the Raven glide down and perch on the roof of the caravan.

CAW!

"Are you going to help or not?" he called out. Sam didn't know what he expected the Raven to do.

The Raven cocked its head, then took off down the alley. Sam dropped his head in despair.

"I guess not," he said aloud.

At The Savoy the saxes wailed, the trombones howled, and so did Barba's Suits. John pulled Vadoma in tight and used her momentum to fling her over his back, holding her over his shoulder by the waist as each foot kicked a suit in the face. John pulled her back over his shoulder, and landed Vadoma right in front of him.

"On the floor!" Vadoma yelled.

John laid Vadoma out with a spin as he kicked his own leg over her head and landed a blow to Suit Four, sending him backwards. The trumpets blared.

"We're kickin' up your heels now!" John hollered.

"Five to go!"

John tossed Vadoma up, down, sideways, and in every other direction. She was a graceful, beautiful weapon. With every turn, a punch to a face. With every flip, a kick, and often two. Every twirl and lift was a mesmerizing flow of the pair's improvised destruction. Through it all, John and Vadoma never missed a beat.

Sam stood in front of Alde, yanking at his bridle.

"Why...won't...you...MOVE?!"

Sam looked Alde in the eyes, but the horse seemed to stare straight through him. Sam threw his hands up.

Think, think!

He tried to will an idea out of his mind.

What will make a horse move?

He felt a quick puff of air across his face and turned see the Raven perched on the top of Alde's bridle. It flapped its wings and twitched its head, trying to show Sam what it had in its beak. Sam held out his hand and to his complete surprise, the Raven dropped a penny into it.

Sam stood with the penny in his hand staring at the Raven, his brain searching.

John and Vadoma are in trouble, I can't get this darn horse to move, and this bird is bringing me pennies?

The Raven squawked, then snatched the penny off Sam's palm. Sam ducked as it flew just over his head and down the alley to Ivan's grocery shop. It landed on the edge of a box of fruit, flapping to get Ivan's attention.

"Hello, bird!" Ivan said with surprise, "What you have?"

Ivan extended his hand, and the Raven dropped the penny, squawked, and looked back at Sam. Ivan stretched his neck to look down the alley and saw Sam standing with Alde. Sam's face was all bewilderment as he witnessed Ivan and the Raven doing business together. The Raven hopped to the apples.

"Clever bird," Ivan said. He picked up an apple and yelled to Sam, "AY!" Ivan threw the apple in such a perfect arc that Sam barely needed to reach out to catch it.

Sam held out the apple to Alde who gobbled it up in one bite. Sam grabbed Alde's bridle.

"That's a good boy! Let's go! Yip yip!"

Alde took off like a shot, trapping Sam's hand in the bridle.

Sam barely managed to tiptoe-run alongside Alde as they burst from the alley. There was no way his legs would be able to keep up. At any moment he'd lose his footing and be dragged alongside the massive horse, or worse, trampled underneath his powerful hooves.

"Up you go!"

Sam felt his trousers rise up his butt again as Ivan heaved Sam atop Alde. Barely managing to look back, Sam saw Ivan brushing his hands off and waving with a smile.

"Trouble!" he called one more time as Sam clung to Alde for dear life.

The Raven swooped down within an inch of Alde's head, then darted left to lead the way. Sam's grip almost gave out as Alde cornered hard to follow the Raven. As Alde's hooves pounded a rhythm at full gallop, Sam heard the busker's accordion getting louder and louder. He managed to look up and see the busker wave, the pitch of his music dropping as it faded behind them.

John spun Vadoma up and over his head, flinging her feet-first away from him. She double kicked Suit Eight in the head before John pulled her back. He spun her again and—

BANG!

The entire room stopped at the sound of a gunshot at the edge of the dance floor.

"ENOUGH!" Barba stood with a pistol pointed at the ceiling. Lazy smoke rose from the barrel into the spotlight. Several Suits held their heads and rubbed their arms as they limped off the dance floor; others remained unconscious and unmoving.

Barba brought his pistol down and aimed at the frozen couple.

"Enough dancing. Let's go." Barba gestured to the door with his gun.

If the moon was out, and there weren't so many people, John could make quick work of Barba and his crew, just like he did Abbot and his men. But tonight there was no moon, and John was just a man. His eyes stayed locked with Barba; two men waiting for the other to flinch. An injured Suit, holding his head, stood up right between them, blocking Barba's gun.

"MOVE!" yelled Barba at his man. The Suit startled, then turned to see the gun pointed right at him. He dropped to the ground, but the dance floor was empty. John and Vadoma were gone. The rest of the crowd was now in a panic, swarming in all directions.

"Don't let them out!" Barba yelled to his men. "The doors!"

"I hope your boy is good with horses!" Vadoma cried as they shouldered though the frenzied crowd.

"*Ahhhhhhhhhh!*" Sam screamed into Alde's mane. He barely clung to Alde's back as they chased the Raven across boulevards, around corners, and through the streets of New York City. Even with the caravan being pulled behind them, Alde never slowed.

Breaking through the front doors, John looked left and Vadoma looked right, but there was no sign of Sam or Alde. From inside, they could still hear Barba and his suits yelling.
"No, that way!"
"The front door, dammit!"
Then, a familiar sound.
CAW!
From the sky between the streetlights, the Raven swooped and streaked past. Alde came around the corner at full speed, a breathless Sam clinging to his back and the caravan careening behind them.
"That's one way to do it," Vadoma smiled. "HATCH!" She called.
Alde slowed the whole shebang to a stop right in front of The Savoy's front doors. Vadoma jumped aboard and grabbed the reins. John was next to her in an instant.
"Vadoma!" the Man in Tails called. From the front doors of The Savoy, he flung both the Pelts and Vadoma's jacket over the crowd and into the air. The Pelts found their owners and wrapped around them tight. Vadoma's coat opened and glided straight to her. In one graceful motion, Vadoma slid her arms into the sleeves and it settled perfectly onto her shoulders. She reached into her pocket and flipped a coin to the Man in Tails.

173

Sam relaxed his grip on Alde's neck and turned to Vadoma, "Maybe I could—"

"No time to waste!" Vadoma snapped the reins and Alde took off again. Sam clutched the horse's neck once more, and the Pelt streamed behind him like a cape.

Barba and his suits burst through the doors just in time to see the back of Vadoma's caravan disappear around the corner. A Ford Model A pulled up right at the curb in front of them. Through the open top, Barba pointed his gun at the driver.

"You're gonna follow that carriage there!" Barba threatened. The driver gulped.

"Get in, boys!" Barba shouted, and four Suits piled in.

The driver hit the pedal and the chase was on.

Sam's eyes were streaking tears as he clung to Alde's back. Streetlights whizzed by, and pedestrians jumped out of the way as they wove between carriages and motorcars.

BLAM!

A gunshot rang out from behind. Sam barely held on as they cut down an alley way. Vadoma reached a hand into her dress pocket and fanned a deck of cards to John.

"Pick two cards!" Vadoma yelled.

"Now?!" John yelled back.

"You know where we're going, yes?"

"Where we're going?!" The alley suddenly emptied onto a busy street.

"LEFT!!" John called out in a panic. Vadoma pulled the reins just in time and Alde made the turn, pitching the caravan up on two wheels. Sam was thrown sideways, but managed to cling to Alde's harness as the caravan straightened out.

"Where are you taking him?" Vadoma nodded towards Sam.

"Forge?!" he yelled back, confused.

"Yes! Picture it and pick two cards! Hurry!"

"Two cards?" John looked with bewilderment at the fan of cards Vadoma was holding.

"YES!" Vadoma shouted. *Why was this so hard to understand?*

She strained a look behind them and saw Barba make the turn out of the alley way. As strong as Alde was, she knew he would run out of steam before the motor-car did.

"Sooner is better!" she yelled as they careened through the streets of Harlem.

John envisioned the tall pines and deep snow of Forge as he reached out and quickly chose two cards, holding them up with one hand.

"Got 'em!"

"Ha!" she yelled over Alde's gallop. "Here we go!"

She pulled the reins hard right to make another corner. A hundred yards ahead, the road T'ed straight into a the side of a seven-story brick building. A massive mural of a woman holding Wrigley's Spearmint Gum smiled at them.

Vadoma gave the reins a crack, "HIYA!"

Sam looked back at Vadoma then toward the brick behemoth.

"Take these!" Vadoma forced the reins into John's empty hand. "Don't stop no matter what!" John looked at the reins, then up at the massive approaching building. Sam couldn't hide the fear in his face as they charged full gallop at the base of the brick wall.

Eighty yards—

Vadoma took a stance and a deep breath. She split the remaining cards, fanned them in each hand, then hurled them forward, buzzing Sam's head as he clung to Alde. The cards

175

rushed forward to just in front of the wall, then swirled into a huge spinning ring. It churned faster and faster until a cloudy darkness formed in the center, a vortex ringed with the rapidly spinning cards.

Sixty yards—

Sam couldn't believe what he was seeing, but John's brain had just put all the pieces together.

"HIYA!" John snapped the reins with one hand and held up his two chosen cards to Vadoma with the other.

Bullets ricocheted from the edges of the brick wall. Alde was full steam ahead. The darkness in the center of the swirl shimmered.

Forty yards—

Vadoma took the last two cards from John in each hand.

"KARTY DROM INANTÉ!!" she commanded as she flung them into the middle of the swirling vortex. The two cards cut across each other and into the center of the darkness. They circled each other rapidly, flinging sparks and arcs of electricity.

Twenty yards— Ten—

"Hold your breath!!" Vadoma cried out.

Alde leapt.

Sam barely had time to blink as Alde's head disappeared into the darkness. The wind on Sam's face stopped. Alde's mane flared out as Sam floated up and off his back. Vadoma grabbed John's arm to hold him down, and her long dark hair flowed as if underwater. Sam felt cotton in his ears and his stomach rose into his throat.

Silence.

A single shot rang out behind them.

Sam turned back at the sound of the gun shot. He saw Vadoma, weightless, fling herself up and on top of the caravan as the bullet leisurely breezed past her. As she stood atop the caravan, the bullet sluggishly advanced, floating toward Sam and Alde.

Vadoma reached out and plucked the two swirling cards from the darkness and clapped them together.

"RESTAURA!" she yelled as she drew her hands apart. The rest of the deck launched from the swirling ring and came flying back to her. As each card joined the others, hovering and spinning between her hands, the portal faded.

The Raven came flying through with a *CAW!,* dodging the final few cards as they whirled past its wings.

Vadoma brought her palms together amidst electric sparks, compressing the deck with a *clap!* The portal was gone. Opening her hands, the deck was stacked perfectly on her palm.

Sam turned his head and watched as the bullet finally passed him and lodged into a pine just ahead.

Where'd a tree come from?

Barba and his car full of cronies found themselves headed straight into a brick wall. The driver slammed both feet on the brake, but it was no use. The motorcar slammed into the wall and the back wheels rose high from the impact, flipping everyone inside up and out of the vehicle. It hung up in the air for a moment before falling back to the ground with a *smash!*

Barba and his men slowly picked themselves up, and looked at the wall with confusion.

What the hell just happened?

19

Frigid air suddenly hit Sam's face as Alde's hooves touched down at a full gallop. The caravan hurtled behind, its wheels barely cushioned by the snow as it landed with a rattle and shake. It was only Alde's powerful continuous pull that kept the whole thing from turning over. From the roof, Vadoma called down.

"Hatch!"

Alde gladly eased his gallop and came to a stop. Vadoma hopped off the top of the caravan and seemed to float down to the ground with grace and ease. She reached up to stroke his back.

"There's a good boy," she smiled. "Always the best way to travel." The Raven came to perch atop the caravan with a *squawk!*

Sam released his grip and was finally able to actually sit up on Alde's back. He looked at Vadoma with confusion, turned his head to the other side of Alde, and puked.

"It's why you hold your breath!" Vadoma laughed. "Being travelled can be hard for your insides."

John turned and vomited off the side of the coachman's box with a pronounced, "Herglkhelhggha!"

Vadoma laughed even harder at John, "I told you! I told you! Ahaha!"

Vadoma shook her head, then looked around to take in their new surroundings. Through the dark, moonless night, she could just make out a large snow-covered field surrounded by woods. Just at the other side, peeking out from the ice here and there, a river flowed at the edge of the field. High in the sky, curtains of green fire from the northern lights streaked silently across the heavens.

"So...this is Forge, then?" She asked as a bright streak dropped from the night sky all the way to the northern horizon. "Nice lights."

John coughed to clear his throat and brought his head up from the side of the caravan, trying to get his bearings.

"We're close to town. This looks like one of Stanchfield's pastures."

The Raven gave a *CAW!* from the top of the caravan and flew ahead.

"Just...follow the bird." He leaned over the side of the caravan to finish what he started. Vadoma shook her head with a chuckle.

"You heard him, Alde, follow the bird," said Vadoma. Alde snorted a cold mist into the frigid night, and tugged hard on the caravan. At least he wasn't in a hurry.

The night woods were thick with fresh snow. Alde's hooves crunched as he followed the Raven's lead from above to the main road running north into Forge. As they came out of the field, the packed snow fell away from the caravan's wheels, and Alde chuffed, happy to be on a more worn path.

Not used to the cold weather, Sam's nose was runny, but the Pelt's warmth kept most of the chill at bay. His stomach was feeling markedly better by the time Alde pulled the caravan down a short row of wooden buildings. Their wheels cut tracks through the fresh snow, making two long lines on either side of Alde's hoof prints. Sam looked back to see John was still hanging his head over the side, recovering from "being travelled."

"Is this it?" Vadoma questioned, unimpressed with the main street of Forge.

John lifted his head from over the edge of the caravan, "Yeah, this is it." The Raven, happy to be home, *cawed* and flew off, its black wings quickly disappearing into the darkness.

Forge was a one road town. If it wasn't for being so deep in the woods, it could be mistaken for one of the many frontier towns that were starting out west. A few two story buildings were set close to the only street, with cabins close behind, each with their own little plots. The cabin windows were all dark, save one on the northern hill just outside of town.

The slightest of winds stirred the trees as a gravelly voice echoed from all around them.

"Evening."

Alde stopped short and sent Sam lurching forward. When he sat up, he saw an old woman standing in front of their entourage, with the Raven on her shoulder. Her right hand clutched a gnarled maple staff. From its the top sprouted a single maple leaf, encircled by slowly blinking fireflies. They cast a glowing light on her breath as she exhaled into the moonless night. She looked at Alde for a moment, then directly at Sam.

She held his gaze for ages before Sam realized she wasn't looking *at* him, she was looking *into* him. In the glowing light from the fireflies, Sam realized her eyes were two different colors. One darker, while the other was as light as the snow. He felt something stir, like he had been missing her. A smile slowly crept across her face.

"It's you," Letha said with the smallest hint of a bow.

Sam's eyes widened and he sat up straight, answering from a trance. His voice was a mix of his own and another. "It is."

"Of course you'd arrive on a horse," Letha chuckled.

"Of course," Sam answered wryly. Letha gave an eye roll as she and Sam shared a laugh. Letha shifted her gaze up to the caravan, and a light-headed Sam fell out of his trance, blinking several times.

"John, welcome home," she offered. "Nice suit."

"Letha," John did his best to put on a smile; his stomach was still inside out. "Good to be back."

"Letha?!" Vadoma asked with surprise. "I've heard that name — You're not...wait...*the* Letha?!"

Letha looked up to Vadoma, then back at the entire caravan, "Nice carriage."

"It's a caravan," Sam interjected.

"Is it now?" Letha smirked. "I think I've seen this lovely caravan before. You wouldn't know a lady named Voshall, would you?"

"Voshall? That's...that's my grandmother's name."

"Grandmother?" Letha paused. "Has it been that long?" Letha's eyes darted as she searched her memories. "Why then... you must be Varbi's daughter, then?"

Vadoma stood and placed a hand on her heart, "Vadoma, daughter of Varbi, daughter of Voshall. Madame, it's an honor."

"Well, it *has* been that long, then..." Letha's voice softened as her memories trailed into a past before Forge. "Oh dear, the trouble we used to...The river..." She looked back up to Vadoma with a grin.

"Letha, my dear," she nodded, also placing her hand on her heart, "The honor is mine." She held Vadoma's eyes and took a breath before continuing. "Seems your timing is perfect."

"Always is," Vadoma responded.

The Raven cooed lightly on Letha's shoulder.

"There you are," she gently stroked the bird. "I've one more job for you." The Raven cocked its head. "Go check on Alma." The Raven scuttled its wings and squawked. "'Sakes,' it's just right over there." Letha pointed to the cabin just up the hill outside of town with the dim light flickering inside. The Raven cocked its head sideways again, and Letha did the same, a mild mocking. "Go on now!" The Raven opened its wings and took off from Letha's shoulder toward the cabin. Letha turned to John. "Seems Constance is bit occupied this evening, John."

"Alma having the baby?" John asked.

Letha nodded, "Should be soon. She started this afternoon. I expect they'll be needin' me before too long."

"Well then, she doesn't need me troubling her," John responded.

"I'll tell her you're here." Letha turned back to Sam. "Lucky for you, we've got the cabin ready for you all."

"Just him," replied John. Letha raised her eyebrows, but knew he'd give her the whole story later.

"Well then, plenty of time to settle in," Letha looked at Sam. "Two weeks before the moon is full again, and you'll be having your Proving Night."

"Proving?" Sam raised his eyebrows.

"Has he not explained anything to ya?" Letha gave John a scolding glance.

"I expected to have a bit more time," John answered. "Vadoma here was a very...efficient...transport."

"These caravan's do travel well," Letha chuckled as she spoke from distant memory. She made a welcoming offer to Vadoma. "We've got a spot in the barn to keep you a little out of the cold and such, if you'd like."

"I'll gladly accept, Madame. Thank you."

"Of course, dear," Letha smiled. She turned to Sam, "Slide on down here, young man, and lead this horse for an old lady, now."

Sam slid from Alde's back, finding his legs quite shaky from being travelled through the portal. He took hold of Alde's bridle and walked the horse along next to Letha. Sam felt a warmth as Letha's hand found his shoulder. She let out a sigh of relief.

"It's good to have you back."

20

Alma could no longer talk through each contraction. She had suspected she would give birth on the new moon, and while it felt good to be right, the birth itself was proving to be even more intense than she anticipated. She leaned on the only chair for support while Yara pressed his palm into her her lower back, just as he had done throughout the aches of the latter part of the pregnancy. His strong and sure presence was the pillar she could let the waves of labor crash upon. Having him here made the birth easier, but easier didn't mean easy, and Alma was hoping Constance had a few tricks up her sleeve to help. For her part, Constance filled the circular wooden bathtub with hot water from the hearth, periodically testing it with a dip of her finger.

A touch hot, she thought. She took the bucket outside, scooped a bit of snow, then felt a shift in the air. She stood, and the Raven was on her shoulder.

"Look who's back," Constance said.

The Raven squawked.

"Good to see you, too."

John had only been gone four weeks, which meant he made good time. She wondered whom he had brought back, and what the other family would be like. She hoped they would have an easy time blending in with the people of Forge. Change was afoot, and with change often comes challenge. John had finished his journey and brought a new family to Forge. Alma was about to do the same.

Alma's moans ushered Constance back inside the cabin with the Raven still on her shoulder. Alma's contraction eased, and when she brought her head up and saw the bird, she spoke directly to it.

"Well, hello there," she exhaled. "Checking on us, are you?"

The Raven cooed. Constance opened the door and nodded for the Raven to leave.

"Go tell her she's welcome to come, it'll be time soon enough." The Raven flapped its wings in protest. "Go on, now, before I let out all the heat," she urged.

The Raven took flight and and swooped outside into the night. Constance closed the door.

"There's a lot going on tonight," Yara said softly.

"I'll say," said Alma. She stood and wrapped her arms around Yara's neck, leaning forward to use him as support.

Constance took the bucket of snow and dumped it into the wooden bathtub. She reached her hand in again.

"Better...It's ready."

Alma took her staff and stood it at the edge of the tub. Yara and Constance helped as Alma stepped into the tub and gently sat herself down. Whether the water would move the birth along or not Alma did not know, but it did help wonderfully with the pressure of the life inside her now making its way out. As the water surrounded her, the baby's weight seemed to lift from her hips.

"That does feel better," Alma said just as another contraction tightened around her. She moaned and Constance brought her head close and hummed with her, matching her voice to Alma's. Constance did her best to follow the intensity for all three breaths before the contraction waned. Alma was getting light headed from the pain, managing only to slur, "That wuz a big wun."

"Yes...yes it was," Constance replied, "Each one brings us closer." Constance stood her staff at the edge of the tub as well. A light knock came from the door, followed by the squawk of the Raven. Constance raised her voice to reach outside.

"Join us, Letha!"

The door opened, and Letha stepped in with the Raven on her shoulder. Fireflies swirled around the top of her staff as she closed the door with a gesture.

"I think you deserve a rest," she said to the Raven. The Raven cawed gently. Letha extended her hand, and the bird walked down her arm pausing at the heel of her palm. "Go on," she encouraged. The Raven took another step and just as its feet touched her hand, it collapsed back into a button-eyed, black sock, as two maple leaves fell to the floor. She tucked the sock into the belt of her clothes, then turned to Constance and Alma.

"The water helps, doesn't it?" she commented. The flicker of the fire glistened in the beads of sweat on Alma's forehead. Alma looked up and met Letha's eyes. Letha knew this look well. It was pain with purpose. Pain without suffering. Alma grimaced and bowed her head. The pressure built and she let out a long, deep, moan. It was the sound that women for millennia have sung to bring their children Earthside.

"Uuunnnhhhhhh…"

Constance, Letha, and Yara matched her note with a hum, the only support they could provide. Their voices followed Alma's and trailed off as the contraction passed. Alma raised her head back up with a soft smile.

"Thank you."

Constance moved the chair next to the tub and gestured for Letha to settle in. Letha stood her staff upright on its own, completing a triangle with the other staffs, each one glowing with fireflies.

Babies have no care for the schedule of their makers, and Alma's little one was taking its time. Over the next hour Alma's groaning grew more intense until she finally looked up to Constance.

"Please tell me it's time to push," she said.

Constance reached into the water to gently check Alma's progress. "You're feeling right for it," she offered. "Time to nudge that little one out."

"I'd rather give a good shove than a nudge," Alma managed with a bit of a smile, just as the wave of the next contraction began to swell. "Here it comes."

"Keep the sound moving," said Constance, "Push it down and out with the babe. Squeeze Yara's hands." Alma reached out and found strength in Yara's grip. Her contraction was strong, and her voice with it, deepening as she bore down and pushed. The primal sound that came from her could have moved mountains.

The baby was between worlds, and so was Alma. The center of the pain was full of stars, the space between contractions quiet and full of anticipation. On the next tightening Alma's push was strong. She felt the impossible release of pain into a euphoric exhaustion. The Mother was born.

187

She released Yara's hands and reached down under the surface of the water, pulling the new life up and into her arms. Yara helped to bring the slippery baby to her chest as it let out a marvelous cry.

"Well, now," said Constance. "There's a loud one!" She shared a smile with Letha as Alma hugged the squirming babe close. Yara's tears were true as he kissed Alma on the head.

Alma smiled through her tears. "You worked hard!" She whispered sweetly. "It's so nice to meet you!"

Letha took in the babe from beside the tub, warmly announcing, "For all the world, appears a girl."

"Of course, a girl," said Alma. "I drank so much dandelion root I thought I'd give birth to a flower!" Constance and Letha both joined in the gentle laughter. Alma brought her head down and touched her lips to the wet wisps of hair on the newborn's head.

The cabin went quiet for a spell as all three marveled at the ordinary miracle that just occurred. It was a moment of sacred silence broken only by the gentle cooing the newborn and the crackling of the fire.

"It's to be done now, then?" asked Yara.

"Before the cord stops," replied Letha.

Alma nodded. Her mind was made up.

"The ancestors thank you. All." Letha added. "I should warn you, she may be a handful."

"She'd take after me then," grinned Yara.

"Destined for greatness," Letha added. The baby cooed as if to agree. "Do you consent to the blade?" Letha asked.

Yara and Alma looked at the baby, then to each other.

"We do."

Letha produced a wide blade, etchings and engravings continuing all the way to its tip. She brought her hand high as the fire caught the glint of a sharp edge. She proclaimed:

A bridge through pain, a destiny gained.

She brought the knife down and sliced the umbilical cord half through.

By mother and child, by blade and hand,
Entwine our souls, our blood demands.

Raising the knife again, this time Letha brought it down across her own palm. Blood immediately sprang forth. She reached for the cord with her sliced hand and held it firm.

Two bloods combine, through cord does pass.
A life continues, a spirit is cast,

As the cord pulsed its final moments of connection between mother and child, Letha's blood shimmered as it laced its marvels into the baby. The new baby opened its eyes wide and turned its tiny head towards Letha. They stared at each other. Letha gave a great exhale of a breath, just as the new babe took a breath in.

The path I am on, I now pass on.

Letha's words seemed final.

The wee babe closed its eyes just as Letha did the same. Letha's hand relaxed. The cord, now empty and still, dropped from her grip and fell into the tub. Both were asleep.

"The rest is coming." Alma said to Constance. She wiggled, winced, and gave another push. "Ah, that's much easier."

"Aye, there's no bones," said Constance as she gently tugged the cord, bringing the placenta to the surface and scooping it out of the water. She took the knife from Letha's sleepy hand and sliced a tiny bit from the edge. She put it to Alma's lips.

"To stop the bleeding."

Alma made a face, but still took the small piece into her mouth and chewed quickly a few times before swallowing. Constance sliced the umbilical cord clean through, then tied a knot close to the baby. She hoisted the cord and placenta together out of the tub and laid both on the dirt floor. She pulled Letha's staff from the ground and pressed it into the placenta. Roots grew around the placenta while the cord rose and fused itself up and around the staff. The fireflies at the top changed from amber to emerald, while the large maple leaf on the staff faded to a deep, deep orange. From above and below the faded leaf, two new small Kelly green buds sprouted.

Constance carefully plucked one of the tiny new buds and brought it to Alma's lips. Alma took it in and chewed it gently before edging the green mash onto her own fingertip. She placed her fingertip into the sleeping baby's mouth and let it suckle the green paste as she recited.

As you are fed, a destiny is wed.

The words came easily. The baby stirred and let out a great cry as the remaining bud on the staff grew and began to stretch into a full leaf. The baby cried again, and the bud on the staff matched the sound, growing even more. With each cry, the color faded from Letha's orange leaf. The baby yawned and closed it eyes. Silence returned to the cabin.

"That went well, I'd say," Constance whispered to Alma.

"I think I've turned into a raisin in this water," Alma replied with a bit of snark. "Help me up." Yara extended a hand to help.

Alma stood on shakey legs as Constance brought a warmed blanket from beside the fire. Yara kept a hand on Alma as she and Constance wrapped the baby and let Alma step out of the tub. She dried herself and carefully shifted to the bed and settled in. Yara offered water and a bit of food before Constance brought the baby back to the new mother.

Constance found another blanket and gently tucked it in around Letha in the chair. Letha stirred and spoke softly.

"John's back. He's in the barn getting settled," Letha quietly reported.

"The barn?" Constance replied. "Well then, looks like my night isn't over yet. You rest dear, I'll go and be sure everything's alright."

Letha smiled as she closed her eyes again, "Thank you, love."

"Of course," Constance whispered before turning back to Alma. "She said John's back and he's at the barn. Is there anything else you'll be needing before I leave you to get your rest?"

"I think we're fine," Alma answered.

"Should you need anything, just tap. I'll be up a while from the excitement of the evening. You did well."

"Thank you," Alma said genuinely. Constance wrapped her cloak around herself and tapped her staff to the ground, bringing fireflies from the walls of the cabin to swirl at its top.

She gave Alma another smile and bow before heading out into the night.

With the babe wrapped in a bundle on her bare chest, Alma took a breath and let her eyes close. Whenever she felt the baby stir, she would open her eyes and see Yara holding watch. Before long, Alma and baby drifted into a deep and timeless sleep, quite worn from the everyday miracle of birth.

21

Once inside the barn, Vadoma unharnessed Alde from the caravan and tied him loosely to a post. John broke the thin layer of ice from the top of the water cistern, filled a wooden pail, and hung it so Alde could easily drink. Sam offered Alde a clump of hay. Vadoma disappeared inside her caravan and came out a moment later with clothes more fitting for a farm instead of an evening in New York City.

Just as Sam found himself yawning and making a spot in the hay to get some rest, the door to the barn opened, and Constance poked her head in.

"Oh?!" Constance remarked with surprise, "Hello there!" While Constance had expected to see John and a new face or two, Letha hadn't mentioned the caravan and horse, or John's fancy clothes for that matter. "Dressed up to make an entrance I see!"

"Took a bath, too!" John said as he stepped forward with outstretched arms. "Up so late, eh?"

"Of course, I am. It's New Moon," Constance's staff stood upright as she accepted John's hug of friendship.

"Ah yes, of course. Tree duty?" inquired John.

"Other duties called," Constance replied. "Alma's got her new one. Healthy."

"A girl?"

"A girl," Constance smiled.

"Perfect," John replied.

"Hurrah for girls!" called Vadoma from her caravan.

"Yes, yes. Hurrah for girls!" Constance let out a laugh as she approached Vadoma. "What a magnificent carriage."

Both Vadoma and Sam responded at the same time, "It's a caravan." Constance laughed again.

"Why yes it is! Apologies, my traveling friend. I see you've arrived in style."

"Is there another way?" asked Vadoma. She held her hand over her heart, "Vadoma, daughter of Varbi, daughter of Voshall."

Constance matched Vadoma's greeting, putting her hand over her own heart, "Constance, Coven of the North. Honored."

Constance shifted her eyes to Sam for a moment, then back to John with a look that said, *Well?*

"This is him," said John.

"Is it now?" replied Constance, making eye contact with Sam. Her eyes were two different colors as well, one the color of dark earth, the other sky blue.

Sam stretched his hand out to Constance, "I'm Sam."

She kept her hand over her heart for a moment before she stepped forward and embraced him. It caught Sam by surprise. Constance was tall, and her embrace was warm. Not as warm as

Fannie's, of course, but still. She held him at arm's length, looking him up and down. She squeezed his shoulders.

"It's lovely to have you here, Sam. We expect great things from you."

"Alde likes him," offered Vadoma. Alde snorted agreement.

"I guess that's a pretty good start," smiled Constance before turning back to Vadoma, "Anything else you'll be needin'?"

Vadoma shook her head, "You've given us a place out of the wind and cold. Our only need now is a bit of rest. Our late arrival forbids me from asking for more. Thank you for the food and water for Alde."

"'Till mornin' then?" said Constance.

"'Till mornin'," Vadoma replied as she bowed and ducked into her caravan. Before closing the door she called out, "Night Alde!" Alde nodded his head and lay himself down in the hay.

Constance gave her attention back to Sam. "Well then, if my lady Vadoma is settled, we'll not have you sleeping in a barn. Let's show you to your cabin." Constance grabbed her staff and led the way out and into the night.

With their backs to the barn, Constance's firefly staff provided a swirling glow as she, Sam, and John tracked a small path into the woods through the snow. In the moonless night, the undulating streaks of green and yellow northern lights stretched across the sky, touching the horizon. Sam stopped walking and looked up in complete wonder.

"Whoa..." His mouth hung open. John noticed Sam's gaze into the heavens and smiled.

"Ahh, it's good to be back." He turned to Constance, "A busy night for the rest of the ladies, eh?"

"For the *rest* of the ladies?" Constance playfully protested. "I think Alma and I were quite busy with the birth, thank you very much!"

John laughed, "No, I didn't mean to—"

"*I didn't mean to?*" Constance mocked with a chuckle. Her eyes fell back to Sam, he was still looking with wonder at the northern lights above.

"Look at him," she nodded to John quietly, "Remember how magical they are the first time?"

"They're magical?" Sam asked.

"They can be. They can both harness and create magic…and so can we," Constance replied.

"You'll learn," smiled John. "Some paths can only be seen in the dark."

On one hand, only the snow on the ground made this place different from his old home many miles south. On the other, John changed into a beast, Vadoma had enchanted cards, and there were magic lights in the sky. Sam wondered if this place would ever feel like home. Sam thought he heard chanting far in the distance that curiously matched the swell and intensity of the lights in the sky. Tilting his head to follow the aurora, Sam felt like he was falling.

Maybe I'm still feeling dizzy from being travelled by Vadoma, he thought. Constance spoke as if she was reading his mind:

"That's a mighty fine caravan Miss Vadoma has, isn't it?" she remarked. Sam brought his eyes down from the sky.

Maybe she doesn't know about the cards, Sam thought. He was excited he could share some of the magic that he'd seen.

"A carriage is just regular, but a caravan is magic."

"Really?" Constance asked.

"She made a circle with her cards that brought us here. Then John threw up."

Constance looked at John. "Did he?"

"Not just *me*," John answered.

"But if you need Alde to move, you gotta give him an apple," Sam explained.

"Good to know," Constance winked at John.

"I haven't been inside yet...the caravan," replied Sam.

"I'm sure it's just as lovely as the outside." Constance paused her steps for a moment and gestured ahead with her staff, "There we are."

In the dark through the trees, a small cabin sat by itself, the snow on the roof glowing a soft green-yellow from the northern lights. They approached the front and John pulled the huge timber braced across the door up and away.

Inside was simple; a bed, a rocking chair, and a small Franklin stove with a few pieces of wood stacked next to it on the dirt floor. A single shelf built into the wall held a row of books and a few small boxes. Between the rocking chair and the bed sat a small table with a kerosene lamp and a tin of matches. Constance stood her staff in the middle of the floor. The fireflies circled a little wider, spreading their golden light into the room as much as they could. Constance gestured.

"Light the lamp, and we can get you settled. There's matches there...aren't those a marvel? So easy."

Sam lit the wick of the lamp and replaced the glass, filling the cabin with a gentle glow. The Pelt relaxed off his shoulders and laid across the bed. Sam swore it looked like it was sleeping.

Constance waved her hand gently through the circling fireflies at the top of her staff, "You all can have a little rest, thank you." They scattered around the cabin as they slowly went dark.

"They do get tired after a time. We all need rest at some point, don't we?" Constance commented.

Sam remembered chasing fireflies with his brother and sister. "Back home they're blue, but I've never seen them do that."

"Blue? Is that so?" she replied. "They must be special."

"Did you train them?" Sam asked.

"You could say that," Constance answered.

Sam looked at the small bed, just big enough for one person. "It's just me then?"

Sam had always shared a bed with his brother and sister. Even for the past two weeks, John was always close by. Now that he was far north in the woods, sleeping all by himself seemed a little unnerving. Constance tried to comfort him.

"Just, until your family—" Constance was cut off with a look from John. He shook his head at her, and she understood that Sam's family wouldn't be joining them. She was sure John would give her the details later.

"Well...'till you can bunk with the boys...You know, John and the rest," she said. John nodded his agreement.

Sam noticed the two long narrow horizontal windows, each a slit following the seams of the log cabin. They were just tall enough to get a hand through and let light in. There was no glass.

"We'll be wanting to keep the heat in," John said as he closed up a wood shutter over each window. As he finished, Constance asked him for a little help.

"John, if you could grab a bit more wood, I'll have a little look-see at our young man here." John stepped out of the cabin

"'Course, ma'am," Sam clanked the door to the stove open and peaked inside. A pile of shavings topped with kindling was already within. He grabbed the tin of matches and struck one against the side of the stove then reached it inside to the edge of the shavings. They smoked, then caught flame with a small *puff* that quickly spread. Sam watched it for a moment to make sure it took before swinging the small door closed.

"Marvelous," Constance stood and pulled the covers back on the bed. "You think you can get a little rest tonight?" she asked as she patted them down.

"Yes, ma'am." Sam knew he wouldn't find it hard to sleep tonight. Hanging onto a horse for dear life while being travelled through a magical lightening tornado resulted in a boy feeling more and more ready for bed.

John came back in the door with an armload of wood. "Not much left to the pile out there, we'll bring some more by tomorrow or the next," he said as he dropped the pieces next to the stove.

"Another thing... Have you been writing down your dreams?" Constance asked.

"Damn," John said under his breath. "The pages blew out on the train so, he didn't have a chance to." He went to his satchel and produced two red cedar pencils, placing them next to the lamp.

"Maybe we can get lucky," Constance pulled one of the books off the shelf and leafed through it, finding a few pieces of old parchment between the pages. "These will do for now, 'till one of us can bring some better paper tomorrow." Her tone implied this would be John's job.

"Any dreams you have, be sure to write them down first thing. Dreams are important to tell us how the blending is going, but a dream's memory often fade. Best to get it down first thing while it's fresh."

Sam had always thought dreams were more than just dreams, but he had never thought of writing them down.

"Also, your old memories, the ones before the bite, will fade more and more quickly," John added. He paused for a moment to choose his words carefully. "Usually your family would help you ground your personal past, but since they aren't here, it's up to you to hold their history. Put down anything you feel is important and would want to remember."

Sam looked at the paper and the pencils. He knew how to read pretty well for his age, but he wasn't confident in his writing. Again, Constance seemed to read his mind.

"If you're still learnin' to write, do your best. If you need to, you can always draw a picture to remind you, and we can help you properly write it down after."

"Yes, ma'am," Sam replied. Constance somehow made him feel like it was okay to be a beginner.

"To keep you safe, I'm going to have John lock this door from the outside. Before you know it, it'll be morning, and we'll be back."

Sam wasn't sure what he needed to be kept safe from, but he nodded anyway. A crackling came from the small wood stove.

"That fire should take the edge off the cold for you," Constance added.

"Should be enough wood for the night," John finished.

A moment of silence settled into the room.

Constance smiled.

"It's nice to have you here, Sam. I look forward to seeing your strength."

Sam felt a longing rise inside him. Like the strength Constance spoke of wasn't quite yet within reach.

Constance tapped her staff on the ground, and the scattered fireflies lit up the crevices all over the cabin. With a rhythmic blinking and flittering, they returned to circle the top of her staff. Sam couldn't tell if she was talking to John or the fireflies when she said, "Off we go."

John opened the door to let Constance out, then stepped close to Sam before offering him a few more words.

"Welcome to your new home."

He brought Sam in for a firm, but short, hug. "Get your rest now. We've got some work ahead tomorrow. We'll see you in the morning. Goodnight."

Sam heard the timber slide into place, locking him inside. He stood and listened as the pair's footsteps slowly receded into the snowy night. For the first time in more than two weeks, Sam was alone.

He went to the door and gave it a small shove. It didn't budge. He looked around the room.

I hope I don't have to pee, he thought.

He added a few of the larger pieces of wood to the fire. As he closed the door to the stove, he paused for a moment, finding the muffled crackling of the fire comforting. If he closed his eyes, it was almost like the fire back home.

He sat on the bed and his Pelt wriggled up and wrapped itself around his shoulders. He reached for his copy of *Huck Finn*, and found a small smile as he opened the pages.

Constance silently counted the steps until she felt they were far enough away from the cabin before she quietly spoke.

"It's just him then?" she finally asked.

"Just him," replied John. "There was no one else to bring."

"Poor thing," added Constance. "Burned to the ground?"

"Just ashes."

Constance let her steps guide her thinking for a few moments.

"We should send a few of the Jacks over each day. It will both get him ready and pass the time. It should make the loneliness of the nights a little easier."

"That would be helpful, I imagine."

"'Course Letha will be around. He'll find a bit of comfort in the connection they'll have," Constance continued.

"'Course."

"Still, it's unfortunate. A rough start."

"Yes." John thought for a moment. "I was able to rein myself in," he confessed. "There was blood, but no killing...there was a fire the next morning. It was no accident."

He thought about how different the trip would have been with Sam's whole family, like it should have been. How there would be more people to welcome into Forge. How Sam would witness the integration of his family, and the integration of his blood inheritance work in parallel. Now, he wondered how Sam was going to fair, becoming his new self without his family close by.

John had seen Sam's inner strength that night in the woods a thousand miles south. Sam had willed himself awake, fought through the unconscious effects of the bite, and made it all the way back to the plantation, simply to make sure his friend, that girl, wasn't hurt. He was shot at and chased with torches. When there was no more room to run, Sam raised his fists, ready to fight the men and dogs that had pursued him. Sam had courage.

He had strength. Sam also had tremendous loss and pain. He was becoming a man.

The silence stretched between Constance and John until she spoke again, as if reading his thoughts.

"*Amor Fati*," she said.

"It's hard this time," John replied. "Perhaps I had too much of a hand in it."

"Your fates were weaved long ago," Constance comforted. John took some solace that perhaps fate guided him more than malice. Constance moved the conversation to John's journey.

"You stopped by Charles and Fannie's? Got the book?"

John padded his Pelt-satchel, "Right here."

"Good, good...It's been quite some time since I've turned those pages. I've never had to put it into practice without Letha."

"I gave it a glance. You're so good you could probably do it without. I mean, you're not Letha, but..."

"Funny." Constance smiled at the playful ribbing. "We've got a little time, but there's still much to do," she said.

"Yes. Yes, there is," confirmed John.

"Lucky for us he's a good worker," Constance offered with another grin.

"Yes. Yes, he is." John managed a smile of hopefulness.

Even with all the work that needed to be done, John was glad to be home. The northern lights grew brighter, and far in the distance, the calm night let a familiar chanting make its way through the trees.

"Shall we stop by the ceremony?" asked John.

"I don't see why not," said Constance.

The chanting grew louder as they approached a large recently cut clearing in the woods. More than a dozen women were walking across the clearing and into the dense forest next to it. Each stopped periodically and planted a staff in the ground as they continued to chant. The northern lights reached down from the sky and touched the earth and circled the trees around them. It seemed both sacred and casual.

Constance stepped into the woods and planted her staff in the ground, matching the chanting of the other women.

John was happy to be home and witness the monthly transfer of spirit as it happened. He felt a hand on his back and turned to see Amasa greeting him with a smile.

"I heard you made it back...in a caravan too? Fancy," Amasa jested. "All good?"

"All good... for now anyway," John answered, "Course there's still work to do, but he's in the cabin. We'll start tomorrow."

"If Arthur picked him, we've got no worries," Amasa said.

John looked up to the sky and smiled, "This is my favorite part."

"Ah...me too," replied Amasa.

They watched as the greens of the northern lights shifted to pinks and reds, then brightened and swirled down around the swaths of trees surrounding them. The changing of colors matched the rhythm of the chanting, shifting to greens and whites as they lapped at the earth, pulling the spirit of each tree up into the heavens until spring, when they would call them back down again.

22

The only road into Forge ended at the calm waters of First Fulton Lake. North from there it was more wilderness, more trees, and more cold. A few wagon trails cut here and there through the woods, but traveling north beyond Forge with any kind of efficiency was done over the water. The old native routes strung lakes together by slow flowing rivers and streams. If the water was high enough, you could paddle clear up to Lake Champlain and up into Canada without having to ever take your canoe out of the water—a good hundred and fifty miles. In the winter, you could do the same over the frozen ice by foot or even by horse and sled.

The road south out of town would bring you into to Utica after a couple days of riding. Turning right would bring you to Albany, fifty miles to the west. A turn left would eventually turn you south, and a couple hundred miles later you'd find yourself on the shores of the Hudson looking across at New York City. On horse, a good ten days in all.

The summers were cool, while both spring and fall were muddy. Most of the logging happened in the winter when the ground was frozen and logs would slide out of the woods and onto the ice of the lakes more easily. The spring thaw brought high water through the rivers and streams, and those logs could be floated down to the mill.

Years ago, as the Jacks cut a path through the forest toward the southern shore of Fulton Lake, they widened the road enough for two wagons to pass. They carefully chose plots for small homesteads, cabins, and a pasture or two, each space tucked and protected against the pines. While the soil didn't lend itself to more than basic farming, the timber traded and sold well enough that the town could sustain itself, and Forge emerged.

By then about a dozen buildings lined the road from the southern part of town leading up to the lake. The first was a two-story home owned by the Goodsells. They also built a carriage barn a few dozen yards off in the back, with an icehouse between the two. A half mile north, the newest building was only a hundred yards from the water's edge, Cohen's Stock & Staple.

Many of the buildings hosted a shop of some kind on the first floor and humble living quarters on the second. The winters were so cold and snowy that living and working in the same house simply made sense. This was the case for the tannery, bakery, blacksmith, and barber, among others.

Cabins dotted the shores of the lake, and some faced the branch of the small river leading south. Most of the cabins belonged to the Witches. Some were for living in, while others were places for ceremony or study.

There was no church in town. This was fine with most folk. After all, there was no mention in the Bible of beastly creatures created by the full moon, yet beastly creatures had a hand in each of the town-folk's lives. The Jacks and Witches insisted upon a code of truth, and found it built trust faster than faith did.

Adhering to the code was a small price to pay for the towns people to always have wood in the winter, Witches to heal any ailment, and powerful men to keep the town safe from danger all year round.

The only other expectations the Jacks and Witches made of the townsfolk was to be well-read and to keep a regular, even if minimal, diary. As such, they kept a strong collective chronicle of the town's history. Records of weather, ice-out, migrations, timber and crop yields, as well as the general goings-on made a good study for the future, or so they were told. As one could imagine, the barber always had the most cutting gossip, while Mabel at the bakery would record the number of pies she baked, but never revealed her recipes. Everyone understood that anything worth doing was worth at least making a quick note about, and all put quill (or pencil) to paper on a regular basis.

Naturally, then, the school house was the main fixture of the town. It was as most schools were of the day, consisting of a large room with an old blackboard, worn-in desk and chairs, and a wood stove in the corner. The bookshelves were so full there was talk of building a library next door soon.

A smaller back room of the schoolhouse held wood storage and other necessities. It even had an "in house" just off the back room, in addition to the traditional outhouse a ways off, to save the children from having to trudge through the snow in the winter.

Other than the comings and goings of a few souls, or an occasional new house or small building going up, not much had changed in Forge for a good century or so. How much Arthur's death and Sam's arrival would alter things was hard to tell. The townsfolk were excited to be a part of history, while the Jacks and Witches wanted to be sure their small piece of the world stayed as true to their roots, and as peaceful, as possible. Even if the future could never be foretold, one change does inevitably lead to another.

23

A narrow slit of morning light snuck though the shuttered window and onto Sam's twitching eyelids. In his dreams, images streamed and flashed.

Swords. Trees. Moonlight. Fireflies. Arabella. Swirling cards. Letha. The Wolf.

Sam sat up into the cold with a start. His eyes traced the room.

Stove...door...roof...cabin.

It took a moment for Sam to remember where he was. The raised scar on his arm itched, telling him something; what it was, he did not yet know.

He got the feeling he wasn't alone. A shadow cut quickly across the sunbeam. Feet tromped a fast rhythm in the snow outside.

Sam got out of bed, pulled the shutter, and strained on tip toe to look out. Seeing nothing, he pulled the shutter of the other window and was startled when a boy's face popped up.

"You awake?" Two huge, excited eyes stared at him.

"Uh... yeah," said Sam.

"Lemme see if I can move the log." The boy disappeared.

Sam heard grunting, wood barely sliding against wood, then the door timber thudding back into place. The boy's face returned to the window.

"I can't hardly move it," he said with disappointment. "Wait! Hold on! I gotta get a leverage."

Sam heard footsteps crunching in the snow, then sounds of dragging, wood piling on wood, and a sudden crash to the ground. The door burst open revealing a muddy-faced lad with a smile from ear to ear, his knit cap barely keeping his unruly hair contained.

"You're here!" he called out excitedly.

Before Sam knew it, the boy was poking and prodding at him.

"Look at your clothes! You're super fancy! Whoa!" Sam forgot he had fallen asleep in his New York City gentlemen's clothes.

"Where's your scar? Is it big? He didn't bite you on the butt did he? Haha!"

Sam tried his best to deflect the poking of the boy, but instead found himself giggling. "Stop that... I'm gonna have to pee!"

"Did you really come into town with a Vatiz?! Did you get to jump through the portal? Lucky! Did you bring anything else with ya?" The boy moved away from Sam and into the cabin. He seemed disappointed that there was only Sam...until the Pelt leapt from the bed and directly onto the boy.

"There he is!" The boy rubbed and wrestled the Pelt as it crawled up and all over him, taking him to the ground by wrapping him in a flurry of fur.

Sam's attention was drawn up and through the open door. He saw a wagon road leading down the hill away from the cabin. A warmly cloaked figure with a staff stood in the morning light.

"Stewart! I should've known!" Letha playfully scolded from afar. The boy peaked out from the cocoon of the Pelt.

"That's Gramma Lettie," the boy said. "Don't worry, I'm her favorite. She's the only one what calls me Stewart. You can call me Stew, or Stewie. My friends call me Stewie."

He pulled his hand out and waved, "Mornin', Gramma Lettie! I let him out of the cabin for ya! Weren't no trouble!" Stew pushed at the Pelt, "Let me go now, I gotta go gentleman Gramma Lettie." The Pelt released him and jumped onto the bed. Stew trotted down the snowy trail and offered his elbow to Letha.

As Stew escorted her to the cabin, Sam watched Letha's feet in awe. In this snowy winter landscape, she was barefoot. Just before each foot would touch the ground, the snow beneath melted away and she stepped on thawed earth. Her staff grew fast roots each time she placed it on the dirt, then drew them up as she raised it for her next step.

"Weren't no trouble?" Letha grinned, "Wasn't any trouble." She corrected.

"Wasn't any trouble," Stew repeated.

"And you're nothing but trouble, my boy!" She laughed as she arrived at the cabin, looking up to offer a greeting, "Good mornin' to you, too, young Sam."

"To you too...two?!" Stew laughed.

Letha eyed the pile of logs and stones Stew had used to pry the timber up and away to open the door.

"What kind of contraption are you building now?" Letha asked.

"A leverage," Stew answered with pride. Letha narrowed her eyes.

"You're not going to leave that mess are you?" she asked.

"'Course not," Stew replied. He quickly started tossing the smaller pieces of wood back to the wood stack. Letha turned to Sam, and he once again was momentarily hypnotized by her separate colored eyes, her blue eye was as light and grey as her hair.

"I hope Stewart didn't wake you. He can be a little... enthusiastic," she smiled. "Did you sleep well?" Sam had to look away from her eyes before he answered.

"You were in my dream, I think," Sam said.

"Was I now? I hope I was nice."

Sam searched his memory, but the details had already faded from his mind, as dreams do.

"I don't really remember," Sam admitted.

"Well now, between your travels, your first night in the cabin, and the new moon, I'm surprised you had any dreams at all," replied Letha. There was a crash from the woods where Stew dropped the last of his "leverage," a length of dead tree.

"All done!" Stew called as he brushed off his hands on his pants.

"So helpful," Letha said with a wink, before stepping inside the cabin. "Let's see if your fire's still going."

Stew produced a small folded piece of paper from his pocket as he followed them through the door.

"I made a list, Gramma Lettie!" he said. "'Member you said if I made a list, I could come along with you into town."

"You actually made the list, now, did you?"

"'Course, I did. Just like you said. We ain't never known of a new Jack coming into town, least that's what Pa says. He says we should make things proper hospitable and all. I wrote down what I thought we needed 'cuz I wanted to make sure we didn't forget nothin' goin' into town."

"Anything," Letha corrected.

"Anything. Forget anythin'," Stew repeated as he unfolded the paper. He held the creased page out for both Letha and Sam to see. There, in the best writing Stew could manage, was just:

Tea

Sam raised his eyebrows, "It's only one thing."

"It's one *important* thing," Stew said seriously as he turned to Letha, "Isn't that right?"

"Indeed, mighty important," replied Letha. "You already brought the syrup, I reckon?"

Stew stared at Letha.

He looked down at the paper in his hand then slowly pulled a red cedar pencil out of his pocket. He put the paper on his lap and pressed more letters into it before holding it up for Sam to see again. Sam read aloud.

Tea
Syrup

"Now it's *two* things." Stew was quite pleased with himself. "I won't forget now, Gramma Lettie."

Stew folded the paper and stuffed it back in his pocket. "Should we go get it?" He asked hopefully. "The syrup? And tea?"

Letha looked Stew up and down, it was hard to tell if Stew was trying to be helpful, or trying to be trouble. Usually it ended up being a little bit of both.

"Stewart, I was thinking: Would it be too much trouble for you to take Sam into town by yourself?"

Yes! Stew's eyes lit up.

He couldn't believe his luck. He was supposed to be in school for a test on the Revolutionary War today, but that was more than a hundred years ago and Stew didn't think it had much all to do with him anyway. He much preferred the stories and history of the Jacks and Witches. *Those* stories he got right from the people that lived them. He'd much rather spend an afternoon with Kofi or Amasa—or Arthur if he was still here. The best stories came from the source, not some book that had *History of the Past* on the binding. Stories in person were exciting and the Jacks never quizzed him about the dates. Most exciting of all, he was right here, on Day One of Sam's story in Forge, no book needed. What could be better than that?

All of this had gone through Stew's mind in a split second before he answered with a smile, "For you, Gramma Lettie, it wouldn't be no trouble at all."

"Wouldn't be *any* trouble," Letha corrected.

"*Any* trouble."

"You don't have anything more important to do?" asked Letha. Stew considered for a moment, choosing his words carefully.

"I'd think that Sam is the most important thing in Forge right now, Gramma Lettie, don't you?"

"I suppose he is quite important. Question is, can you handle something this important?"

"Of course, Gramma Lettie."

"That *would* be helpful, Stewart. It means I could take my time today and drop in to see Alma...make sure she and the baby are well, then meet you back here."

"I like being helpful," Stew smiled.

For her age, Letha liked to think she was fun, but she knew she wasn't "Stew" fun. She fancied the idea of Sam spending a little time with someone his own age, and sending the boys on an errand or two was better than letting them wander aimlessly.

"He'll be needin' other things besides tea," Letha continued. "A couple shirts, boots...Having a bit of bread on hand from Mabel's isn't a bad idea. Could do with a knit hat and socks... work trousers and such. It's quite a bit."

Letha looked at Stew, expecting him to add to his list, but Stew pointed at his noggin.

"I got it, Gramma Lettie, I know all what to get."

Stew was still doing his best to contain his excitement at getting to bring Sam into Forge for the first time. It's not everyday you get to show someone your hometown, after all. "Pa has me runnin' errands today anyway. I can do both at the same time. That's even more sufficient."

"Efficient," Letha corrected.

"*Efficient*," Stew repeated. "More efficient."

Letha looked back and forth to Stew and Sam several times before making up her mind.

"Off you go then," she finally said. "Be sure to stop by Rahm and get him measured for those boots. He'll be needing 'em, no doubt. And back here before dark, with the tea and all the rest."

"Of course, ma'am, of course," Stew let his smile creep out more than he meant to. Letha raised her voice a little to make sure Stew was listening.

"Listen, Stewart. While's the sun's already up, the moon won't be long. Even though it's just a sliver during the day, it could be a little strong for him. You bring him right back here if it's too much, yes?" Letha locked eyes with Stew, making sure he understood. "It's important."

"Yes, of course, Gramma Lettie. I'll bring him right back... an' we'll be back 'for dark, ma'am. Promise to truth."

The Pelt sat straight up, hoping to go too. Letha smiled.

"Guess you better go along too...keep him warm and all," Letha said. "Go on."

The Pelt leapt from the bed onto Sam's shoulders and wrapped him up.

"Off you go then," Letha said to Stew.

Stew bolted out the door in his excitement, leaving Sam standing, staring at Letha.

Stew's head poked back in. "Well, ya comin' or not?!

Sam followed Stew along the snowy wagon trail as it wove its way through the winter woods towards town. It didn't take long for the questions to start.

"Where'd you get your fancy clothes?" Stew asked. Sam looked down at his black vest, still buttoned, and the matching dark coat and trousers that Fannie had given him. He did look a bit out of place in the snow.

"I got them from a friend of John's in Washington D.C." Sam's foot slipped on the snow, making him do a quick dance step before finding his balance again.

"Whoa! Here...walk in Gramma Lettie's spots," Stew advised with a gesture towards Letha's footprints. He continued with the questions excitedly, "From Fannie and Charles?"

"Yes. You know them too?" Sam gingerly hopped into the snowless steps Letha had left.

"I ain't never met them, but Charles'll send a book up for me from time to time, him being one of the Holders and all."

"The Holders?"

"You seen all his books, didn't ya? In his house? John says it's like a library."

"In the front room." Sam recalled the wall of books as he entered their house.

"I guess. I ain't never been," Stew confessed again. "He's got all the history and everything, for all the people of Forge and the Jacks and such too. He's one of the Holders of History."

"He let me borrow one," Sam said. "A book."

"Which one? You good at readin'? I'm pretty good too, though I still gotta sound out some words sometimes. Writin's more tricky."

"When I'm doin' my letters, I get my d's and b's mixed up," confessed Sam.

"Me too!" laughed Stew, "They always look right when I'm doin' 'em!"

Sam understood. It was good to have a new friend.

"I gotta get better at my writin'," Stew continued, "so I can start givin' Charles me and Pa's story too."

"Charles gave me *Huckleberry Finn*," Sam said.

"*Huck Finn*! I read that one, *Tom Sawyer*, and a bunch of his other ones too. That Mark Twain's pretty good, eh? I like the frog story and all the pictures he puts in."

Of all the things Sam could have in common with someone, he was surprised that it was a book that they both shared.

They moved from under the scraggly winter canopy into open fields, where some cows and a few horses milled about, diving their snouts into the snow, looking for a leftover bit of growth. Sam was grateful for the steps Letha had left; he was able to stay out of the snow entirely.

"How does she do that?" Sam asked. "Melt the snow when she steps?"

"You should see in the spring," Stew answered. "Them footprints'll be full of flowers. Not just Letha's either, all the Witches."

Sam stopped. "*All* the Witches?"

"'Course. There ain't just Gramma Lettie. Wait, you didn't think it was just Gramma Lettie, did you?" Stew answered. "Every Jack's got one. They usually go together, like brother and sister."

Brother and sister. Sam suddenly felt mixed up inside. He missed Ruthie and Ben. He felt alone.

Stew could sense something had shifted.

Sam's silence hung in the still winter air.

They walked the length of the field quietly until they reached stone wall with a wooden gate. Stew opened it to let them through and latched it behind them. He stood with his hand on the gate for a moment.

"Sorry 'bout your family," he offered. Stew took a breath to say more, but it didn't feel right. Instead he quietly lead the way across the next field, letting their footsteps fall uninterrupted for a while on the earth and snow. When he broke the silence, it wasn't another question. Instead Stew offered something about himself.

"My Ma ain't around no more neither. She got passed just after I got born."

Sam took it in. The snow crunched beneath their feet as the two boys walked side by side, crossing into a warm patch of sun in the center of the field.

"Sorry, 'bout your Ma," Sam said.

"Yeah, me too," Stew replied quietly. "Gramma Lettie's pretty good to me though, you know? So I'm glad I got that."

"She seems nice," Sam replied.

Stew seemed to be searching his mind. "You...You can borrow my Pa anytime you need...'s no trouble." Stew paused, then smiled. "I always wanted a brother."

A brother, Sam thought. He had lost his family only two weeks ago and had been in Forge not even a day, yet Stew was already starting to make it feel like this could be home. Sam smiled.

"Would I be your younger brother or older?" Sam asked.

"Don't matter to me. You're a little taller so...older?...even though I'm the smart one," Stew laughed.

Sam laughed too. It felt good. Stew had a gift for making everything feel a little lighter. They both let the lightness lead them through a growth of well trimmed trees, finally cresting a small hill.

A slight wind made Sam put his hands into his pockets and his fingers encircled a tiny column.

Oh yeah...I forgot, Sam thought as he pulled it out.

"What's *that!?*" asked Stew, eyes wide. Sam pointed at the text on the wrapper.

"It says right here, Tootsie Roll, but Fannie called it a midgie," said Sam. "She put a couple in my pocket before I left."

"Is it good?" Stew asked.

"Sure is," Sam replied. He pulled both the ends, slipped his finger under the wrapper, and pulled out the chocolate candy. "We can share it."

"Really!?"

Sam pulled and twisted the roll apart and handed half to Stew.

"It's a little chewy," Sam explained as he bit into his half. Stew put his up to his nose, then put it in his mouth. He immediately closed his eyes and smiled.

"That's *really* good," he said.

"Sure is," replied Sam with a smile of his own. For a split second, he felt like Fannie had her hand on his shoulder.

Sam had been so focused on the candy that he hadn't noticed they were overlooking a small valley. Stew swallowed and gestured ahead.

"There's town."

Forge was laid out in the distance before them, a few sprawling two story buildings along a short, slightly curved main street that lead to a bridge stretching over a half-frozen river. Unlike the bustling streets of New York City, there were no electric streetlights, no people selling newspapers, and no motorcars. Across the river, instead of buildings taking up the skyline, a ridge climbed high, edged with naked winter branches stretching to the sky like roots pulling down the cold from the gods. The hillside looked as if it had been shaved. A swath of timber had been taken and piled along the edges.

Against the open sky and the snow, the smoke that leaned from each chimney made Sam feel warm. It's scent reached up the hill.

Stew gestured again, this time towards the sky.

"There's the moon, too." The thin sickle of moon rose to the southeast. It would chase the sun across the sky all day. Sam felt a warmth in his scar.

Even with the washed out palette of winter before him, the colors in the town seemed a little more vivid. Sam picked up the scents of bread, leather, and wood, and sounds seemed more distinct than mere moments ago.

He glanced at Stew.

He must feel it too, Sam thought.

Among the sounds, there was a faint mechanical whining that seemed to be coming from the building by the river.

"What's over there?" Sam asked, pointing.

"The saw mill," replied Stew. "Got a circular saw a few years ago. Cuts a lot quicker now." Stew blinked, "Wait, you can hear it, can't you?"

"Can't *you*?" Sam asked.

"Nope," Stew said with a smile. "That moon's making you sharp."

Sharp.

That was exactly how Sam was feeling. Sam thought it was simply being in a new place that made everything more acute, but Stew insisted it was the moon.

"Yeah, that's the moon alright. You feeiln' alright? Not ornery or nothin'?" Stew asked.

Sam shook his head. Stew looked him up and down.

"You look fine to me...Let's go," Stew smiled and lead the way down the hill towards town.

They were soon making their way straight down the narrow main street. While the morning cold kept most inside, Stew

223

happily shouted to the few people starting their day, "Good morning!"

Sam got the feeling that Stew was quite pleased to be the one to show "the new boy" around town.

Each person Stew greeted would linger on Sam for a moment or two, then bow to him. Sam would nervously bow back. He didn't recognize anyone's face, but each person felt familiar, and strangely so did the town. A piece of him somehow felt as at home as back in South Carolina.

"Sorry I'm not doing a proper introduction to everyone," Stew whispered. "It would slow us down too much, 'specially if we stop in there." Stew pointed to a small shop with a short, stocky red and white striped pole. The barber shop. Sam knew getting the dish took much longer than a haircut, and today Sam would be the dish.

Sam smelled something delicious in the air just as Stew took an exaggerated breath through his nose and smiled. "You hungry?"

Stew walked up the steps to one of the shops and straight in the door without knocking.

As they entered, Sam was struck by a blast of heat and the scent of baker's yeast. In front of them was a rack of rising dough, and further along towards the back, Sam saw a large, brick baking oven. A lady had her back turned and called over her shoulder without ever looking up from her work.

"Mornin'! I'll be right with ya!"

"Mornin', Miss Mabel!" Stew called back.

"Stewie! Just who I've been looking for on this cold morning! My woodbox is almost empty...Bring me a few more armloads from the back, would you, dear?"

"'Course," replied Stew as he motioned for Sam to follow. Stew stepped all the way through the shop, past the brick baking oven, and out through a back door. Sam slipped again on the packed snow outside, flailing his arms before catching his balance on the substantial wood pile. His slick-bottomed shoes from the city simply weren't cutting it here in the snow. Stew stacked wood into Sam's arms.

"Miss Mabel'll give us some cinnamon buns if we help...least she usually does for me. I don't even think she noticed you," Stew said excitedly as he finished piling wood onto Sam. Stew loaded his own arms up and stepped inside with Sam close behind. He dropped the armload of wood with a splintering thud into the woodbox, then watched as Sam did the same. When Mabel heard the second landing of wood, she called out from around the corner.

"You got a friend with you today?"

"Sure do!" Stew called.

"Good then!" Mabel's voice carried from around the huge oven. "You should be able to fill that box faster!"

"Sure will!" Stew called back as he and Sam stepped back outside. They were dumping their second load into the woodbox when Mabel called out again.

"You hear if Alma's still in labor, or do we have a new one?"

"A girl!" Stew called out.

"A blessing for sure!" Mabel called back. Sam could hear the happiness in her voice. "Alma's good?!"

"Yes ma'am!" Stew called as he and Sam went back outside for a final armload.

"I guess it was quite a night...I hear Arthur's new blood came into town last night, too," Mabel called out. "On a fancy carriage even!" Stew stared at Sam for a moment and smiled.

225

"That's you she's talking about! She don't even know it's you in here with me!" Stew whispered.

"It was quite a sight from what I can tell!" he called back.

"You get a chance to get out there and meet him yet?"

"Oh yeah, yeah! Gramma Lettie asked me to run out and grab a few things for the cabin, you know?"

"Oh sure, no one's been in that cabin for a while, let me wrap up an extra loaf or two to take up to him. He can leave 'em outside to freeze. They'll keep till spring as long as the squirrels don't find 'em. He'll be hungry after the journey. Let him know Mabel baked 'em...I wanna make a good impression!"

Mabel hadn't once looked up from kneading the dough. Stew was having trouble containing his laughter.

"Of course, Mabel, I'm sure he'd love that!" he called back.

"What's he like?" Mabel asked, "Is he handsome?"

Stew's eyebrows went up.

"Oh, very!" he called back, giving Sam a wink. Sam tossed the final load into the wood box. He flexed his arms at Stew. "Strong too!" Stew called again, barely containing his laughter. "All done Mabel! Filled the box up good we both did!"

The smells of Miss Mabel's baking had worked their way down to Sam's stomach, tickling his hunger. During the whole conversation, Mabel had never looked up from her work, and with her back still turned and rolling dough, she once again called out to Stew.

"Two loaves in the bag for the new Jack! And I left you a cinnamon bun in the paper there. One for your friend too! They got raisins today!"

Stew grabbed the bag of bread and one of the buns from the front counter. He nodded to Sam to grab the other. Sam carefully picked up the the cinnamon bun, wrapped in brown paper, managing to only drop one raisin from the folds as he turned towards the door.

"Ain't a bad start to the mornin', is it?" Stew said to Sam as his butt pushed the door to the bakery open. He called out one last time to Mabel, "Thank you, Miss Mabel!" He made eyes to Sam to do the same.

"Thank you, ma'am," Sam shouted.

Mabel's ears perked up. She knew everyone in town, but she'd never heard that young man's voice before.

Who's that?

She finally pulled her hands from the dough long enough to turn towards the front door just as it closed, catching only a glimpse of Stew and Sam through her window.

Back on the frozen main street of town, the warmth of the cinnamon bun was working its way through Sam. He had to force himself to eat slowly.

"Good, ain't it?" said Stew.

"Mm-hmm," Sam nodded as he chewed.

Stew was glad to see Sam enjoying the treat from Mabel.

"How long you been here, Stew?" Sam asked. "In Forge?"

"Long as I can remember," he said.

"When was your Proving Night?"

"*My* Proving Night?" Stew laughed. "No, no, no. I didn't have a Proving Night. I ain't never been bit... not a proper wolf bite anyway, like you."

"You don't have a bite?" Sam asked with surprise.

"Well, I mean, I've been bit by lots of stuff; garter snakes, horses, ducks, even an angry beaver once. But not proper *bit* bit, like you. I'm just the same as everyone else in town."

227

Sam had seen John's scar, so he had assumed everyone in town was like them.

"So...people in town know about the..." Sam couldn't think about how to describe it, so instead made a snarled face and raised his hands like claws, making a quiet *rawr-rawr* sound. The Pelt rose on Sam's shoulder's making Sam look taller.

"'Course everyone knows," Stew assured him. "Not everyone got bit is all. The Jacks is the only ones that been bit," Stew confirmed. "That's why they're Jacks. Hopefully you'll be one too."

Hopefully? Sam thought.

"Are there a lot?" Sam asked, "Of...Jacks?"

"Jacks?" Stew replied as he counted in his head, "I don't know...twelve...thirteen?"

On their journey north, it was obvious to Sam that John's transformations were something to be hidden. Yet here was a whole town of regular folk that presumably knew all about John, Sam, and all the other Jacks. No doubt these regular folk knew about Letha and her magic too. The way word spread in small towns, they'd soon all know about Vadoma.

"Where are they?" Sam asked, "The Jacks?"

"They're all out at the logging camp," Stew answered. "They'll come into town from time to time, or send me or my Pa out for supplies and all. But we're all just regular here in town, no Jacks."

Stew pushed open the door to the next shop with his shoulder. "I was gonna do your trousers and stuff next, but maybe let's do your boots first," he said.

Sam felt a jerk backward that almost pulled him off his feet as he passed through the door. Getting his balance, he realized that the Pelt had spread itself in the doorway and was trying to pull Sam back outside. Stew turned and rolled his eyes.

"He don't like this store," he said. He gestured inside to the saddles, shoes, gloves and other leather goods hanging from large nails on the walls. "Just have 'im wait outside, should only be a minute."

"Alright," said Sam.

He stepped back outside and gently pulled the Pelt off his back and placed it on the snowy bench outside the door. Sam said the only thing he could think of:

"Stay?"

When Sam reentered the shop, his nose was filled with the pungent smells of tanned leather. From behind a waist high table stood a man with dark olive skin, striking features, and a very full, black beard. The man looked up from his work as Sam greeted him.

"Mornin', Mr. Rahm!! I brought Sam in for some boots!" Stew called.

"Mornin', Stew," he replied. He looked Sam up and down, "Sam, eh? Back already? That was quick." Rahm stabbed an awl into his table before offering his hand. "Nice to see you, Sam. Shoes off." Rahm pulled out a large swath of thick leather and tossed it on the floor. "Let's look at your feet."

The shoes Fannie had given Sam were fine shoes, if a touch big, but it was obvious they weren't cutting it in the northern ice and snow. Sam didn't want to slide his way through town.

Sam pulled off his shoes and stood on the piece of leather. Rahm took a grease pencil from behind his ear and traced each of Sam's feet.

"Should have them ready in a day or two, well before your Provin'," Rahm promised, He gestured to Sam to put his city shoes back on.

As Sam tied his shoelaces, he saw that Stew had managed to get his foot caught in a stirrup of one of the saddles laid on a saw horse.

"Just a sec," Stew said as he tugged as his boot. Rahm rolled his eyes and reached down to pull Stew's boot out of the stirrup. Stew hopped a few times and caught his balance.

"Thanks, Mr. Rahm!" Stew smiled.

"Go on now, before you get yourself stuck in something else," Rahm playfully chided.

Back outside, the Pelt climbed up onto Sam, who still had more questions for Stew.

"So...Your Pa's not bit either?" Sam asked.

"Nah, but he helps them out at camp, cookin' and such. They call him Soup."

Sam's father's name was Sam, and his father's father's name was Sam... as far back as he knew, it was all Sams. His brain stopped for a moment. "Soup? Your Pa's name is Soup?" he blinked.

Stew nodded, with a smirk.

"Your Pa's name is Soup," Sam repeated. "And you're Stew?"

"Fun, huh?" Stew answered with a giggle.

"Time for your tea," Stew held another shop door open. Sam stepped in and recognized Constance from the night before. It was good to see at least one familiar face this morning.

"Well, good morning, Sam."

"Mornin' Miss Constance," Sam replied. There was no floor in this shoppe, instead a mix of clovers, grasses and other low greenery covered the floor. Constance moved about the shoppe barefoot, yet she seemed to glide above the ground as she moved. Stew unlaced his boots and was soon barefoot and wiggling his toes in the green. Sam followed suit and kicked off his shoes as well.

"Mornin', Miss CC!" called out Stew. "Gramma Lettie said I may as well pick-up some more tea since I brought Sam into town."

"*You* brought Sam into town?" Constance asked with a smile. "Well, aren't you lucky! School's okay with it?"

"Gramma Lettie said bringing Sam to town was important," Stew replied.

"That is true...I'm in the middle of a mix for Alma, so you'll have to give me a minute," Constance explained as she continued her work. "You stop by and see the baby yet, Stew?"

"Not yet," Stew said. "They ain't fun much when they first come out."

Constance let out a laugh, "They do get to be more fun as they go along. You turned out pretty fun, right?"

Stew shared the laugh, "Sure did!"

Sam finally got his shoes off and his feet touched down on the green earth. Unlike the tingling that had been coming from his scar, the ground seemed to infuse him with a feeling of comfort. It was easy to relax here.

Constance pulled clear jars of dried ingredients from shelves, and darkened clay pots on low racks. At the top of her staff was an impossibly balanced wooden bowl where she poured or placed the ingredients as she talked. No matter how many times she picked up and placed her staff, neither it nor the bowl ever even hinted at falling over. Just like Letha's staff, it pushed down and pulled up roots with each each movement.

"How do you feel right now, Sam?" Constance asked. "Is your scar itching much?"

Sam had only noticed his scar once Stew pointed out the moon rising. He hadn't thought much of it since. "Not too much itching, really," Sam replied. "It tingles from time to time." Of course, the suggestion made him reach over and scratch it.

"That's good," Constance reassured. "It's going to get a little worse as each day—and night—passes. You'll be wanting the tea tonight, no doubt. And a little stronger as we go. Did you sleep well?" she asked as she reached for another ingredient.

"Fine," Sam replied.

"No dreams?" she asked.

"Some...I guess...I don't remember them so much now," Sam confessed.

"It's still a new place for you, and no doubt, new dreams too. I'm sure you'll remember more as you settle in," Constance assured him. "You'll be smart to start writin' your dreams down. You might surprise yourself at what you already know."

Constance scanned the shelves for Alma's last ingredient.

"There we are," she said, opening a jar of dried black elderberry and dropping a couple pinches into the bowl. She walked to her shoppe counter and poured the herbs into a mortar. She took the pestle and beckoned Stew to come over, handing it to him.

"Make yourself useful," she said. Stew took the pestle in hand and stuck his tongue out as he began to grind down the ingredients. Constance turned to Sam.

"Now, young man, we should make enough for a day or two. Then we can change it depending on how you feel. Sound good?"

232

Sam nodded. He wasn't quite sure what he was agreeing too, but Constance had been a comfort to him when he arrived in Forge last night, and he felt he could trust her. She looked Sam up and down.

"I supposed we could start with Arthur's mix," she said. Sam felt a small rise from inside. A sort of familiarity with something. Constance offered Sam an empty wooden bowl. "Could you hold this for me?"

She moved to each of the shelves and pulled a little of this and a little of that, placing each ingredient into the bowl in Sam's hands. The strangely familiar smells of each one filled Sam's nose. It didn't take long before she paused her work.

"That's what we usually did for Arthur," Constance said as she put her hands on her hips. "Anything in particular that you feel like you need?" Constance gestured to the shelves of ingredients behind her. She had learned long ago that mixes were far more potent if the subjects was allowed to pick a few of the contents for themselves.

Sam glanced down at the bowl of aromatic items in his hands. He looked up at the wall of jarred herbs and powders in front of him. He searched his brain and remembered his mother used to boil horsemint when he and his siblings would occasionally fall ill.

"Do you have...horsemint?" Sam asked.

"I *do* have horsemint." Constance traced her eyes down the wall and pulled out a large glass jar. The small narrow piped petals were faded from their usual bright pink to a dull grey. She tossed several into the bowl. "Anything else?"

Sam shrugged his shoulders. "Why is everyone asking about my dreams?" he asked Constance.

"Dreams ain't just dreams," Stew answered.

"Aren't," Constance corrected.

"Aren't just dreams." Stew stuck out his tongue as he pressed hard to grind Alma's ingredients. "They can talk to ya' that way too sometimes...in your dreams."

"Dreams can be a glimpse or an insight into past, present or future," Constance continued. "And especially for you...it could be a way that you experience your merging with Arthur. It's not the only way, but it's one way, a common way."

"She means Arthur can talk to you through your dreams," Stew summarized. "Smooth, huh?" Stew stopped grinding and thought for a minute. "Sometimes Miss CC'll make a dream tea for me, and it helps me with seein' my mum again, even if it's just in my dreams and all." Stew smiled at Constance.

Sam's mind started swimming with the idea that he could see his his family again, even if it was in his dreams.

"It takes a while to get the dream mix just right for each person," Constance explained. "We can do that for you too, if you'd like. But let's just see how this one takes first, alright?"

Sam nodded.

"Good. Anything else?" She asked again, looking into Sam's bowl. Sam shrugged, and Constance beckoned him to follow her back to her table where Stew was still grinding.

"That should be fine, Stew," she said, taking the mortar and emptying the ground contents into a small square tin. She turned to Sam, "Your turn."

She poured the new ingredients into the mortar and pushed it in front of him. "Take your time. The more fine, the more potent."

"Grind, grind, 'til it's fine," said Stew. Constance gave him a little chuckle.

234

Sam took the pestle and pressed it hard down into the mortar. It crunched as it pushed through the herbs and into the rounded bottom. Unusual yet familiar smells triggered memories from so long ago that Sam wondered if they were his. He shook his head, re-gripped the pestle, and pressed as he moved it in circles.

While he ground his own tea, Sam got an earful from both Constance and Stew about the town of Forge. There was still an actual metal forge in town, though it was fired up less and less lately. The town had changed industries from iron to lumber almost a hundred years ago but still bore the name of its origin. Now, Forge was known for timber, lots of timber, and it all belonged to a man named Stanchfield who owned all the land the town was on, as well as the mill, and all the land the lumber was being cut from. Stew said Stanchfield owned so much land, "You could walk clear to Canada without leaving it."

Turns out Arthur had saved Stanchfield's life in a snow storm many years ago, and as a repayment, Stanchfield let Arthur not only live on the land, but work it too. The money was split right down the middle. Word got around to other wild men and their Witches that there was honest, hidden work in the North Woods, and Stanchfield was soon hosting more and more Jacks until they and their kin stuck around long enough to make Forge an established town.

All in all, Stanchfield had about a hundred people or so that were either working in his woods, or in Forge supporting the work in the woods. Outsiders were encouraged to leave, and if they didn't take the hint, found themselves down-river. Anyone that lived in Forge stayed until they left the earth itself. The codes of truth and honor the Jacks lived by gave them purpose right to the end. Those who couldn't stay true were asked to leave, and it they didn't were told to.

Stew didn't say it directly, but Sam got the feeling that Letha and Constance weren't the only two women in town that carried a magical staff.

"That should do it," Constance said as she glanced into Sam's mortar. She poured his mix into another tin and labeled both with a grease pencil, "Alma" and "Sam." She handed Sam his and offered the other to Stew.

"Drop this one off to Alma on the way out of town," Constance said to Stew. "You'll save me the trip."

"Yes, ma'am," said Stew with a smile.

Several stops later and Sam's arms and Pelt were full as he and Stew finally started the walk back towards the cabin; he now had trousers, a shirt, the tin from Constance, and two loaves of bread. They took the same road back up to the small overlook where Sam got his first view of Forge. As they crested the ridge, Stew turned and looked back.

"So that's Forge...most of it anyway," he said. He jostled the items he was carrying, piled them onto Sam, and held up the tin with Alma's name on it. "I gotta trot these down to Alma's."

Off the knoll, another trail led down to a cabin amongst the trees. It looked to be a little bigger than the one Sam was in.

"Should only take a wiggle or two."

"Wait," Sam said. He had a question that had been bothering him all day and thought he should ask Stew before they got back to the cabin.

"Everyone knows about my Proving Night?" he asked.

"'Course they do! It's exciting! There hasn't been one, in a looong time. None of us regular folk ain't never seen one. I

236

mean, the Jacks and the ladies probably have, but not no one in Forge...so...it's exciting, right?"

Stew raised an eyebrow at the blank look on Sam's face.

"You're excited, right?" Stew asked. "It's less than two weeks away!"

"I don't know," Sam replied. "I don't know what happens. Is the Proving...like a test?"

"I guess...kinda...it's the night you meet your Witch." Stew smiled as he turned and walked down the trail, leaving Sam by himself.

My Witch?

Sam watched as Stew got smaller on the trail, knocked on the cabin door, stomped the snow off his boots, and stepped inside.

Sam stood by himself in the cold, the Pelt wrapped around him. His breath rose and matched the smoke that started to spew a little more strongly from the cabin's chimney. A breeze moved the trees. Some of the leafless branches squeaked as they rubbed together. Suddenly Sam felt very, very alone.

Then, he didn't.

In his bones, Sam felt something, somewhere, watching him. In moments, crows filled the trees, yet not one of them made a sound. It seemed impossible that there were so many. Each of their heads was turned so one eye looked at Sam.

His spine tingled. All the hair on the Pelt stood up. A dark, musty smell filled his nose.

"You're welcome!" Stew called as he forcefully closed the door to Alma's cabin, spooking the crows into flight.

Stew skipped up the hill towards Sam.

"Well that's done," Stew said as he joined Sam. "What're you lookin' at?" Stew followed Sam's gaze to the disappearing flock. "Whoa, so many!"

Sam turned to agree, but his eyes were drawn up into a tree behind Stew.

"There's some more right there," Sam said. Stew turned and saw that just above him, in the long bare branches of an oak, more crows jumped from branch to branch.

Stew carefully counted, "One...two...three...four—"

"Eleven," Sam interrupted. The crows gave a caw then spread their wings and followed their brethren into the sky.

"Eleven? You sure?"

"Pretty sure."

"I know that one is bad, and two is good, but...I don't know 'bout eleven." Stew shrugged then started on the wagon trail back towards Sam's cabin. "Gramma Lettie will tell us..."

As if on cue, the Raven swooped down and landed on Sam's shoulder.

"She must be checkin' on us," Stew said. The Raven clicked its beak. "You can tell her we're almost back." The Raven squawked and took off.

Stew continued. "You like the cabin? I swept it out last week, and brought a little wood up, put some kindling in the stove too."

"Sure," Sam replied. He wasn't going to tell Stew that sleeping in the cabin, or anywhere, all alone was a new experience. The strange dreams he was having didn't make things any better.

"Is the cabin mine? Is that where I'll be staying from now on?" Sam asked.

"I expect you'll go out to loggin' camp once Proving Night's done," Stew continued.

"Loggin' camp?"

"It's where the Jacks are...when they're loggin'."

"Cutting down trees?"

"Yeah...is there another kind of loggin'?" Stew asked sincerely. Sam shrugged. "'Course, loggin' camp ain't just about the loggin'...well, it's mostly about the loggin', but it's useful for the Jacks to stay hidden too. Naturally, depending on when and where the moon is, they got different states of fur and such. Out there you don't gotta worry about other people seeing... when you... change...you know? It's easier to stay hidden out there."

"Why can't I go out there now?" Asked Sam.

"'Cause you haven't proved yourself yet."

"Yeah, I know, but why do I have to...prove myself?"

"'Cause... it's Provin' Night." Stew didn't understand what Sam didn't understand. "You gotta prove yourself first."

"Like I gotta pass a test?"

"Yeah, yeah," Stew was relieved that Sam was finally getting it. "It's like a test."

"Did *you* take the test?" Sam asked.

"I'm not bit, 'member?"

"Oh..." Sam thought he had at least one piece put together. There *were* more people like John, only they were all out at logging camp. Sam still had questions.

"Well...What about everyone else? Everyone in Forge?" asked Sam. "Do they know about the Jacks? About Proving Night?"

"Sure do," replied Stew. "We're all part of the Pact."

"A Pack? Like a pack of wolves?"

"Haha! Pack, pact!" Stew laughed. "It's pact like...like a deal," Stew thought for a minute. "Like a oath."

"Like keepin' your word?" Sam asked.

"Yeah, like keepin' your word."

"How do you get into the pact?" Sam asked.

"You get brought here, like John brought you."

"So…John brought you here, too?" Sam asked.

"Nah, Me and my Pa got brought here by Arthur a long time ago. We'd both be dead if it wasn't for him. Arthur was too late to save my Ma though. That's the way my Pa tells it anyway."

"Did your Pa get bit too? Or did he…just…get here because Arthur?" Sam asked.

"He got here 'cause Arthur. Pa said he'd do anything for Arthur to pay him back, for savin' his boy…that's me. My Pa said he could cook, and Arthur thought that was a fine idea as they didn't have a proper cook up at camp at the time, they was just takin' turns."

"So…wait…your Pa's at logging camp, but he's not bit?"

"Well…no."

"So, your Pa, he didn't have a Proving Night?"

"No, you only get that if your bit."

"But he's a Jack?" Sam asked.

"No, he ain't a Jack, he ain't bit. He's the cook at loggin' camp."

"But I thought only Jacks were at logging camp."

"Well, it's the Jacks camp, but my Pa is up there too, 'cuz he's the cook, he don't cut no trees."

"So…is he in the Pact?"

"Yeah! Yeah! Now you got it, he's in the Pact like me!"

"So if you're in the Pact, or you do the Proving Night…then you can go out to loggin' camp?"

"Yup…that's it!"

"Okay," Sam said, though he needed a second to let it all sink in. "So the Jacks…it's like a secret that everyone knows?"

"Everyone in Forge," Stew clarified. "There ain't no secrets when everyone tells the truth. That's a rule of the Pact: Always tell the truth."

"You ain't never lied?" asked Sam. Stew stopped and looked Sam in the eye.

"No."

Sam's gut told him that Stew meant what he said, but something wouldn't square in his head. "If you never lied, then how do you keep the secret?"

"Secrets and lies are two different things. You can keep a secret without having to lie."

Stew said it with such confidence that Sam didn't question it.

"You mean Mabel...with the bakery...she knows?"

"'Course she does. Rowan saved her a while back. Rahm got himself saved by Amasa. "

"Who's Amasa?"

"Best river driver you ever seen."

"What's river driving?" Sam asked.

"Driving logs down a river, 'course."

Sam nodded understanding, even though he didn't. He had more questions, but he wasn't sure any of the answers would make sense. He was glad that Stew started walking again. Soon, Sam's cabin came into view.

"It's gonna be a Blue Moon, you know, in thirteen days...on your Provin' Night," Stew said. "That means you'll be extra strong." Stew looked ahead and called out, "Hey Gramma Lettie! Back before dark, just like I promised!"

"Promise to truth," said Letha.

The scar on Sam's arm started to itch.

"There was crows, Gramma Lettie, lots of 'em," Stew reported. "They all took off, then we counted eleven. Well, Sam counted eleven."

"Eleven...hmm."

"What does it mean?" Stew asked, wide eyed.

"Uncertain."

"Aw, I thought you'd know."

"No, Stewart, eleven is uncertain...not sure...could be bad or good."

"Well that ain't no help," Stew wobbled his head in disappointment."

"Isn't," Letha corrected.

"Isn't any help," Stew was starting to sound exasperated.

"It seems we're not the only ones that know about Sam being here. Glad I sent the Raven to check on you." Letha turned to Sam. "Let's heat that stove up. It's tea time."

Inside, Stew and Sam made quick work of lighting the fire and setting up the single chair for Letha.

"There's a pot there on the wall. Pull it down and pack it with snow," Letha said. "Press it down a few times, a lot of snow is only a little water."

Sam pulled a long handled pot off a nail in the wall, stepped outside, scooped it full of snow, then pressed it down to compact it. He did this a several times until he had a full, well-packed pot.

Sam placed the pot on the stove and watched the snow melt as the fire took hold. Letha was right, for all the snow he packed into the pot, there was barely an inch of water in the bottom. Sam had to make a few more trips outside before Letha thought there was enough water to add the herbs.

"That's enough, now we'll wait until it just starts to bubble," Letha instructed. "In the mean time, show me your loot!"

Stew made a big show of the shirt, trousers, wool coat, tea, and the loaves of bread. Stew laughed as he retold the story of going in and out of Mabel's unseen, even though he was talking with her the whole time. When the telling was done, Letha looked and saw that the bubbles were starting to rise from the bottom of the pot and dance their way to the surface.

"Let's see that tea," Letha asked.

Sam produced the tin that Constance had given him, the "Sam" written on top was a bit smeared from being carried all day. Sam pulled the top off and the smells from Constance's shoppe filled his nose again. He handed the tin to Letha, but she waved it away.

"Go on," she said. "You can do it yourself."

He brought the tin above the rising steam and slowly spread the ground herbs over the water in a zig-zag pattern, enjoying how the boiling bubbles made the herbs jump from side to side. Each herb left a winding trail of color as it sank.

"Stewart, you want to run along, or you wanna teach the lesson on tea?" Letha asked. Stew looked at the floor.

"I ain't so good...aren't so good at teachin', Gramma Lettie."

"Course you are," Letha replied. "You taught Sam a great deal about all the people today, didn't you? You taught him all about town, and where to get supplies."

"He sure did," assured Sam.

"That was just showing him around, that weren't proper teachin'."

"Wasn't," Letha corrected, "And yes it was. Some of the best teaching and learning need no book at all."

She glanced back into the pot. "We'll give it a good few minutes, then we'll pour it off, add the syrup, and have a drink."

Stew's eyes went wide. "Darn," he said.

"Stewart. You did remember the syrup, didn't you?" asked Letha.

"We got all the other things done, Gramma Lettie!" Stew protested. "Miss Mabel, Mr. Rahm..."

"You did, you did," Letha grinned. "Not to worry. It'll work just the same." She made a little face at Sam, "Hope you like bitter."

Stew hung his head. Sam said the only thing he thought would help. "I don't mind bitter. Momma used to say that bitter's good for your heart."

"Really?" asked Stew.

"Sure," said Sam. It was the truth. He remembered how his mother used to chew on burdock root and claim it was to help her heart.

Sam was happy it seemed to make Stew feel a little better. He didn't mind bitter. Sure,.it wasn't his favorite, but he didn't hate it either.

Sam felt the scar on his arm start to itch more. Maybe it was the heat from the fire, or having three people inside but the cabin, but he was suddenly feeling very warm.

"As the sun goes down, the moon'll pull on you more and more. You'll feel it, even when it's just a tiny sliver."

Letha caught Sam's eye. Her look soothing him the same way as when he arrived in Forge.

She took her eyes from Sam, and the soothing faded as he felt the heat rise inside himself again. It was similar to the sharpness he experienced earlier with Stew when they first looked over Forge. Now, it seemed to be building.

"I felt it this morning, when the moon came up," Sam explained.

"He said he felt sharp," Stew added.

"Sure, sure. Now that the sun is down, that sharp'll get more and more...edgy," Letha raised an eyebrow and smiled as she finished the metaphor.

"Sharp...edgy," Stew nodded as he returned the smile.

"How come when you look at me it's better?"

"There's a few tricks in these old bones," Letha said. "Since you're feeling so sharp, let's see if we can make you dull again, huh? Grab a tin cup there and pull a scoop out."

Sam took a cup from the shelf above the stove and gently dipped it into the pot. He brought it up to his lips, feeling the steam rise up through his nose before he took a cautious sip.

Sam knew what bitter was, but this was something else entirely. He thought that Letha must be playing some kind of joke. There was no way liquid could be so dry.

Letha let a little chuckle escape. "I told it you was bitter. How do you feel?"

Sam was so pre-occupied with the feeling in his mouth that he didn't even notice that the sharpness had eased, and he was feeling more himself, even without the stare-down from Letha.

"Better," Sam responded.

"Sorry about the syrup," said Stew again. "That doesn't look like it tasted very good."

"It doesn't taste like anything, except dry," said Sam.

"I'll get the syrup for you tomorrow," Stew said, "Then it'll be easier to take, for sure."

I can't imagine it being any worse, Sam thought.

24

As the sun brought the orange of morning, Sam was running through a forest in his dreams. Trees fell in his wake, almost hitting him as they boomed and crackled to the ground. He tripped and fell, then looked up to see a tree thundering down upon him. Sam suddenly sat upright and fully awake.

Just a dream.

The door to the cabin was already cracked open, and the sun drew a line of bright yellow across the floor.

Who opened the door? I would have heard them, wouldn't I?

Outside, men's accented voices called out to each other.

"That'll do! We'll pile 'r up!" one called with an Irish lilt.

"Go on and get the horses fed!" another accent shouted. Sam didn't recognize either voice, he listened again but only heard the clomping of hooves slowly moving away from the cabin.

Sam looked down to see a pencil in his hand and unintelligible scribbles on several loose pages of paper. If they were words of some kind, they were impossible to read. Turning the page over, he saw more swirls, but there was one letter he could manage to make out. It was the first letter of a signature at the bottom of the page; a single, large "A."

The splintering sound of wood being stacked startled Sam. Suddenly, he had to pee.

Now.

Sam took careful, quick steps to the door and cautiously pushed it open. A sled full of split wood was being emptied by two men. It didn't take much imagination to conclude that these two flannel-clad blokes were lumberjacks. One was pale, red-haired, and bearded; the other was dark like onyx. Soon, Sam would meet Rowan and Kofi, but now, as they turned their backs to grab another load from the wagon, Sam bolted behind the outhouse to pee.

Rowan stopped pulling wood, "You hear somethin'?"

"I hear you stoppin' the work," Kofi fired back.

"No—listen!" Rowan grabbed Kofi's arm to keep him still. Sam's last dribbles landed on a few exposed leaves behind the outhouse. Rowan looked at Kofi. "'Zat a snake?"

"A snake in the middle of winter, man?" Kofi shot back.

Sam stood behind the outhouse in silence, *Should I come out now?*

"It came from there," pointed Rowan with a hushed tone.

Kofi shook his arm loose from Rowan's grip, "There ain't no snake in the outhouse, man!"

Rowan timidly approached the outhouse, reached out, and whipped the door wide open. There was only an empty seat.

"I told you... Nothin, man," said Kofi. The door slammed shut, instantly revealing Sam standing behind it.

"Bejeezus!" leaped Rowan. Kofi laughed so hard, he dropped his armload of wood. It took him a moment to catch his breath enough to greet Sam.

"Sorry, sorry! We didn't expect anyone to be here, is all," Kofi explained. "We thought you'd be off with Letha or John or somethin'."

"I haven't seen her yet today," remarked Sam. He reached a hand out, "I'm Sam."

"'Course y'are," Rowan took the offered hand. "I'm Rowan, this here's Kofi." Sam stopped for a moment when he realized that both Rowan's red and Kofi's black hair had a white streak running through it, just like John. Sam finally took Kofi's hand to shake it, remembering that he heard their names from Letha the night before.

"We just stacking it over there?" Sam asked as he stepped towards the wagon and started getting an armful for himself.

"Helpful 'i'n he?" said Rowan.

"More 'n you," fired back Kofi. Rowan and Kofi looked at Sam, then each other, and got back to work. Kofi grabbed the pieces he had dropped as he was laughing. "Stackin' it just right there next to the cabin."

Once Sam's arm was full, he grabbed a piece with his free hand and walked the load quickly to the long stack of wood. He added his armload to the stack with a splintered *thud!*

The three of them made quick work of the sled's contents. As Rowan brought the last armload to the newly stacked wood pile, he turned to Sam.

"Should be enough for two weeks, eh?" he said.

"More 'n enough," remarked Kofi.

Rowan looked down the wagon path for anyone approaching. "Still no Letha? Well, then, she shouldn't mind if we steal y'away for a wee bit, then, should she?"

Sam liked Rowan's lilting accent.

"Y'ever throw axes?" Rowan grinned as he reached to the side of the sled and brought out two weathered examples. "King'll be back with the horses 'fore too long. We got time for a toss or two."

Sam figured that throwing axes meant just that, but he'd never done it before. Kofi and Rowan could see the look of uncertainty on his face.

"Ain't nothin' to it," offered Kofi before giving a side eye to Rowan. "Anyone can beat red-beard here."

Rowan rolled his eyes, "You have one lucky day and all of a sudden..."

Kofi smiled as he took his axe, "I wouldn't call it luck so much as jus' bein' better."

Rowan gripped his axe and purposefully halting Kofi's playful jibs, calling out the target.

"Third pine on the right!" Rowan rocked a little, taking a step backwards, then forwards, raising the axe up and letting it gently fall to his side to find his rhythm. Anyone could see he was taking his time.

"Get on with it, man!" called Kofi.

Rowan was all concentration as he finally brought the axe up and over his head and flung it forward with a swing of his arm and a flick of his wrist.

The axe wheeled through the air, flipped half a dozen times and stuck into the tree with a *thunk!* Rowan didn't smile, but instead raised his eyebrows and looked directly at Kofi, "How 'bout that?"

"Smug are we?" replied Kofi, sliding his axe in his hands and making a show of feeling the weight and balance of it before dramatically taking two steps forward and flinging it towards the same tree. It sunk right next to Rowan's. Kofi smiled.

"How about *that*?"

"*I'm* smug?" Rowan said with a laugh. He looked at Sam, "Where's your axe then?"

"Axe? I don't—I don't have one," replied Sam. Rowan and Kofi quickly realized their mistake.

"Right," Kofi said. He shrugged his shoulders at Rowan with a hint of *oops* before turning back to Sam. "The axe comes after your Provin'." He leaned into Sam and whispered just loud enough for Rowan to hear. "Guess you'll just be watchin' me win today then."

Sam followed as Rowan and Kofi retrieved their axes.

"I get an axe after my Proving Night?" An axe sounded exciting to Sam.

He'd seen John with his two axes as they traveled. For tools that were so heavy, John swung and chopped with them precisely and effortlessly. He saw the same casual precision from Rowan and Kofi.

—-

The last time Sam had seen that kind of relaxed mastery with a tool was when he helped his father work on the roof of their shack. Sam would hold a shingle in place, while his father tapped a nail once or twice to set it. Then with an effortless swing, his father would raise his hammer and bury the rest of the roofing nail into the shingle with one perfectly landed strike. There was something wonderfully strong, relaxed, and satisfying about the simple whack of the hammer to the nail.

"These a' roofin' nails," his dad had said when he noticed Sam watching with keen-eyed interest, "Ten pennies take another whack or two."

WHACK! Rowan's axe sunk into the next tree trunk, bringing Sam back to the present.

—-

"Aye, no axe 'till after your Provin' Night, your first night," said Rowan. They arrived at the tree with the axes embedded in it.

"Ah, the first night," Kofi looked a little wistful. "Wouldn't want to go back there for sure." He pulled his and Rowan's axes from the trunk of the tree and handed Rowan his.

"What's so bad about it?" Sam asked.

Rowan and Kofi shared a look between them, *How much should we tell him?*

"'Tis a bit itchy for one," said Rowan. Kofi burst out with a laugh that could only come from understanding.

"Ah, yes, itchy for sure," Kofi made a big deal of scratching his arm. "Like the burning kind."

"Like when you've got a scab on your elbow, and ya just can't leave it alone," Rowan continued, "And you just want to scratch, but it burns at the same time, so it feels bad, but at the same time good."

"Or like the heat of the fire ants that stings and burns, but at the same time, you're all eye's open and alive," Kofi added.

"Like a wool coat in the summer?" asked Sam.

"Worse," Rowan said.

"Much worse," added Kofi.

"Like being wrapped in sheep?" asked Sam.

Rowan and Kofi erupted in laughter, they dropped their axes and leaned on each other.

"Aye!" Rowan managed to get out, "'Tis like being wrapped in sheep!"

Amidst their laughter, Rowan managed to pull up his sleeve almost up to his shoulder to reveal his arm to Sam, showing a long scar just above the elbow. It was even more pink than Rowan's already pale complexion.

"Good one, eh?" Rowan said with pride.

"There's mine," Kofi pulled his shirt up from his waist and revealed a large scar on his ribcage. "Where did he get you?" Kofi asked.

Sam pulled up his shirt sleeve. "Here." Rowan and Kofi both looked at Sam's scar. Sam felt a strange kinship knowing he shared something physical with them both. "And on my leg too," Sam said, patting his pant leg.

"Ya got bit twice?" Rowan raised his eyebrows.

"You only got bit once?" asked Sam with a smile. Kofi laughed again and slapped Rowan on the back.

"You don't have to win everything, man," said Kofi.

"When did you get bit?" Sam asked.

"Oh, it's been a while now," said Rowan.

"A long while," answered Kofi.

Kofi pulled his axe from the tree and pointed with it, calling out the next target. "The fir there, twenty paces off." Rowan stepped forward for his turn.

"Itchy like a sheep," Rowan chuckled under his breath as he took aim.

Kofi gave Sam a wink. He waited until Rowan was mid-throw and let out a, "Ba-a-a-a," just like a sheep. Rowan's axe went flying off to the right of the target tree as his laughter took over again.

"You bastard!" he jested at Kofi.

Kofi shrugged and smirked as he stepped up and took aim.

Rowan turned and whispered to Sam, "See there, Sammy, sometimes you just use a little distraction."

Just as Kofi raised his axe to throw, Rowan raised one leg slightly off the ground and let out a long fart, with a little upturned-lilt at the end, as if it was a question. Sam's eyes went wide. Kofi stopped, smiled slightly, and shook his head. He raised his axe again and threw it strong and fast, thunking into the tree.

"There's a mighty fine one," Kofi said. Sam wasn't sure if he was referring to the throw of the axe or the fart. They all walked towards the next tree, Rowan stepping ahead a bit to collect his axe from his missed throw.

"You've got questions, then? About your first night? You're Provin' Night?" Kofi asked as they walked.

Sam shrugged his shoulders. Of course he had questions, but being put on the spot made his mind draw a blank.

Kofi turned to Rowan, "Jesus." Kofi scrunched his nose as the smell finally drifted to him. "Been digging at the mushrooms again?"

"It's healthy," Rowan said.

Faint, in the far distance, a stick broke. All three of them turned their heads towards the sound. Kofi noticed that Sam had turned too.

"Well, look at that, you're already hearin'?" he asked. Sam wasn't sure how to answer, as far as he knew his hearing was fine.

"Never stopped, I guess," Sam answered. Kofi smiled at Sam's wit.

"Can ya hear better than before the bite, I mean?" Kofi clarified.

"Do ya know how far can ya hear from?" Rowan asked.

"How far?" Sam had never thought about it.

"Aye," said Rowan, and he took off on a run into the woods.

"Jesus," Kofi said, "Anyone can hear that ruckus." Soon, the ruckus stopped as Rowan turned back towards them.

"Can ya hear this, Sammy-boy?" Rowan whispered from a good fifty running paces away.

"Sure," said Sam loudly.

"Keep goin'!" yelled Kofi in the direction of Rowan's voice. They heard the crashing fade as Rowan made his way even farther into the woods, soon out of sight through the trees. Kofi couldn't tell if Rowan had stopped, or if he had faded out of hearing range.

Kofi was surprised when he heard Sam yell, "Yuh, I hear you." Kofi hadn't heard anything. He looked Sam up and down as he barely made out Rowan purposefully crashing away from them again.

Kofi looked towards Sam a few moments later. He, himself, hadn't heard anything for a least thirty seconds.

"He's still going," said Sam, "Wait, he stopped." Sam waited for a bit, then said purposefully loudly, "I HEAR YA!"

There was a howling laughter far in the distance, followed by Rowan's voice yelling "Son of a *bitch*!"

"You've got a good ear on ya," said Kofi. "No one's going to be surprising you!"

"It ain't the hearin' that's tricky," replied Sam, "It's the listenin'… Least that's what Momma used to say."

"Ah, that's a good one," remarked Kofi as he thought for a moment. "Be nice with your sister!" Kofi jested with Sam, "That's what *my* mother would always be sayin'." He gave a chuckle at the end. They shared a bit of a laugh as Kofi started to pick up the sound of Rowan returning, now a couple hundred yards away.

Something in Sam's face told Kofi not to ask about Sam's family. Kofi, Rowan, and the rest of the crew had already learned about their fate. Each man in the crew had a past, and such things were only offered, never pried. Kofi knew that he should let Sam take it one step at a time.

Sam found it interesting that out here with these two strangers, he had already thought of his family twice. Once his father, and now his mother. Maybe it was the nights he'd spent alone. Maybe it was because Rowan and Kofi laughed so much, but he didn't feel sad remembering them.

"What's her name?" asked Sam. "You're sister."

Kofi was surprised by the question, but had no qualms about answering. "I had many sisters, but that one was Kappa," he said.

Sam seemed to breathe in the name for a moment, "Kappa, that's nice," he said. "Mine was Ruthie," he added.

Was.

Kofi wasn't sure what to say, so he left the space open for listening instead.

"There was a fire," Sam said. His eyes bounced from tree to stone to snow. He didn't know where to look.

Rowan returned and noticed the stillness between Kofi and Sam. Kofi dropped his axes to the ground. The good natured joking stopped.

In the stillness, tears crested Sam's eyes and fell down his cheeks.

"A brother too," he said softly. "Ben."

The wind stirred the trees nearby and a swirled leaves around Sam's feet.

Rowan and Kofi placed a hand on each of Sam's shoulders. Kofi was the one to speak, "If it's a comfort to ya, they're not all gone."

"Feels like it most days," said Sam. He wasn't ready to tell them how his dreams were filled with visions of them burning with Sam always feeling helpless.

Rowan spoke next, "Blood bonds us, and you share the blood of your family, so you're a bit of them too. They're closer than you think." He and Kofi breathed in and out together, and Sam felt a warmth spread from his shoulders. He could smell it.

Grits. Cornbread. Butter.

He looked around but his tears blurred his vision. He couldn't make sense of where the scents were coming from. It smelled just like his mother's kitchen on Sunday mornings before church. Around him he saw wisps of his mother at the stove and his father pulling the top from the cast iron to reveal cornbread. His brother and sister shoved each other into their shared chair at the kitchen table. They only got cornbread on Sundays, after all.

"Careful, now. Pan's hot," his father said. Ben and Ruthie used all their might to not reach out and touch the shiny crust on top. Sam placed tin bowls on the table for everyone while his mother brought the other pot with grits, and scooped some out for each person. His mother sat. His father used the butter knife to cut into the hard crust of the cornbread and gave each a piece, serving Sam's mother first, like always.

No matter how much he blew on it, Sam would always bite it too early and burn the roof of his mouth. He would give anything to burn his mouth in that very kitchen again.

He heard the distant *caw!* of a raven. His vision blurred. He blinked, and as his eyes cleared, the wisps of his past were gone, and he was back in the north woods. He was standing with Rowan and Kofi, each of them still with a hand on his shoulder.

"Not so far away," said Rowan with a gentle smile.

"I could… It smelled like my kitchen on a Sunday mornin'," Sam said.

"You're lucky you didn't smell Rowan's wind instead," said Kofi. A small chuckle rose from Sam, as he wiped his tears with his sleeve. Kofi and Rowan reached for their axes.

"Sounds like King's hitching up the sled," said Rowan. "We best get back too. Letha'll be casting a spell on us if we're keeping ya for too long." All three turned back towards the cabin.

As the cabin came into sight, Letha was standing just outside the door, looking at the pages of weird writing Sam had found that morning. Letha looked up as they approached.

"King had no reason to wait for ya, so I sent him off."

"'Course," Kofi said.

"I hope you all had fun," Letha said with a smile. "Thanks for your help. Now off with ya. Sam and I got business. The moon will be up soon."

"Yes, ma'am," Rowan replied. He and Kofi gave Letha a bow and extended a hand to Sam.

"Be seein' ya soon." Rowan winked as they turned and stepped away. Sam and Letha watched them walk down the trail left by the sled in the snow. Letha held up the pages in her hand.

"Looks like you've been busy."

"Me?" Sam shrugged his shoulders. "Wasn't me that wrote that, ma'am."

"Anyone else in that cabin last night?" Letha asked.

"No, don't think so."

"Well, then. Could only be one person that wrote it then, huh?"

"But—"

"Maybe you don't *remember* writing it," Letha added. Sam couldn't make sense of what Letha was saying. "You've heard of sleep walking, now, haven't you?"

"Yes, ma'am," answered Sam. "Walkin' always seemed a funny thing to do in your sleep."

"There's lots of funny things people do in their sleep," Letha said. "Seems your's is writing."

Sam had never written in his sleep before. As far as writing went, he would only practice his letters when his mother would make him after church every Sunday.

"My writin' ain't nothing like that," Sam told Letha. "I'm good at my name and the Lord's prayer, but that's about it." Sam looked over the pages again. "That writin'...if that's writing... truth be told, ma'am, I can't read it."

"Is that so?" asked Letha, looking back at the pages. "To be honest, it looks like scribbles to me too," she smiled. She gestured to the door of the cabin. "Let's get out of the cold and see if there's any heat left in that fire."

Sam opened the stove door to find a few coals still glowing. He grabbed a little kindling, stacked it carefully, and blew on it until the glow popped into a flame. He threw a bigger log on top of the kindling stack.

"Should be just a minute," he said to Letha. "For the fire." Letha traced her fingers across the cabin door where a few horizontal lines were recently carved into the logs. Sam had the

258

familiar feeling again, like he knew Letha somehow. Like the night before, she seemed to read his thoughts.

"Did you feel like you recognized me? When you arrived?"

Sam was surprised at the question and equally so at his honest answer, "You looked like someone that I know, but I've never met you before."

"That's quite right. *You've* never met me, but the one that bit you knows me well." Letha chuckled to herself, "It's funny we sometimes call it new blood...'Course it is new to you, but it was old when it was here last. Arthur had lived a long life before he left this world."

"Rowan said the Wolf left me with more than this," Sam pulled up his sleeve to show the scar on his arm.

"Yes, yes, he did. More scars and more hope," Letha answered. Sam thought for a moment.

"The Wolf's name was Arthur, then?" Sam asked.

"You could see it that way, yes...both the Wolf and the man." Letha replied. This conversation was actually going much more smoothly than she expected. "Would you like to know what Arthur's trying to tell you?" She pointed at the papers. "I think you'll find it entertaining at the least. Arthur was good for that," she explained with a smile.

Sam looked at the pages in Letha's hand. For a moment he thought that it was actually quite funny that he was writing notes to himself in the middle of the night, especially since he couldn't even read them.

"I s'pose," Sam finally answered. "I'm almost done with *Huck Finn.*"

"Well now," Letha replied with a smile. "I think you're going to find these words even better than our friend Mr. Twain's."

She patted the bed next to her and Sam sat. Maybe with her help, he could make sense of these swirls and scratches after all.

Letha put her finger down on the page to guide her eyes and took a deep breath. She squinted.

"This...well...I—Uh—" Letha stopped short. She turned the page over and saw the large letter "A" at the bottom.

"Well, that must be his signature, 'Arthur,' yes? Yes...yes... but the rest..." Letha scanned and turned the page over again, "This...well...hmm." She slowly traced the crisscrossed lines on the page, thinking; *these scribbles really are impossible to read.*

"I was sleeping when I wrote it," offered Sam.

Letha laughed.

"It was dark too," Sam continued.

"Ha," Letha chuckled, "Yes, I suppose it was." Her eyes rose to the ceiling as she thought for a moment. "Well...I imagine these things take time...yes...yes...no worries here." She held up the pages as she spoke. "This...these are a good sign that Arthur is...he's trying. We can't expect to get it all lined up on the first night now, can we?" Letha smiled, she seemed pleased with her answer. "As the days and nights come, I'm sure these scribbles will turn into something we can actually read more easily. We'll soon be able to make sense of it...yes...no worries."

Letha set the pages aside and smiled at Sam. Something about her tone made him think she was saying the words out loud for her own benefit as much as his.

"Well, then, I'll be off here in a moment. Do you have any questions or anything before I go?" Letha asked.

Sam stood up and started re-stacking the small pile of wood next to the stove. He always found that moving helped him think, and sure enough a question popped up.

"I can split the wood myself if I had an axe. Kofi and Rowan said I'll be getting one."

"An axe? Of course, of course, yes," Letha replied. "You'll be getting your axe after your Proving Night." Sam was pleased.

"Well, thank you, ma'am," he paused for a moment before asking, "Could I borrow one before then?"

Letha smiled. "I supposed Stew could get his hands on one for you."

Sam had no doubt Stew could get his hands on lots of things.

25

Sam woke in the middle of the night with a shiver.

The fire must be low, he thought.

He rose from his bed and opened the stove, finding the smallest of flames barely flickering atop a pile of coals. He grabbed a handful of kindling and a couple small logs and quickly piled them onto the coals. He leaned down and blew a few times before the strands of birch bark caught, lending flame to the rest of the kindling.

He let the fire burn and build for a moment in front of him, feeling the heat on his hands and face. The flames cast a deep yellow glow into the cabin. In the shadows near his bed, an old man stood with a wolf at his side. Sam blinked, and they disappeared. He shook his head, then turned back to the fire and poked it with a twig before throwing it on top of the growing flames. Just as he closed the door, the wolf appeared on top of the stove ready to pounce. Jaws wide, it jumped at Sam. He threw his arm up and the wolf's teeth closed on it. Sam felt a burning all up and down his arm as the wolf evaporated into his scar. Behind the stove, the old man stood tall, a smile appearing from behind his long beard.

Sam sat up in his bed. The dim light from the windows told him morning was on its way. His eyes searched for the bearded man, but instead found the room empty. He pulled the covers back and got out of bed to check the fire. Reaching for the door of the stove, he realized he was holding a pencil, just like yesterday morning. He placed it down on the bedside table, finding new pages of scratches and swirls. He squinted in the soft morning light to see if he could find any pattern in it. He was surprised to find that amidst the unreadable scribbles, there were straight lines. They crisscrossed the entire page, making angles here and there, some even crossing multiple times to make triangles and other geometric shapes. Again, aside from the lines on the page, the only thing that he could make out was the big "A" of the signature.

Sam stared at the page for a long time, trying to make some kind of sense of it. Eventually, his eyes blurred, making the lines and shapes move on the page.

Stew's voice called from outside, "Morning Sam! Brought you another bun from Mabel's!"

"Thanks!" Sam yelled back as he shook his head to get his eyes to focus again. He dropped the pages on his bedside table and opened the stove to stir the ashes inside, hoping to find an orange coal that could easily catch.

The timber clomped out of place, and the door opened to reveal Letha. Stew was close behind with a warm smile and a warm cinnamon bun. In fact, the cinnamon on Stew's face showed he'd already finished his while he was on the way.

"Thank you," offered Sam as he took the baked goodness, smelled it, and took a big bite. He was starting to really like the mornings.

"Can I show him?" Stew asked.

"Of course," replied Letha, nodding to Stew. "We have something that Arthur left for you." Sam silently hoped it was the axe he had asked Letha about, but instead he watched as Stew handed over a small, flat, wooden box.

Sam pulled off the lid easily and discovered a selection of wooden pieces of all different sizes and shapes inside. There were mostly triangles and trapezoids, with one flat diamond among them, fourteen pieces in all.

"It's a *loculus*," Stew said. "Neat, huh?"

Sam quickly realized the shapes looked a lot like the angles and crossed lines on this morning's pages. He grabbed the papers and offered them to Letha.

"They look kind of like these," he said. Letha was surprised to see the plethora of lines and shapes upon the page. She had expected the same illegible strokes as the previous day.

"Well...huh," Letha commented with a smile. "Looks like someone knew I was coming." A clatter made Letha and Sam turn to see that Stew had dumped the pieces out onto the bed.

Stew turned a few of the pieces in his hand. "These look older than the ones they have up at camp...wait..." Stew's eyes grew. "Is this Arthur's?"

"Yes," Letha replied.

"Whoa," Stew replied. Letha turned to back to Sam.

"It's a Greek puzzle. It's simple enough; make a square using all the pieces. If you need, you can use the top of the box as a frame." Letha flipped the cover of the box and placed a piece in the middle. "Off you go."

Sam sat on the bed and placed a second piece next to the first, then a third, filling the top of the box until he had no more room, yet still held a piece in each hand that wouldn't fit.

"A good first try," said Letha.

"Yeah, you just missed two. I usually have three or four that won't fit," said Stew.

"How do you do it?" asked Sam.

"I usually just keep tryin' till I get lucky," replied Stew.

"Yes, yes, there is luck," Letha chuckled. "There are many ways to solve it, hundreds in fact. I could tell you a few, but it's much more fun to find your own way."

She could at least give me a hint, he thought.

As he stared at the pieces, his vision started to shift, but instead of blurring, each piece seemed to wiggle and move on its own, reminding him of the pages this morning.

The pages.

This morning's pages flashed through his memory. Sam flipped and shifted each piece this way or that way until he had arranged them into a perfect right triangle. Letha watched him place the final piece.

"Well, look at that," she said with a nudge to Stew. Letha pulled one of the pages from the bedside table, and dropped it next to the triangle Sam had made. The lines and shapes sketched on the page matched the very same lines making up the triangle Sam had completed. "Arthur never liked making the square either. He liked the triangles better."

This is a good sign, Letha thought. On his own, and perhaps with a little of Arthur's influence, Sam didn't use the edges of the box, or the lid, to make his shapes.

"Arthur made triangles, too?"

"Yes, yes, he did," Letha said wistfully.

"What else did Arthur make?" Sam asked as he shifted the pieces.

"He made Forge, didn't he Gramma Lettie?" Stew interjected.

"Well, I suppose he did," Letha replied. "Him and many others."

"Did he make the Wolf?" Sam asked.

"What's that now?" Letha asked.

"Did Arthur make the Wolf that bit me?"

"Did he make the…" Letha was a little surprised by the question. This was something John should've explained already. "Yes and no," she said. "He had his part in it, and so did I. Could've only done so much without each other. Like a lot of things, some spells work better together."

As Sam rearranged the shapes, he spoke aloud, putting the pieces of the last few weeks together at the same time. "Arthur is the Wolf that bit me, but he's also a man. He was like John: he changed."

"Correct," Letha said.

Sam pushed another piece into place. He had almost completed a square. "When he was a Wolf, he bit me. Then the Wolf died, so now he lives…inside me?"

"Very close," remarked Letha. "The Wolf wasn't Arthur, but it was a vessel for his blood and spirit long enough to find you. Arthur's human body was, and still is, here in Forge." Letha looked down to see that Sam had made a square, but again was holding two extra pieces. "Your journey with Arthur has only started."

Sam pulled apart the square and started again.

"Everyone says I have a Proving Night coming."

"Ten days!" Stew added. "When you meet your witch."

"On the full moon," Letha continued.

"That's the same as when I got bit. A full moon."

"Yes it is," replied Letha. "Sounds like you've put quite a bit together already."

"Were you Arthur's witch?" Sam asked.

"Yes. And I still am," Letha replied.

"So, you were married?" Sam asked.

"No, no, no," Letha laughed. "God, no. A Witch and her Wolf are never married. It's not like that," Letha thought for a moment. "You had a sister, yes?"

"Yes," Sam replied.

"It's like that...It's even deeper than being married. You share blood."

"So, if I have Arthur's blood, you're like my big sister?" The idea felt comforting to Sam.

"Sister?!" Stew laughed.

"Listen to you!" Letha said with a laugh of her own. "Maybe more like a grandmother, wouldn't you say?"

"An older sister?" Sam laughed.

"*Very* older!" added Stew. Letha gave an incredulous look at him before continuing.

"There are many ways to think about it," she said. "Some think of it as a bow and arrow. The power is in both being together and in the separation."

Sam thought for a minute.

"He smiled at me this morning, Arthur did," he said.

"What was that?" Letha raised an eyebrow.

"In my dream this morning, before the sun," Sam gestured towards the stove. "I was checking the stove and he was standing there, then he smiled before he disappeared. The Wolf was here too. He jumped into my scar."

"It sounds like he's trying to get to know you," Letha replied.

"Can he do it in the daytime?" Sam asked. Letha laughed.

"Messages come in many ways. Could be something around you that you notice, like a stone in the right place, or a swirl in the water that looks like something. It could be dreams, feelings, thoughts... you may even have a sort of inner talk with him. Usually, you have to be patient and open. Do you think he was trying to tell you something this morning?"

"About the puzzle, I guess?"

Letha thought for a moment. "Maybe there's more to the puzzle than we think." Sam watched as Letha silently looked at both the pages and the puzzle. She wasn't thinking; she was opening to receive an answer.

"Ah... there it is...," she smiled. "One of the unique things about this puzzle is there is more than one way to solve it, more than one way the pieces fit together and still make a shape."

"Sure," said Sam. He was already almost finished making another shape.

"You're doing the same," continued Letha. "You will integrate both Arthur and the Wolf in your own way. You must make the pieces fit, but it isn't up to me how they go together, it's up to you. But if they don't all go together in time...," Letha drifted off.

Even as he was listening, Sam's hands and mind had kept moving. He placed a last piece down to complete a perfect square and looked up to Letha with a dose of confidence.

"I'll put them together," Sam assured her. "It's in my blood."

26

In the middle of the next night, Sam woke to the scar on his arm burning. When he pulled the covers back, he saw small hairs growing from the scar itself, then spreading down the back of his hand and onto his fingers. His fingernails ached. The only respite was to dig his hands deep into the earthen floor of the cabin. It reminded him of the soothing feeling he had so many times in his own garden. Digging seemed to pull a soothing coolness into his body. Each reach brought him deeper and deeper into the earth until it seemed to swallow him up completely and everything went dark.

Sam blinked his eyes open to the sound of the timber being lifted. He was lying on the floor, next to a deep hole that had been dug in the middle of the earthen floor. Stew pushed the door open and morning light flooded in.

"Nine days 'till your Provin—Whoa!" Stew's eyes went wide when he saw the huge hole next to Sam.

"I don't…" Sam looked down to the dirt all over his body and hands, "I was dreaming I was digging."

"Looks like you weren't just dreamin'," Stew said with a smile. "We'll tell Miss Constance and Gramma Lettie before you dig a hole clear to China. Prob'ly need stronger tea."

Sam rose from the ground and brushed himself off the best he could. Stew picked up the pages next to Sam's bed. There still wasn't anything legible.

"Still got nothing here, huh?" he commented. "Wait, that kinda looks like an 'O' there… and a little 't',"

"Guess so," Sam said as he looked over the page. "It'll be nice when I can actually read it."

Stew set the pages back down on the bedside table, then moved to the door and held it open. "You ready?"

Sam was grateful at the invitation to head to town again, not just for town's sake, but he had more questions and Stew always seemed to have an answer. The Pelt leapt up onto Sam and they were on their way.

"Can I ask you something?" Sam said as they started down the trail. "About Forge?"

"'Course," Stew replied. "I know everything."

"If my family was still alive, they would've come up here too? With me…to Forge?"

"Well, that's what the books say." Stew was unsure why Sam was asking. If Sam was missing his family, Stew didn't want ot say anything to make it worse. Luckily, Sam asked another question.

"Would I still be in the cabin by myself?"

"Probably," Stew replied. "That's 'cuz they don't want you hurtin' no one while you're still waiting for your first night. It's the safest thing. Can you imagine what your Ma & Pa would do if you were diggin' holes in your sleep?" Stew laughed.

Sam laughed too. He thought how he used to growl and playfully chase his brother and sister while they squealed with delight. They would be squealing for a very different reason if he sleep-buried them in the dirt floor of his cabin.

"So...there hasn't been a new Jack in a while then, huh? When was the last one?"

"A long time...longer 'n when my Pa and I got here," Stew replied.

"But...I guess I'm not really *new*-new, 'cuz I got Arthur's blood and all...I'm new but not, kinda."

"Yeah..." Stew thought for a minute. "It's kinda like you got Arthur's hand-me-downs, and everyone is wanting to see how they fit."

They crested the hill overlooking Forge, and Sam's eyes brightened as he saw Alde slowly pulling Vadoma's caravan down the main street.

"Vadoma! Alde!" Sam called out as he ran down the hill. Vadoma waved as she pulled Alde to a stop.

Sam trotted up and scratched Alde's jaw and long face. The Pelt jumped off Sam's back and worked itself up and onto Alde until it sat up like a saddle and rider at the same time.

"How are you, boy?" Sam said affectionately. "Mornin', Miss Vadoma!"

"Morning my good Sam," Vadoma replied. "Who's your friend?"

"This is Stew," Sam replied with a nod over his shoulder, expecting Stew to chime in with a, "Good mornin'," but instead there was only silence. Sam turned to see that Stew was looking up at Vadmoa with a dumbfounded half-smile on his face.

"Guess he's never seen a caravan like yours," Sam said, but as he followed Stew's gaze, he realized Stew wasn't looking at the caravan, he was looking right...at...Vadoma.

Stew seemed stuck, like he couldn't move.

"Nice to meet you, Stew," Vadoma finally said.

Stew stared. His smile grew.

"Stew?" Sam said. "Stewie?"

"Wha?" Stew finally snapped out of his trance. "Uh...I... uh..."

"Nice to meet you, Stew," Vadoma repeated. Stew looked back at Vadoma, then Sam. He dropped his head and made a deep bow.

"The honor is mine, your highness."

"Your highness?" Sam questioned.

Stew's reply came as a whisper, "Just look at her! The horse, the fancy wagon..."

"It's a caravan," Sam corrected.

"Caravan...the fancy caravan...her eyes...she's gotta be a princess or a queen or somethin'!"

Sam looked up to Vadoma and gave a shrug. Vadoma gave Sam a wink and a smile, then sat up extra straight.

"Rise, young Stew," she said. Stew brought his head up. "Young Stew, could you guide Alde?" Vadoma asked.

"Of course, m'lady," Stew responded in his deepest voice. "To where does...doth...my lady wish to go?"

"I've been invited to Miss Tena's school house to give a lesson on traveling and travelers," Vadoma replied.

Stew stopped short. Of course, he wanted nothing more than to escort Vadoma, but he sure didn't want to be seen at the school house.

"M'lady, the school house is only there, past Rahm's shop," Stew gestured gallantly.

"Excellent. Would you guide my horse along the way?" Vadoma asked. Stew swallowed his unvoiced objection and gave a small bow.

"I must confer with young Sam." Vadoma gestured for Sam to join her in the coachman's box. The last time Sam had traveled with Vadoma he was hanging onto Alde for dear life. He much preferred the idea of an easy ride down main street. He jumped up and settled in next to Vadoma as Stew took Alde's bridle and started to walk.

"How are things?" She smiled. "Stew seems nice."

"He is pretty fun," answered Sam. He was going to say more, but was stopped short by the sound of children from the schoolhouse running toward Alde and the caravan. Their excitement boiled over with "Oooohs!" and "Ahhh's!" as they approached.

"Watch out now! Don't get run over!" scolded Stew. "We'll be over at the school house in a jiffy, you can see better then." Stew did his best to shoo the children, and in another fifty yards, they were in front of the schoolhouse.

"Stew!" called Miss Tena. "There you are! I suppose this explains your tardiness. Being helpful?"

"That's right, Miss Tena, I was bein' helpful this morning," Stew replied.

"He's being very helpful, ma'am," agreed Vadoma. "He guided me promptly to the school house. He is no doubt a man of letters and a gentleman at that."

"What's a man of letters?" Sam asked, but before Vadoma could answer, Stew was announcing their arrival.

"May I resent Miss Vad—"

"*Pre*-sent," Miss Tena corrected.

"*Pre*sent," Stew took a breath. "May I *pre*sent Her Highness Miss Vadoma, and her trustee steed horse, Alde, and her magnificent carriage-van."

"Good morning Miss Vadoma!" the children chimed, followed by a mix of "Good morning Horse! Morning Mr. Alde!" Miss Tena made a show of looking the caravan from end to end before addressing Vadoma with an appreciative smile.

"Nice to meet you, I'm Miss Tena. And who is this other new face?"

"I'm Sam, Miss Tena," Sam replied. All the children surrounding the caravan stopped and looked up at Sam. A soft murmur made its way through the young crowd.

"That's Sam!?"

"It's him!"

"It's Arthur!"

Sam hadn't realized he would hold any fascination with the kids. His presence seemed to catch Miss Tena by surprise as well.

"Well, now, what an unexpected surprise! Say 'Good morning, Sam!'" she instructed the children.

The children all followed suit with a collective, "Good morning, Sam!"

"Good morning…everyone," Sam responded. Giggles scattered among the children, along with a series of hushed questions.

"Shouldn't he be bigger?"

"Why doesn't he look like Arthur?"

"I wonder where his scar is!"

Miss Tena brought the attention back to herself. "Now, now. Let's not pester our new friend Sam with too many questions.

Miss Vadoma is the one we invited here today, isn't she?" Miss Tena gestured to Vadoma in the coachman's box. "Who can tell me what Miss Vadoma is sitting in? I'll give you a hint. It's *not* called a carriage-van, it's called something else!"

The children shouted answers.

"A wagon?"

"A long wheel?"

"A cart?"

"Cart is close!" replied Miss Tena.

"It's a *caravan*," Stew correctly remembered.

Miss Tena looked at Stew with a hint of surprise, "Did everyone hear that? It's a caravan! And a beautiful one isn't it?" Calls came from the children again.

"I like the colors!"

"The wood birds look so real!"

"Red is my favorite!"

Vadoma, used to drawing a crowd, pulled out her deck of cards, held them high, and called, "Who wants to see a trick?" She turned to Sam and Stew and spoke through her smile, just like she had that night at The Savoy. "Get out of here while I have them distracted!"

Sam pulled Stew's arm, and nodded his head towards Constance's Tea House and Apothecary, "Let's go!" he called.

"Thank you, my lady," said Stew softly with a bow. He let go of Alde's bridal and he and Sam slipped away.

Moments later they were taking their shoes off to wiggle their toes in the green that covered the floor of Constance's Apothecary. Sam's Pelt, fur side out, rubbed itself this way and that.

"I see the school children are quite interested in Vadoma," Constance commented.

"Who wouldn't be? Isn't she somethin'? She's pretty interesting," said Stew as he craned his neck to look back out the window. Instead of getting another glance at Vadoma, John strolled up, blocking Stew's view before entering the shoppe.

"Morning all," he said as he entered. "Here for more tea, are you?"

"I drank the last yesterday," replied Sam.

Stew was still looking out the window. "You think Vadoma likes tea?"

John looked over his shoulder out the window as well, "She seems to be well traveled, I'm sure she'd love some." He turned and raised an eyebrow at Constance and said slyly, "Probably something with flower petals." John chuckled. "Just stopped in to see Alma, she's tired but seems happy enough."

"Ya got dandelion root, Miss CC?" Stew interjected.

"Dandelion? Sure...second shelf, third from the right," she reported automatically. Stew reached up for the jar and took out a few dried roots and placed them on the ground. "Can you step on these, Miss CC? "

Constance walked over the green of the floor, placed her foot over the roots, and pressed down a little. When she stepped away, it only took a moment for three full yellow dandelion flowers to grow up from the floor.

Stew reached forward and plucked them from the ground. "Thanks Miss CC!" he exclaimed. He bolted out the door without even putting on his shoes. Sam watched as Stew held out the flowers for Vadoma with a bow. Even through the glass of the window, Sam could hear the squeals of delight from the children surrounding her. As Stew turned and headed back to the

Apothecary, the skip in his step was matched by his ear-to-ear smile.

"Well, now look at that little charmer," said Constance as she pulled a bowl to start filling it for Sam. "There's no end to the wonderful trouble of that one."

"Soup wouldn't have it any other way," commented John.

"Brrr!" Stew shouted as he came back in and spread his cold bare feet into the green of Constance's floor.

"Better hope she puts those flowers in her caravan before they freeze," John said.

"She will, she will," Stew replied with confidence.

"Of course she will," said Constance before turning to Sam. "How sharp you feeling?" She asked.

"You waking up at night?" asked John.

"He dug a hole. Right in the middle of the cabin," Stew chimed.

"Yeah, seems like I'm all over the cabin at night," Sam confessed. "Even scratching at the walls sometimes."

"No pain though, right?" she continued.

"Not so much," Sam replied. "More like an ache."

Constance was pulling ingredients from the shelves as she murmured, "Aches...aches... let's see.. ah there." She pulled a jar marked "Willow" off the shelf and placed a few pieces of its bark in the bowl above her staff.

Sam's nose didn't recognize the smells. *She must be adding something new,* he thought.

"Step on up to the mortar here, Sam," instructed Constance.

"Grind, grind 'til it's fine," said Sam with a smile as he gripped the pestle and pressed it into the mortar.

"'Til it's fine," Stew repeated softly. "Mr. John, there anything else we should be gettin' for Sam and all? At Cohen's or anythin'?"

It was obvious Stew wanted to head into Cohen's Stock & Staple, the biggest, and only general store in town.

Years ago, Moses Cohen had been peddling tools and other goods from a horse and sled in the early spring when a late blizzard caught him by surprise. Blinded by the wind and snow, he lost his way and night soon engulfed him. Lighting a lamp proved impossible, and without knowing it, he mistook the edge of the smooth, frozen lake for a snow covered road. He realized his mistake too late and fell through the thin spring ice; sled, horse, and all.

Lucky for him, he was only a hundred yards or so from the logging camp. Above the storm was a full moon and the keen ears of the Jacks heard his crackle through the ice and cries for help. Still in the dark of the storm, he found himself, his horse, and even his sled hoisted from the water and onto shore. Most of his wares were even dredged up and tossed back on his sled. It wasn't until he was sitting in the lumber camp among the Jackwolves, with the oil lamps and open fire casting their light, that he realized he'd been rescued by a most beastly sort.

Maybe it was from being on the brink of death, but Cohen showed only gratitude that night, offering anything he had in his sled as payment for saving him, his horse, and his livelihood. Of course, Arthur and the Jacks would have none of it, insisting on paying him for a couple knives and much needed soap.

The next morning as Cohen took his leave, a more human looking Arthur asked if he could possibly get several hundred feet of chain. They needed to chain up logs in the lake and hold them fast before spring thaw was fully underway. They needed it

278

soon and Arthur explained that "the timing wasn't right" to send someone from camp all the way to Albany. After seeing their beastly forms the night before, Cohen understood. He was happy to oblige, and asked if they would be needing anything else he could bring back. With lightheartedness, Arthur and the boys replied that there was "always something."

Always something was enough for Cohen, and he had a busy spring. He not only supplied the chain and other wares to the Jacks, but acquired a plot of land in Old Forge from Stanchfield. It was only steps from where First Fulton Lake drained out into the river that cut through the town. With both the lumber and the help of the Jacks, he erected Cohen's Stock & Staple in time to sell pickling jars and the like to prepare for winter.

What the people of Forge couldn't make or grow, Cohen brought up from Utica or even further away. So good was he at anticipating what people would need from day to day and season to season that the saying around town was, "If Cohen doesn't have it, you probably don't need it."

Today, John suspected Stew wanted to peruse those well stocked shelves at Cohen's. Soup, Stew's father, always had something on order that Stew could pick up for him, but there was a rumor that Cohen also had a new set of pocket knives on display. How could a boy resist?

"Your Pa have anything waiting for him at Cohen's?" John asked.

"Pork and beans," Stew replied. "A new smooth stone for sharpnin' the knives too, I think. Something about a couple pounds of nails too. Always somethin'."

"Always somethin'," John replied. "Go along then. I can finish up the tea here with Sam. If you leave right now, you can be back up at camp well before dark."

"But...I..." Stew was hoping to get a little more Sam time.

"You'll have more time with Sam, don't you worry. You get the pork and beans up to camp. Hunting's been scarce and the boys'll be hungry."

"Alright," said Stew. Still, there was a little disappointment in his voice. He wanted to bring Sam in to see all that Cohen's offered. Still, he took John's suggestion and started to put his socks back on.

"You see the new pocket knives yet?" John asked.

Stew's face lit up, "No!" He slid his foot into his boot and called as he went out the door, "See you tomorrow, Sam! Thanks again for the flowers, Miss CC!"

Even though Constance had added more and more into Sam's mortar, he had already ground it all into a fine powder.

"This good?" he asked Constance.

"Great."

"Actually, we aren't going to make it back to Sam's cabin for a while," John explained. "Any chance we can boil some right now?"

"Of course, of course," Constance replied. "I've already got some water on for myself." Constance took the kettle from her fire and poured it into a ceramic cup. She glanced at John. "You too?"

"You think?" John asked.

"I think." Constance winked at Sam, "You're not the only one who needs a little tea to keep them straight from time to time." She filled another cup and set it next to Sam's, then spooned a scoop of the ground herbs into each one. Sam liked the way the colors spread into the water. He could smell something different in this mix as the steam drifted up from the cup.

"I added a little lavender and yarrow — to help with the aches and your dreams," Constance remarked as she emptied the rest the mortar into a small tin and handed it to Sam. "We'll see how it works and adjust when you run out again in a few days, alright?"

"Alright," Sam replied as he blew on the tea to cool it.

"Here," Constance said, as she opened her door and reached out to break off a small icicle from her own roof. "Stir it with this."

Constance turned back to her shelves as Sam stuck the icicle into the tea and made lazy circles with it. In no time, it was cool enough to drink. He pulled the icicle out, handed its partially melted form to John, then drank the whole cup down in one go. Sam's face seemed to shrink with the bitterness on his tongue.

"I'm gettin' used to the bitter, I think," Sam said as he blinked and tried to get the moisture back into his mouth.

Constance didn't have the heart to tell Sam that the small jug she had just pulled from the shelf was full of maple syrup to sweeten the tea. John took a small sip of his tea and made an even worse face than Sam did. He pushed the cup away politely.

"Thanks, but uh..." said John.

Constance rolled her eyes at John before addressing Sam. "See you again in a day or two."

"Thank you, Miss Constance," said Sam. The Pelt jumped up and onto his back. John's Pelt did the same, and they were out the door.

Sam followed John straight back over to Vadoma and the school children. John, like any of the Jacks, was usually a welcome treat for the them when he dropped into the schoolhouse from time to time, but today all eyes were on Vadoma and her cards. John was able to walk right up to Miss

Tena without a single child wanting a ride on his back or a toss in the air.

"Mornin' Miss Tena," John said quietly. "Looks like the kids are getting a learnin' today."

"Shhh," Miss Tena gently scolded. Her eyes were transfixed on Vadoma's cards. John decided to finally look over to see what the fuss was about when he heard Vadoma call out a card.

"It was the what?"

"Nine of diamonds!" the children all chimed in together.

"Oh... so, not *this* card," Vadoma held up a seven of clubs.

"Nooo," the children collectively said.

"Well, then, maybe it's that one." She pointed to a young boy in the group. "Check your hat." The boy's eyes went wide.

The children were rapt while the boy pulled off his knit cap and found a card inside. The nine of diamonds. The children erupted in equal parts applause, cheering, and variations of "How-did-she-do-that?"

"She's pretty good," said Miss Tena to John.

"Not a bad dancer either," replied John.

"Is that right?" asked Miss Tena before turning back to the young crowd. "Alright, children, alright," she called. "Miss Vadoma can't spend all day with us. We've got more lessons! Say your thank-you's!"

A mix of gentle protests and *thank-you's* sounded as the school children drifted back to the schoolhouse. A few continued to look over their shoulders, though Sam couldn't tell if they were looking at Vadoma or him.

"Where were you in your lessons?" John asked Sam as Miss Tena walked the children away.

"My lessons?" asked Sam.

"You had any schooling?" John asked.

"No," said Sam. "My Ma taught me to read, write, and such. I can count to a hundred. I know my two-plus-two's and all."

"Sounds like a good start. When we get a chance, we'll have Miss Tena spend a little time with you...see where you need work."

"I'm sure *you* need some work," jested Vadoma at John.

"We all do...we all do," replied John. "How are you finding things in town?"

"Alde here is getting a little restless," said Vadoma. "He's used to being on the move."

"I'm sure. A caravan *is* built for traveling," said John.

"How long until your big night? The Proving Night?" Vadoma asked Sam.

"Another nine days, I think."

"I'm not sure if Alde will last that long," replied Vadoma. Alde turned his head and gave a snort.

Sam hadn't expected Vadoma to stay, but now knowing she may leave gave him a tinge of wistfulness.

"Don't leave without saying goodbye," John said. "If nothing else, it looks like it may break Stew's heart."

Vadoma smiled, "He wouldn't be the first."

"Or the last, I'm sure," added John.

Vadoma laughed. "You headed someplace important today, or do you want a card trick like the kids?"

"Sam's got a lesson," replied John, "though not at the schoolhouse." John's smirk betrayed a bit of mischief.

"Not all lessons are in books, eh?" said Vadoma. She clicked her tongue, shifted the reins, and Alde pulled the caravan back towards the barn. John invited Sam to walk up the main street of town with him.

"Stew show you the lake yet?" asked John.

"I've seen it from the hill there," Sam gestured to the hill he and Stew crested each time they came into town. "Never seen one frozen like that before."

"Yeah, I don't imagine. You've got to be careful. Most spots in the lake are alright, but where the water moves faster the ice can be thinner. Falling through isn't fun. We'll show you how to test the ice."

"Walking on ice... kinda like walkin' on water, huh?" Sam offered.

"Sure is, and your new boots'll help." replied John. Sam looked up to see Cohen's Stock & Staple on the right as they turned at the edge of the lake. They walked the shoreline towards where the river emptied out, then turned left again to walk downstream. "What about trees and timber? You swing an axe much?"

"Not much," Sam admitted. He had chopped plenty for the family fire, but the swaths of cleared land he'd seen in the hills around Forge told Sam the cutting the Jacks did was more intense.

"You'll soon be swinging one a lot more. After we fell 'm, we drag 'em out onto the ice, where they stay all winter. In the spring, when the lake thaws, the water does the work, and we float 'em down into Forge or further down river and cut 'em up."

"They just float down?"

"Not always, jams happen all the time."

"Jams?"

"Log jams. The logs get bunched up and won't move, so we have to get out into the river loosen 'em up. Untangle them."

"Do you use boats?" asked Sam.

"If the river is wide enough, boats called bateaus," said John. "If the river narrows, and everything gets stuck we have to drive them down."

"Drive them? The boats?"

"The logs."

John stepped to the edge of the river south of Forge. It was maybe thirty yards across, the water moving fast enough to keep the winter freeze at bay. Downstream it turned and widened, making an eddy where logs had gathered and lazily floated around and around. John and Sam approached an older man standing a few yards from the shoreline. His hair was grey enough that it was hard for Sam to tell if he had a white streak like John, Rowan, and Kofi. He was singing a happy tune to himself as he arranged a stack of collected sticks and wood into a pile for a fire. He looked Sam up and down and asked a question instead of a greeting.

"Can you swim?" the man asked. Sam looked at the man, John, and the river before answering.

"Yes?" Sam's response came as a question, not because he couldn't swim, but because he didn't want to. The snow on the banks of the river told him the water was frigid.

John gestured with his head, "This is Amasa."

The river driver, Sam remembered Stew saying. He offered his hand. "Good mornin', sir. I'm Sam."

"Glad you're here, Sam. The day-moon will be up in a bit. Then we'll start."

"Start...?"

"Logs," Amasa replied, looking towards the eddy.

"Those logs?" Sam pointed to the cut timbers slowly circling on the surface of the river. Each was thick but short, maybe four feet in length.

"Those logs," Amasa replied with a smile.

Anything and everything Sam could think of involving logs in a river meant being wet and cold, neither of which he was looking forward to.

Amasa made his way down the shoreline toward the circling eddy. He sprang off the shore and landed atop one of the floating logs. For a man into his grey years, he was incredibly nimble. He jumped to a second one, then a third. He made it look easy, balancing perfectly on one log for a while until leaping to another, then the next, whistling all the while. If the logs weren't there, he'd have looked like he was dancing a jig.

Maybe this could be fun, Sam thought.

Amasa moved with expertise along the logs all the way out into the river. Arriving at the outer edge of the eddy, he gave a *whoop* for emphasis as he turned and started to make his way back. A few moments later he was all the way back to shore, his fast steps making his last log spin as it grazed the shoreline. He expertly hopped off and stepped up the riverbank to Sam and John. His boots had never even touched the water.

"Nothing to it," Amasa winked.

The scar on Sam's arm started to itch. He recognized a restlessness in his body. Amasa glanced east to the day-rising moon, a slightly larger crescent than the day before, "There's the moon. Your turn."

"Go on!" urged John as he made walking fingers up his own arm.

Sam cautiously stepped up to where the circling logs bumped the shoreline. Amasa offered a little advice.

"Keep your feet moving. When you end up in the water, don't panic... Just breathe," he said.

"I don't wanna end up in the water," Sam said.

"Nobody does," responded Amasa.

Sam stood on shore and watched for a moment as the logs bobbed and floated slowly by. He carefully extended one foot and touched a log. It sunk a little. He brought this foot back and looked over to Amasa.

"Any time," said Amasa with a smile of encouragement.

Now or never, Sam thought.

Confidently, he took the same foot and stepped onto a log. The second he put weight on it, he slipped off sideways and plunged into the river. Even with the water only waist deep, the cold stabbed his legs and he felt his heart stop. He immediately tried to get back on the log from the water, but all it would do was spin. His only choice was to wade through the circling logs back toward shore. The current was slow but strong, and the timbers pushed and shoved at him, trying to pull him out into the river. Even only a few feet from shore, this first battle with the floating arsenal was one that Sam was barely winning.

When he finally shoved his way close enough to shore, Amasa offered a hand and hoisted Sam up and out of the water. Sam was out of breath and bent over with his hands on his knees.

"Not bad," Amasa said with a smile. "Not too good either, but a decent first try."

Sam stood and looked out over the logs, then back at Amasa. He had made it look so easy.

"Ready for another go?" asked Amasa.

Sam looked for some kind of rhythm in the bobbing up and down, but the logs had no regular or predictable action. It was a fallen tree free-for-all.

I can't step on them, Sam thought. *Maybe I can jump on one. Two feet.*

Sam found a new spot at the edge of the water, waiting patiently for just the right log to float into place.

No...wait...

Wait...

Not yet....

That one!

Sam jumped with both feet and landed dead center on a log. He stood up.

That's bett—

He flailed his arms, balancing precariously for only a second, maybe two, before he slammed down onto the log and dropped into the water again.

This time Sam didn't touch bottom until the water was all the way up to his chest. Wedged between two logs, he tried pulling himself back up, but each effort would only spin his tenuous grip loose. He had no choice but to fight through the floating pillars again to get back to shore, and fight he did. The deeper water and stronger current made a wall of pressure against him. With each step the timbers he was getting battered and bruised by the timbers. It took everything in him to fight through the water-logged mass, his scar burning with each effort. After what seemed like an eternity, he finally grasped Amasa's outstretched hand again.

Soaking wet, Sam flopped on his back in the snow on the riverbank as the Pelt came over and poked at him.

"Looks like it's time to light the fire," Amasa said. John nodded.

"I guess we should go back to the start," Amasa said. "You ready for a lesson?"

Now he wants to give me a lesson? That would've been nice a few minutes ago, Sam thought. He managed to catch his breath and stand, though his soaking wet clothes were having their way with him.

Amasa dropped in up to his thighs and drew a single log away from the circling eddy. He prodded it toward a calmer part of the shore.

"On you go," he called as he waded to one end to steady it.

Sam tried to shake off the cold as best he could before jumping out onto the log. Even with Amasa holding the end with two hands, Sam just barely managed to stand on the thing.

Amasa loosened his grip and Sam felt the log start to turn. He flailed his arms and splashed down into the stabbing cold water once more. Without the other logs pummeling him, he managed to quickly get to his feet.

"Again," said Amasa as he held the log steady.

Sam fought the shivering in his body that somehow made his legs both wobbly and stiff at the same time. He remounted the log for a brief moment before slipping and falling in once more.

"Again."

Try after try, Sam could manage to actually stand tall without falling off until Amasa loosened his grip. Sam would find himself in the water again, and often smacking the log on the way down. Instead of shivering, everything was now going numb. Sam found it harder and harder to move his stiffened joints as the cold penetrated deeper and deeper.

A biting wind rose up from across the river. Sam's body tightened against the gusts. He was stiff, wet, and out of breath.

"Come on over and dry off for a spell!" John called to him. While Sam was falling and splashing into the water, John's fire had grown as tall as a man and was putting out enough heat to warm an entire company. Sam looked at the fire, then back out

289

at the logs. Amasa stepped up and out of the water, and headed towards the fire.

I can get this, Sam thought. He looked back at the eddy of circling wood. Under all the cold, a heat stirred deep. It rose all the way up into his head where he felt a shift, an impression, a sound. A voice that wasn't his own entered his mind.

Control the log. Fast, light feet. Stay on your toes. Find the rhythm.

Sam unclenched his arms and fists that had braced him against the freezing air. He walked down the shoreline, back to the swirling eddy of wood. He waited for the right log to circle into place.

GO! The voice called inside his head.

Sam leapt forward. The instant his foot touched the top of a log, the voice barked out:

Run!

Sam did just that, running in small, light, quick steps all the way to the end of the log when the inner voice rang out once more:

Jump!

Sam hurdled into the air and onto a second log, still running at full speed. His arms stretched out, waving and flailing to balance.

Ha! Yes! The inner voice celebrated inside his head. *Well DONE!*

Sam was ecstatic. "HA!! We got it!" he called out loud.

John and Amasa stood wide-eyed in front of the fire. "Well, I'll be," managed Amasa.

Sam ran faster and faster across the logs, speeding straight at the outer edge of the floating circle—and without knowing how to stop, he dumped himself straight into the river.

The water was much, much deeper. Sam disappeared under the surface, the air squeezed out of his lungs. The current soon pulled him beneath the logs, and try as he might, his feet couldn't find bottom to push up and out of the frigid depths.

The thumping of the logs was deafening as they bumped each other just above his head. Shifting shafts of light reached through the gaps of the logs, striking Sam's face as he fought the current. His lungs burned, his skin was pierced with cold, and try after valiant try, Sam couldn't kick powerfully enough to drive his arms up and onto a log. Against all his efforts, his joints went stiff and—

He sank...

...and sank.

His feet touched the rocky bottom. In one final tremendous effort, he launched himself up and between two logs. He wrapped an arm around each one and looked up to see Amasa standing above him, a foot on each log, keeping them steady.

Sam gasped for air as he held on.

"Breathe." Amasa showed him with exaggerated inhales and exhales. Sam did his best to match Amasa's breathing, but the cold had pulled the air and strength out of him.

On shore, Sam's Pelt was having trouble sitting still next to John. "Staaaayyy," John said.

Even with Amasa's example, Sam's breathing gave way. His limbs gave up. He closed his eyes as he lost his grip and sank under again.

"Dammit," Amasa uttered.

Underneath the surface, Sam rested in surrender. No matter what his mind wanted, no matter what the voice in his head wanted, his body had had enough.

Just as darkness started to envelope him, he felt the water swirl and suddenly was rising up and up. He was pulled between two logs and into the light of the day. He felt himself swing and was over Amasa's shoulder. Amasa was running over the logs; they were nothing but a blur as Sam watched them pass underneath.

Amasa plopped Sam next to the blazing fire. The Pelt wrapped itself around him and immediately Sam felt its warmth. In all of Sam's life, he had never been so cold or more grateful for the heat of a fire.

Sam looked out over the circling logs in frustration and wonder. Amasa had made it look so easy, like he was dancing over them.

"I heard a voice in my head," Sam explained. "I thought I could... it said I could—"

He heard John over his shoulder. "Just take a second and warm up. Then you can try again." It was going to take more than a second for Sam to warm up.

"Could I take the fire with me out there?" Sam managed to joke.

John had a quick laugh and added more wood to the fire. A silence settled over them for a moment as Amasa held his hands out, warming them.

The Pelt squeezed firmly around Sam, and he felt tingling where the logs had bestowed bruises upon him. He stared into the dancing flames of the fire, mesmerized. The flickering matched a feeling that was rising inside him, yet like a flame, it was impossible to hold.

Sam blinked and shook his head. He looked toward the river, where the logs floated slowly around in their great circle.

It's all moving.

Everything was moving: The fire. The river. The logs. Even the cold wind in the air. Sam looked out over the water. He had tried to balance atop the logs but the only success he experienced was when he was running.

Keep moving.

He threw off the Pelt and went to the edge of the river. Amasa and John blinked at each other before John yelled to him.

"You alright?"

"Ain't nothing alive that don't move," Sam yelled back. The men looked at each other with surprise at Sam's confidence.

Still on shore, Sam started running in place with his knees high when his own voice came through his mind.

I must look like an idiot.

Sam took his running feet from the shore right out onto a log. Right, left, right, left.

To his surprise, he could feel the subtle shifts in the direction of the log as it wanted to roll this way or that. He didn't try to run forward or backward, but instead focused on adjusted the landing of each foot ever so slightly, making the log roll one way, then the other. He was in constant motion and was never quite balanced, yet he actually felt in control. The current took him and the log out into the river, at the outer circle of the eddy. He looked up to John and Amasa, who were standing on the shoreline looking rather impressed.

"HA! I GOT IT!" Sam yelled. With his next step, he caught his toe on the log and plunged back into the water.

As he sunk up to his chest again, the other voice in his head came through, *Best to keep your eyes on the logs for now.*

Sam laughed as he fought his way back to the shore where John and Amasa were waiting.

"That was almost a quarter of the way around," said Amasa. "Starting to get the hang of it, eh?"

"Ain't nothing alive that don't move," said Sam.

"Well now, 'Ain't nothing alive that don't move,'" laughed Amasa.

"I was tryin' to stand still on the logs, but that's not how it works. The river's alive, it moves. So, you gotta keep moving. "

"Well now, you're right...it does work best if you keep movin'." Amasa gave Sam a look up and down. "Ready for another go, or you need a little more time by the fire?"

Sam spent the better part of the rest of the day alternating between the heat of the fire and the cold plunges between the logs. Slowly but surely making a little more progress throughout the day. He did eventually make it all the way out to the edge of the eddy, but never all the way back. There's only so much a boy can learn in a day, after all.

27

The next morning, Sam woke again to find a pencil in his hand and scribbled pages scattered about. When Letha arrived, it was Rahm from the tannery that helped to pull the timber away.

Rahm held out the boots he had made. "Try these on."

Sam noticed a pattern of small spikes poking through the bottom of the sole. Letha answered Sam's question before he even had a chance to ask.

"Logger boots. They're what you'll be needin' day to day," remarked Letha.

They're what I was needing yesterday for the logs, Sam thought.

His slid his foot into the boot and wiggled his toes. It fit well enough. He slid on the other foot and stood up, feeling the spikes sink down into the dirt floor of the cabin.

"Go on, now, walk around a bit," Letha pointed to the door.

Sam found Stew waiting outside. "Oh!! Nice!" Stew called when he saw the boots. "Let's test 'em out." He took off into the woods and Sam bounded after him. Stew jumped and leapt off of roots and the sides of trees.

Sam followed him tentatively at first, but when he discovered how when the boots gripped the terrain, Sam was soon bounding after Stew. He never thought footwear would make him feel like he was more grown up, but it sure felt like he stood a little taller in those boots.

"They feel alright?" Rahm asked as Sam and Stew returned.

"Yes, sir," replied Sam.

"I made them a little big. You're still growing. Hoping to get two seasons out of them. Here's your kit." Rahm handed Sam a small canvas bag filled with wax, polish, and a horse bristle brush. "If you're not sure, Stew can show you how to keep 'em nice."

"Thank you, Mr. Rahm," said Sam.

"'Course," Rahm replied. "Be sure to take 'em off before the moon and all. Don't want you bustin' through 'em. Luck to you." He gave a quick tip of his hat to Letha and turned back towards town.

—-

It was still dark on the seventh morning when the sound of the door timber roused Sam from his sleep.

Curious, he thought. He sat up in bed and heard the door barely creak open. Then footsteps outside... no, foot *stomps*, rather, on the ground. *Sounds like horses,* he thought. A second later, he heard a distinct snort confirming it. *Maybe Alde got out.*

He swung his feet over the side of the bed and threw on his new shirt, trousers, boots. The Pelt lazily wrapped itself around

296

him. Sam stepped outside, but there were no horses, nor another soul in sight.

He made his way behind the outhouse to pee and then walked around the entire cabin, but he was alone. No John, no Letha, no one. The sound of a horse's *chuff* perked his ears.

"Is that you, Alde?" Sam said aloud. He stepped into the woods as the dark of night gave way to the orange of morning.

The cabin itself was out of sight when he stepped around the trunk of a pine to find two magnificent horses, both even bigger than Alde. They kicked at the cold, frozen ground, finding a root or two, then raised their heads while they chomped. Each a shade of brown, one had large white splotches along its body while the other had only a single white patch on his head, the rest of his coat a lighter auburn.

Sam didn't want to spook them. He stood and simply watched as the rising sun peeked through the trees. Against the light, the horses's breath circled up and away from their long faces. One, then the other, looked right at him.

I guess that's as good an invitation as any, Sam thought.

Sam approached the horses carefully but confidently, watching their ears, and soon found himself only a few feet away from the splotched one. It looked Sam up and down, then took a few steps away.

Sam chuckled. "Easy there. Easy," he said quietly. He stepped closer again, making it right up next to the horse. Instead of moving, this time it turned its huge head and watched Sam place a hand on its tall shoulder. It was warm, and Sam could feel its muscles twitching as he rubbed it this way and that.

"Good morning, big guy," Sam said.

He pat the horse firmly up its neck until he was scratching its long jawline. The horse stood still, then slowly leaned its head into the scratching.

"There we go."

Sam heard the other horse's hooves and turned to see it walking towards him. "You want some too?" he said aloud as he turned. Soon he was scratching down each of their backs. *After all, who doesn't like scratches?* he thought to himself. *Just like dogs.*

Sam worked his way forward and back on the second horse, then noticed both horses weren't eyeing him anymore; they were looking up and out in the same direction. Neither was moving. Sam followed their gaze and caught a slight movement between the trees. There was barely the faint sound of steps on the ground, but he couldn't quite see precisely who, or what, they were coming from.

One step.

Another.

A doe came into view through the trees. It was relaxed and unafraid, stopping to sniff the ground from time to time. It brought its head up and finally looked directly at Sam and the horses. All four were frozen in place for a moment, until one of the horses *chuffed* and spooked the doe. It raised its white tail and leapt away, bounding behind the trees until it disappeared. Sam could hear its rhythm on the ground as it made its way further and further into the forest, soon fading into nothing.

Well, that was neat, Sam thought to himself. He returned his focus to the horses to find they were motionless and staring.

What is it this time? Sam thought as he peered into the forest again.

A stocky Asian man stepped out from between the trees in the distance. Behind him, Letha appeared, staff in hand. The Asian man gave Letha a small nod and look of approval, then made two clicks with his tongue; the ears on both horses perked up.

He gave a short whistle, and the horses trotted away from Sam through the trees. Even with their massive size, there was a gracefulness as they moved. Sam thought this was the best start to a day he had had in Forge so far.

The horses arrived at the Asian man's side and he turned to lead them away. Letha gave them a quick pat as they passed. Their shapes were soon lost between the trees, just like the doe. Letha approached Sam.

"Who was that?" Sam asked.

"The horses?"

"The man."

"King. You'll meet him soon enough." Letha gestured that they should walk back towards the cabin.

"And the horses?"

"Wonderful aren't they? King has a remarkable gift for those animals. Good workers, just like you." she smiled.

"What are their names?"

"Tolbo and Od," she replied, "I've brought you more tea, even stronger this time."

That means it tastes even worse, Sam thought.

"Which is which?" Sam asked.

"Which is what? Which?"

"The horses."

"Oh, Tolbo has the big spots," she responded. "You'll be seeing them again soon, after your Proving. When you get to meet the rest of the boys."

The rest of the boys. Sam wondered if there would be more boys like him or Stew; boys his age. *Was there some kind of school, or a group of young apprentices?* He realized Letha was so old that she called everyone, even John, "my boy" or some other term of endearment. As such, there was no telling from Letha if there would actually be boys, or men folk. Sam was left wondering.

"Let's have a look at what you wrote in your sleep last night," she said. "Maybe today we can make sense of those scribbles."

But once they were back in the cabin and Letha had the pages in hand, all she could do was to raise her eyebrows and comment, "Well...maybe tomorrow."

—-

As each new tomorrow came and went, the sleep-writing never became more legible. There were more curves, and even a few unique shapes that hinted at new forms for the loculus pieces, but there was never anything that Sam, or anyone else, could discern—besides the ornate "A" of the signature.

Sam secretly hoped that it wasn't his own lack of penmanship that was the issue. "Reading and writing" tended to go together, but he had done much more reading than writing, even though "more" didn't account for much.

Sam instead did find confidence being helpful around town as the days passed. Each morning Stew would arrive and announce how many more days till Proving Night.

Sam appreciated the countdown, and Stew's excitement for Sam's "big night" did bleed off a little. Still, Sam found himself growing more nervous as the days passed.

Just like the days back home, Sam found the time moved faster when he was busy, and he and Stew had a routine that he happily settled into. They'd head into town and spend the better part of each morning lugging wood to the woodboxes around town. Mabel's treats always made her the first stop, but they would eventually help anyone that needed it, even Miss Tena.

Some days, Stew would say that Amasa was waiting by the river and Sam would spend a part of the day trying to master the logs, but always ending up wet and cold. Luckily, Stew or John always had the fire going so he could try again and again.

Constance was a daily stop, with a slightly adjusted tea formula. During one of these visits, as Sam was grinding away at his herbs, Stew produced a paper with scribbles of his own and placed it on Constance's table. The entire page was filled with line after line of the alphabet.

"You practicing your letters?" Constance asked.

"She said I'm a gentleman and a 'man of letters,' Vadoma did...and that's what a man of letters does; he writes letters." Stew folded his arms across his chest, smiling. It was obvious to Sam that Stew was right.

As Stew's luck would have it, Vadoma and Alde came trotting down the main street of Forge, passing right in front of Constance's shop. Stew grabbed his paper and was out the door in a flash. Sam stopped grinding to look out the window as Stew bowed deeply.

He handed the alphabet paper up to Vadoma. She looked with surprise, before carefully folding and tucking it into her cloak pocket. She bowed to Stew dramatically, then nudged Alde along. Stew came back into the shoppe beaming.

"She liked them," Stew beamed. "She said she'll keep them close as she travels."

Sam wondered where and when Vadoma would be traveling. While Alde and the caravan seemed to naturally fit into the setting of Forge, Sam got the impression that Vadoma didn't like to stay in one place for too long.

The days in town gave way to evenings at Sam's cabin where Letha or John would be waiting with something to eat for Sam before sending Stew on his way and making sure Sam was settled in for the night.

Once they left and dropped the timber in place, Sam would add a bit of wood to the fire, drink a little more tea, then sit on the bed and open *Huck Finn*. Within a few pages, he would be so lost in the story and the fight to keep his eyes open, that he could never remember actually falling asleep.

In the middle of the night, he would twitch himself awake in the strangest positions, like once at the edge of the bed, tongue out, licking his scar. Or on another night, twitching awake with his face pressed against one of the narrow windows, like he was trying to get out. Each time he would breathlessly come to, look around the room and blink, as he slowly put the pieces of his life back together.

The Wolf bite.

The burned house.

The train with John.

The cabin in the snow.

As he gained control of his mind again, he would steady his breathing, and would feel grounded, more like himself. He would find comfort in checking the fire, getting into bed, and twisting the knob of the oil lamp. He'd watch the flame shrink until the cabin went went dark.

Sleep would come fast, and his dreams would fly through his mind. His childhood, his travels, then places he never knew, but faces he felt like he did. A younger Letha. Back in Charles' library, a man with a beard named Fredrick. He would experience recurring scenes of green pastures, horses, and rain. They were images of some other life. He dreamt of people that he hadn't met yet, but knew he would.

On the fourteenth morning, Sam woke to find precise circles traced over and over on the pages in front of him. It was a grand departure from the lines and small curves that he had written in the preceding weeks. Sam stared at them for a long time. He could tell they meant something, but the insight that he longed for was still illusive.

Sam could hear Stew singing a tune as he made his "leverage" to move the timber away from the cabin.

"Tonight, tonight, he'll finish the bite!
Tonight, tonight, it's Provin' Night!"

"You ready?" Stew said as he pulled the door open and let in the morning light.

"What do make of these?" Sam gestured to the pages on the bed as he laced up his boots.

"Them's moons. Seems 'propriate...seein' how Provin' Night's a full moon and all."

Sam knew that Stew must be right.

In town, Proving Night was on everyone's mind. Mabel made an extra special "Moon Bun" for Sam. It was sweet with a yellow center, and Mabel made Sam taste it right there in her bakery. If it wasn't for the heat coming from the oven, Sam was sure that Mabel blushed when he said it was delicious.

Rahm stepped out of his shop and reminded Sam to take off his boots before sundown. Rahm didn't like to make the same boots twice.

The banter of the school children reflected Proving Night as well, with whispers of, "He doesn't look any different yet," "I hope he makes it," and even, "Good luck!"

Stopping by to see Constance, Sam was surprised that he wasn't required to grind any herbs. Instead, Constance handed him the usual tin box, but gave him instructions to open it after the sun went down. Adding pointedly, "We'll see you in the morning."

Sam had asked all the questions he dared about Proving Night, but even so he felt a mix of excitement and nervousness throughout the day. Proving Night had been approaching for the past two weeks. Every day Stew would remind him how many days were left, while the simple advice he had received from John, Rowan, and Kofi, was to "stay strong."

28

Since Arthur's death six weeks ago, Letha's feelings of restlessness had churned more and more each day.

Fate had closed in. Tonight would be Sam's storm.

Letha's knock was right on schedule.

"Come in!" called Alma.

Letha set her staff in the floor of Alma's cabin, then came close to the new mother as she fed the baby.

"She looks healthy," Letha said.

"She's had a good latch from the beginning." There was a lull while Alma contemplated the separation she would soon have from her baby. Letha could feel Alma's hesitation and gently reminded her of the significance of the evening.

"Even among full moons, ours is special tonight." Letha reminded her.

Alma looked down at the baby nursing at her chest. She knew. Letha knew, and somewhere deep inside, Alma was hoping that the babe knew how special she and the night both were.

The baby's full belly soon made her drift off to sleep, and Alma wrapped her in a small quilted blanket. A short walk later, they arrived at the frozen shore of Fulton Lake. The skies above were clear as the orange of sunset began to ombre the sky.

Yara was standing on the snow covered ice in front of a makeshift dog sled. He invited Letha to sit. Once comfortable, Alma placed the wrapped baby into Letha's arms before standing on the back of the sled. She playfully yelled "Mush!" to Yara.

Yara pulled the sled across the ice with confidence. Before his daughter was born, the hands of destiny had already began pulling at her fate. Tonight, the moon would pull too.

29

Full Moon

"You're prob'ly gonna need a lot of wood," Stew said as he dropped yet another armload into the cabin.

"This seems like a lot," Sam replied, looking at the stack almost as tall as him.

Stew nodded with his hands on his hips.

Sam was more than happy with the wood pile, but wondered if Letha and John would soon be arriving.

He watched as Stew fiddled with a piece of birch in his hand. Stew slowly peeled the bark off then tossed each long strip into the fire to watch it flame.

The Raven swooped in from outside and perched at the foot of the bed. It eyed both of the boys.

Caw!

"I know, I know." Stew rolled his eyes. He scratched the Pelt then gave Sam a slap on the back. "Good luck tonight!"

"Thanks..." Sam didn't know if he felt excited or nervous, or both.

"Come on, Raven," Stew said.

Sam watched him walk the path away from the cabin under the ombre sky as the orange faded to blue.

Where are Letha and John? Sam wondered.

His stomach growled. He hadn't eaten since Mabel's in the morning and was feeling particularly famished. He'd grown used to Letha or John bringing a bit to eat when they stopped by at the end of each day. Sleeping was always easier on a full stomach.

The wind shifted and swirled snow from the roof down and around him.

It'll be even colder tonight, Sam thought. *Maybe one more load.* He went to the wood pile and loaded his arms.

Sam dropped the load of wood next to the stove and kicked off his boots. When he opened found and opened the tin of tea from Constance, all there was inside was a single dried maple leaf.

The door closed and the timber slammed into place.

"John? Letha?!" Sam called out, but there was no answer. He gave the door a shove, but as always, it wouldn't budge.

"JOHN?!" he called out louder.

Silence.

So this is Proving Night.

The Pelt came and wrapped around Sam's shoulders. Sam immediately felt more calm.

"I thought there'd be a test, or something. Maybe more logs with Amasa," Sam said to the Pelt. He sighed.

After adding a couple pieces of wood to the fire, Sam lit the oil lamp and picked up *Huck Finn.* His stomach let out a small growl he tried to ignore. He flipped open to a dog-eared page toward the end of the book:

"I couldn't bear to think about it; and yet, somehow, I couldn't think about nothing else."

Sam's ears perked. There was a *creak!* in the distance. Then a *crackle!* Sam turned his head to hear better. An avalanche of sound barreled toward him. Cacophonous crashing and a thunder erupted so loud that Sam felt it come through the ground. Then all went silent.

Before Sam's mind had time to discern the source of the sound, the first blade of moonlight cut through the long narrow window, a silvery beam stretching from the heavens, directly to Sam.

His face flushed with a heat that seeped into his veins and spread through his entire body, then flooded into his scar. In seconds it felt like it was on fire. He dug and scraped his fingernails into it, triggering a painful relief for a moment before his arm changed under his scratching. The scar was expanding. No, not the scar—there was a dark, thick fur burning up his arm and onto his shoulder.

Sam jerked his arm away. He could feel the roots of hair searing, expanding, and pushing out from each follicle of his skin, boiling up his arm, shoulder, and down over his back.

Sam's vision went double as his skull shifted and grew. He choked as each vertebrae in his neck relocated. He ground his teeth as his jaw extended and the shape of his skull elongated. He was being scorched from the inside, as if the sun had set directly into his veins. His organs roiled and pressed at his ribcage, forcing it to widen. Every bone in his arms and legs

309

burned as they stretched and pulled his ligaments from their roots. His fingers shrank as his nails narrowed and sharpened.

Falling to his hands and knees, Sam released a guttural groan that grew into a powerful howl. The last of the hair blazed its way across his chest and down his legs, completing the transformation.

Sam lifted his eyes to see the enormous full moon filling the window. It was undeniable. It was powerful. It made him boil from the inside with rage that was impossible to quench.

His nose flooded with the pungent scents of pine, smoke, horse, manure, earth. Through the thickness, subtle threads prodded at his brain. One smell pulled at him, driving a hunger into his core. His mouth watered.

Deer.

He turned his head, calibrating exactly where the scent was coming from. He moved his ears, now ringing with the tiniest of sounds.

There.

Narrow, careful footsteps pushed into the snow somewhere in the distance. Sounds that matched the smell; the steps of a doe.

He looked at the door of the cabin.

He wanted out. Now.

He charged the door. The entire cabin shuddered as his new strength boomed into the night, but the door didn't budge. He let out a growl of frustration, then backed up and slammed the door again. The timbers blocking the door held firm. With each repeated effort, he only left claw marks in the dirt of the floor.

Dirt.

He reached down to the base of the wall and pulled the earth. New muscles flexed as he cut deep into it with his claws. The smells of soil filled his head; worms, grubs, fermented vegetation, underground fungus—each had their own scent as they were pulled into a pile behind him.

It wasn't long before he was reaching far under the wall of the cabin and breaking through to the surface outside. He drove himself into the hole, wedging his shoulders against the sides of the tunnel. He tried to push forward with all his might, but the wall of the cabin above didn't budge. He was stuck.

His scar surged heat and urged him to push. A voice came from deep within.

Let.

Me.

Free.

He growled through gritted teeth. With a savage burst, he pushed up with his newfound ferocity. The entire side of the cabin rose on his back. He shrugged his shoulders and drove forward.

BOOM!

The cabin crashed back to the ground behind him.

He stood free in the open air. The light of the moon glistened blue off his black coat of fur.

He felt strong. He felt powerful. He felt *alive*. The Pelt crawled out from the hole and flung itself up onto Sam's back.

His entire brain filled with the smell of his prey, and the hunger took over. There was no doubt which way to go.

North.

Sam's legs and arms worked in unison in his new form as he barreled ahead on all fours. Pull, push, pull, push. He felt every fiber of his muscles as they stretched and pulled, propelling him powerfully onward. The smell of the deer grew stronger as the forest blazed past. He felt the wind on every hair that had risen out of his body. He felt at home. Sam was a dark shadow rushing through the moonlit forest. The chase was on.

A mile away, the unsuspecting doe poked its nose into the fallen snow, looking for a bit of undergrowth.

Sam eased his pace as he got closer and the scent dug deeper into his head. His ears picked up the crunch of a single leaf—and he froze. Sam's new animal instincts were taking over. He turned his head and inhaled slowly. It was near.

Through the shadows between the trees, his keen eyes caught just the glimpse of movement. Sam stopped. There it was again, the flitting of a short, white tail. The deer. A doe.

Without making a sound, Sam dropped his head low and pushed his paw gently into the snow. Each precise step brought him closer...and closer.

He crouched, ready to pounce.

The deer stepped into a shaft of moonlight in front of him.

Sam vaulted out of the shadows and into the air, but the deer's reflexes were too sharp. Sam landed in the snow, where the deer should've been. As the doe leapt ahead, Sam's instincts drove him into the chase. He bounded through the snow, up onto tree trunks and off rocks, leaving claw marks wherever he touched. He launched himself off a boulder directly at the deer, but again, it was too quick and his teeth only grazed its hind quarters, leaving a shallow gash. Sam tumbled head over tail into a snow drift.

Sam shook off his fall and renewed his chase, swinging wide to get ahead of the deer. Several seconds later, the deer stopped and looked back, its ears perking up and twitching from side to side, searching for any sound. Sam slowed his approach and stayed in the shadows, frozen. He picked up a new scent in the air.

Fear.

It was invigorating.

Sam heard a faint pounding getting faster and faster. He smiled when he realized it was the racing of the doe's heartbeat.

The deer stepped forward, turning its head repeatedly to scan the moonlit forest. Sam timed his movement with the deer, silently bolting from one shadow to the next, staying hidden as he tightened the distance between them. In his mind's eye, Sam replayed the deer leaping away. This time, he would anticipate the deer's darting and pounce ahead. He calculated the terrain, then adjusted his line of approach. He once again crouched and waited for the doe to step into the perfect place for a hidden attack.

Patience.

The doe's ears flicked as it took one step, then another. It cautiously poked its head between two tall birch trees, and Sam launched himself in the air with his mouth wide and teeth bared. The deer spooked, but with nowhere to go, jumped straight towards him.

In an instant, jaws were clenched around its neck.

Sam's teeth sunk deep into the thick hide. He tasted the hot metallic blood as it filled his mouth and eased down his throat. The deer thrashed and struggled, but it only helped Sam's teeth cut deeper—until they crunched into bone. Sam shook the deer and could feel the neck dislocate and *snap!* The fight was over.

He had made the kill.

He felt powerful. Proud.

Sam felt a shift in the structure of the neck between his teeth; the bones of the spine were moving, fitting into his mouth differently. Sam swallowed the blood that ran down his throat. One gulp. Two. The pressure of the its pulse weakened with each fading heart-beat.

The doe twitched one final time as Sam lay the limp body on the snow before him. Its smell was changing. The scent was less wild. There was an earthen quality to it, a deepening that was somehow familiar. Sam released his jaws and stepped back.

He looked up.

Left.

Right.

Then down at his kill.

Something wasn't right. It stirred in a peculiar way.

The deer's beige-brown hair was blanching and sloughing off. The blood-stained hair of the neck fell away to reveal pale skin. Where the neck was bitten was shedding hair while the top of the deer's head was growing it. Something else was being revealed from underneath as all the brown body hair fell away.

Sam snorted and sneezed. He shook his head aggressively to try to clear his brain; the small part of him that was still human was trying to make sense of what his eyes saw. Looking down again, it was undeniable.

On the red-stained snow in front of him, sparsely covered in the remaining hair of a deer, lay an old woman. Her grey hair spread around her head, her lifeless eyes stared into nothing. Above her shoulder on her neck, a gaping wound. She didn't move. No pulse. Letha.

The world slowed. Sam's own breath filled his ears. One breath. Another. A third. He exhaled a mist that hung in the air like a still, small cloud. One by one, small sparks of light crackled as they emerged from the trees nearby. They gently floated through the hanging mist of Sam's breath, pulling tiny translucent trails as they lingered and swirled above Letha's body. Each in turn delicately fell onto her pale skin before gradually fading out.

Letha lay in front of him without the light in her eyes, without the smile on her face.

In the valley of his heart, all Sam's sorrow and regret emerged. Swelling from deep within, it finally found its escape with a prolonged howl of lament.

The bawl from his throat drowned out his human thoughts, and his beastly instincts washed back over him. His hunger returned. His feeling of power returned. It was intoxicating to stalk his prey, to kill. His stomach growled as he anticipated his hunger finally being satisfied. He brought his tongue out and dipped his head to taste the blood again, but—

His ears twitched. Was it a voice? A cry?

A new scent drove into his animal brain. He searched the forest. His senses pulled at his nose and ears, luring him away from his own prey. He needed to kill again.

The sound, there it was again...and the smell...*there*!

His legs sprung, and the world around him was a blur of speed. Behind him, the naked trees of winter bowed towards Letha's body.

With each stride forward, Sam's new wolf form was leaving human thoughts behind. The deeper he went into the woods, the deeper he went into his new animal self. The small string of Sam's own consciousness that was connected to the beast was wearing thinner and thinner.

The passing timbers of the forest opened to a clearing in the snow. Towering blocks of stone stood tall in a wide circle, while one lay in the middle on its side, an altar of rock.

A shaft of blue-grey light from the moon cut through the trees and directly onto the altar. There was movement; squirming. On a bed of pine boughs lay the tiniest spotted fawn. It seemed an offering to the wolf, to Sam. It was another life he could easily take. A new taste to experience.

His belly was still empty. Without eating his first kill, his hunger was still unsatisfied. The blood had yet to dry on Sam's snout, and there would soon be more. The fawn bleated in search of its mother. His ears filled with the sound.

The spots on the fawn shifted as it inhaled, a new breath filling its tiny lungs. It bawled even louder. It almost sounded human.

He stalked the edge of the stone circle, creeping closer and closer to the fawn. Different than the doe in the woods, it was helpless. It didn't move. It must've sensed Sam, the wolf, was close. It's own instincts told it to stay alive; it must stay still.

Sam barely maintained a thread of control over the wolf within. He stopped and stared at the fawn in front of him. He shook his head and snorted loudly, trying to get the scent out of his nose. The fawn shimmered in the moonlight. For a moment it seemed like it wasn't there at all.

This little morsel had no protection. It would be effortless to kill, so young that it didn't even run. It had cried out for its dead mother, even with death standing before it. It was defenseless. Sam lunged and felt a pang of disappointment when it didn't move. What fun is it to hunt something that won't be chased?

Sam's tenuous thread that connected him to himself was beginning to give way. He could barely hold on.

Sam circled the altar again, inching closer to the fawn.

The smell.

It seeped into his brain as Sam licked his snout. The fawn let out a small whimper. The moonlight glinted off the welled up tears in its eyes. All Sam could feel was a wanting, a yearning to taste those very tears, to taste its fear.

He stepped closer, looming over his tiny prey.

Its mother was dead. So was his.

The fawn was alone. So was he.

Rage filled him.

He would tear the fawn apart, like his family was torn from him. He wanted to swallow the loneliness and bury it deep inside this mighty beast he had become. He would never be hurt again.

He could feel the fawn's breath, he was close enough to lick it.

Taste.

His mouth watered and his stomach growled at the hint of the tender meal. The fawn didn't move. A fleeting thought from the recesses of Sam's mind rose, *It thinks I'm its mother.* Sam's tongue wrapped around the fawn's tiny head and touched its tear-filled eye.

Sam's entire being shuddered at the salty taste. He pedaled back as the tears turned so cold they burned his throat as he swallowed. It mixed with the blood from the doe, like a great fermented poison that curdled inside of him. His stomach churned into knots, freezing him from from the inside out.

His beastly form weakened, he curled over, breathless from the pain. Every gasp for air only pushed another wave of pain deeper. Tighter. Darker. His heart beat slowed.

This must be what it's like to die.

His body twitched.

At least I'll get to be with my family.

He stopped fighting.

A voice, from an unknown space within, instructed him, "Breathe."

It was the voice of Arthur.

Sam opened.

Air rushed into his lungs. From his brow, a streak of white erupted from the roots of his dark fur. Burning cold, it blazed from above his eye over and down the back of his head, his shoulder, and pushed into his scar.

His heartbeat returned, pushing a warmth through his entire body. His senses were suddenly overwhelmed, like they were being used for the first time. He heard every movement in the night, from beetles clicking their wings, to the breath of mice digging in the snow. He felt the Earth's slow hum beneath his feet, grounding him into it. Colors he had never seen before danced against the darkness of the night. Trees pulsed with a dark hue. Auras stretched from every branch, small spots glowed through the snow and scurried under the surface. Sam raised his head, his eyes filled with sapphire moonlight.

He felt his ankles shorten and his legs lengthen until he was standing upright. His claws retracted as his paws stretched into palms and clawed fingers. The fur on his body was still thick, and his muscles ached to move, but he felt more human and less like the wolf that he had been struggling to control. He finally had a hold of himself again.

Sam finally exhaled.

Amber fireflies rose out of the ground through the snow and swirled to the altar, their light turning blue as they crossed into the moonlight and engulfed the fawn. Sam blinked as he looked into the center of the glow at the...*baby?*

Tears streaked its cheeks as its cry pierced the night.

Sam scooped up the baby, cradling it against him. The Pelt swung around him and wrapped around the baby, protecting it from the cold.

Keep her warm.

The baby calmed as Sam pulled her close. He brought his head up and perked his ears, searching the forest for any threat. More fireflies seeped up from under the snow and circled around them.

The baby fluttered her eyelids open and fixed her gaze on Sam. At first Sam thought her eyes were the deep color of the ground at first thaw, but he watched as one iris began to change before him, from the outside in, turning from brown to an icy blue. Sam felt a warmth return to his center. He knew, from deep within, that this small helpless creature was somehow his.

Out of the darkness of the northern sky, the ribbons of the aurora burst forth. Sam and the baby sat at the center of the henge bathed in a silvery moonbeam, surrounded by the dancing lights.

Behind Sam, next to the altar, stood Letha's staff. Fireflies rose and glowed blue as they circled the top.

He remembered the lullaby his mother used to sing to him and his siblings. It rose up and out of him without a thought, and Sam found himself singing to the baby. His voice was pure, and his pitch was true.

The last leaf on Letha's staff fell. In its place, a new bud sprung forth, the edge thrumming with light.

—-

As the sun broke through the dawn, the Jacks and Witches made their way toward the henge. They anticipated two possibilities from the night before; either there would be nothing but blood stains and the Jacks would have to hunt Sam down, or—

On the ground, Sam sat with his head bowed over the baby. His Pelt was curled around them both as he softly sang a lullaby.

Alma exhaled with relief as Sam looked up.

"Morning, Young Sam," said Constance gently.

"Well look at that," marveled Alma.

"There it is," remarked John.

They were all looking at Sam's hair. In his human form, the blaze of white remained.

"What is it?" Sam asked, trying to look up at his own head.

"You have a wonderful streak. It looks dashing," Alma answered.

Sam reached up and touched his hair, but it didn't feel any different.

"I'm glad to see you made it through the night," Constance said gently. "As did she."

"Her eye...it changed color...she..." There was so much going through Sam's mind.

"She saved you." Alma completed the sentence for him.

Sam knew what Alma said was true. This baby had somehow tamed the ferocious beast he had become, though he couldn't fathom how.

"She's your Witch," explained Alma. "She's your *Tether*. She is the one person that will keep you connected to yourself, and will help you control your power as it grows...as you both grow."

My Tether, Sam thought.

He looked down at the baby and searched his mind through the murky memories of the previous night.

"Letha," he said under his breath.

"Letha?" Alma asked, scanning those that had gathered. Letha's staff stood next to the stone altar. "Where is she?"

Sam had so many strange, realistic dreams over the past weeks.

It must've been...a bad dream.

"Letha?!" John called out.

"Letha?!" others called, but there was no answer.

"She should be here," Alma said. "It's the most important part."

Maybe it wasn't a dream.

A dread filled Sam. He wanted to flee, but he was frozen in place.

Stew came running from the woods, tears streaming down his face. "Help! It's Gramma Lettie! I found her! Oh, Gramma Lettie! She's—"

"She's dead."

All heads turned.

The voice was Sam's. His mind wasn't swimming anymore; it was drowning.

"I think I—killed her—I couldn't stop myself—I was the Wolf —she was a deer—then she wasn't—the moon—I couldn't stop. It happened before I found her—"

"You *killed* Gramma Lettie!?" Stew cried.

"I'm so, so sorry, I—"

John stepped forward. "Every witch has her way." He placed a hand on Stew's shoulder. "We knew she needed to join Arthur."

"But she didn't tell me," Stew replied. Constance drew Stew close.

"Would knowing have made it easier, or would you have tried to stop her, or stop Sam? It was as she wished, or it wouldn't be."

"But I'm her favorite." Stew was quiet.

Kofi stepped forward, "I imagine you always will be."

Sam hoped that somehow, some way, Stew would forgive him.

"Having her gone won't be easy," said Constance.

"I'm gonna miss her." Stew looked at the sky, "I'm gonna miss you Gramma Lettie!"

"We all will," said John.

"Truth," Alma reached for the baby. "She's not gone, but passed on. Like Arthur passed on to you, Sam."

"I thought Letha would be my witch," Sam stated.

"Wait," Stew's eyes darted as he tried putting the pieces together. "Letha was Arthur's witch, then Arthur passed onto you...Letha had to pass on to someone too. So she passed on—or in—*into* the baby. She was doin' that the same night you got to Forge! So—it ain't just Gramma Lettie that—"

"Isn't," corrected Constance.

"It *isn't* Gramma Lettie that's your Witch, it's the baby!"

"My Witch also means...she's my Tether." Sam surprised himself with how confidently he spoke.

Alma turned to John, "I think he's Proven."

"I think he is too." John addressed Sam directly. "You've made it through your Proving. Still got quite a bit to learn, though."

Sam allowed a feeling of relief to find him. "I made it."

"You both did," replied Alma. "You are a living part of both Arthur and Letha's sacrifice, a crucial part. And you should always hold your Tether tightly when your change comes."

A turbulent mix of sadness, remorse, and hope filled Sam. Only a few hours ago, he had taken a life, that of their lovely Letha. But now he had a place, a people, and a purpose. He felt that it was his duty to protect and nurture this baby. This small one that tethered him to himself and to his deeper meaning.

"You have strong blood in you," John paused for emphasis. "Arthur was a formidable, noble man. His blood-borne power will add to your own birth-borne strength as you grow."

Sam's thoughts went to his father and his family. It had barely been a month since fire had taken them, and now here he was; surrounded by new, destined kin. Sam knew he would never be alone, but there was still much to learn. Starting with the little one he held.

"What's her name?" Sam asked.

"We've given her the name Cadi," Yara answered. "But you should give her a Tethered Name."

Sam hadn't ever named anyone or anything, before. Looking down at the baby, he felt nervous. His mind searched for something special to call her, the one who had brought him back from the beast. He wanted a name that tied them together, like brother and sister.

He remembered this special full moon and the fireflies of his old home.

"I can name her anything?"

Yara nodded.

Sam closed his eyes and took a deep breath.

"Blue."

As though recognizing her new name, Blue squirmed and let out a small coo. Alma and Yara met eyes as the name swirled in the air between them.

"Ah...Blue," Alma smiled.

"That's a fine name for the little one," remarked Yara.

"Yes, yes it is," added Constance.

Sam handed the baby to her parents, "I think she might be hungry."

"Well now, come here, Little Blue." Yara smiled as he took the baby from Sam.

Sam stood and his Pelt wrapped around his waist. Even with the snow all around, he didn't feel cold. Instead, he felt John's hand on his back.

"Well done."

30

As the morning stretched over the henge, Sam met the rest of the Jacks and Witches. There were so many that Sam couldn't remember all their names, but he could see the connection in each pair. Each Jack had a blaze of white running through his hair, and each Witch revealed eyes that were different colors.

Sam could feel the ease between the men and women. When they spoke it was neither the affection or frustration of husband and wife, but the banter of a brother and sister. They were like siblings that had journeyed through many years together. There was a lightness that led to easy laughter, while underneath there was also protection and pride.

It had been many, many years since a Witch and a Wolf had departed the Earth. Arthur's death began *The Passing* while Letha's death marked the end of her last spell. Each passed their wisdom on. The transference was complete.

Today would close the circle for all to see. Arthur and Letha would be laid to eternal rest, their spirits carried on through Sam and the baby Cadi Blue.

For now, the Jacks and Witches each went separate ways to prepare for the funeral. The Witches followed Sam's tracks from the night before into the woods, Constance carried Letha's staff reverently. Before long, they arrived where Letha's body lay, still encircled by bowed trees. Constance placed Letha's staff upright into the ground. At the touch of each Witch's hand, the trees stood straight again. In the snow, Letha's body lay peacefully curled in a halo stained in red. Solemnly, the Witches prepared Letha's body to be moved. Dressing her in her a woolen cloak the color of dusk.

The Jacks quickly found their way south through the woods to the sandy, snow-covered shore of Fulton Lake. They would spend the rest of the day cutting and lugging wood to make a raised, flat funeral pyre. Logs were stacked chest high for the edges, while the middle was filled with smaller dry wood and piles of pine cones for hot, strong burning. Narrow timbers would be laid across the top where Letha and Arthur would soon rest.

Many hands made for quick work, and before long the pyre was almost complete, giving Amasa and King a chance to harness Tolbo and Od to the scoot, a flat logging sled. A tug on the reins from King sent them into the woods with all the Jacks following behind. It was time to collect Letha and Arthur.

As they walked, the Jacks periodically reached out with their axes to slice down a pine bough or two. Sam would shuttle them up to Amasa, who used them to line the sled as they travelled.

The Witches were waiting when King, Amasa and the Jacks arrived where Letha lay. They gently placed her onto the pine boughs, leaving enough room for Arthur, then laid her hands, one over the other, on her chest.

The Witches watched in somber silence as the sled and Jacks disappeared into the woods.

Even before arriving at Arthur's vault, the Jacks could see there was something missing in the skyline, and sure enough, when they arrived, the old majestic pine lay on its side, cut clean through.

They carefully kept the muslin sheet wrapped around Arthur as they pulled him from the vault, then tucked the pine boughs tightly around both bodies. It wasn't until then that John noticed something was missing.

"Where's his axe?" John asked.

Amasa stepped back into the vault, but came out empty handed. The Jacks took turns shrugging; no one could imagine why it was gone.

"Is that it?" All the men followed Rowan's gaze towards the freshly felled pine. Arthur's two sided axe was stuck deep in the huge, flat stump. The Jacks exchanged disbelieving glances.

"Who's the joker, eh? What's it doing over there?" Rowan asked.

"He can't be buried without his axe, wouldn't be right," Kofi said. Kofi purposefully walked over and grabbed the handle with one hand, expecting to easily pull it free, but instead was jerked back when it wouldn't budge. The other Jacks had a chuckle as Kofi re-gripped with two hands and pulled, but the axe stayed in place. Rowan couldn't help himself.

"You want I should pull that out for ya?" He jested.

"I'd like to see you try," Kofi fired back. The other Jacks egged Rowan on as he took the handle in his hands and pulled. But all that happened was Rowan's face got red enough to match his hair. He finally let go and rubbed his hands on his pants before trying to grip again.

John raised a hand.

Good-hearted cheers rang out as John stepped onto the stump. He reached for the handle, but stopped himself, as if he just remembered something. He looked at Sam.

All heads turned. Sam felt the Jacks' eyes on him as they stepped aside, giving him a clear path to the axe. He reluctantly came forward, but John stopped him at the foot of the stump.

"You'll be last," he said to Sam. He then raised his voice to the rest of the Jacks, "Each makes a go of it!"

Over the next several minutes, the air was full of manly sounds of great effort and energy as each took a turn stepping up to the axe and pulling with all their might, but none could make it move. Not even John.

At last, Sam took his place next to the axe. Now closer, Sam could see the etchings on its face. Some looked to be on purpose, while others were earned from years of use.

"I just pull it out?" Sam asked John.

"If you can," John answered.

If Kofi and Rowan couldn't pull it out, there's no way I can do it, he thought. Sam could hear the voices of the Jacks whispering to each other.

"This'll be something, eh?"

"It's Arthur's axe, after all."

"You think he'll do it?"

The air around Sam swirled, picking up loose leaves and snow. Sam put his hands around the handle, it felt like it was buzzing. He took a deep breath, and everything went quiet. Sam felt calm, like holding the axe was as natural as could be.

He pulled, felt a release, and the axe was free.

Sam looked to John in disbelief, but John was smiling with pride, just like the rest of the Jacks.

Sam looked at the axe, centered among the crevices and etchings, the same "A" stood out that had been in all of his morning pages.

"Take good care of that, and it'll take care of you," John said.

The weight of the axe in Sam's hands seemed more than material, he could feel the weight of its history, as if it had its own stories to tell and lessons to share. Sam knew the axe would be with him for many, many years, just like it had been for Arthur.

From the vault back to the pyre at the southern shore was a simple enough trip; a wide trail lead down the east side of the lake, then crossed a few streams before it bore right and opened up next to Cohen's Stock & Staple. They were in no rush. The final ceremony wouldn't start until sundown.

Stew spent the better part of the day making sure the success of Sam's Proving Night spread to all the townsfolk. With an uncharacteristic seriousness, he also told them a pyre was being built and would be lit at sundown, with all the Jacks and Witches in attendance. Sure enough, well before dusk, the town's shops and houses were emptied as the shoreline surrounding the pyre became filled with people.

Most of the town wondered if Sam had visibly changed after the full moon of Proving Night. As he helped the Jacks put the finishing touches on the pyre, the townsfolk whispered excitedly about Sam's new streak of white hair. It was a sign, like all the other Jacks, of the beast he carried within.

To Stew's dismay, there was no sign of Vadoma. He had stopped by the barn where her caravan was usually parked, but found it empty. He even followed the caravan's tracks in the snow to the edge of town where they suddenly just stopped, as if she vanished into thin air. Stew hoped she'd be back. After all, he had more pages full of letters to show her.

Just before sunset, King pulled the scoot out of the woods and next to the pyre. The Jacks collected around the sled, and made a small bow to the two bodies. Then, as if on cue, each of the Jacks headed into the woods. John turned to Sam and tugged his sleeve.

"Off we go now." John beckoned Sam to follow. He and the rest of the Jacks would use the cover of the woods for their transformations. This moon was special. It would be Sam's first full transformation following Proving Night, and his first transformation while Tethered.

Sam would also be in the company of the other Jacks during their moon-driven change, as he would for many months to come.

With the Jacks in the woods, Constance motioned for the Witches to form a circle around the pyre. She started a rhythmic, methodical walk, each foot brushing the ground before purposefully stomping down, sounding a firm *thump*. After each step she voiced a momentary hum that sent a subtle echo across the frozen lake. The other Witches joined in turn, and soon all their movements synchronized, slowly and purposefully stepping in rhythm.

Thump...Hum.

Thump...Hum.

The townsfolk were not often called upon to share in the magic of the Jacks and Witches. The folk-magic they practiced and passed down in their families had the power of repeated story, but not the potency of the Witches' spells. But on an occasion like this, the combination of folk and Tethered magic would create a ceremony worthy of Letha and Arthur.

The townsfolk added their numbers to the rhythm and the growing sound that echoed throughout the valley. The pounding of so many feet quickly left the entire sandy shore bare of snow.

Thump...Hum.

Thump...Hum.

The growing sound reached through the trees and into the woods, where John stopped walking and turned to Sam.

"This'll do," John said. "Boots off. Your change tonight will be different, but the same. You're Tethered now."

The rhythmic chanting from the Witches and townsfolk steadily filled Sam's ears as he unlaced his boots. He felt a coolness touch the base of his neck, traveling down his arm and leg to both of his scars. Each tingled heat as hair sprouted from the rough skin. He looked to the sky and found the beams from the rising moon. Sam grabbed his stomach as a scorching pain took over the center of his body and pulled him to the ground. A fear came over him that he would again lose control like the night before. His chest tightened. His breath stopped.

In his windless silence, he heard the other Jacks transforming too. The sounds of their grunts, groans, and scuffling on the earth were all around him in the forest.

Sam felt each new hair break through his skin. His bones ached as they extended and thickened, stretching his tendons and sinews past his human limits. He curled into a ball as his organs shifted and grew into a new, larger ribcage.

His mind flashed with images both familiar and strange. He was chasing the sheet music, then the Wolf was biting into his leg as he saved Arabella. There were the ashes of his house and the overwhelming emptiness of loss, then Letha's motionless body in front of him, staining the snow red.

His Pelt wrapped around him tight, and Sam felt the emptiness and pain in his center soften. A shadow blocked the moonlight and Sam looked up to see John's werewolf form silhouetting the moon. After his own arduous transformation, Sam had a new appreciation for how relaxed John appeared.

"Breathe," instructed John.

Sam took a deep breath as the Pelt released around him. The burning in his body eased, and unlike the wild, animalistic, and unpredictable night before, Sam felt like he had a hold of himself.

"You ready?" John's voice had an implied expectation.

Sam stood like a man. He looked down to see himself covered in thick hair, with limbs and legs, hands and feet that looked more animal than man. He felt a connection to the wild, but still had control of his mind.

He howled.

Close by, another howl answered, then another, as all the Jacks joined in a cacophonous chorus that twisted through the trees and traveled down the ice to the funeral pyre, meeting the Witches' chanting.

The bellowing anthem of the wolves signaled the beginning of the ceremony. The Witches and townsfolk stopped their rhythmic circling with a final stomp.

The Jackwolves returned to the hushed murmuring of the townsfolk. Each one took a position next to their tethered Witch. Seeing a Jack or two in beastly form wasn't completely uncommon, but never had the town seen all of the Jacks gathered together looking so ferociously feral, standing with their Witches. The air was thick with the forces of Forge, both folk and feral.

King pulled the sled forward as Alma handed a sleepy Blue to Sam, then helped Constance and a few other Witches take Arthur's wrapped body from the pine boughs on the back of the scoot. They attentively placed him on one side of the funeral pyre.

The Witches stepped back and Sam handed the dozing baby back to Alma. He then joined John, Kofi, and Rowan as they delicately took Letha's thin frame from the back of the sled. Her hair was carefully draped to hide the wound on her neck. A few pine boughs stuck to her robe as they brought her to the pyre.

The sight of Letha's body brought an audible gasp from the crowd. She was the well-loved matriarch of not just the Witches, but of the entire town, yet she had told no one about her plan. Every one had been focused on Sam's success on Proving Night. No one had realized this full moon would also bring Letha's death.

As he helped move her to the pyre, Sam felt heavy hearted with the guilt from taking Letha's life. He now knew it was all meant to happen the way it did, but he was still grappling with the fact that her death had been at his hand. He didn't think he was a killer, and he hoped he wouldn't become one.

At the same time, he was trying to focus on the honor of being one of the few called to lay her body to rest. He had never handled anything or anyone as carefully as he did in this moment.

As he eased Letha into place, Sam had a moment to study Arthur's motionless figure. He looked frail and gaunt, not like the regal, and even intimidating Arthur who visited him repeatedly as an imposing phantom, Wolf at his side, in the dead of night. Here, covered in a thin muslin sheet, he was motionless and pale, his spirit long left. He seemed a faded, ghostly apparition, an apparition who's last drops of blood now ran through Sam.

Sam's eyes fell to the cut on Arthur's wrist. Curiosity getting the better of him, Sam touched the red line. A jolt of recognition charged up his arm and darkened his vision. A glint of silver flashed across his mind's eye as he heard faint echoes of Letha's chanting voice.

Sam blinked and his eyes were back on Letha as she lay atop the pyre. Under her crossed hands, Sam noticed something. Shifting her arm, he found a black sock with two buttons sewn where the toes should be. Sam gently pulled it from her robe, climbed down, and moved away from the pyre. He looked at the sock curiously before holding it up to Alma.

"What's this?" Sam asked. "It looks like a sock."

"Ah," Alma smiled. "Yes, yes, it is a sock. That may come in handy in a few years, thank you." Alma took it and tucked it into Blue's swaddle. Blue squirmed and smiled.

John stepped forward in front of the funeral pyre and turned to address the crowd. The light of the moon fell sharply across his face as he spoke.

The Path of the Raven
Has come to an end.

All birds must land.
As the Raven has flown,
So must spirit.
Death leads to birth
In this life or in another.

Heads nodded in the crowd.

Arthur's breath lasted centuries.
He was strong, persistent, and kind.
Sam's breath now lends heart to Arthur,
as Arthur did to the one before him.

Letha's magic lasted equally so,
Blue will grow, and Letha's magic will rise again.
Blue, we welcome you.

In Alma's arms Blue cooed. John smiled before continuing.

Truth is the highest virtue,
It sows trust and connects us
To the most potent magic.

John turned to Sam.

Truth is the path
From who you were
To who you will be.
Know your truth and
You will not need to find the path,
You just need never lose touch with it.

335

"Sam, what is your truth?" John asked directly.

Sam felt a glow from within, different from Arthur's instincts that had been filtering through him for the past days and nights. This glow was closer to the center of his own soul. Whispers echoed from his family's past and spun through his mind.

His father had told him that work would bring him into adulthood, and his mother said his voice would bring him to many new places. Here he was, a thousand miles from his old home. He had proven he was ready. Sam felt a life of new possibility before him. Now was the time for his voice to speak his truth.

Sam could feel his father's hand on one shoulder, and his mother's on his back. He stood a little taller. A sense of calm confidence settled over him as he spoke.

"I am the son of my father,
Who gave me strength.
I'm the son of my mother
Who gave me music.
I am the brother of Ben and Ruthie,
Who gave me laughter."

"These are the truths of your past, and will always be," John responded. "You will come to know that you are more than this Sam of the past. You will become a new Sam. You will be more than you ever imagined."

"Stew?" John gestured towards the pyre.

Holding a makeshift torch under his arm, Stew pulled a small tin of matches from his pocket and lit one. It flared, fizzled, and was out before he could touch it to the head of the torch.

"Dang it," he whispered under his breath. Stew hunched over the next match, trying to protect it. This time, he managed to get the match to the torch. It barely caught, smoldering and throwing off puffs of grey smoke without any signs of a flame cutting through. Stew blew on the torch again and again, but his breath only made more smoke.

Constance gave John a wink and waved her staff in Stew's direction. A quick, short wind blew, and a flame finally burst forth.

"Ha!" Stew whispered with excited relief. He held the torch out for Sam to take.

Sam gripped the torch and stepped forward to the funeral pyre. His brain and body could not find how to feel. He was overcome with regret from the loss of his family. There had been no ceremony, no funeral, at the end of their lives. There had been only himself, John, and his neighbors to stand in the ashes of the fire that had taken them. All he could do was accept this new family and his new destiny.

Sam turned to see all the citizens of Forge focused on him. They had been witnesses to Sam's daily comings and goings in these past weeks. He had carried wood for Mabel, shoveled snow for Miss Tena, and brought hay for the horses. He felt connected to them all.

With a mix of reverence and remorse, he touched the torch to the pyre. This was the end of Letha and Arthur, lives taken and given.

The flames caught quickly, soon crackling and flinging sparks into the sky. Among the stars, spirits took to the heavens. Flashes of fire and smoke shifted intensity and color. The familiar flares of yellows and oranges turned to blues, greens and even purples. Sam had never seen fire so beautiful.

There was a shift on the frozen lake. One wolf, then another, emerged from the darkness beyond the pyre. Each one staked a place in a circle around the growing fire.

In the spaces between the flames, Sam caught the movement of ghostly human shapes. They swirled and flickered this way and that, like his mother and father dancing in the kitchen of their home. Smaller flamed figures flitted around them, like children chasing each other.

Sam only blinked once, but they were gone. His eyes searched the next few flashes of flame, and he saw Letha's and Arthur's ghostly figures floating up into the sky. High in the air, the northern lights intertwined with the flames of the pyre, connecting the heavens and the Earth.

Sam knew in his bones The Passing was now complete, and so was he.

The fire crackled and sparked while the gathered crowd stood in silence. Sam took in Alma, the baby Blue, John, Stew, as well as all the Jacks and Witches. With all eyes on him, Sam inhaled, stood tall, and spoke.

"I am the Blood of Arthur,
Tethered to Blue,
Brother of Wolves,
Son of Forge."

The entire town was there to witness this beginning of new life.

338

Sam felt a shift in the air as the first wolf around the pyre howled. Immediately it was joined by the Jacks and the rest of the pack.

Stew called out, "Yeehaw!" Cheers erupted.

Through the yells and hollers, Sam felt an uneasiness he couldn't explain. He realized it was because the ground beneath their feet was trembling and rocking. The wolves scattered back into the forest just as a crackling crescendo shattered the frozen lake. A sudden tempest propelled the pyre through the broken ice and thrust it into the middle of the water. The northern lights whipped down and touched the fire, making it grow and glow brighter and more radiant until all on shore had to shield their eyes or look away.

Suddenly, it was dark.

Sam looked out to the lake, but the pyre was gone. The reflected moonlight on the churning ice-water was the only sign it was ever there.

Stew would tell this story for years to come.

—-

Music and merriment filled the logging cabin that night. The large table was pushed back and piled with Mabel's baked goods, jams and jellies, and smoked meats Soup had been working on for days. To make room for the dancing, the benches had been pushed back too. Boots stomped, spoons clanged, and sticks slammed on pots and pans while Amasa's fiddle sang a jig. There was no way Rowan, Kofi, or any of the Jackwolves could sit still, and they had no trouble finding willing dance partners. A dozen Pelts flung like capes from one partner to another, adding flair to every movement. Turns out, John wasn't the only one who knew how to lead. Ladies were twirled, children were playfully tossed, and yelps of laughter filled the air.

Sam noticed that Stew's dancing, even without a discernible pattern, was very enthusiastic and somehow still on rhythm.

Somewhere in the night, John took Sam aside and wordlessly handed him the book, *Le Morte D'Arthur,* from Charles' library in D.C. The music was calling Sam too much for him to be able to sit and read, so he climbed up and placed it onto his new bunk, just above John's. Reading would have to wait until the quiet of the morning.

As Sam climbed back down from the bunk, Stew tapped him on the shoulder. Kofi and Rowan flanked him with smiles.

"You wanna try the Contraption?"

"The what?" Sam asked.

"It's like a running contest," Stew explained.

"Is it finally going to work?" called John with a smile.

Outside, fifty yards or so away from the logging camp, Stew revealed his most recent prized work of genius. Many trips back and forth to Cohen's and countless hours spent testing had resulted in quite a contraption, indeed. A fifteen-foot log of an arm was set on a short axis with several stone-filled burlap bags tied to the end as counterweight. Far on the other end two ropes linked to a large leather catch that held a sizable woven ball. The whole thing was positioned in a way to be aimed out over the lake.

"I pull this, and it launches the ball way out. First person to get it and bring it back gets a point. First person to get five points wins." Stew said, "Easy."

Sam looked the contraption up and down and thought for a minute.

"Like...fetch?" He asked.

"Well...yeah," said Stew.

Kofi and Rowan nodded excited agreement. Stew took the release into his hand, Rowan and Kofi scrunched down into starting positions. John braced a foot against a tree. Stew counted down.

"Three...two...*one!*" He pulled the release and the arm flew up, launching the ball fast and high over the lake. Instantly, Kofi and Rowan bounded after it.

"Ha! I knew it would work!" Stew exclaimed.

John's eyes widened with surprise as his claws dug into the bark of the tree, and he sprung after them.

The chase was on as Sam jumped with an explosive force, launching himself high into the air. He landed on two feet and ran as fast as he could after Kofi, Rowan, and John.

Faster.

Sam's thought initiated another shift, and his body transformed with intention into something less like a man and more like a wolf. He reached his front arms forward, pulling the Earth under him before pushing it away behind. Each stride felt more powerful as he lost any features of a man and became all wolf. No longer limited to running on two legs, he was sprinting on all fours.

It felt good. Every muscle pulled, twitched, and relaxed as he tried to gain on John. He felt his ears pull back on his head and the cold air around him pull on the hair that covered his body. He was closing in.

The faster he went, the more Sam felt sheer bliss. At the edge of the lake, he broke out of the woods just as he caught up to

John. Within two strides on the lake, Sam's front paw slipped on the ice and sent him tumbling and sliding to a stop on his back in a snow drift.

He shook the snow off, as a wolf would do, only to see John stopped with his shoulders shaking, a witness to his not-so-graceful fall. John's Wolf head tilted skyward, and Sam couldn't tell if it was a howl or a laugh that left his throat. In truth in was more the latter.

Sam gave a small howl himself, as the rest of the Jacks blazed past after Stew's ball, still arching through the air. John renewed his sprint while Sam found his footing. The ball finally landed on the frozen lake, skidding across the slick ice. John glanced over his shoulder to see Sam trying to keep up.

Still a lot to learn, John thought. *This will be fun.*

31

As Sam drifted off to sleep, he thought of his own father. How he would have been proud to see that his son was making his way in the world. Sam consciously decided to focus on that feeling of pride instead of sadness as he closed his eyes for the first time in his new bunk, strangely comforted by the ballad of snoring men around him.

At sunrise in the logging camp, the Jacks grunted and groaned in their bunks as they returned to human form. Sam felt an internal pulling as his body contracted, like he was packing a coil that wanted to spring forth. When his mind cleared, the first thing he recognized was the smell of breakfast.

He turned over in his bunk to see John stacking wood next to the stove. Stew stood at the cook top steadying a large cast iron pan while Soup chopped and tossed in pieces of fatty meat that sizzled and smoked as they slapped down. The father and son worked smoothly and effortlessly together.

Sam sat up and was surprised to find a pencil gripped in his hand along with two scribbled pieces of paper in bed with him. He collected them and realized there were more than just the usual scratches and squiggles. For the first time, there were actual, readable words, written in a masculine calligraphy.

Sam dropped down to the floor and went to the stove, holding up the pages to Soup and John.

"Look!" he said.

"What's that you have there?" asked John.

"They're not just scratches and such this morning...it actually looks like words."

John took the pages as Soup looked over his shoulder. Stew strained to peek from underneath.

"That's Arthur's signature for sure!" Stew said as he pointed to the underside of the page with a spoon.

"Looks like Proving Night brought more than fur," John said as he handed the pages back. "Arthur is finally coming through. I'm sure you'll find something useful in there."

Sam looked down at the swirled writing. It was much more fancy than the printed *Huck Finn* he was used to. He wasn't sure if he should read it right away, or if he even he could.

"Go on. We'll finish making breakfast," John encouraged while he stocked the stove. As Sam passed his bunk, the Pelt reached out and slid onto his shoulders. He opened the cabin door, stepped into the cold, grey morning, and sat on the well worn log bench outside.

He turned the two pages in his hands. At the bottom of one, in strong strokes, was Arthur's signature, the familiar, ornate "A" the first distinct letter.

This must be him. This is Arthur.

He wondered what great things would be held in the words. He turned the page back over to the front and took a breath. He began to read.

Dear Sam,

Your father has told me much about you...

Acknowledgements

I have many people to thank on this first self-publishing journey, which was as much of an adventure as Sam's. First and foremost, it would be at the least impolite, and at the worst a travesty if I didn't properly thank my lovely wife and extremely patient editor, Alice. To be concise, this book wouldn't be even close to what it is without her help.

Another huge thanks for both my family and my in-laws, who've been incredibly supportive of my creative pursuits. A shout out to my kids, who put up with character arcs and plot lines over dinner, car rides, and every other waking second.

Thanks to Marco Garcia and Marc Ryan who told me to go for it. Thanks to D'Marco Farr and Ellen Cater, for giving it an early read.

To Joe Luna and my fitness fam at 1440 Athletics and Fitness, you guys are all badass and the most supportive group of sweaty people I've ever come across.

Thank you to Sheila Hatcher. You know why.

Thanks to Tim Byrne for capturing the spirit of the story in his cover art and Rodney Hatfield, marketing guru, for guidance and spreadsheets. (Thanks Reedsy.com!)

There is also a long list of many that I've never met, who are a piece of this journey in one way or another, ranging from the flying fingers of Steven King, to the emotional intelligence of Brené Brown, to the efficiency of Tim Ferris, to the tenacity of David Goggins, to the masculine compassion of Jason Wilson.

And finally thanks to Jim Scolari, whose gift with words I could only ever strive for. I wish you could've read it in person.

For book club and teacher resources, visit the following:

www.readmoonshine.com/resources
www.teachmoonshine.com

Find and Follow us!
@magentacreators
@readmoonshine
@maxisallwrite
@makingmax

About the Author

Photo credit:
Alice Kuo Shippee Photography

Max Shippee grew up in rural Maine and knows the woods well. His own journey took him to Hollywood, California by way of Oklahoma, Nevada, Texas, DC, and even Bali, Indonesia. For the last 20 years, he has been busy as an actor, a gym owner, a husband, and a father. Along the way, he's had some stories brewing in that silver-haired head of his. He thought he best write them down. You can find his spontaneous science-fiction installments on Reddit, and now, *Moonshine, The Series* has begun with *Path of the Raven*.

www.ingramcontent.com/pod-product-compliance
Lightning Source LLC
Chambersburg PA
CBHW032000130726
47903CB00012B/201